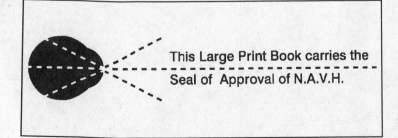

SMALL MERCIES

SMALL MERCIES

EDDIE JOYCE

THORNDIKE PRESS

A part of Gale, Cengage Learning

GALE
CENGAGE Learning·

Farmington Hills, Mich • San Francisco • New York • Waterville, Maine
Meriden, Conn • Mason, Ohio • Chicago

GALE
CENGAGE Learning®

LIBRARY OF CONGRESS CATALOGING-IN-PUBLICATION DATA

Joyce, Edward.
    Small mercies / by Eddie Joyce. — Large print edition.
        pages cm. — (Thorndike Press large print basic)
    ISBN 978-1-4104-7853-5 (hardcover) — ISBN 1-4104-7853-X (hardcover)
    1. Children—Death—Fiction. 2. Bereavement—Psychological aspects—Fiction. 3. Large type books. 4. Domestic fiction. 5. Psychological fiction. I. Title.
PS3610.O97S63 2015b
813'.6—dc23
                                        2014049328

Published in 2015 by arrangement with Viking, an imprint of Penguin Group, a division of Penguin Random House Company LLC

Printed in Mexico
1 2 3 4 5 6 7 19 18 17 16 15

For Martine

CHAPTER 1
SOMEONE WHO ISN'T BOBBY

Gail wakes with a pierced heart, same as every day. Her mouth is dry. She reaches for the glass of water on her nightstand, but it has warmed in the night. Next to her, Michael gently snores away last night's fun.

She can never sleep in on Saturdays. Friday nights? She's useless, like someone drugged her. They order a pie, usually pepperoni but plain last night for Lent. She eats two slices, drinks two glasses of Chianti, and is asleep on the couch by eight. Before he leaves for the Leaf, Michael drapes a blanket over her inert body. He wakes her when he gets home, no later than eleven these days. He helps her up the stairs, the beer on his breath gone stale with the walk home. She barely wakes, has just enough energy to get her tired bones beneath the covers. He says something nice, kisses her forehead.

She's always up with a start the next

morning. She doesn't need caffeine or an alarm clock; a shapeless guilt propels her into the day. Before she steps out of the shower, she's already in full swing, making lists, mental notes. What needs to be done. Today, tomorrow, this week, this month. She'll write it down later. She dresses in the stillness, sitting on the bed, the comforter muffling the energy required to slip on her socks. An occasional snort from Michael is the only reminder that she's not the solitary soul in the world.

A quick look in the mirror. Not for vanity, not anymore, but for its older sister: dignity. She makes sure she's not a total mess, that the clothes she slipped on in the dark don't clash. Brown corduroys and a long-sleeve faded green T-shirt. Good enough.

Her energy is tested as soon as she leaves the bedroom. Bobby's room is across the hall and as much as she'd like to, she cannot pass it without entering. It hasn't changed since Bobby got married and moved out. He took most of his things, but the room looks the same. The bedroom of a grown child living at home. The bed is made, the window cracked open. A faded poster of Patrick Ewing, sweat drenched and intimidating, hangs above the bed. He is leaping to block a shot. She nods to him.

Patrick, how are we this morning?

Fine, Mrs. A., fine. Can't seem to finish blocking this shot. Always inches away.

Keep at it, Patrick.

Will do, Mrs. A.

She sucks in a breath of air, closes her eyes, tries to remember what it was like to be in this room with her son. He was barely ever here. To sleep and that's all. The older boys had to share a room, but Bobby got his own. She can't remember how it worked out that way. One of those things. No explanation, no reason: a fact of the family conceived in temporary convenience and cemented by the simple passage of time. When one of the older boys objected — Peter, it would have been Peter — it was too late.

"I don't mind, Mom. He can have it. I'll switch or Franky can move in with me."

Easy as a hammock, her Bobby boy. But they didn't make the switch. The youngest gets the hand-me-down clothes, the half-broken toys, gets picked on and left behind, gets teased and tormented. He would at least have his own room, even if he didn't want it.

Besides, she didn't want Peter to get his way. He was fourteen or fifteen. Cock of the walk. Already entitled, not in a rich-kid way

9

but expectant. He worked hard, no sense denying it. He studied too, even though it came easy. He practiced — football, baseball — even though that came easy too. But he expected the world to open wide for him, knew that one day he would storm the castle and fuck the princess and drink all the wine, because he was smart and athletic and handsome and diligent.

And he wasn't wrong, as it turned out.

But he didn't get the room. She remembers now: a list of reasons, a presentation at the kitchen table. A smug little smile at the end, satisfied at the brilliance of his own logic. The shock and hurt when she said no, without giving a reason. She wanted the little prick to taste some disappointment. Strange how you can hate your own kids at times.

She walks over to the short bookcase that sits below the window. A handful of basketball trophies rest on top of it. One has been knocked over by the breeze from the window. She picks it up, inspects the placard: MOST IMPROVED PLAYER, FARRELL JUNIOR VARSITY 1990–91. Bobby held this once, cherished it. She places it in an upright position, slides its marble base into the proper place among its compatriots.

A few years back, Michael broached the

topic of maybe using the room for some-thing else. Another guest bedroom or a home office or maybe a game room for the grandkids. She stared at him, blue eyes unblinking, until he simply ran out of words. He never raised the issue again.

Some days she thinks he was right. The room doesn't conjure anything, doesn't evoke any particular memories. It simply reminds her of Bobby's absence and she hardly needs a room to do that. It has inflicted pain, this room, on a few morn-ings, when she's walked in to find someone lying in his bed and, for a moment, experi-enced a flicker of obscene hope, quickly extinguished when she realizes it's Franky and he's slipped in here, drunk and melan-choly, while they were sleeping, spreading one sadness over another. She closes the door on those days and lets Franky sleep. When he sneaks away in the morning, hung over and embarrassed, she washes the sheets and remakes the bed and feels Bobby slip a little further away.

Mostly, it's a distraction. A pause — maybe five minutes, maybe an hour — keep-ing her from her day. Like today. So it's time to wish Mr. Ewing good luck and get on with it. She makes the sign of the cross and leaves the room.

Then she's down the stairs, a tornado doing all the little household things that have gone undone during the week, all the things she should have done the night before. Everywhere she goes, the house staggers back to life: the washing machine swigs, the dishwasher soaks, the coffeemaker sputters and spits. The lighting of bulbs marks her path through the house. Bathroom, hallway, stairwell, kitchen, living room, front porch. The wooden floors groan up at her as she goes; the bones in her ankles and feet respond with unsettling clicks. The trash is removed, the paper is brought in.

Voices from the radio slip back into the kitchen, oblivious to the fact that they've been silenced these sleeping hours. A mundane news station. Nothing political, nothing angry. Just the traffic, the weather, the happenings of the five boroughs, New Jersey, Connecticut, Long Island, Westchester. Something that makes her feel like she's part of a community. A large, rambling, fractious community, but a community all the same.

There was a stabbing in Yonkers, a fatal drunk-driving accident in Garden City, downed power lines in Massapequa. There are feel-good stories: an anonymous donation to a food pantry in Mount Vernon, a rescued dog in Canarsie, a kidney donated by a stranger to a sick child in Flushing.

How awful. How wonderful. How frustrating. The traffic, always bad somewhere, even at this hour, even on a Saturday. The newscaster lists the times like a hostess at a restaurant assessing the wait for a table. Fifteen minutes at the Holland inbound. Twenty outbound. Thirty minutes at the Lincoln outbound. Forty-five inbound. An hour at the GW Bridge, in either direction.

Most mornings, she barely pays attention. It's something to move things along, keep her company. The voices on the radio float to Gail wherever she is in the house. They grow lower, disappear, reappear, are drowned out by the dryer, grow stronger, disappear again. Her ears perk only if the radio mentions something local.

An accident on the West Shore Expressway. Another bias attack down in Port Richmond. A kid from Prince's Bay wounded in Afghanistan. When this happens, which isn't often, she stops her bustling and listens.

On this morning, there's nothing happening. The borough is silent.

She's in the kitchen now, inspecting the fridge. It always seems emptier than it should be, but whenever she fills it, she ends up throwing away half the food. They don't have three ravenous teenage boys eating around the clock anymore. The fridge is like the house: emptier than it used to be. Nothing can change that.

She looks into the cupboard to make sure she has Alyssa and little Bobby's favorite cereals. She's holding a box of Honey Nut Cheerios when a report catches her attention: a home invasion the night before, in someplace called Moriches out on Long Island. Two men broke into the home of an elderly couple. The man was a World War II veteran, eighty-three years old. They beat him senseless. He's in a coma, but they interview his wife, whose fear is palpable, can be felt through the airwaves. One man has been apprehended, but the other is on the loose.

Gail hopes a cop — an angry, hungover cop — finds him in a cold, low place, shoots him in the stomach, and leaves him to rot under a pile of wet leaves. She can see the cop plain as day, walking silently, his gun drawn, chilled breath spilling out before him. A spike in the back of his head from too much whiskey the night before. Anger for this and for something else. A score that was never settled. Chance to make things right. The assailant unaware, some low-life junkie starting to come down. The cop's almost there.

Good Christ, where do these thoughts come from?

Moriches. She's never been there, never even heard of it. But now it has a feel, now she will remember it. Moriches, where elderly World War II veterans are beaten to snot and renegade cops administer street justice.

She likes the woman, the wife of the veteran. Her voice, her manner: they belong to a different time. Gail tries to focus on her. A pity what happened. How scared she must be. Moriches. When Tina gets here, she'll ask her to look it up on the computer, point out where it is. She wants to know where it is, to see it placed on a map.

Gail hasn't been to most places she hears of on the radio, but each summons a feeling. She likes some names: Lynbrook, Mamaroneck, Dobbs Ferry. She doesn't like others: Sayville, Passaic, Scarsdale. She was shocked when Michael told her that Scarsdale was a well-heeled town. The name sounded tough, like a run-down mining town. A scar in the earth, scars on the faces. She never would have guessed.

When there's nothing left to do, when nothing else can be tidied or straightened, she sits at the table and waits for Tina and the kids. She spreads the *Advance* across the table and sifts through it. This is more intimate than the radio, deserves more focus. A community of millions siphoned down to a few hundred thousand.

Between articles, she looks out the large bay window at the front of the kitchen. The morning is gray, the sun up but stuck behind a fleet of low-lying clouds. The other houses on the block are dark. The street is still. The whole neighborhood sleeping off the week.

The block hasn't changed much in the forty years they've called it home. Fewer trees. Less open space. A handful of new houses that don't quite fit in. Otherwise, Wirra Lane has largely escaped the overdevelopment that has plagued the rest of the Island.

A blank moment in the mind. Her thoughts drift to Franky. She hopes he's holding down his latest job, hopes he's still on the wagon. She hasn't seen him in a few weeks. Hasn't heard from him in a few weeks, come to think of it. Maybe he's met someone. God, she hopes he's met someone. The right girl would make him tow the line. The right girl would make him straighten out his act.

Of course, the right girl would be too smart to get involved with him at all.

It wasn't always that way. There was a time, not so long ago, when Franky was half a lady's man. Handsome in a roguish way. A glint of trouble in his eyes, sure, but charming. She was sitting at this table one morning, dawn coming on, when a car pulled up. Franky and Bobby were both living at home, taking summer classes at CSI and wearing out their elbows at every bar on Forest Avenue. They'd been out the night before. Gail had heard them come in, after four, stumbling down the hallway into their bedrooms.

At least, she thought she'd heard them — the two of them — but it wasn't like she'd done a bed check. She couldn't fall back to sleep, so after an hour of trying, she wandered downstairs to get a start on the day. And here was a car, pulling to a stop quietly, and there was Franky in the passenger seat, leaning over to make out with the girl who was driving. He got out of the car and closed the door softly, was walking up the path to the front steps when the girl — black hair in a ponytail, toned, long legs in jean shorts — got out of the car and chased him down, holding a slip of paper. He turned back, gave her another long kiss, and tucked the paper into his pocket. He waved as she drove off, then walked into the house, happy and oblivious, looking like a man who'd just gotten laid, which was probably the case. He didn't notice Gail sitting in the dark.

"Was that Kerry Cole?" she asked, hoping to startle him. Gail recognized her from the *Advance*. She'd been a soccer star on the Island a few years back, had gotten a full ride to Notre Dame, must have been home for the summer. He sat down across from Gail, a smirk on his face.

"T'was, Mother, t'was," he said, in a fake Irish accent. "A fine girl."

He retrieved the slip of paper from his pocket, spread it on the table. Gail saw the name Kerry, a telephone number below it. Bobby would have been embarrassed and Peter annoyed, but Franky was nonplussed. Proud, if anything. And Gail felt a strange pride too. She could see a girl like Kerry Cole falling for Peter. But Franky? Who was taking his sweet time getting through community college? Whose great ambition was tomorrow night? Whose ideal reading was two pages of box scores in the *Post*?

Yet there she was, chasing Franky down to hand over her number. Making out with

18

him in the front yard like it was her last day on earth. As a mother to three boys — three men now — Gail had gotten used to a certain amount of locker room banter over the years. Still, it was an odd thing to be happy that your son had maybe screwed above his station. But she was happy. And proud.

"Slumming for the summer?" she asked, regretting it immediately. She meant it in a teasing way, but with Franky, she had a way of being cruel without always intending to. He didn't flinch though.

"What can I say, Mother? There's no accounting for taste."

He smiled. He wasn't drunk, wasn't even tipsy. He was glowing with the unlikelihood of his conquest. He was past the age where Gail could give him a talk about precautions, about being careful. And God help her, she could think of worse things than Franky knocking up a sweet, smart girl like Kerry Cole.

"You should call her, Francis," she said, trying not to sound too insistent.

"I'm starving," he responded.

She fried up some bacon and scrambled some eggs, sat there with him while he ate it. The smirk on his face creased into a smile.

"Fine girl. My ass."

He had to spit the eggs out into a napkin because he was laughing so hard. She said it to him for the next few weeks, their own private joke. He could be so easy sometimes. He had his moments.

He never called, despite Gail's nudges. Gail didn't see Kerry Cole again until her wedding was announced in the *Advance* some years later. By that point, Gail had endured a host of mornings with Franky: mornings where he needed to be helped out of a cab, mornings where she found him passed out on the front lawn, mornings when he didn't come home at all, and, of course, the morning when he called and told them in a slurred ramble that he'd been arrested.

There were even a few other mornings where he got dropped off by a girl. None of the girls was Kerry Cole, but he didn't lack for companionship. He still had a certain appeal, still had his looks. Sitting on a bar stool — a drunken, ruined memorial to his dead brother — Franky probably did well with a certain brand of barfly.

Some women love reclamation projects.

On the counter, the coffeemaker ceases its pleasant babble. She makes a pot for Michael; she prefers the Starbucks that Tina brings with the bagels. Michael complains.

"It's too expensive, it tastes burnt."

Gail doesn't care. She likes the taste. She'd rather have one good cup of coffee than four crappy ones. Michael is a big tipper, would give his last dollar to a friend, but he's cheap in ways that perplex Gail.

Not cheap. Frugal. Saves his money on coffee so he can leave five-dollar tips for surly bartenders. Doesn't make sense to Gail, but that's all right. Not everything about your husband should make sense. Took her years to realize that. If she were teaching a class to prospective brides, that would be her first piece of advice.

Don't expect everything he does to make sense.

Michael is out of bed. The weight of the house has shifted with him. She knows what he's doing now, as sure as if she were in the room with him. A stiff walk to the bathroom, followed by a hasty flip of the seat and a long, contented piss. Regimes have fallen during Michael's Saturday morning pisses. She can tell how many beers he had the night before by the length of his piss: ten seconds for each bottle.

Gail hears the shower start. Short piss.

Michael must have been a good boy last night.

The reshuffling of the house's order — another body in the mix, another consciousness released from slumber — always startles her. It's like a second waking, equally abrupt but more demanding. The day has been on tracks, sliding toward its start, and now it has arrived. Soon the house, enormous in its emptiness, will shrink with the day to accommodate Michael, Tina, the kids. Gail always misses the stillness as it recedes.

The morning has caught up with her. Time to get down to business. She grabs a pad of paper and a pen. She thinks for a moment, tries to conjure the date.

March 12th.

The ides of March are nearly upon us. She stopped teaching last year, but this would usually be the week her eighth-grade honors class started *Julius Caesar.* She tried to time it right, have them read the ides of March line on the ides of March. The little things matter when you're teaching. You'll do anything to keep them interested, keep them reading. Over the years, a few parents complained that Shakespeare was too advanced for eighth graders, even smart ones. But Gail always thought it was perfect for middle schoolers. It dealt with friendship, betrayal, conspiracies, honor: all the same things they were starting to struggle with in their own lives. Besides, kids needed to be pushed, not coddled.

Busy time of year. St. Patrick's Day. The start of the NCAA tournament. The Cody's pool. Bobby's favorite week of the year. Her blue-eyed boy with the Italian last name and the map of Ireland on his face, wearing his fisherman's cable-knit sweater, the one Gail bought for him in Galway, to every god-damn St. Patrick's Day parade in the tri-state area: Manhattan, Hoboken, Bay Ridge, and, of course, Forest Avenue. The sweater slowly accumulating brownish stains from spilled Guinness. Watching basketball for days on end. He used to say it was like they took everything good and crammed it into one week, except for Thanksgiving and the night before Thanksgiving.

What about Christmas? she would ask.

Overrated, he'd pronounce. Other than your food, Mom. Overrated.

Wait till you have kids, she'd think. Wait until you watch them fly down the stairs on Christmas morning.

She writes "to do" next to the date and makes a few short dashes on the left side of the page, the assignments to be added.

-Cleaning supplies.
-Cold cuts.
-Call Peter about Wednesday.
-Bobby Jr.'s birthday party.

A single dash lies companionless at the bottom of the list. There was something else. She was thinking of it while she loaded the dryer. Her memory's not what it used to be, but she knows when she's forgotten something. She taps the pen at the empty space as though the item might write itself if prompted.

Ah well, if it's important, she'll remember it soon enough. The dash will not be lonely for long.

The lists aren't as long as they used to be. She remembers a time when she couldn't make lists at all, when the next thing to do just presented itself, usually before the previous thing had been done. One of the boys with a bloody nose and hungry to boot, one of the boys waiting to be taken to practice. The phone ringing, someone needing to be picked up at the movies. An ice pack fetched, ziti reheated in the microwave. In the car, dropping one son off at the gym, picking another up at the movie theater, the third in the back, a hostage to the situation, holding the ice pack to the bridge of his nose in one hand and a Tupperware container of leftover pasta in the other. The moviegoer gets into the car, two of his compatriots are halfway in before he asks.

"Can Jimmy and Steve come over?"

Of course they can. Their friends were always welcome, the house always open. Gail fed a small army of boys, weekend after weekend, year after year.

It would have been Bobby with the bloody nose. Bobby having to tag along with her as she ferried the older boys all over the Island. Gail adjusting the rearview to look at him, just the two of them in the car.

"You okay, captain?"

That or something like it.

A smile in response, a wad of tissue sticking out of one nostril. No bother, Mom, his smile would have said. Right as rain. The patience of a saint, everything an adventure. When he was a boy, when he was a man.

Gail sets aside the incomplete list and picks up the paper. Somewhere on the block, a car alarm rings out in protest as a sleepy-eyed neighbor fumbles for the right button on his key chain. When the alarm is silenced, Michael's footsteps are on the stairs. He walks into the kitchen, yawning and happy.

"Good morning, beautiful."

"Good morning yourself."

Michael looks good for a man "on the back half of the back nine," as he describes himself. His face is still pleasant, always on the verge of a smile, even though life hasn't spared him from sadness. He opens a cabinet, takes out a red FDNY mug. He pours himself a cup of coffee and drizzles in a splash of milk. He kisses Gail's cheek and sits next to her, his gaze out the window.

"So, what's the world got in store for us today?"

"Same as always." She licks her finger, turns a page. "How was the Leaf?"

"Same as always."

He smiles.

"Who won the game?" When she fell asleep on the couch, Duke was losing to Virginia Tech by six points at the half.

"Duke pulled away in the second half. Too big."

"Shoot. So when do they do the draw?"

"You mean the selection show? Tomorrow night."

"You and the boys putting in a few entries this year?"

He frowns in mock exasperation.

"Why do you ask questions that you already know the answer to?"

"For the same reason you keep entering a

pool you'll never win. I enjoy it."

He smiles again.

"Touché."

The Cody's pool is an institution, a March Madness tradition. Its genius is its simplicity. Pick the four Final Four teams. Pick the champion. Pick the total points of the final game. Ten dollars an entry. Seems easy, but if you lose one Final Four team, you're out.

Kansas loses in the second round? There go eleven thousand entries, more than a hundred thousand dollars. Syracuse goes down, a buzzer beater in overtime? A quarter of the pool is finished. Done. See you next year. People come from all over — Jersey, Brooklyn, the city, even Connecticut — to put in their entries. Last year, the pot was over a million. In cash.

She teases Michael, but she loves the pool. A special lottery for the Island. The teachers at school put in a few sheets. So do the guys behind the counter at Enzo's. Franky and Bobby used to sit, at this very table, for hours, eliminating certain teams, elevating others. They'd pool their money with a few friends, put in a few sheets of picks. They'd revise their picks over and over. If only they'd approached their schoolwork with that intensity, like their older brother did.

After Peter went away to college, he called

home with his entries every March. By the time he was a senior, his friends wanted in. Two of them even drove down with him for that first crazy weekend. They drove straight to Cody's and put in their entries. They watched the games all weekend in the basement. Franky and Bobby down there with them. Nonstop basketball. Explosions of noise every few hours. Michael sat in the kitchen with her, said he was going down to see what happened. He didn't emerge for a few hours. When he did, he was glowing with the easy energy of male camaraderie, like after a good night at the Leaf.

Only this was better. This was his blood, these were his boys.

Gail cooked and sent the food down with Michael. She kept it simple: food to fill stomachs, food to soak up beer. Chicken parm, sausage and peppers, small armies of penne, pork roasted in sauerkraut. She had to make a few hasty trips to Enzo's for replenishments, for bread and cold cuts. The amount they consumed.

A lull in the action, between the afternoon games and the night games. They filed out of the basement, stretching and boasting, ready for more of the same but in a different location. Peter and his friends over the legal age, Franky close enough for the Leaf.

But not Bobby, the straggler again, left behind with his mother. A senior in high school but still the young pup.

Gail was angry with the other boys, angry with Michael. Couldn't they just stay in the basement? She'd get the beer herself. They could drink it by the caseload downstairs. Keep Bobby involved, part of the crew. But Bobby could have cared less. Never bothered.

Mom, would you care if Tina came over and watched the games with us?

With *us*?

Of course not.

Gail glances at the clock on the microwave. Half past nine. Tina's late.

"What do you want to do for dinner tonight?" Michael asks.

"I was thinking I'd make your mother's lentil stew, the one with the sausage. One last belly warmer before the weather turns."

He sips his coffee.

"You sure you want to cook?"

Gail folds the paper, takes off her glasses.

"Why? You have another idea?"

"Thought maybe we could drive into the city, down to Chinatown, go to that downstairs place we used to take the boys to, the one with the great dumplings."

"Michael Amendola. Will wonders never cease. What about the toll on the bridge?"

"Keep teasing me. Very nice. I try to expand my horizons and you tease."

"Drive to Manhattan, eat dumplings. Next thing, you'll be saying we should get sushi."

"Why not? I'm turning over a new leaf, Goodness. Sushi. Falafel. Pedicures and yoga. Understanding and compassion. Out with the old, in with the new. They can put mosques on the moon and I won't make a peep."

"Interesting. Doesn't sound like this new leaf will have any room for the old Leaf."

"Let's not go crazy. It's a process, turning leaves. Can't get rid of the old one until you make sure the new one works. Best to start with something simple. Like dumplings."

They laugh together. It's nice when they can cheer each other into the day.

"Actually, sounds like a great idea. Change of pace."

He shakes his head, rolls his shoulders.

"Doesn't even have to be Chinatown. Little Italy's down there too. Either or."

"Whatever. Something different."

He stands.

"Good."

A familiar car slows on the street in front of the house and turns into their driveway.

The car rolls to a stop and the passenger door opens. Alyssa shuffles out. She is twelve, on the cusp of so many things. She lurches toward the house clutching her phone, eyes riveted to the tiny screen. Bobby Jr. skips out of the rear door, his black hair flopping as he darts in front of his sister. He waves excitedly to them through the window.

Tina brings up the rear, carrying a tray of coffee and looking frazzled. She nods at them through the window, a grim smile on her face.

"She's lost weight," Michael says.

Michael's observation, upsetting for a reason Gail can't pinpoint, lingers for a moment until the front door flies open with Bobby Jr.'s weight and he explodes into the house, the jacket already sliding off his arms. He wriggles his arms free and the jacket drops to the floor in the doorway between the porch and the living room. He leans back, croons.

"The trickster is here."

He breaks into a giggle, lets Michael tousle his hair before sliding into Gail's arms.

"Missed you, Bob-a-loo."

"Missed you too, Grandma."

He smells like Cheerios and milk. He has

his mother's dark hair, but everything else is his father. The blue eyes, the goofy grin, the constant good humor. His smooth cheek feels young against her cragged counterpart. He'll be nine in a few days. She's been looking forward to his birthday party for weeks. Next Sunday, just the family. A barbecue in the backyard, like the good old days. She releases him and he skips back to Michael for a high five.

Alyssa follows her brother in, her perpetual pout a slap in the face after Bobby's infectious jubilation. Other than a splash of acne on her forehead, puberty has not yet touched her. Her body is painfully geometric, a collection of straight lines, hunched shoulders, and stringy brown hair. Gail hopes she's a late bloomer.

Tina comes in last. Usually she restores equilibrium; her pleasant but weary demeanor striking the middle ground between the moods of her children. Not today. No, today her heart is clearly with Alyssa and this troubles Gail. Tina's unhappiness will have substance, will have something real behind it.

She looks at Gail with a pained expression, like a parent about to explain some unpleasant reality to a child. And then Gail knows, the answer presents itself, like a twig snapping after a few moments of pressure.

It's the only thing that makes sense.

Tina doesn't bother with a preamble. She doesn't try to explain. She doesn't mention Bobby. As soon as they're alone — the kids safely planted in front of the television in the living room, Michael out running errands — she says it, confirming what Gail already knows.

"I met someone."

Gail looks over at her daughter-in-law. Tina's hands are trembling and she steadies them by pressing them down, fingers splayed apart, on the tabletop. Gail reaches over and squeezes Tina's shoulder.

"Good for you, Tina, I'm happy for you."

Not a total lie, but it sounds false to Gail even as she says it. She *is* happy. But she's sad too. No sense denying it. She was afraid this would happen even as she hoped it might. She thinks there should be a better word for this feeling. *Bittersweet* doesn't capture it. This is different. This is happiness and sadness entwined, flowing through you at the same time. Gail is sure there is an Italian word for this feeling, some word that Maria, her own mother-in-law, would have known. Some little word that sounds exactly the way she feels.

Tina has more to say, but Gail doesn't want her to say anything. She doesn't want her to make promises she might not keep. Already she can feel distance growing between them. Already they are protecting themselves, protecting each other, from what is to come. Tina starts gathering herself to speak. The shrill, insistent sounds of Saturday morning cartoons blare in from the living room.

"Tina, I know how much you loved my son."

Tina hugs her and Gail notices that she *is* thinner. She gained weight after Bobby was killed. Her small frame didn't carry it well. All the chub went straight to her face and her rear, made her look heavier than she was. But she's slimmed back down; she nearly has the figure she had when Gail first met her, when Tina was a teenager. Even Michael noticed. She should have known. She feels a protective flutter in her throat.

Bobby Jr. walks into the kitchen.

"Mom, can I have a doughnut?"

Tina is sniffling and Gail dries her eyes with her shirtsleeve. Bobby's eyes shine with embarrassment. Gail summons a smile. The poor kid has spent half his life walking into kitchens full of crying women.

"Everything's okay, Bob-a-loo. We're just

crying about a silly thing."

"Were you talking about my dad?"

"Kind of, yeah."

"Come here, sweetie."

Tina slides around the table, opens her arms for a hug. Bobby looks down at his shoes.

He needs a male influence. This is probably a good thing. Tina's mothering him too much, trying to shelter him from the world that took his father. It's a fine line. You want to protect your kids, but you can't go too far. If you shield them from everything, they never learn to fend for themselves. Michael used to worry that she mothered Bobby too much. Her baby.

"He'll be like a turtle without a shell, the world will bring a hard boot down on him and he won't know what to do."

It was a hard boot all right.

Alyssa shuffles into the kitchen, eyes still glued to her phone. She looks up, assesses the situation, and frowns.

"Why is everyone crying?"

It is a complaint, disguised as a question.

After Tina and the kids leave, Gail sits at the table for a long time, processing this turn of events. She has questions. Of course she has questions. Loads of them. She can feel them piling up even as she tries not to think of them. Her mind starts spinning with possibilities, each of them unpleasant to contemplate. She sees Tina in a wedding gown, the kids on vacation at Disney World with a new dad, the whole family moving to San Francisco.

Yes, she has questions. She has more questions than she can bear.

But the answers, the important ones, are already there. He's a nice guy and he's good with the kids. And it's serious, has to be. Tina has dated a few other guys over the years. Gail knows this even if nothing was ever explicitly discussed. Tina never said anything because it wasn't ever serious enough to warrant a conversation. The fact of the conversation means it's serious. The fact that it's serious means he's a nice guy and good with the kids. She could noodle this stuff out if she tried.

So, he's nice and good with the kids and it's serious. She'll learn the details soon enough. No sense worrying about things you can't control.

She knows this is right — that she shouldn't worry — but she knows that she will. The questions will not vanish. The answers will not satisfy her. She can feel the happiness of this ebbing, the sadness rising, morphing into loneliness. She needs to do something, anything, to distract herself. She needs some relief from her own thoughts.

She stands, looks out the window. It's still gray out, one of those ominous half days, a bridge between darknesses. She puts on a jacket, feels an anticipatory shiver run from the back of her shoulders down to her thighs.

Maybe later she'll look up that Italian word that Maria would have used. Maybe she'll just make up her own word.

Before she leaves, she looks back down at her to-do list. The final, solitary dash sits abandoned on the paper. She picks up the pen and gives the dash a companion.

It reads:

-Tell Bobby.

CHAPTER 2
THE BEST DAMN PIZZA
IN THE WORLD

Tina sets her lips in a gentle circle and applies a bright red lipstick. She inspects her reflection in the bathroom mirror, unsure whether the color suits her. Or the occasion. Even the simplest decisions — what lipstick to wear, hair up or down — are vexing her tonight. She hasn't felt like this since high school: the fluttering stomach, the anticipation that borders on dread, the head turned to sieve, unable to hold a single thought.

You haven't dated since high school, her reflection reminds her. *Not really.*

Only this isn't high school, when emotions were the only thing that mattered. More than school, more than family, more than friends. When you could feel something so deeply, so purely, without any comprehension of its true capacities. To change you, your life, the things that matter. To bring new souls into existence.

No, this isn't high school. The real world infringes, insists; a dozen anxieties jostle for priority in her head. The kids, Bobby, Wade, tonight, tomorrow morning, waking in a different bed, another man beside her, Gail judging her. She knows this last image is crazy, but she can't shake it. It keeps showing up at the end of a sprint through half thoughts. She is lying in Wade's bed and he is in the bathroom. She can see one of his pale naked buttocks atop a long, spindly leg, but the bathroom door bisects him, hiding half of his body. The tap is running; she can hear it. The sheets on his bed are lime green. Tina lies on top of them, luxuriantly naked, and Gail watches her from a doorway, shaking her head and frowning.

The whole thing is ridiculous. She's never been to his apartment, never seen his bare ass. And she prays to God that he doesn't have lime green sheets.

This isn't high school. Why then can she hear Stephanie shouting at her from the bedroom? Twenty years pass and you wind up in the same place, more or less. In your bathroom talking about guys. She hears Stephanie call Vinny an asshole a few times, but she's not processing it. It's noise floating around her.

She's thought about calling Gail half a

dozen times, even flipped open her cell phone once to do it. She told her about Wade this morning, but it felt like she held something back. What is she supposed to say, though?

Gail, in case I wasn't clear this morning, I'm planning on sleeping with this other man who I told you about. Tonight. Okay with you? Fine, we're clear then. Okay, I'll let you know how it goes.

"Are you even listening to me?"

Stephanie has crept into the bathroom while she was preoccupied.

"Jesus Christ. You scared the shit out of me."

"So you weren't listening to me?"

"Sorry, Steph. I'm just distracted." She points to her lips. "Too much?"

"Not if you're gonna give him a blow job on the way to the restaurant."

"So yes, definitely too much."

She starts blotting off the lipstick.

"Might be a good thing. Ease the sexual tension right off the bat. That way you can both enjoy your dinner. Well, maybe not you, depending."

Stephanie does this, pushes the conversation toward sex, tries to make Tina uncomfortable. She's done it since high school. The smallest details of Stephanie's sex life with Vinny are conveyed to Tina, who long ago learned not to share in kind. Instead, she employs a simple trick to swat away intrusive questions: redirection. Stephanie is always eager to talk about herself.

"You were talking about Vinny and a Jets game."

"Jesus, I'll just start over."

Stephanie closes the toilet seat and sits on it. She removes a pack of cigarettes from the pocket of her sweatpants, takes one out, and places it in her mouth.

"You mind?"

"No," says Tina as she flicks on the exhaust fan. "Don't let the kids see you."

"You want one?"

She would *love* a cigarette. But she knows she shouldn't. She waves her hand no. Stephanie tosses the pack onto the marble counter that Tina is leaning against. She lights the cigarette, takes a drag, and exhales up toward the vent. The whiff of burning tobacco sets Tina's fingers tapping on the marble.

"So, back in December, Vinny took the boys to a Jets game. As usual. It was freezing out and I was trying to make sure no one gets frostbite or hypothermia and they're all 'yeah, yeah, yeahing' me, you know, like I'm the asshole. I says, 'Vin, it's gonna be fifteen degrees out and windy and they're not gonna have eight or nine beers to keep them warm, Vin,' and he says, 'Yeah, yeah, Steph, yeah, yeah, I heard you the first time,' and he winks at the boys and they all laugh. And then they run out of the house and I watch them pull away in the Denali and they're all smiling, thrilled to be rid of me. All three of them smiling because they're finally rid of the nag. And you know what? I felt exactly the same way.

"Anyways, I straighten up a little bit and then I go upstairs to draw a bath. My Sunday ritual when they're at the games. A nice warm bath, a little one-on-one time with the removable showerhead."

"Steph."

"What?"

"What if one of the kids hears you?"

"You're such a prude. They're not so innocent, they see everything on the Internet these days. You'd be surprised."

"Whatever."

Stephanie leans past Tina, taps the ash out in the sink.

"Do you really do that whenever they're at the Jets games?"

"I pray every night that the Jets make the play-offs. Or that Vinny gets season tickets to the Mets."

Tina forces out a laugh. Stephanie has been watching too much reality television; her jokes sound rehearsed.

"So anyways, I go up to the bathroom and I see Vinny's facial hair in the sink. Like caked into the sink with shaving scum. A ring of little black and white hairs. And I think, Getting old, Vincenzo, because of the white hairs, and then it hits me. T, I can't tell you how pissed I was. Normally, I'd just run the tap and wash it out, but I was so disgusted. I smeared some of it on the mirror so he'd be sure to know I saw it when he got home."

Stephanie stops, takes another drag.

"So he forgot to clean up after he shaved?"

"Exactly."

Stephanie nods, as though the point of her story should be obvious to Tina.

"Okay. That's gross but . . ."

Stephanie smiles, a little secret on her tongue. One she wants to share. Tina knows the drill. She waves her hand in a small circle, attempting to move the story along.

"So?"

"So I fucked Tommy Valenti."

Tina reaches over and shuts the bathroom door.

"You did what?"

"Fucked Tommy Valenti. Twice. Well, one

time we fucked and then the other time, I gave him a blow job in the parking lot of the mall."

"You're joking me."

"No, I ain't."

Tina doesn't believe her.

"You're telling me you slept with —"

"Fucked."

"Tommy Valenti because Vinny forgot to clean up his shaving scum before he went to the Jets game. What am I missing?"

Stephanie takes another long drag, lifts her shoulders in mock incredulity. "Who shaves to go to a football game?"

"I don't understand what you're telling me."

"Tina, answer one question for me."

"Okay."

"Who shaves to go to a football game?"

"I have no idea what that means."

"Well, I do."

"You're a lunatic. Vinny shaves before a football game and that means he's cheating on you."

"Cheating on me *again*. And yes, yes it does."

"That makes no sense to me."

"Well, that's because Bobby probably never fucked around on you."

Tina's mind catches on the word *probably*.

44

She looks at Stephanie, who's sitting with one leg crossed over the other and inspecting the soft pink polish on the toenails of her closest foot. A wave of disgust passes through Tina as she looks at Stephanie's midriff, a patch of tanned, toned skin exposed between gray sweatpants and a white tank top. She remembers how Stephanie used to flirt with Bobby, touching his chest or his arm, right in front of her, especially when she knew Vinny was fucking around. She remembers Bobby enjoying the attention.

Slut, she thinks and then feels terrible.

"Does Vinny know?"

Stephanie looks up.

"God, no."

"Isn't Tommy Valenti married?"

"Jesus, Tina. Already with the judgment?"

"What? I'm asking. I can't ask? Forget it."

"Yes, Tommy is married, but he says his wife . . . they have an understanding. She fucks around too. They have an open marriage."

"Do you believe him?"

"I don't know. You know what? I don't care."

"Jesus, I mean, Jesus. I don't know what to say."

"T, Vinny has been fucking around on me

45

for years. Years. When he was working on the floor, God knows."

"I know, but I thought you said that mostly stopped. You know, after he stopped working in the city."

"I thought it did. But I guess I was wrong."

Stephanie's sneer softens. Her eyes well and her lower lip starts to quiver. Tina knows this transformation, from angry defiance to wounded and heartbroken. You could set your watch by Stephanie's mood shifts.

"What kills me is I can see her. When I close my eyes, I can actually see her. Some little whore in a Jets jersey, giving him head in the back of the car at a tailgate. My boys know her. Shit, Tina, they probably jerk off while thinking about her. How fucked up is that?"

"Pretty fucked up," Tina says flatly.

Another sordid episode in the highly repetitive saga of Stephanie and Vinny's marriage. In a month or so, Vinny will confess to a minor slip and promise to change his ways. The promise will be accompanied by a gift of some kind: a fur coat or diamond earrings. After an indeterminate period during which Stephanie will continue to punish Vinny by carrying on with her own affair and by generally making his life miserable, a second gift will be proffered. This gift will ensure the cessation of Stephanie's vengeance-seeking dalliance and a temporary return to marital bliss for the DeVosso household for a proscribed period of time, determined principally by how long Vinny can keep his dick in his pants or alternatively, how long he can hide from Stephanie the fact that he is not keeping his dick in his pants. The bliss period was the worst for Tina because it required listening to Stephanie describe the graphic details of her reinvigorated sex life with Vinny.

At least that's how it used to go. Ever since Vinny lost his job on Wall Street, the quality of his gifts had gone south, along with their ability to placate Stephanie. Vinny had come to lean heavily on his ability to avoid getting caught. Tina had little doubt that, in the future, Vinny would discard his shaven hairs with the care of a gangster disposing of a body.

Stephanie starts crying. She tears off a sheet of toilet paper and dabs at her eyes.

"I'm not a bad person, T."

"No, no. I didn't say that."

She's heard this all before, but tonight it's a welcome distraction from her own thoughts.

Stephanie takes a final drag and extinguishes the butt under the tap. She retrieves the pack and takes another cigarette out. The tiny white cylinder is too perfect for Tina to resist.

"Give me one."

"Really?"

"If not tonight, when?"

She plucks a cigarette from the pack, lets Steph light it for her. She sucks the smoke deep into her lungs and exhales with relish. It's her first cigarette in three years.

"So what's gonna happen with you and Tommy?"

Stephanie sits back down on the toilet.

"Nothing. Just having a little fun. How's the cigarette?"

"Bliss."

Bobby used to hate that she smoked. He used to nag her about it, even though she was only a social smoker, barely a pack a week.

It's the worst thing you can do, he'd say, it's poison.

Is that so? What about beer, Bobby? Or shots of Jameson?

It's different. They don't destroy your lungs, they don't give you cancer.

So she stopped smoking in front of him. She only smoked around certain friends,

Steph or Amy Rizzo or Maggie Terrio or when she visited her sister in Jersey. She'd smoke a single cigarette when she got home from work. Walk into the backyard with a Marlboro Light and a glass of wine, let the day's bullshit float away in tiny puffs of smoke. Whenever they were out for drinks, she'd sneak away from him, find a compatriot to tuck outside with, even before the asshole of a mayor banned smoking in bars. Bobby hated it, especially when her partner in crime was a guy, even his own brother Franky. The only thing that ever made him jealous.

He'd pull her aside half an hour later, when their friends were up at the bar.

What the fuck were you two talking about? A little drunk, the slurring coming on, the belligerence along for the ride.

What?

Outside. I saw you laughing outside with Stevey.

Fucking Christ, Bobby. Relax.

Tipsy herself, glad to see Bobby the jealous one. For once.

You'd love it, T. I'm sure you'd love it if I snuck outside with Amy and you saw us falling over laughing. Yeah, you'd fucking love it if I was outside with Amy. Or Steph.

She's pretty sure Bobby said that: Or

Steph. He must have said that at some point. They fought about it more than once. He knew what buttons to push, even if he only pushed them when he was drunk.

When she got pregnant, she quit. Easy, no fuss. She didn't have cravings, even after Alyssa was born. Not really. Here or there. After a few drinks, sure. Sometimes when she was driving. But for the most part, it was easy enough. Cold turkey.

One night, right before she got pregnant with Bobby Jr., they were all out at the Leaf: Bobby; Franky; Bobby's father, Michael; Amy and Timmy; maybe even Steph; a few other guys. A big crew. A few tables pushed together in the side room. They were celebrating something, she can't remember what. Gail was watching Alyssa. Michael was drunk and jovial, telling stories about the boys growing up. Everyone feeling pretty good, backslaps and smiles. Franky smoking like a chimney, right next to Bobby.

"Jesus Christ, Franky."

"What?"

"You're blowing the smoke right in my face."

"Okay, sensitive. You're in a fucking bar. Deal with it."

"You want to give yourself cancer, fine. But spare me."

The whole table snickered, little grunts of disapproval at Bobby's sanctimony. He got up in a huff, strode to the bathroom. Franky waited until he was out of sight, handed everyone a cigarette, and gave instructions. The table went quiet, waiting for Bobby to come back to launch the prank. He sat down, still pissed but sheepish about it.

"Hey, Bobby, my bad. I shouldn't blow the smoke in your face. Seriously, my bad."

Franky reached a fist over, looking for a bump from his brother, an official sign that all was forgiven. Bobby smiled, that goofy grin he could never contain, and gave his brother a pound. A beat passed. Then Franky and everyone else at the table, including Tina, brought cigarettes up to their lips in unison. Franky lit his and passed the lighter to Tina. Bobby stood up, grabbed his jacket, and stormed out the door as the whole table laughed.

Tina followed him outside.

"Bobby!"

He was halfway down the block. She had to jog to catch him. She wasn't wearing a jacket. It was cold; her breath shot out in plumes. She stood in front of him.

"Bobby, it was a joke."

Over Bobby's shoulder, she could see that Franky had stepped out of the bar, was slowly walking toward them.

"Go back inside with your friends. I'm going to get Alyssa and then I'm going home."

He stepped around her. The street was empty, all the stores shuttered. She stepped in front of him again. She was still clutching the cigarette and the lighter.

"Bobby, are you fucking kidding me? Don't do this. Don't ruin the night. It was just a joke. I'm your wife. I love you."

He leaned down, his expansive blue eyes came to rest right in front of hers.

"You're a bitch."

He stepped around her again and this time, she let him go. He walked off in the direction of his parents' house and didn't look back. She turned around and saw Franky retreat into the Leaf. She smoked the cigarette Franky gave her alone, outside the bar, rubbing her arms to keep them warm. When it started to rain, she went back inside the Leaf.

Five months later, Bobby was dead.

She thought about that night often in the years after Bobby was killed. After the kids were in bed, she'd smoke half a pack a night in the kitchen alone, cursing him.

I'm a bitch, Bobby? Cigarettes are bad for you? Fuck you, Bobby. I'm still here. I'm still

*here and you're fucking dead, Bobby. Run-
ning into burning buildings is bad for you,
Bobby. Cigarettes are fucking dandy.*

She'd wake in the middle of the night,
lungs raw, and beg his forgiveness. Smoke a
cigarette in bed and ask him to forgive her
for that too. Every night for almost two
years. The cigarettes in the kitchen, the
curses in her head. Tougher to quit the
second go-round. Tougher because she
needed to quit this time, needed to quit for
the kids. It took a few tries. She used the
gum.

Someone knocks on the bathroom door.
Tina sneaks a last drag and then stubs her
cigarette out in the sink. She turns the
faucet on and splashes some water on the
smeared ash. Stephanie stands and lifts the
toilet cover; Tina drops the butt into the
commode. Stephanie lowers the lid, sits
back down on top of it.

"Who is it?"

"Alyssa."

"One second, sweetie," says Stephanie.

Stephanie wipes her face one more time,
stands up. Tina takes a swig of Scope and
spits into the sink. A languid haze of blue
nicotine smoke lingers, despite the vent.
Tina opens the door. Alyssa stands on the

other side, a sour look on her face. She looks at Stephanie, whose eyes are still swollen from crying.

"Jesus, everyone is crying today."

"Alyssa, enough. What do you want?"

"Were you guys smoking in here?"

Stephanie raises her hand.

"Guilty as charged."

Alyssa eyes her mother.

"I let Aunt Stephanie smoke one cigarette, Alyssa. She won't smoke any more tonight. Right, Steph?"

"Right. My bad. Won't do it again."

Alyssa rolls her eyes, a practiced gesture of exaggeration.

"We're hungry. Can you order the pizza?"

"Sure. What do you want, Steph?"

"Whatever is fine with me."

Tina reaches for her wallet, takes out some money, and hands it to Alyssa. "There you go."

Alyssa hesitates. "Aren't you going to order it?"

"Alyssa, the number for Vertuccio's is on the fridge downstairs. Dial it. Tell them what you and Bobby want. Give them our address. When they come, pay and give the delivery guy a tip. This is not rocket science."

"Okay, okay, don't have a shit fit."

"How many times do I have to tell you about the language?"

Alyssa shuffles away, saying something under her breath. Tina shouts after her.

"Were you eavesdropping?"

She hears Alyssa lumbering down the stairs. Stephanie walks out of the bathroom.

"Sorry."

"Not your fault. Thanks for taking the bullet on the cigarette."

"Do you think she heard?"

"Maybe a little, but not the whole thing. She stomps around like an elephant. We would have heard her."

"How's she taking this whole Wade thing?"

"Menzamenz."

"She get her period yet?"

After thirty years of friendship, Tina no longer bothered trying to discern a logical pattern to Stephanie's questions.

"No."

Stephanie shrugs.

"God got my kids mixed up. She's built like her father, she's already taller than me. Meanwhile, little Bobby got my genes. He's a sprite."

"Any boys?"

"No, not yet. I keep praying she'll wake up one day with some shape, a set of tits, something."

"Life isn't fair." Tina chokes back a dirty look. Stephanie wouldn't know the first fucking thing about being the ugly duckling, wouldn't know about being tall and lumbering or short and flat-chested. Since the sixth grade, she's gotten plenty of attention from the boys.

Tina checks the time. Wade should be here any minute. She's not ready. She walks back into the bathroom. She grabs another lipstick, something more demure.

"Are you nervous about tonight?"

"I am."

"Have you guys . . . ?" Stephanie makes a slapping gesture with her hands.

"Have we what?"

"Fooled around yet."

"No."

"Really?"

"Really."

Stephanie drapes herself inside the door frame.

"Tina, have you fooled around with anyone since Bobby?"

"Jesus, Steph, no."

Stephanie adopts a look of mock surprise.

"What about Tommy Patek?"

Four years ago, Tina went out on a few dates with little Bobby's baseball coach. His wife had run off to Florida with her trainer and left him with two young kids. He was a nice-enough guy with stale breath and a fragile psyche. On their third date, he took Tina to a Spanish restaurant in Mariner's Harbor. He excused himself to go to the bathroom as soon as they sat down. Fifteen minutes later, Tina's cell phone rang. It was Tommy, calling from the parking lot. He was rambling and Tina suspected he was drunk. He said he was confused and that he couldn't keep seeing her, that he had left money with the maître d' for her dinner and a cab home. Then he hung up.

Tina ordered a carafe of sangria, a shrimp and chorizo appetizer, and seafood paella. She asked for the check halfway through her second carafe of sangria. When the embarrassed waiter brought it over, she opened the black check holder to discover the crumpled twenty Tommy had left her sitting on top of a scribbled bill.

There was no fourth date.

"We made out on his couch one time. His seven-year-old daughter walked in on us just as he was getting to second base."

"Oh, very high school. Role playing. You slut."

Tina doesn't respond, keeps applying the new lipstick.

"You're lying." Steph presses.

"It's the truth."

"So you're telling me you've never slept with anyone beside Bobby." She lowers her voice, down to a hoarse whisper. "I don't fucking believe you."

"I didn't say that. Jesus, I don't want to talk about this. Not tonight."

"C'mon, Tina."

"I'm trying to get ready. Jesus."

"Was that his name? He-zeus? Was he Dominican?"

"Enough. Junior year, Bobby and I broke up for like three months, when I was away at school. I don't even remember why. Anyway, I went out with this other guy, Dave McKinley, a few times."

"You and the Irish guys."

"He wasn't Irish, he was Scottish. And Bobby is half Italian."

"So what happened?"

"We had sex twice. The first time I was drunk and the second time he was. Nothing special, no big deal."

"Did you ever tell Bobby?"

"No."

Tina sometimes wonders what Bobby did during the three months they were broken up. She asked him when they got back together that summer. He said he got drunk with his friends same as usual, confessed that he made out with Chrissy Nolan in the back of the Leaf one night, but that was it.

He was probably telling the truth. Bobby was incapable of deceit. Capable of calling her a bitch. Capable of drinking more than he should. But not a lie. Not a big one anyway.

When he asked her the same question, she lied. She never mentioned Dave McKinley or the other guy that she dry humped for a week. She said she'd focused on her studies, gone to the gym, some other bullshit. She acted hurt at the Nolan revelation, as if it were a huge betrayal, even though they were broken up, even though she'd done far more than Bobby.

And he believed her! He spent the whole summer trying to make amends, treating her extra nice. All because of a drunken make-out with Chrissy Nolan.

And what does she wish today? That Bobby had fucked Chrissy Nolan. Fucked her senseless. Fucked her for two months straight. So he didn't go to the grave having only slept with her. So that Bobby had as much joy and sex and fun in his life as possible without betraying her. She visualizes it sometimes, a naked Bobby trying to manage Chrissy Nolan and her long colt legs in the back room of the Leaf. It always makes her laugh.

Good for you, Bobby, she thinks.

Doesn't stop her from shooting Chrissy Nolan nasty looks every time she sees her. Doesn't stop her from enjoying the fact that Chrissy Nolan is no longer thin and spry but thick and desperate, that her skin, once as pale and delicate as an eggshell, has grown ruddy with age and alcohol, that the alluring brown locks have become a mess of short, tangled hair dyed blond on the cheap.

"So you haven't gotten laid in like nine years?"

Stephanie is swinging from side to side in the door frame. Tina regrets this entire conversation, regrets having asked Stephanie to watch the kids in the first place. She should have asked Amy or Gail. But Amy's in Florida and Gail, well, she couldn't very well ask Gail.

"I would have fucked half the Island by now," Stephanie says ruefully.

No doubt, Tina thinks.

The doorbell rings.

"So what's this guy Wade like?"

Tina thinks for a beat and then answers.

"He's different."

"Meaning?"

Tina hears the front door open downstairs. She hears Bobby Jr.'s excited hello. She can't hear the substance of Wade's reply, but the tenor of his voice soothes her. She wants to be away from Stephanie, in the car with Wade. She's missed him, she realizes, and that's both scary and reassuring. Stephanie walks out into the hallway, shouts to Wade that Tina will be down in a few minutes. She reenters the bathroom with a grin.

"He's cute."

Tina is almost done. She flexes her eyes taut, applies some eyeliner.

"And rich."

"Steph, how could you even tell that?"

"Tell me I'm wrong."

"I don't know. He lives in Manhattan. He's friends with Peter."

"So he's rich."

"I guess so."

Why is she doing this, making her feel bad? What difference does it make? Why is she denying it? Yes. He's rich. So what?

"So that's what you meant when you said 'different'."

"That's not what I meant."

She turns, done with the mirror.

"How do I look?"

"Hot. Classy."

Tina looks down. She bought a new outfit for the night. A simple black dress. Prada.

She tries to remember whether she ever wore anything this expensive when she was with Bobby. Probably not. They were kids. She feels like a fraud. She wants reassurance from Stephanie that what she is doing is okay, that it's not a betrayal, that nine and a half years is an appropriate amount of time, that Bobby would be okay with this. But she's cautious about showing Stephanie a softness. Something in Stephanie's behavior tonight makes Tina think of fishes being gutted.

"What is he anyway, Wade? Another mick? Definitely not eyetie."

"He's nothing." She shrugs. "You know, American."

Tina takes a red silk wrap out of the closet. Another new purchase. The receipt from Saks flashes in her head, four digits before the decimal. Only two items: the dress and the wrap. Absurd. And then the thought, impossible to resist, that the money for these things, things intended to impress another man, is a direct result of Bobby's death. She wouldn't have shopped at Saks while Bobby was alive; she barely knew it existed. Bobby's death made her a different woman, in more ways than she could have guessed. Almost everything about her has changed, but the guilt remains.

Stephanie grabs Tina's purse, puts the pack of Marlboro Lights in it.

"For later," she says with a wink. She hugs Tina and kisses her cheek. "Have fun."

"Thanks, Steph."

"Where is he taking you anyway?"

"Some place in the city. Per Something."

"Per Se?"

"That's it."

The expression on Stephanie's face is equal parts admiration and envy. She raises her right hand, rubs her thumb over the tips of her index and middle fingers in a quick, repetitive motion.

"Oh yeah, he's loaded."

Tina feels better when she's in the car with Wade. His presence calms her, takes her out of her head.

"Sorry about Steph."

When they came downstairs, Wade was sitting on the couch, watching television with Bobby. He stood up, introduced himself to Stephanie. After she shook his hand, she touched the fabric of his tan blazer and gave Tina a knowing glance. "Cashmere," she'd said. And then added, "Very nice," in case her point hadn't been caught.

"Sorry for what?"

"You know, the whole cashmere comment."

He laughs. The jacket suits him. So do the blue tie and the BMW. He's not trying to be something else. This is him. He has money, he won't shove it in your face, but he won't hide it either. He's not ashamed.

"I'm sorry I'm a little distracted. She told me tonight that she's having another affair. Well, maybe not an affair, but that she screwed around with one of her husband's friends."

"Wow, you had some day. How did everything go with Mrs. Amendola, by the way?"

She finds it endearing that he calls Gail Mrs. Amendola. She has to remind herself that Wade knows her, that they may have even met for all she knows. It's hard to imagine that; they seem to belong to different worlds entirely. But she is his good friend's mother. He's probably heard Peter complaining about Gail for years. Sometimes she finds it comforting that they have this preexisting connection; sometimes it makes her uneasy. Tonight is one of the uneasy times.

He's driving without her guidance, making his way to the West Shore Expressway. She would have taken Hylan, then Father Capodanno to the bridge, but what's the difference? Six one way, half dozen the other.

"It went fine, I guess. I don't know. She's tough to read sometimes. Did you ever meet Gail?"

"Once. In college. At graduation. A few of the families went out to dinner. I doubt she'd remember. There were probably fifty people at the dinner. We were all at different tables."

He pauses, glances over at her. He's tucked his upper lip into his mouth, his bottom teeth are gnawing on the indrawn flesh. She doesn't know all his ticks yet, but she knows this one. He's hesitating, trying to decide whether to tell her something.

"Go ahead," she says.

"Bobby was there too. I met him. I remembered that the other day when you told me you were going to tell Gail."

"Oh, I didn't know that."

"Yeah, I'm sorry."

Sorry for what, she thinks, sorry you met my dead husband before he was dead? Or my husband? Sorry you told me? Sorry you didn't tell me sooner? Or just plain sorry? Probably the last. There's no easy way to talk about this.

"That's okay. He must have been what? A senior in high school?"

"I think so. I remember Franky was teasing him about his girlfriend."

"You mean me."

"I guess so."

"That's crazy."

"I know."

She does a few swift calculations in her head, trying to line up certain events in relation to this meeting between Wade and Bobby: before or after. She slept with Bobby for the first time in April of their senior year. 1993. April 16th. At her house. Her parents away for the weekend. Peter's graduation was in the middle of May. When Wade met Bobby, Bobby was not a virgin. They'd already made love. For reasons she cannot fathom, this is important to her. Crucial. Her panic subsides.

"I remember Peter telling me that Bobby and Franky were pretty close. Closer than he was to either of them."

"Yeah, Bobby and Franky were tight. They were always together. Franky kinda went off the deep end after Bobby was killed."

How is Franky going to react to all of this? She's been so worried about telling Gail, but Franky is a different story altogether. He sees every little thing as an insult when it comes to Bobby's memory; this will be a mortal sin. She's always sensed that Franky

66

had notions about maybe taking his brother's place. Never stated, of course. Just a sense. But Franky's darker thoughts have a way of making themselves heard.

Not tonight. She will not worry about this tonight.

"I'm sorry, but can we talk about something else."

"Of course . . . tell me about your friend's affair."

She gives him the condensed version of Stephanie's story: the Jets game, the hairs in the sink, Stephanie screwing Tommy Valenti. Wade listens to the whole story before rendering his verdict. He doesn't interrupt like Bobby would have, peppering the story with exclamations of "No shit" or "Get the fuck outta here." She can't help herself; she catalogs their differences.

"Well, you can't argue with her logic. *Who* does shave to go to a football game?"

"She's crazy, but I'm guessing she's not wrong. Vinny's a scumbag."

She feels self-conscious, a little coarse, a little Staten Island, using that word. She reminds herself that Wade is a grown man who has certainly heard worse, no matter what kind of jacket he wears.

"He used to work on the floor of the stock exchange. He was a specialist; I think that's what they were called."

"Oh, Stephanie is married to *that* Vinny. The specialist."

"Yeah. How did you know that?"

"I remember Peter telling me about it. How some guy he knew from Staten Island got jammed up in the specialist investigation and he had to get him a lawyer."

"Yeah, Petey was too concerned with his own image to take the case himself. Can't have the gindaloons from Staten Island roaming the halls at his precious law firm."

Wade grimaces.

"I'm sorry, I know he's your friend."

"It's okay. In fairness, though, it's really not the sort of work he does. I don't think he handles that kind of criminal stuff. Not for individuals anyway. And on top of that, it was probably best for Vinny to get a lawyer he didn't know."

That's what Peter told Stephanie, but Tina always thought it was bullshit. An excuse not to deal with Vinny.

"How's Vinny doing? Peter told me he didn't end up getting indicted."

"No, he didn't, but there was another trial. The SEC, maybe? The whole thing ended up costing them a bundle. Vinny's not even working now. I think he just day-trades."

"I'm sure. Those guys had the rug pulled out from under them. There's nothing left down there. They don't need the Vinnys of the world anymore. All the exchanges, it's the same thing."

Wade sounds wistful. He has a way of talking that makes Tina feel secure, as if she's in the hands of someone who has things sussed out. Who knows which path the world is going down and has prepared himself. He doesn't have Bobby's hard-charging physicality. His masculinity is more subtle, but he can protect and provide.

That's what Tina really meant earlier when she told Stephanie he was different. She doesn't think of Bobby every time she looks at Wade. The few other guys she dated or considered dating — the city workers and the union members, the business owners and the blue collar drinkers, all the Staten Island boys who lived their entire lives on a slab of land large enough that they forget it's an island — all those guys, they were just bad copies of Bobby. Inadequate copies. He was the absolute best possible version of that man, the absolute best. To try to love some lesser version of him would be the greatest insult to his memory she could imagine. If she wanted to feel love (and she was still young and wanted to love and be loved in return), she needed to meet someone who didn't feel like a cheap imitation of her dead husband.

But how do you do that when all you meet is thirty tiny variations on the same theme? The same bodies sustained by pasta and bread and meat; thick of neck; firemen and cops and sanitation workers, and the occasional accountant or lawyer thrown in for good measure; Italian or Irish or maybe something else but not likely; good men mostly, solid, dependable men who work hard and don't expect much of the world, but men who you look at across the table and think only this: you are not Bobby. You will never be Bobby.

You don't. So she stopped trying. Until her dead husband's older brother called her and said, I have someone I'd like you to meet, and she demurred, and then he said, He's a widower, his wife was killed in a car accident three years ago, and she thought, What the hell, and so they had one dinner and he made you laugh with his unexpected sarcasm and old-fashioned manners, then they had another and he made you laugh again, and then they had a few more dinners and then he met your kids. . . .

"Have you spoken to Peter lately?"

Wade's question suggests news of some kind.

"No, not really. Why?"

"I think he and Lindsay are going through a rough patch."

"Bullshit. The Stepford couple?"

"I think so."

He sounds grim, like a doctor giving an unfavorable prognosis. Tina wonders whether Gail knows. Peter's the successful son, lives in Westchester, partner at a law firm. Gail always jokes that he's gone lace curtain, but she'd be crushed if something actually impinged on his perfect life. Marital problems are for people like Stephanie and Vinny, not Peter and Lindsay.

"Maybe I shouldn't have said anything."

"No, it's not that. I just hope I didn't put too much on Gail's plate today. And Peter's the golden boy, never does anything wrong."

He reaches over and grips her hand.

"Sorry."

Stephanie's teasing has stuck in Tina's head; she was trying to turn this into something base, something vulgar. Not sex but money, Stephanie rubbing her fingers together. Tina looks out the front windshield and sees the blue span of the Verrazano approaching.

"Do you care if we don't go to Per Se?"

"I guess not but . . ."

"Get off at this exit. Here. Now."

The urgency in her voice surprises her.

"Jesus."

He swerves toward the Lily Pond Avenue exit, cutting in front of a low-slung Camaro. Tina watches the car's passenger window slide down. A Hispanic teen in a Yankees hat nonchalantly gives them the finger as the car reaccelerates away from them and climbs toward the bridge.

"We have to cross over. Go back the other way. Make a left here."

Wade makes the left and after a few hundred feet, he pulls onto the shoulder, puts the car in park, and turns on the blinkers. They are parked underneath the onramp to the bridge, a half mile of quasitunnel. A few cars zip past, but the traffic is light.

"Where the fuck are we going?"

His usually placid face is curled with annoyance. Tina hasn't ever seen him angry. She unbuckles her seat belt, leans over, and kisses him, shoving her tongue into his mouth. His anger fades and he responds in kind. She pulls away, a little, so their eyes are inches apart.

"Only to get the best fucking pizza in the world."

She kisses him again, closes her eyes, and lets the world narrow to the entwining of their tongues.

Denino's is packed. A throng of people stand in the crammed entry-way, waiting to be seated. Families spill into one another at long planks of connected tables. Crews of oversize men squeeze into booths. A large group of teenagers sits in prim tribute to times gone by: girls on one side of the table, boys on the other, the space between them heavy with hormones. Old and young, sweaters and jeans, earrings and chains, pitchers of beer and soda, silver plates with bubbling pies, the air thick with the smell of garlic and oregano. A raucous, semicommunal pizza party; every soul in the room content.

Tina and Wade slide past the crowd in the hall. The woman at the hostess stand — ancient, white-haired, Italian — gives Wade the once-over before taking his name. Wade navigates them to an empty stool at the bar, turns it so Tina can sit, stands next to her as they wait. He orders a pitcher of Bud. Every few minutes the music stops and a name is announced. *Esposito, party of four. Esposito, party of four.* The bar is packed. A few of the guys glance at Wade, scoping the jacket and tie. He stands out, no doubt, tall and upright in a room of stocky and hunched, but if Wade feels out of place, he doesn't show it. Tina is overdressed as well, but no one seems to notice or care. When the pitcher arrives, Wade has to take out his wallet to pay. Tina can't help thinking that Bobby would have had a twenty already in hand.

Crowley, party of eleven. Crowley, party of eleven.

"So this is the famous Denino's," Wade says as he fills their glasses.

"Peter used to talk about it, I guess," says Tina.

"Oh, just a little."

"It's not Per Se, I know."

Wade loosens his tie, unfastens the top button on his shirt.

"That's okay. After the make-out session in the car, White Castle would have been fine."

Tina laughs, feels giddy. She nearly crawled on top of Wade in the car and got the act itself over with, out of the way. Another obstacle removed. But she held back, a grown woman's urges losing out to the vaguely virginal desire to mark the first occasion as special. The truth is that he does it for her, excites her in that way, in a way that no one since Bobby has, even though it's for different reasons. She reaches a hand over, puts it on his chest.

"I feel like I'm back in high school or something."

"Shit, I wish I knew you in high school."

She laughs again. Wade flashes a thin, crafty smile, satisfied that he can amuse her.

"No, you don't. I was a prude."

Donato, party of six. Donato, party of six.

Tina finishes her beer. Wade refills her glass. A few minutes drift by. The smell of the place has woken her stomach. She's hungry, hasn't really eaten all day. The beer is already affecting her, her mind is floating alongside the hum of the room.

Alderson, party of two. Alderson, party of two.

"That's us."

They walk back to the hostess stand, Wade holding the half-empty pitcher and their glasses. The ancient woman walks them to a small booth, does a perfunctory wipe of the tabletop, and drops a stack of paper plates and silverware on the table. A waitress in a black T-shirt comes over. Wade defers to Tina.

Tina orders: a pepperoni pie, another pitcher of beer. Wade removes his tie completely, tucks it into an interior pocket in

75

his jacket.

"What kind of name is Alderson anyway?"

"High WASP. My father's people came over on the *Mayflower*, but my mother was off the boat from County Leitrim. Came here by herself when she was nineteen."

Tina smiles. Stephanie was right; she must have a thing for Irish guys. Or half-Irish guys. She waits for Wade to continue, to explain how his parents met, but he doesn't say any more. She is unaccustomed to having to ask questions about the parents of the man she's dating. Every man she ever dated, his whole life was right in front of her. In plain sight. Nothing needed to be said. It was simply known. This is another thing she likes about Wade: there are things she doesn't know.

Wade is looking around the room, soaking it all in.

"My mother would have loved this place."

The pizza arrives with an abrupt clatter; the waitress slings a grease-stained pizza stand in the middle of the table and drops a tray on it. She slides a container of Parmesan cheese and a container of red pepper flakes under the tray. The cheese on the pizza sizzles; the pepperoni have curled into tiny basins of oil.

"Careful, that tray is hot," the waitress

chides as she whirls away.

Tina slides a slice onto a paper plate, blows on it, and hands it to Wade.

"Give it a minute. You'll burn the top of your mouth if you eat it now."

He does as she says. He takes a bite of the drooping angle of the slice.

"Verdict?"

"Delicious."

"Not good enough. Best you've ever had?"

"The best I ever had?"

"Yeah. Say it."

"I'm not sure. Pepe's in New Haven is . . ."

Tina picks up a fork, brandishes it in the direction of his eyes.

"I'll tell you what, Tina. It's the best damn pizza I ever had."

After dinner, they walk slowly up a sloping street to where the car is parked. It's misting out, a rain so fine that it doesn't fall so much as hover. When they get into the car, they kiss until he pulls away.

"I'm not sure what that was about," he says.

"What do you mean?"

"I mean, I feel like that was some kind of test."

Tina feels embarrassed at her transparency. She stammers a soft disagreement.

"Not exactly."

"It's okay if it was. But you should tell me what you're thinking, what's bothering you."

"I guess we should have just gone to Per Se."

Wade brings his hand to her cheek, draws her eyes up and away from the floor of the car.

"Tina, it's okay that we didn't go to Per Se. I'm glad we came here. So is my wallet. But I'm not entirely sure where your head is. I'm thinking maybe we pushed this too fast too soon for you."

"No, it's not that. It's just that you're very different from Bobby and that's a good thing. I just wanted to know that you were alike in some ways too."

"Okay, so it was a test?"

She doesn't recognize the look on his face.

"Yeah, I guess so."

He looks out over the dashboard. A family passes on the sidewalk, the father carrying a grease-stained white paper bag with leftover slices. Wade puts the key in the ignition, turns on the wipers.

"So, how'd I do?" he asks.

"You ate five slices of pizza."

"So?"

"I like a man who leaves empty plates in

78

his wake."

Wade kisses her, a long passionate kiss intended as a prelude. His hand slides up the outside of her dress, to the base of her breast. Tina feels a flutter in her stomach. Outside the car, a few teenage boys hoot as they walk by in hoodies and jeans, oblivious to the rain. Wade leans over and honks his horn, startling the onlookers. They laugh up the street, gesticulating and hollering back at the car. Tina whispers in his ear.

"Take me home."

He looks disappointed for a beat until she clarifies.

"Your home."

The drive into Manhattan is agonizing. The rain picks up and the traffic slows. There's an accident on the BQE, closing a lane. Tina has too much time to think about what's going to happen. The flutter in her stomach turns into a pit. She calls Stephanie to check in, make sure the kids are all right. She whispers, pretends she's in a restaurant. They're fine, of course, and how is Per Se? Out of this world, another course just arrived, let me run. Wade raises an eyebrow when she hangs up.

"Don't ask."

The traffic thickens to a derby at the rise

in the BQE just before the Battery Tunnel; four lanes of cars jostle, connive, and try to funnel their way down to two. During the week, tempers would flare, but Saturday night is more patient. The city is right in front of everyone, the night still impossibly young.

Wade lives in Battery Park City. Tina knows this route well: after this merge, the steady crawl under the Promenade, the right onto the Brooklyn Bridge, staying right to take the FDR downtown. Getting to the city this way is a test of nerves: get right but spend as little time as possible in the right. You have to push and probe, test the resolve of others, flirt with collisions at every second. It's a miracle there aren't more accidents. She hates driving in the city, but it's more than that tonight.

They will drive and not see what should be there. She will not look so she doesn't see what isn't there, what should be there. They will drive around Ground Zero, trace a little semicircle around Bobby's grave. They will both try not to think about what is not in front of them. The tension in her body vibrates up and out of her, into the car, pulsing in the air.

The car has passed the crest of the hill; Wade needs to get over one more lane, needs a Good Samaritan or someone texting or a stalled car.

She can't do this.

"Wade, please . . ."

A guy in a busted Taurus slows down, lets a space open between his car and the bus in front of him, waves them in.

"Wade, I think I need to go home."

"What?"

A van with Chinese lettering on its side accelerates on their left, then abruptly veers in front of them, an insane dash across two lanes into the waiting space. Wade hits the brakes. Tina slides forward, but Wade reaches one hand over and corrals her in place. A few horns honk. The offending van is absorbed, part of the stream of traffic. The space closes.

"Oh, fuck this," Wade says, and then steers the car left, away from the throng, toward the empty toll booths for the Battery Tunnel. With his right hand, he searches the center console for an E-ZPass. He winks at Tina.

"I think we can spring for the toll. The bread at Per Se would have cost as much."

Tina pushes a long breath out. The car pauses at the booth and then glides down to the mouth of the tunnel.

"What were you saying?" he asks.

"Nothing," Tina says. "Never mind."

The car shoots into the tunnel, a blur of white tiles.

It's bad before it's good. They have to stop twice because Tina is overwhelmed and doesn't think she can do it. When they're naked together for the first time, she recoils from Wade's touch and turns away from him. She cries because despite it all — the years and the loneliness and the mourning, how she felt in the car earlier and what she wants to do now, the breeziness fueled by a few pitchers of beer, the knowledge that she's waited and been faithful, not just to Bobby but to his memory, been respectful and decent beyond what others expected, beyond what others did, that she's been a widow worthy of a hero because that's what Bobby is, will always be, despite the fact that she loves, *actually* loves, the man she's lying next to, and he loves her, she knows that too, even though she's not sure why, despite the fact that she's entitled to this, that she's earned this — despite all of that, she still feels shame, still feels this is a betrayal.

Wade is patient and kind and does nothing wrong. After a few minutes, he reaches for her naked back, leans to whisper something soothing in her ear, and she hears a shrill pantomime of her normal voice snap in the air.

"Don't touch me."

Tina feels the warmth of his body retreat, hears his breath, still patient, on the other side of the bed. The tears swell into body-wracking sobs. She pulls her knees up to her breasts. Whenever she closes her eyes, a different image of Bobby appears: playing basketball as a teenager, at the bar of the Leaf ordering a round, holding Alyssa in the hospital, in his gear at the firehouse. She opens her eyes, focuses her gaze on a spot on the wall. She tries to banish all memories from her mind. Before she can be with Wade, she has to be alone, has to be without Bobby.

Leave me alone, she thinks, for a little while.

She releases her legs, straightens them. She thinks of nothing but the physical reality of the moment: the slight chill in the room, the softness of the pillow, the fabric of the bedsheet draped on her nipples, a strand of hair caught in the corner of her mouth, the scratchy soreness of her eyes from all the crying.

This is a physical act, she tells herself, nothing more. Like going to the bathroom or eating.

No, it's not, she thinks. That is ridiculous beyond words. It is something more, has to be, or else you would have done it a lot sooner. You waited for a reason, Tina. You waited for the right person and you're lying in bed with him.

She thinks of Wade: the tensile rope of his runner's thighs, his spare chest with ribbons of thin hair, the surprising thickness of his penis, a pleasant contrast from his leanness everywhere else. An impulse to compare Wade and Bobby, to line their naked bodies beside each other in her mind's eye and catalog the differences, arises; she has a vision of Stephanie asking scandalous questions of comparison. She fights these thoughts off. She will not do that here. Everywhere else but not here.

She thinks of Wade again: the smell of him, his way. She visualizes their kissing episode in the car earlier, his hand finding the curve of her ass through the dress, the moistness between her legs as he fondled her. She feels the moistness returning. She reaches her hand backward across the bed, searching for his groin. He slides over to accommodate her reach. His erection has dwindled, but it responds to her trembling fingers.

When he swells solid in her grip, she turns and straddles him, pushing down on his chest with her free hand. Her other hand is still holding his cock, fully erect now, and she lowers herself onto it. She stops, her body clenching as it adjusts to a distantly familiar sensation; the pain lessens in spasms. When he's fully inside her, she starts to ride him. He reaches around the middle of her stomach, his fingers nearly touching across the small of her back. The physical dynamics are awkward — he is tall and she is short and this is their first go — but they settle into a pleasurable rhythm. Tina's tears return involuntarily and Wade stops moving when he notices. He starts to say something, but she kisses him, urges him on, takes control of their fucking, because she wants this, she needs this, needs to feel alive again, to sweat and to thrust and to fuck, to feel him throbbing inside of her, to cry and to scream and to come.

And she does. She has a ferocious orgasm that sends shudders up and down her body. The intensity of it sends her nails digging into the wiry muscle of his biceps, drives her teeth together in a jarring gnash. She remembers to breathe and the feeling expands and she puts everything into it and lets go. It crests and slowly descends; she feels like she's floating backward through a door toward humanity.

Her orgasm surprises Wade too, who comes in response, his fingers tensing as they slide down and grip the cheeks of her ass. She feels his stiffening spurt and slithery retreat; even after he's gone soft, their groins are still joined in sticky, wet congress. Tina feels an urge to hike her sex up to his face and grind her groin over his mouth, to have his hands on her ass as she careens toward another orgasm. She doesn't want to stop, doesn't want to start thinking again.

"Jesus Christ," Wade says, breathlessly. "Holy shit."

She feels the world returning.

"Holy shit," he says again, reaching a hand up for her tears.

Her crying becomes a wet giggle. She leans down and kisses him, then lays her head down on his chest. The room has a fecund stink, the smell of sex. Tina yawns, suddenly exhausted.

"Tired?" he asks, half jokingly.

"Long day," she says and then, through a hazy euphoria, she remembers how it started, with her telling Gail and the heartrending look on Gail's face. Then Bobby is back in her head and Stephanie is asking her questions in the bathroom and

Alyssa is frowning at her smoking and Bobby Jr. needs something. So before the whole crew can get properly started and ruin this moment, she tucks herself under Wade's arm, closes her eyes, and falls asleep.

Tina wakes with a shiver. She feels Wade's body coiled behind her. They fell asleep in a loose spoon, his hand is still draped over her shoulder. She's still naked and the thin bedsheet isn't much cover. She lifts his arm gently, slides out of bed, and retrieves her underwear off the floor. As she's putting them on, she spots the shirt he was wearing earlier, draped over an easy chair in the corner. She slips it on, like she's seen in movies but never actually done herself. Bobby almost never wore dress shirts. The shirt is comically long on her, like a night-gown; the hem sits below her knees. She closes a few buttons and pads into the kitchen.

He has the fridge of a wealthy bachelor: a six-pack of Stella, a bottle of half-empty white wine with a French label, a few hunks of cheese in the crisper, and a white bag holding restaurant leftovers. She wants cold pasta, a handful of rigatoni with gravy. Maybe a sliver of chicken parm and some almost-stale bread. She closes the fridge.

It was pretty damn good. One romp has awakened a hunger almost ten years in the making. Part of her wants to go back to bed, wake Wade, and do it again, but another part wants to be alone for a bit, to enjoy this nothingness, this leap between two lives.

She looks around the apartment. She didn't get the grand tour earlier. It's modern, a little austere. Lots of clean lines and sharp edges. She doesn't want to be nosy, but she has a restless energy that defies the hour. She walks through the living room to the second bedroom. She opens the door and flicks on a light.

The room is a mess; cardboard boxes lie scattered on the floor. A desk sits under a window that looks out onto Jersey. A sliding glass door next to it leads to a terrace. The white wall across from Tina holds three swaths of paint: robin's egg blue, a deep yellow, and a barely there gray. The room is stuck in a transitive state; it sits heavy with the weight of unfulfilled expectations.

A daybed sits against the wall opposite the window; a solitary box leans precariously, one corner off the edge, frames of pictures jutting above the rim. Tina walks over and sits on the daybed. She lifts the open cardboard box onto her lap. It's filled with pictures of Wade's dead wife, Morgan.

Tina's seen Morgan before — she and Wade had shown each other pictures of their deceased spouses on their third date — but these pictures are more intimate.

Here's Morgan and Wade at a fancy ball of some sort: Wade next to her in a tuxedo, she in a stunning red dress. Here they are in a restaurant: she's hoisting a glass of red wine in a jokey toast and Wade is rolling his eyes. She's beautiful, an athletic blond girl from Northern California with a touch of mischief in her eyes. A Stanford grad, an architect.

Tina looks through the pictures and each one summons the same question: How could the same man love this woman and love me?

One particular photo draws Tina in. Morgan is alone in this one, wearing hiking gear: thick socks and clunky boots, an oppressive backpack, a sweat-stained tank top. Her hair is pulled back in a ponytail and her lips are pursed in a tight smile under sunglasses. She's sitting on a large stone and behind her, Tina can see the white trunks of trees.

The Morgans in the other pictures are unaware, anchored to the moment of the photo, but this one *knows* somehow. Knows that another woman will be looking at this very picture one day. The look on this

Morgan's face is one of reluctant acceptance. It unsettles Tina, but after she stares at it for a minute, it's oddly comforting.

Some part of Wade will always belong to Morgan in the way that some part of her will always belong to Bobby. That's the way it has to be. It's not even a sadness. It couldn't be any other way; their losses bind them to each other. Sure, it's other things as well, but without their losses, there's little chance they would have found each other in a thousand years. It's okay to admit that. Their losses were the most important events in their lives. There's no shame in loving each other for the way they carried them.

Tina thinks back to earlier in the night on the BQE. She was so consumed by her own emotions, it didn't sink in that they were almost in a car accident. He reached his hand across like he could actually prevent her from going through the windshield. Morgan died in a car accident on the Cross Bronx Expressway, driving up to look at a house for sale in Rye. They wanted a yard and a family to fill it. She was thirty-four, having trouble getting pregnant. The coroner said death was instantaneous, she didn't suffer.

Small mercies.

She lifts the photo to her mouth, kisses

the sunglass-ed image of Morgan.

"I'm sorry," she says. She puts the photo back in the box and sets the box on the bed.

She wants to punctuate this moment, singe the night into her memory. She remembers the pack of cigarettes that Stephanie left in her purse. She goes back to the kitchen, finds her purse, and fishes a cigarette from the pack. She lights it on the stove top and then goes back to the office. She opens the sliding door and steps onto the terrace.

It's cold outside. The rain has stopped, but the cement on the terrace is still wet beneath her bare feet. The terrace extends around the corner, back around to where Wade is still sleeping in the master bedroom. A covered gas grill and a few throaty pigeons are her only companions.

Tina can hear the city below. She walks to the corner of the terrace. Even at this hour, thousands of tiny lights illuminate the city. She can see the harbor through other buildings. She can see Brooklyn, the Verrazano, the ferry terminal, the hilly North Shore of Staten Island, the last-century industries of the Jersey waterfront. She feels the flesh on her legs ripple with goose pimples. She takes a drag of the cigarette.

She's never felt smaller than she does at

this moment. The enormity of the city, the space and significance of it, overwhelm her. She sees herself from a mile away, a fleck of nothing on one terrace on one floor in one tall building of thousands.

She lowers the lit end of her cigarette into a puddle on the railing. She flicks the stub out into the cold air and watches it plummet into the cradled space between buildings.

The color of the night is shifting from black to deepest blue. Dawn is coming. The daylight will break over Long Island first, make its way over the boroughs, illuminate Staten Island last. Her gaze fixes on Staten Island and its low, whispering darkness. The only place she's ever called home. She wishes she could hold back the dawn, prevent the light from crossing the Verrazano, hold back the day and its inevitable sadnesses for all those she loves.

But her wishes are useless. The dawn's march is steady, executed without mercy or cruelty, and even this colossus of a city is powerless against it. In mere minutes, the dawn has passed and left the pristine blueness of a perfect day in its wake.

CHAPTER 3
A QUARTER COME TO REST IN A QUIET PLACE

Gail is already awake when first light reaches the house. She skimmed through sleep, like a stone skipping over water. Strange dreams skittered away when she woke, the retreat of their dark tendrils leaving her anxious. She shifts to a sitting position, massages her closed eyes with the palms of her hands.

She puts on an oversized FDNY sweater and a pair of gray sweatpants, walks across the hall to Bobby's room. She lies on his bed, hoping to cajole her body into another half hour of shut-eye, but it's useless: she's up. Nothing short of a case of Chianti will remedy that.

She goes downstairs to the kitchen, takes a Tupperware container out of the fridge, grabs a fork, and sits at the table. She uses the side of the fork like a knife, carves off a sliver of meatball. She goes back to the fridge, finds a container of sauce, and pours some in with the meatballs. She stares, bleary-eyed, out at the street. It rained in the night; she could hear it from bed. The street is still slick with it and the air smells thick and lush.

They didn't go into the city last night. She told Michael she was too tired. She didn't tell him about Tina's new fella. Soon enough.

A pocket of drizzle descends on Wirra Lane. Across the street, one of their new neighbors, Dmitri, runs out from the old Grasso house to his car. He is thin, tall, Russian. The wife, Ava, seems nice; her face always carries a smile, but she speaks very little English. They have two young kids, a boy and a girl, with dirty-blond hair and the pinched faces of the frequently disciplined. The family moved in two years ago, after the Grassos moved to a retirement home in New Jersey.

"The last stop," Sal Grasso told them on the day they moved out. Michael laughed. Gail bit her lip so she wouldn't. Sal's wife, Carla, punched Sal's shoulder.

"Stop saying that."

"What?" he said, as one beefy hand rubbed his enormous gut and the other brought a cigarette to his mouth. "How long you think I got anyway, babe?"

It was hard to argue with Sal. He was an

obese, two-pack-a-day smoker charging hard on seventy, with two heart attacks in his rearview, possessed of a complete unwillingness to make any lifestyle changes at "this stage of the game," as he put it.

But the joke was on him after all. Three months after they moved, Carla was dead. A massive stroke. The one thing Sal had never counted on was outliving his wife, who was a decade younger and infinitely healthier. The last Gail had heard was that he'd moved out to Vegas to work as a blackjack dealer, something he always wanted to do. Go figure.

The Grassos had been good neighbors: friendly, not too nosy, helped you in a pinch. Invited Gail and Michael over for drinks every year sometime around the holidays. They reciprocated with a barbecue once a summer. Close, but not too close.

The Russians aren't as friendly. Michael gave up after inviting Dmitri to the Leaf one night. Dmitri said he didn't drink, didn't even thank Michael for the offer. A little brusque in his decline. That was enough for Michael.

"Even the fucking kids are unfriendly."

Gail feels differently. These things take time. She was a stranger here once. A newcomer in a place with a distaste for newcomers. That newcomer sat at this same table, waiting for Maria.

She runs her free hand over the surface of the table. They've had the table since they moved in: a gift from Maria and Enzo. The oak bears the nicks, bruises, and stains of forty years. So many words — angry, joyous, sad, hopeful — have passed over it. This table has heard more secrets than a confessional box. So much news. Even Tina's nugget from yesterday.

What was it that Maria used to say?

The news of the world passes between women in kitchens.

Gail can't remember the Italian words, only the lilt of Maria's voice, the hand gestures and pauses, the wooden spoon used to punctuate the point. The real news of the world: births, deaths, sicknesses, affairs. Whenever Gail had a bit of news, she told Maria here in this kitchen. And vice versa. Gail had no daughters of her own, no special confidante to pass news along to. There were friends, of course, but it never felt the way it did with Maria.

Until Tina. They've spent a good bit of the past ten years at this table: talking, crying, commiserating. Tina sat with her at this table on the night Franky was arrested. Two days after Christmas. No one had seen him since Thanksgiving, when he showed up drunk to Peter's house. They didn't have any details but Gail knew it was bad. Franky had called Michael and Michael had called the only lawyer he knew: Peter. There was nothing to do but wait. So Tina waited with Gail. Had a friend stay over to watch her own kids, sat here through a long, eerie night, holding Gail's hand, both of them sneaking glances at the phone. It finally rang a little after six in the morning.

Peter said that Franky was being held in the Tombs, would be arraigned later that morning, would probably be released later that day, but they might need to line up some money for bail. Peter had already hired a good criminal lawyer, someone who knew state courts, handled street crime.

"What did he do, Peter?"

"He beat the shit out of a cabby outside the ferry terminal in Manhattan. Broke his nose."

"Why? Why would he do that?"

"He says the guy said something about you."

"About me?"

Her stomach churned. Bile climbed into her mouth.

"About his mother. Like, 'fuck your mother,' something like that. Who the hell knows, Mom. He's not making a ton of sense."

After Gail hung up with Peter, Tina heard her confession. She was responsible for Franky getting arrested. What she'd said to him at Thanksgiving had precipitated this incident. But it was more than that. She blamed herself for everything that was wrong with Franky. She'd failed him from the start, had never known how to be the mother he needed. She'd cut him too much slack except on the few occasions when he really needed it. She dismissed Tina's protestations to the contrary.

"I'm a horrible mother, Tina. Don't ask my advice on raising kids anymore."

Tina didn't listen. She came to the table again and again, seeking Gail's counsel. When Alyssa was being teased at school, beyond the usual adolescent girl nonsense. When Bobby was having trouble reading. When Alyssa was driving her nuts with her moodiness, which was pretty much all the time. Nothing terrible, thank God. Just the everyday trials and tribulations of motherhood, complicated by the absence of a father. Gail's advice was simple, reassuring.

Be patient. This will pass. All kids go through an awkward phase. Bobby was a late bloomer too. Let them make their own mistakes. You're doing a great job. You're a great mother.

It wasn't always about the kids. One day, Tina was in a nasty mood, had even snapped at Gail a few times. When the kids were out of the way, Gail sat her down, asked her if something was wrong. Tina's face tensed for a moment, but then she started to laugh.

"How can I say this, Gail? I'm . . . frustrated."

"About what?"

Tina raised an eyebrow, coughed suggestively.

"It's, uhh, it's been a while."

The news of the world passes between women in kitchens.

That's what Maria said, one of the things she used to say anyway. She said other things too, mostly advice on how to raise kids, the advice that Gail passed along to Tina years later. Gail listened to every word, soaked in every suggestion. She'd gotten no guidance from her own mother. Constance had only ever said one thing on the subject.

"Don't have kids, Gail."

Inside a diner on Third Avenue. A lit cigarette in one hand and a spoon in the other, alternating sips of tomato soup with drags from the cigarette.

"What?" Gail asked.

"Don't have children. They'll bring you nothing but unhappiness."

Gail flinched. She searched her mother's eyes for knowledge. Was this a sick joke? Did she already know somehow?

No. Her face was earnest, the advice as sincere as it was impossible to follow. Gail was already pregnant and about to move to Staten Island and sitting there, miserable and nauseated, for the express purpose of telling her mother those two things. She'd told her about the move first, which was a mistake, because it prompted her mother's remark. She didn't know about the pregnancy; she was referring to the move. Of course she was. Everything that was done in the world was done for the purpose of hurting her mother.

Gail bit her lip. She should tell her mother about the pregnancy. It would explain things. This was not abandonment. They were seeking a better life for their child, something so fundamental it could explain the history of human movements on the planet. Her mother should have understood that.

But something held her back: fear. Not for herself, but for the child she carried. Her first maternal instinct. Protecting her unborn child from the words of its grandmother. Gail and her mother finished their meals in silence. When they stepped out of the diner together, Constance would not take her arm. A warm September night, the last gasp of summer. The streets of Bay Ridge were bustling, people out and about. The sun had slipped from sight, but the clouds above glowed an apocalyptic red. Men stood outside bars, hoping for a last glimpse of skin before the weather turned. Excitement, bordering on panic, in the air.

The men in the street stared at Gail as she passed, as if she were some rare beauty, which she knew she wasn't. Her looks fell somewhere between plain and pretty. Reddish hair, but not the luxuriant fire of a movie star, just a dull auburn that most people mistook for brown. A smattering of freckles haphazardly strewn across her face. A lack of curves generally, highlighted by the near absence of breasts. In high school, the boys used to tease her, call her a pirate.

Like a pirate, Gail.

With your sunken chest.

Get it? Ha ha.

Her eyes have always been her saving grace, capable of conveying emotion with a bracing intensity. A watery blue, cool and pure. Some girls spun and their skirts lifted ever so slightly; others leaned and left a but-

101

ton loose. Gail stared.

Once, when her tormentors called her a pirate, she fixed her eyes on the their ringleader, Andy Tormey, whose confidence flagged in the ferocity of her stare. A few weeks later, Andy stuck his tongue in her mouth behind the brick outhouse on the playground on Ridge Boulevard. When he moved his hand up toward the tit that he'd joked wasn't there, Gail laughed but absorbed the lesson: play to your strengths. After that, she did all that she could to draw attention to her eyes. She was never as popular as the girls with big chests or the girls who let the boys fiddle under their skirts, but she got her fair share of attention. And the jokes about her chest ended, especially after she dumped Andy before he could get his hands up her shirt.

No beauty queen, but she's okay with that.

The men stared anyway. They ignored the ring on her finger, the old woman at her side. They will disregard a stroller too. Michael was right; there were better places to raise a family.

She stared back at the men, hoping to embarrass the more brazen oglers. They laughed but looked away.

The remainder of the walk was slow and silent. Constance shuffled along and Gail followed a pace behind her. They reached her mother's building. Her parents lived on the third floor and she usually helped her mother up the stairs, but Constance turned to her at the building's entrance. They hadn't spoken a word since the diner. Through her mother's glasses, Gail saw her own eyes, the one gift her mother had given her without condition.

Constance's eyes were older, but held the same power as Gail's. She found Gail's gaze and held it.

My husband is a drunk. One of your brothers is in Vietnam, another is a junkie, and I don't know where the third is. Probably dead. I lost a child, your sister, when she was two. You are my youngest child. You are all I have.

Gail nearly faltered.

"Mom, I . . ."

"Yes, Gail?"

She smelled the soup on her mother's breath, mixed with cigarettes. Another wave of nausea hit her. She found a reserve of strength somewhere.

"Do you need help getting up the stairs?"

Constance didn't answer. She walked inside and closed the door behind her.

Three weeks pass. They haven't spoken. No calls. No visits. Two nights before the move, her father calls.

"Everything all right, Goodness?"

"Everything's great, Dad."

"We haven't seen you. Everything all right?"

"Grand."

"Okay then. Maybe I'll see you Saturday before mass?"

She hadn't told him.

"Sure, Dad. See you Saturday."

If she had, he would have asked Gail to meet him at Kelly's or Leggett's or whatever shit hole he was still welcome in. He would have tapped the stool beside him and picked a quarter from his pile of change on the bar. A smile. Always charming, never belligerent. "Feckless," that's what her mother said, a "feckless man." Feckless, like it was the worst thing someone could be.

And maybe it was.

"Okay, Goodness," he would have said, "we'll spin this twenty-five-cent piece here and if it comes up heads, you leave for that godforsaken place. But if it's tails, you stay here, among the good Christian souls of Bay Ridge."

Because that's what he did when she was a kid, whenever Gail was sent to fetch him at this or that saloon.

"Okay, Goodness, heads we leave. Tails,

we stay for one more."

And then he'd spin it. It would take a few tries sometimes, but then he'd send it roaring and it would shoot down the bar, ricochet off the mug of some startled inebriate, fly off the wood, and come to rest in some dark patch of the floor.

"Go look, Gail, which is it?"

She would lean down, her back blocking his view of her inspection.

"It's tails, Daddy."

" 'Course it is."

Then he'd push his empty mug across the bar for a refill. He'd hand Gail a Coke in a small glass bottle. She lied because it was better to sit there with him happy than to walk home with him sullen. Better to put off the shouting for as long as possible. Better to get a Coke than not get a Coke. So it was always tails until her mother got wise and started sending her brother Tom instead of Gail. Tom was simple. He reported the results of the coin flip honestly, without consideration for what might be best for himself or his siblings.

Anyway, that's how Gail feels in their new house, like one of her father's flickering quarters come to rest in a hidden corner of the booze-soaked wooden floor: spun in Bay Ridge and rotated right over the Verrazano

Bridge and come to rest in this forgotten place, this fifth of five boroughs.

She can't get comfortable, has never lived in a house before. Takes some getting used to, being in a place with more rooms than people. Their old apartment was tiny, just a kitchenette with a bedroom barely large enough for the bed. They lived there for three years, saving every penny so they could afford the down payment on a house. This house. Her house.

Her house. Doesn't feel that way. Every wall is covered in hideous wallpaper: garish yellows, greens, and oranges. Nicotine stains cover the ceilings in the bedrooms and bathrooms; the old couple who lived here must have smoked themselves into the grave. Every day, she smells the ghosts of cigarettes smoked long ago in a new spot: in the cabinet next to the fridge, at the top of the stairs, even in the emptied-out shed in the backyard. Whenever she catches the scent, she thinks of blue smoke drifting out from between her mother's brown teeth and her stomach churns.

Michael says he can't smell anything, that she's imagining things. He doesn't understand, couldn't understand. She can smell the brown mustard he'd smeared on the sandwich he'd eaten for lunch. She can smell the can of Schaefer beer Mr. Greeley, their new next-door neighbor, drank before he walked over to welcome them to the block. She can smell the chicken pot pie he'd had with the Schaefer, the Ivory soap he cleans himself with.

The nose of a pregnant woman is a wondrous curse.

Pregnant. Another thing she doesn't feel. Well, most of the time. An occasional dab of nausea, precipitated by nothing at all. The supercharged sense of smell. And the other thing. But that's it. Only in the last few days has she noticed a change in her stomach; the gaze of her belly button has drifted up, its bottom half pulled out ever so slightly by a nascent bulge.

The pregnancy. It is the reason for the house, its expedited purchase, the loan from Michael's parents, the awful dinner with Constance, the silent walk home, the disorienting move.

She goes days without seeing a soul. No one to talk to. She draws stares at the market. Tight smiles that don't linger. She can almost hear slack returning to cheeks when her back turns.

The house is cold and creaking. She stays in the kitchen with the occasional dash to the toilet. The phone sits in its cradle, no hint of agitation. In Bay Ridge, she had her friends and her job. Waiting tables wasn't glamorous, but it passed the time, kept a few coins in her pocket. Michael doesn't want her to work. He wants her to rest, to get the house ready. She can't rest and she can't ready the house either. There's too much to do; it overwhelms her. So she sits and she looks out the window or reads a book, and when Michael comes home every day, he looks around at his unchanged home a little confused but says nothing.

She looks out at the trees; their black, barren limbs sway menacingly at dusk, threatening to choke the street itself. A few hundred feet away, an empty lot stands rife with them, foreboding and defiant. The whole place makes her long for the dense certainty of concrete.

Michael is always at work, either at the firehouse or with his father, making a few extra bucks, putting a dent in the loan. His father owns a shop: part butcher, part deli. Enzo's Italian Delicacies. They make their own sausages, their own soppressata and fresh mozzarella. When Michael comes home from the store with a grocery bag full of food, Gail makes him shower, a quick rinse, but it does no good; she can still smell the meat and blood on him. He cooks and pleasant aromas — garlic in olive oil, the fry of onions, fennel, and pork sausage — fill the house, mask the stink of sinew and tendon on him. She watches him cook and feels useless.

He is excited.

"I bet it's a boy."

"Maybe."

"It's a boy. I can tell."

"How?"

"Girls take their mother's looks."

"So?"

"You still look beautiful."

They go straight upstairs, dinner unfinished, because when she isn't sick to her stomach, she wants Michael desperately. This is the other thing besides the nausea and the nose. She thinks of little else. And when he isn't around, she pretends that he is and touches herself, gently but still. She worries that something is wrong with her. He worries that they might hurt the baby, but the doctor assures her that sex is perfectly safe.

What about being so horny that you can barely read? Is that safe too? She doesn't ask these questions.

When they finish, she cries. The hormones are fiends: happy, sad, feisty, horny, withdrawn, hopeless, angry. All in the space of thirty minutes. Ping-ponging from one to the next with no discernible pattern. Michael tries to comfort her, asks her what's wrong.

"I'm lonely."

She is lonely, yes, but also unhappy. A new feeling for her. She's never been unhappy before, not really. Her mother hoarded the entire family's unhappiness so the rest of them simply pretended it didn't exist, despite all the evidence to the contrary. Gail couldn't wait to get out, get away, and now that it was done, what?

Unhappiness.

"You'll meet people. It takes time. Besides, in a while, you'll have all the company you need."

He rubs her stomach. She is already ready for another go. She feels out of control. No, that isn't it. Controlled by some other part of her, one she never knew existed.

"I miss my mother."

Words she never thought she'd utter. He frowns, furrows his brow.

"Hey, I have an idea. What if my mom came over, kept you company?"

"Michael, she doesn't like me."

"Of course she does."

"She doesn't speak English."

"She does. It's broken, but it's English."

"Broken?"

"Okay, it's fucked up beyond all repair."

Gail giggles and her breasts heave. The pregnancy has given her boobs. Michael reaches over and fondles one. He kisses her nipple.

"She can teach you how to cook."

She slaps the unshaven cheek grazing her nipple.

"Are you trying not to get laid?"

"All's I'm saying is you're always saying how you'd like to learn how to cook."

"I know how to cook. Open can, pour."

"Man cannot live on soup alone."

"Bread alone."

"Whatever." He rolls up on one shoulder, earnest as an altar boy. "Give it a shot, Gail. For me."

She rolls her eyes, pulls him to her.

"Okay. Now shut up and fuck me again."

She thinks, *I don't say things like that.*

A black car stops in front of the house and Maria gets out. Enzo beeps the horn and the car slowly rolls back into motion. Enzo drives like a man who learned to drive late in life, overly cautious, fixated on every detail. He performs a slow, precise K turn. The street is a dead end.

Maria ambles up the steps, one giant

smile. She is a short stout woman with a ruddy face, a long thin nose, and stringy gray hair. She wears glasses that enlarge her eyes and give her face a slightly grotesque appearance. She looks like the den mother for a house of goblins. Enzo is handsome and dignified, despite his line of work and age. Gail would love to know how they ended up together.

Gail opens the front door, manages a smile. Maria hands up a bag of groceries from the store. She uses the railing on the stairs, helps herself up. She seems ancient to Gail.

"Grazie."

She gives Maria a tour of the house. They walk from room to room. Gail comments on the first few rooms, speaks of their plans and designs, but after a while she stops, frustrated by Maria's silent scrutiny. Maria inspects each room with the intensity of a drill sergeant: she knocks on doors, she flushes toilets, she opens and closes windows, she kneels down to peer under beds. They finish in the kitchen. Maria looks at Gail.

"Needs work."

"Yes, you're right. It needs work. We . . ."

Gail's voice drifts and she turns to hide a leaking tear from Maria. For a moment, she's afraid she might start sobbing in front of this woman who clearly dislikes her. Maria takes a hold of Gail's arm; her fingers are surprisingly thin and delicate.

"Is very nice. Very nice. But . . . uh . . . needs work. Good?"

Gail nods.

"Good? Good."

Maria puts on a white apron and produces a tiny knife with a chipped black handle. She starts taking things out of the grocery bag and putting them on the counter. Garlic, onions, a can of tomatoes, a few stems of parsley, sausages. She takes out a chopping board and goes to work, all the while using the little knife. She moves quickly. The kitchen gets heavy with smells. They're like the smells that Michael's cooking produces but heftier, more elaborate.

Gail tries to follow what Maria's doing. The can of crushed tomatoes is opened and poured into a pot with olive oil and garlic sliced so thin it's translucent. Another burner is lit, sausages are tossed into a pan. Maria adds things to the pot, she adjusts burners. A film of sweat appears on her forehead. Gail watches as a bead rolls down her nose and drips into the pot as she's stirring it. She laughs. Maria turns, smiles, rolls her shoulders as if to say, "Hey, it happens."

The aroma in the kitchen adds layers, blends into a whole with distinct notes. After a while, Gail realizes she's no longer watching what Maria's doing. Instead, she's watching Maria: the crooked smile on her face, the lips moving silently, words in another tongue, conversing with ghosts. She's watching someone who loves what she's doing, who's transported by it. She's seen this look on Michael's face.

The pot is on a simmer. Maria slides some cooked sausage and meatballs into it. She lowers a wooden spoon into the sauce, tastes it. She reaches for the salt, throws a handful into the sauce. She chops some herbs, drops them in too. There's no recipe, no set of instructions; Gail will never learn to cook like this. It would take another lifetime, a different mother. Michael will have to learn to deal with canned soup.

A natural pause in the process. Maria ushers Gail to the new table, a housewarming gift from her and Enzo. She tears an end from a loaf of bread, dips it into the sauce, and hands it to Gail. She breaks off another piece for herself. She removes the cork from a half-full bottle of homemade wine. She ferrets out two glasses from a cabinet, pours a few mouthfuls of wine into each. She sits at the table, in a full sweat. Gail can smell her, an earthy funk, under the heavenly aroma of the sauce. Gail takes a bite of the soaked bread. The sauce hasn't simmered long enough yet, but somehow witnessing its construction makes it more delectable than usual.

"Delicious."

"Grazie."

Maria pushes the glass of wine across the table at Gail, raises her own.

They haven't told his parents yet, haven't told anyone yet. Michael is superstitious, wants to wait until she's three months along. He allowed her to tell her mother to explain the move and she didn't even manage to do that. And it doesn't seem possible that something is growing inside of her. She could say that she didn't feel like a glass, that she didn't drink in the afternoon, that she wasn't feeling well. She could even take a sip, couldn't hurt, and Lord knows she needs it. Maria holds her glass out, waiting. Gail pushes the glass away.

"Maria, I shouldn't. I'm . . . we're expecting."

A quizzical look. She doesn't understand. Gail thinks of a dozen euphemisms to explain, but none will help here.

"You know, I'm pregnant." She points to her stomach. "With baby."

Maria's expression changes. She understands. She removes her glasses, puts them on the table. She stands abruptly, spilling a little wine. Gail stands in response, uncertain. Are they going to hug? Maria walks in front of Gail, grips her arms. She kneels on the floor and kisses Gail's stomach very gently. Twice. When she looks up at Gail, her eyes are brimming with grateful tears.

And suddenly the pregnancy feels very real to Gail.

After Peter is born, Maria comes every day. She doesn't need to be asked. She knows Gail is overwhelmed, that Gail's mother will give no help, that her own son is working most of the time and trying to sleep when he isn't. She knows that tending to infants is tedious, endless work: they eat, they sleep, they shit, they cry. She knows that the tender moments of immeasurable joy are surrounded by hours of frustration and anxiety and uncertainty. She knows that the soft purple of a newborn's closed eyelids makes every mother think of death and drives her to do the silliest of things: wake a sleeping baby. She knows that caring for an infant requires the energy of the young and the patience of the old.

She also knows that Enzo will grow impatient with driving her to Michael's house every day, so in the winter months before Peter is born, she forces Enzo to teach her how to drive. They practice on the street in front of Gail's house, the car drifting into snowbanks. Gail stands and watches from the kitchen, her hands snug around the ball of her stomach. She sees Enzo's frustrated gesticulations in the passenger seat, Maria's shoulder shrugs in response. She tries not to laugh. Maria is learning how to drive so she can come help Gail. When she thinks about this, her eyes well up and her chest throbs with gratitude.

When she's not learning how to drive, Maria teaches Gail how to cook. Sunday gravy, eggplant parmigiana, chicken cacciatore, osso buco, a lentil stew with sausage. Gail picks up a little Italian, surprises Maria a few times with a few words or a phrase. They develop a language, a means of communicating: some Italian, some English, a few hand gestures. In the quiet moments, Maria kisses her own hand, reaches over and touches the bulge of Gail's stomach.

A host of incremental improvements occur in the run-up to the baby's arrival: Gail's cooking, Maria's driving, the state of the house. Michael and his friend Dave Terrio, who everyone calls Tiny, work on the house on the weekends. They finish the baby's room with two days to spare.

The tiny, spattered, shrieking pink wonder that Michael lays in Gail's arms has a shock of black hair.

"He looks like a Peter," Michael says, and Gail agrees.

Gail stands at the kitchen window, holding Peter in a swaddle and waiting for Maria. The black car staggers to a stop. Maria gets out and struggles up the front steps, trays of food balanced on her beefy forearms. She kisses Gail, lays the trays on the counter, and takes her grandson. Gail goes for a walk, gets some fresh air, runs some errands. When she gets back to the house, Peter is asleep and Maria is cooking. They sit at the table and eat. A few soft whimpers from the nursery upstairs crescendo into a wail. Maria stands, but Gail waves her back into a chair. She wants Maria to climb the stairs as little as possible. Something in Maria's gait is off; there's a flaw in the ambulatory machinery, one that she manages to hide unless she's climbing stairs. Gail glides into the nursery, eager to see her baby boy. He smiles up at her with marble eyes, the tears already drying on his cheeks.

They become a well-oiled machine, the

two of them: a cooking, cleaning, baby-tending machine. They spend every day together, for months on end. At night, Michael teases her.

"How is your new best friend?"

"She's a lifesaver. I don't know what I'd do without her."

"What do you talk about all day?"

"We don't talk."

"You don't talk."

"Not really. A little bit here and there, but it doesn't matter. It's nice between us."

"Good. I'm glad," he says through a yawn.

"Michael, what's the matter with your mother? The way she walks, something's not right. I think it's her hips. Has she had them checked out?"

"She's always been like that. She doesn't talk about it. I think it's her back. She had an operation once when I was a kid. I don't really remember why. Just remember my father taking me to visit her in the hospital."

"How is your dad? Must be nice spending all this time together at the shop."

"Nice?"

"Yeah, isn't it?"

"Standing behind a counter all day with a man who can't speak English, cutting pork chops, grinding meat? No, *nice* is not the word I would use."

"Jesus, Michael, he's your father."

"Would you want to spend every day with your father? Or, better yet, your mother?"

"No, but your father is nice. Pleasant."

"So everyone tells me."

There's something off between Michael and his father, something missing. They love each other, but it's almost like Michael is embarrassed by Enzo. Enzo is a simple man, sure, but then so is Michael. Gail doesn't quite understand their relationship. It is clear that Enzo loves it when Michael works in the shop; it is also clear that Michael hates working in the shop. Gail has no idea why things are this way. In her mind, a job is a job, and selling meat is a lot less dangerous than fighting fires. She wishes Michael would follow his father's path, but even as a young wife, she knows that trying to change him is futile. He loves being a firefighter.

"Anyway, it helps pay the bills right?" Michael says, eyes closed.

He yawns again and this yawn reminds Gail that she's exhausted as well.

The days are long, but the years fly by.

Another saying of Maria's, roughly translated by Gail. She agrees with the first, is unsure of the second. But sure enough, days turn into weeks and weeks into months and months into a year. They celebrate Peter's first birthday in the newly cleared-out backyard: Michael and Gail. Enzo and Maria. Tiny and his new girlfriend, Peggy. They sit at a red picnic table that stands in the shadow of the house. A dusty patch of newly seeded dirt leads down to a crumbling wooden fence that divides Michael and Gail's property from the house behind theirs. The weeds have been pulled, the decrepit shed removed. An adolescent red oak tree stands on the line between their property and the Greeleys'. Michael talks about a space to grow tomatoes, maybe a chain-link fence to replace the wooden one. Gail brings out a platter of roasted lamb shoulder with potatoes, carrots, and onions. The compliments flow in Maria's direction. She shakes a finger at the rest of the table, points it at Gail. Enzo laughs and slaps Gail's back. Michael smiles, inebriated and proud. Gail blushes. She wants to hold onto the moment in all its messy splendor.

A birthday cake is retrieved from the fridge. Enzo sings "Happy Birthday" in Italian. His voice is obscenely bad. The whole table laughs when he's finished. A man wanders around the side of the house, looks a bit unsteady. It's a bright windy day, everyone squints in the sun. Gail brings a hand above her eyes.

"Mr. Greeley?" Michael says. They invited a few neighbors over for cake. "Where's your wife?"

"Goodness," Gail's father says, his reddened face coming into view, "where's that grandson of mine?"

Her father, Sean, sleeps on the couch, his head thick with Enzo's wine. In the morning, Gail cooks him bacon and eggs. He eats with alacrity. Gail pushes more bacon onto his plate.

"You learned to cook, huh?"

"Among other things."

"Nice place you have here."

"Thanks."

"Tommy turned up."

"I heard."

"He was in California, in San Francisco. Brought a girl home with him. She's up the pole. Your mother is tickled."

"Is she now?"

He sighs, pushes away from the table. The corners of his mouth are yellow with egg yolk.

"I have an idea, Goodness."

He reaches into a pocket, pulls out some change. He flips through the coins, finds a quarter. He holds it up to her between his index finger and his thumb. She takes a good look at him. The booze has finally caught up. His eyes are runny and his chin trembles; the skin on his face has a purplish hue, like the veins are trying to escape his slowly drowning skull. She fights off the thought that her child could be infected by his sickness.

"You remember this game, Goodness. Heads, you stay here. You don't come see your mother or Tommy or his new wife. But if it's tails, you come back with me today and you let this go. We put it behind us. Okay?"

He pushes his plate aside. His fingers have lost their dexterity. After a few failed attempts, he gets the coin spinning. When he does, Gail swings her hand down on the table, covering the quarter with a resounding slap and startling her father. He looks up at her confused, like she's a bartender who's cut him off for no good reason. She doesn't bother pretending to look. Her eyes blaze down at the withered shadow of her father.

"It's heads."

She gets pregnant again. Exhaustion is this pregnancy's song. Peter's newfound ability to walk exacerbates her fatigue. Maria picks up the slack. She sends Gail to the couch for naps, occupies Peter, keeps the refrigerator stocked.

Tiny proposes to Peggy. She starts coming around to visit Gail. She's a little chatty for Gail's taste; she's flighty and lovesick. But like Gail, she's another Irish girl, soon to be married to an Italian. She grew up in Woodside, knows all about those melancholy apartments with their booze-soaked lassitude and the silences that leak into decades. And like Gail, she can't believe her luck in exchanging that world for this one.

Michael is skeptical.

"I don't get it."

"What do you mean? She's nice."

"Tiny's always had an eye for the cheerleaders, the prom queens. It doesn't figure."

"Why, because she's a little chubby?"

"She's a little chubby, she's not much to look at, she talks too fucking much, she's Irish."

Gail flicks his ear with her middle finger.

"Hey, that hurt."

"Good."

She turns away from him in mock anger

"How could I not love the Irish? My son is half Irish. And my other child."

He slides a hand around her, rests it on her protruding abdomen. The baby kicks and the flesh on Gail's stomach ripples. They giggle together.

"Boy or girl?" she asks.

"Girl," Michael says. "A feisty girl. Just like her mother."

Francis arrives in a February snowstorm. Colicky, more fussy. Difficult from the start. He doesn't sleep for more than an hour at a stretch. When Michael works nights at the firehouse, Maria stays over and helps Gail. Their exchanges grow testy in the wee hours when exhaustion and the oppressive neediness of the infant conjure moments of pure insanity. They apologize to each other in the mornings and laugh at their lunacies. Reconciled, they savor together the sparse smiles and gurgles and coos given by the reason behind their nocturnal bickering. They mark the progress of his older brother with wonder: the vocabulary, the awareness, the intelligence.

"Speciale, intelligente" proclaims Maria about the precocious young Peter. Gail has no way of knowing, no point of comparison. Her firstborn seems bright, but she's sure every mother thinks that way.

She gets pregnant a third time, a mere five months after Franky is born. When she miscarries, Maria is the one who drives her to the hospital. Maria is the one who calls Peggy to come watch the two boys. Whenever Gail cries in the months that follow, Maria hugs her and cries with her. Some days, Gail catches Maria crying by herself, dabbing her eyes with her sauce-stained apron. When Gails asks her about it, Maria simply says *nulla,* nothing, and smiles.

Michael is an only child.

One day, that thought floats into Gail's head while she watches Maria struggle to make it up the front steps.

More birthday parties are held. Tiny and Peggy buy a brand-new house seven blocks away. Other neighbors drift into their lives: the Grassos, the Landinis, the O'Tooles, the Dales, the Hudecs. Joe Landini is a cop; Sal Grasso is a transit cop. Mike O'Toole is a firefighter. Tom Dale works for sanitation. Terry Hudec is an assistant principal at a school in Bed-Stuy.

None of the wives work, except Jenny O'Toole, who works two days a week at a hairdresser on Hylan Boulevard. There's always someone to drop in, always someone to watch the kids in a pinch. They all have children as well, mostly young. It's a good block; when Mrs. Greeley passes away, all the wives take turns dropping in on Mr. Greeley with a tray of food and a six-pack of Schaefer. He complains about the fuss, but he's too grief stricken and lonely to refuse the hospitality. They were two months away from their forty-seventh wedding anniversary.

"I never ate this good when Sandra was alive. Strictly meat and potatoes in the kitchen, God rest her soul. Where'd a blue-eyed colleen like you learn to cook?"

"My mother-in-law, Sam. I married Michael for his mother's cooking."

"Thatta girl. I'll tell you something." He beckons her closer with a conspiratorial gesture. "Yours is the best. You got those ginny girls beat on the food."

"Nice of you to say."

"But Diana Landini wears them low-cut blouses, so she's my favorite."

He winks. She laughs and shakes her finger at him.

A year later, Gail and Michael are sitting at the kitchen table on a crisp spring morning when they hear a shrill shrieking. They look at each other confused until Diana Landini comes tearing out of the Greeley house and runs across their front lawn. Michael is up and out the door in a flash. Gail watches as he passes Diana and runs into the Greeley house. The quickness of his actions shocks Gail, thrills her. She often forgets that her husband is a man of action.

Diana is out of breath and pallid. Her breasts heave with exertion, threatening to slip out of her blouse. Her dramatic entry frightens Franky, who immediately melts down, and his meltdown, in turn, upsets Peter. Gail tries to calm the three of them. She fetches Diana a glass of water, lifts Franky to her hip, and slips Peter a cracker. Diana finally gets the words out.

"Mr. Greeley, I think he's . . . I think he's . . ."

"The kids, D. The kids. It's okay. I understand."

Gail looks toward the house. Michael has already seen a bit of death, she knows he has. In Vietnam. In burned-out buildings across the five boroughs. He's carried dead men, felt the weight of their forfeited hopes. He will do what needs to be done.

They sit there, wordless, until a fire engine thunders down the street. An ambulance follows shortly after. Neighbors step out of houses, wander over. Michael talks to the firefighters, leads them inside. When he walks back to the house, Maria comes limping across the front lawn. She had to park down the block because of the commotion. Michael walks up to her, explains what happened. Gail watches her make the sign of the cross as she stares at the house. They come inside.

Michael smiles at the boys and says simply, "He's gone." Diana starts sobbing. When Peter asks who's gone, Michael kneels down and hugs him.

"Mr. Greeley's gone. He went away, to a better place."

Michael retrieves a bottle of whiskey from the basement, pours a small measure for himself, Gail, Maria, and Diana. When they finish it, he walks Diana home.

In bed that night, he tells Gail that he found Mr. Greeley in his ugly brown chair, mouth agape, an uneaten plate of ham steak and fried eggs in his lap. He was already gone by the time Michael got there.

"Heart attack."

"It's terrible. So sad."

"Oh, I don't know. To go suddenly, no suffering, at seventy-four? While staring at Diana Landini's tits? I'd sign for that."

She hits him and he laughs.

"Pig."

She's wanted to crawl into bed with him all day. The only meaningful protest to death. She climbs on top of him and lets go of her dark thoughts. When they finish, Michael spoons her from behind, whispers in her ear.

"Pig fucker."

When Michael falls asleep, she gets up and checks in on Peter and Franky. She lingers over them, touching their hair and watching the tiny, restless spasms of their sleep.

She sweats through her third full pregnancy. A brutal summer starts early and leaks into October. She wakes sweating, falls asleep in a sheen. She spends her days leaning into the fridge or standing in front of the giant fan that cools the living room. Peggy is pregnant as well, a month further along; she comes to Gail's house and they sweat together, with ice cubes on their tongues, the backs of their necks, under their arms.

While Gail sweats, Maria coughs. She starts coughing around Memorial Day and is still coughing on Labor Day. It's a thick, phlegmy cough, sounds like her lungs have been filled with the wrong fuel. Every day, Gail asks her if she's okay.

"A cold," she says. *"Nulla."* Nothing.

She rubs Gail's stomach to change the subject. Maria thinks it's a girl. Gail thinks Maria may be right, especially if it's true that girls steal their mother's beauty. Her face is gaunt one day, puffy the next. Her legs ache with varicose veins. Even her translucent eyes seem dim and drab. She perspires like an obese sultan and the older boys, conscious of impending change, hang all over her.

In the fall, Maria's cough turns sharp and painful. The phlegm disappears; her mouth seems to pull sound from an empty chamber. One morning, Gail sees a red spot on the handkerchief that she coughs into and insists that she see a doctor. Not tomorrow or next week. Today.

"It's nothing, *nulla.*"

Gail doesn't accept this answer. She drives Maria to the appointment herself, her swollen stomach grazing the steering wheel. The doctor tells her it's viral bronchitis, nothing too serious. He suggests using a humidifier, drinking tea with honey and lemon, and taking Tylenol for the pain. Gail drives Maria home, stopping at a pharmacy to buy a humidifier. She sets up the humidifier in the still, dust-flecked bedroom of Maria's house. She tells Maria that she should stay home for a few weeks and rest. Maria says that Gail needs help, that she can't manage the two boys alone in her condition. Gail tells her that she'll need more help when the baby arrives, that she'll need a fully rested Maria without any cough. Maria lies on top of the bed, acquiescent, and this frightens Gail a bit.

"Are you okay? Do you want me to stay?"

"No, no, no. *Nulla.*"

"Stop saying that. It's not nothing."

Maria reaches for Gail's stomach.

"Bambina. Bella bambina."

"If it's a girl, I'll name her Nulla, after her stubborn grandmother."

Maria laughs, provoking a coughing fit, which brings her torso off the mattress. Gail eases her back down. She kisses Maria's forehead.

"Rest."

After Gail starts the car, she has a moment of uncertainty. She turns the engine off and reenters the house, as quietly as she can. She takes the stairs slowly, her bulk bringing a few groans from the wood. She doesn't want to scare Maria, wants to make sure she's okay. She pushes the door to the bedroom in a few inches. The soft light of late afternoon sun is muffled by the curtains; the humidifier spews moist air over the bed. She hears Maria's labored breathing, a few staccato coughs. She sees the dark bulk of her body turn in search of comfort.

Gail exhales. She is a mother, prone to

checking on her charges, even when there's no reason. Maria is resting. All may continue. She leaves the house as quietly as she came. She pulls the car delicately out of the gravel driveway, hoping not to disturb Maria. By the time she picks the boys up at the Landini house, her mind has moved on to a host of trivial concerns: what to make for dinner, whether Michael has to work this weekend, what to get the new neighbors as a housewarming gift.

She doesn't think of Maria again until Enzo calls that night and tells them through rolling sobs that he came home from the store and found Maria cold and lifeless in their bed.

Bobby arrives in the shadow of Maria's death, two months after she is put into the ground. His tiny body is pressed to cheeks streaming with tears, equal parts joy and grief. All look at him and think of Maria and how she would have loved to hold him. He spends his first day in this world without a name; they have been too busy, too guilt ridden and grief stricken, to worry about names. If it was a girl, the name was easy. But a boy?

Gail lies in the hospital bed, worn out in every way. Michael sits in a chair, holding his new son, trying to be happy. In the hallway, Enzo moans and shakes, his grief disturbing the happy idylls of the surrounding families and their brand-new bundles of joy. Tiny arrives with flowers. He is a new dad himself. His daughter, Maria, is a month old. Fatherhood suits him. He's gotten a touch thicker above the belt and below the chin. Enzo sees him and hugs him with vigor, crushing the flowers between them. He shepherds Tiny into the room. Tiny kisses Gail, lays the pressed bouquet on her lap. He takes the petite, placid wonder into his arms. He asks for a name.

Michael and Gail exchange a nervous glance. The boy needs a name. He does not know their sorrow. He has done nothing to deserve this. From the hidden recesses of her brain, Gail remembers Maria sliding a photo across the kitchen table to her. Something she wanted to share. A fragile, faded, black-and-white thing, with dozens of fold lines crisscrossing the two people depicted: a young girl dressed in a blazer and skirt. Large glasses on a long thin nose. No classic beauty, but a touch of eccentric comeliness. Maria. A boy, a few years older, stood behind her, blithely handsome, on the verge of masculinity. His hands folded across his chest in mock defiance. Gail pointed to him.

"Enzo?"

Maria shook her head, carefully turned the flimsy, yellowed paper over so Gail could see the writing on the back: Roberto e Maria. Lecca. 17 aprile 1931.

She turned the photo over again, pointed to the boy.

"My brother."

"Roberto?"

"Si. *Morto.* He died in the war."

"He was so handsome, Maria."

Roberto. Robert. Bobby.

"Gail?"

Gail looks to Michael for guidance. His eyes are tired, blank; no name is resting on his tongue. Tiny looks nervous for a second. She speaks without thinking.

"Robert. His name is Robert Enzolini Amendola. Named after Maria's brother, Roberto."

Tiny smiles, relieved. Even Enzo looks happy.

"Wonderful. Hello, little Bobby. Little Bobby Amendola."

It sounds right. A good name. Anyone named Bobby Amendola is gonna turn out fine.

"Gail?"

She goes to see Enzo weeks later, finds

135

him in the attic with dried sausages on strings hanging from the rafters. He's drinking his homemade wine and cutting pieces of sausage with Maria's knife, the one with the chipped black handle. Bobby is there, these things — the smell of that attic, the slicing of that sausage, the slosh of Enzo's wine — they slip into him. He is tiny, but he absorbs them.

"Gail! Gail!"

She feels hands on her arms. She looks up and Michael is leaning down, his face in front of her. Not the addled, sleep-deprived father of three with no name on his tongue. Not the bold man of action who raced next door. Not the handsome, tireless dervish who fixed this house, worked two jobs, and satisfied the carnal needs of his libidinous, pregnant wife. No.

A tender old man with fear on his face, worried about his wife. How long has he been here? Crease lines converge on his eyes. When did he get so old?

He's dressed for church, slacks and a collared shirt. He goes because she asks him to. Sometimes he doesn't and she understands that; some Sundays she doesn't want to go herself, but she does anyway.

"Are you okay? You're not dressed. Is

everything okay?"

A bit of fatigue in his voice. This isn't the first time he's had to pull her out of a daydream. She tells him it's harmless, an idyll, but she can see big words scrolling across his forehead: *Alzheimer's, dementia.*

"I'm fine. I need to talk to Tina."

"Tina?"

"Yeah, I need to explain. I need to tell her about Maria. I never told her about Maria. Not really."

Michael looks confused.

"Maria. My mother?"

"Yes."

"Gail, you're not making any sense."

"I know. It doesn't matter. I can't explain it."

She starts going through the kitchen drawers. She finds the paring knife, still chipped, the blade long gone dull. Michael sighs, a long, pointed gesture of exasperation.

"Look, are we going to church or not?"

"No."

He tries to suppress a smile. He's still a child in this way. Let him play hooky from church. Give him ice cream, beer, pizza, two seconds of naked tits in a movie.

"I'm going to change then."

"Fine."

She puts the knife in her bag, slips on a

jacket and sneakers, and dashes out to the car. The air is cold, still dewy; another gray day, makes her long for the blazing crispness of early autumn. She could call, but she wants to do this in person. Sit at Tina's table and explain. What exactly? She's not sure, but Tina will get it, Tina will understand.

Their lives didn't overlap. Maria never saw Bobby's face, never held his hand. She's always known this, of course, as a mathematical matter — one life ended before the other began — but she's never really understood what it meant. He grew up eating the dishes that Maria taught Gail to make. The mother he always knew was different because of Maria, had already absorbed the gentle lessons of motherhood she bestowed. He sat in an attic strewn with sausages with his grandfather when he was three weeks old. These are all things Tina should know.

She drives faster than normal. She's holding something slippery and precious and she needs to get to Tina's house before it slides away.

A year after Bobby was killed, Tina was in a low, angry place. Her parents were retiring, moving to Florida. They'd put it off for a year to help Tina after Bobby's death, but now they were moving forward. Selling the house and moving away. Tina was furious. She railed at them, night after night, at Gail's table, the tears streaming down her face.

"A fucking year, Gail? A fucking year? They gave me a year. Almost to the god-damn day. 'We've done our bit, T. Now we have to get on with our lives. Welcome anytime.' Oh jeez, thanks. Sure, we'll drop in every weekend. Thanks a lot, fuckwads."

Gail laughed at the familiar malapropism.

"That's a Bobby word."

Tina poured herself a large glug of Chianti.

"It sure is."

"You can't be mad at them, Tina."

"Fucking A, I can't. They're moving to a golf course, Gail. They don't even fucking golf."

She cursed like a sailor in those years.

"What am I supposed to do? With a one-year-old and a kid about to enter kindergarten?"

Gail reached a hand over.

"Tina, anything you need. Anything at all. Michael and I aren't going anywhere. Anything. You want to move in here? Done. You want to drop the kids off every day? Done."

"Thanks, Mom."

"You're welcome."

Tina raised a hand to her face, pushed some tears into her skin. She exhaled.

"Well, I need two things right now. I need a cigarette."

She fished a pack out of her purse. She cracked the window behind her.

"I didn't even know you smoked," Gail said, genuinely surprised but without judgment. She found an ashtray hiding in the back of the cupboard, behind a Cornell baseball coffee mug.

"I sneak, when the kids are asleep. I know I have to quit."

"All in good time. I'm surviving on cheap red wine and ziti. What's the other thing you need?"

"I need a Bobby story, one that I haven't heard. Tell me a Bobby story, Gail."

Gail wasn't sure what she was asking.

"A story about Bobby, in other words?"

"Yeah, my therapist, she says I need to explore my grief, need to let it expand, not try to diminish it before its proper time. So I figure I have cried and wailed over everything I know about Bobby. I have relived everything we did together. Everything I can remember anyway. I have grieved for all of that. Now, I want to grieve over the things I didn't know. Tell me a story about Bobby that I don't know."

"A Bobby story?"

"A Bobby story."

It became their little tradition together. Whenever one of them got low, she would ask the other for a Bobby story. A story would be told, they would laugh or cry together, and then they would hug. Gail would sit up some nights, trying to remember little snippets from Bobby's childhood so she'd have them ready for when Tina asked. She even wrote a few down in a black and white notebook so she'd be sure to remember them. The time Bobby snuck a communion wafer home from church. The time he was telling the whole family about his biology project and accidentally kept saying *orgasm* instead of *organism.* The time the boys fought the Garsini brothers at P.S. 8 because one of the Garsinis had pushed Bobby for no good reason. Franky jumped in to defend Bobby and then Peter jumped in to defend Franky. All three of them sitting in the kitchen that night, giggling and holding ice packs to their heads. One with a black eye, one with a bloody nose, one with a fat lip. Bobby happy as a clam because his big brothers had come to his defense.

She even told Tina about the time Franky and Peter left Bobby behind down at the beach at Gateway and she found him there crying, astonished that his brothers could be so mean. He was ten, maybe eleven, and it was the first time she saw him really angry, except for a few tantrums he had as a toddler. She told Tina the whole story too. She didn't leave out her own failure that night. She let it serve as a lesson to Tina: how you punish your children is as important as whether you do. Never be cruel, even when they are.

And the things she learned from Tina. Little insights into what Bobby was like as a husband and a father. How he adored his daughter. How he loved his brothers, admired Peter and had eternal patience with Franky. She reaffirmed what Gail already knew: that her son was basically happy, an easygoing, kindhearted soul.

With flaws. Tina didn't hide those. She told a few stories about his temper, about nights when he had a few too many. She told Gail that they fought the night before he was killed because he'd been at a bachelor party that weekend in Atlantic City and still went out to watch the Giants game with Franky. That when he came home, he was tipsy and tried to apologize, but she wouldn't have it, and that when he left for work the next morning, she was still mad at him. That when he died, she was still mad at him.

Just when you think the sadness can grow no larger, your son's widow tells you that — no, confesses that to you — and the grief pushes through a door you didn't know was there to occupy a space you didn't know existed. When you lose a child, you know the grief will be overwhelming and harrowing, but you half expect it to be monotonous. A single, horrible note that you can't get out of your head.

But it's not. It has dimensions, it has depth. It changes and transforms. It hits you differently each day. You owe it respect in some ways. You have to mourn everything: the flaws as well as the virtues, the bad moments as well as the good. You have to turn over every rock and embrace the individual sadnesses you find underneath. The Bobby stories did that.

Together, Tina and Gail gave grief its due.

She parks the car on the street in front of Tina's house, a modest, high-ranch home, surrounded on both sides by ridiculous Roman-columned monstrosities. Bobby bought a house half a mile from his parents. All he ever wanted was the life they had.

She will tell Tina a Bobby story, the first

Bobby story, the prelude to all the others. She will tell him about Maria, who kissed her stomach, and Enzo, who grieved in an attic, and Sean, who spun his quarters, and Constance, who told her not to have children and wouldn't cross a bridge to see them when she did. She will tell her about Diana Landini's blouses and birthday parties at red picnic tables and how she miscarried and she caught Maria crying by herself, even how sex crazed she was during her pregnancy with Peter. She will tell her how Tiny Terrio, who she knows, whose daughter is a friend of hers, asked a question and ushered Bobby's name into the world. She will tell Tina all of this and Tina will understand. Tina will hug Gail and everything will be normal again between them.

And when it is, Gail will ask her about the man she met. It's only fair. She will ask her and listen to Tina's answers and she will be happy for her.

She walks up the front stairs and rings the doorbell. One of Tina's neighbors, a man, picks up his paper and waves it at her in hello. The front door opens and a woman answers, wearing a long white T-shirt that extends below her waist. Gail flinches, uncertain.

"Mrs. Amendola?"

Gail hears small feet scampering toward the door. Bobby Jr. leans into view.

"Grandma!"

"Bob-a-loo."

She leans down and hugs him. Milk and Cheerios. They should sell it as cologne.

"Tina's not here."

Gail's eyes move up to the woman she now recognizes: Stephanie DeVosso. Friend of Tina's. Stephanie's legs are a deep, settled brown. In March. She stretches her arms in a long yawn and her T-shirt lifts, revealing skimpy black panties. Gail can see the mound of Stephanie's pubis in relief against the silk fabric of her panties. She bites down an urge to take Bobby to the car and drive away.

"That's okay. I was just passing by. I thought I'd take a shot."

"I'll tell her you stopped by."

"Not necessary, Stephanie. I'll call her later."

She kisses Bobby, who races back inside.

"Later, Grandma-ma-ma."

Stephanie looks after him. When he's out of sight, she puts a hand to the side of her mouth and whispers.

"She spent the night with Wade."

Now he has a name.

"Of course. I forgot. Sorry to bother you,

Stephanie."

Gail turns and walks down the stairs. She remembers a rumor she heard somewhere, something Michael brought home from the Leaf. She turns, calls back to Stephanie.

"Meant to ask you, Stephanie. How's your friend Jenny doing? Jenny Valenti?"

Stephanie's teeth shift behind closed lips. "She's fine."

"Good. I saw her mother a few weeks ago at Enzo's. Said she's really struggling with the whole mastectomy. Must be tough, for a woman that age. You know, with a young husband."

Gail's eyes narrow. She holds them on the younger woman until the woman looks away.

"Must be," Stephanie says, eyes down.

"Yes, well, we all have our crosses to bear. Have a good day."

Gail doesn't look back as she walks to the car. She drives to a nearby strip mall and parks the car. She looks at herself in the rearview mirror. Her eyes are drained and red.

"Silliness," she says to her miserable-looking reflection. "Pure silliness."

Her cell phone rings. Tina's number. Stephanie must have called her. She hesitates, unsure whether to answer. She clears her throat, tests her voice. No point putting this off.

"Hello?"

"Gail? It's me."

"Hey, Tina. How are you?"

"Is everything okay? Stephanie said you came by, needed to talk."

That colossal bitch.

"No, it was nothing. I was driving around and thought I'd stop by. I should have called first."

"No, Gail, I'm sorry. I should have . . . I wasn't sure how to . . . Christ, I'm sorry."

"Tina, it's okay. It's my fault. I'm sorry."

"I would have asked you to watch the kids, but I didn't think, I mean, I wasn't sure . . ."

Tina's voice trails off. Gail wonders where she is right now. Manhattan? Connecticut? New Jersey? She knows nothing about this man, Wade. She didn't even know his name until a few minutes ago. For all she knows, Tina could be lying in bed with him as they're talking.

"I'm really sorry, Gail."

"Nothing to be sorry about, Tina. Stephanie shouldn't have bothered you."

"Well, the bitch just couldn't resist ruining both of our mornings."

They both laugh.

"I needed that, Tina. Thank you. Let me

let you get back to your —" Man? Other man? New man? Lover? — "day."

"Wait, I was going to ask you something later, but I may as well do it now."

"Sure, anything."

She hears Tina exhale, can visualize her trying to formulate the question.

"Would you mind if Wade came to the party on Sunday? For Bobby Jr.'s party?"

Gail almost asks who Wade is and then she remembers.

"That's next weekend," she says, without meaning to sound irritated.

"I know. I know. I just thought that it might be a nice way for Wade to meet everyone."

"Sure, Tina. Of course. He's more than welcome."

Tina asks if she is sure.

"I am," Gail says, though she is not. Her voice lacks punch, it's like water in a puddle. She feels disconnected from the world, from this conversation. If this man is coming to her house in a week's time, she has things to do. People to tell. She has to tell Bobby, of course, but the other boys as well. Michael, Peter, Franky. These will not be easy conversations. Tina is asking too much. A week to tell four men news it will take them a decade to accept? Too much, too soon.

"Are you still there, Gail?"

"Yes, Tina, sorry, I got distracted."

She'll start with Peter, start with the most sensible one. Maybe he can tell her how to tell the others. Maybe he can help her figure out a way to tell Franky.

"Are you sure you're okay with this?"

"Yes."

"Are you sure there wasn't something you wanted to tell me?"

"It was nothing," Gail says, thinking *nulla*.

"Okay, I'm sure we'll chat during the week. Have a good one."

"You too, Tina."

She closes the phone. A week from now, a stranger will step into her house. Before that can happen, she has to tell the boys, all of them. No small task.

Gail opens the car door and steps out. The cool air is bracing, revives her a bit. She looks around the shabby little mall. It was brand new ten years ago and now it's dilapidated: a dingy deli surviving on Lotto tickets, a walk-in slice joint with Mexicans behind the counter, one abandoned storefront, and a narrow little diner that looks to be a week away from going under.

She peers in the window of the diner. Two old Italian women — glasses perched above bony noses, scarves wrapped around shrunken heads — chat at the front table over coffee and danishes. One of them turns to Gail, gives a friendly nod. Gail waves back, thinking of Maria. She should have told Tina about everything, just rambled on about all the things she never told her. It wouldn't have been perfect over the phone, but that doesn't matter. She should have told her.

A voice rises in her head. The voice has a smoker's rasp and speaks perfect English. And between each sentence is a pause long enough to spoon a mouthful of soup.

What were you going to tell her anyway, Gail?

That he was conceived in response to death and born in its shadow? That you named him after a man — a boy — who died young? That you gave him a cursed name, a condemned name? One that was doomed to be etched in remembrance. Bobby Amendola. A firefighter's name, if ever there was one.

You could have named him George or Fred or Paul or Kevin. You could have given him a butcher's name, Enzo, or a drunk's name, Sean.

You could have given him any of these names and he would still be alive.

One final pause.

Or you could have listened to me, those

many years ago, when I told you that, one way or another, your children will rip the heart from your chest.

CHAPTER 4
A FRESH START

On Monday morning, Peter Amendola is woken by the sounding of the Staten Island ferry's horn as it eases away from the southern tip of Manhattan and slips into New York Harbor. The sound — a brief, low rumble — has woken him most of the mornings he's stayed at Alberto's apartment, even before he knew what it was. He groans and shifts to a sitting position on the couch, rubbing his eyes. He lifts his Black-Berry from the glass coffee table in front of the couch and checks the time: a little past six. He walks to the window to watch the ferry's progress. He knows its path well, knows the feints and turns of its twenty-five-minute voyage. He spends half his time in this apartment watching as one ferry leaves and another arrives, passing each other. A crowd of them at rush hour.

Back and forth, on and on, again and again.

He used to love the ferry. It was the quickest way to get to Manhattan, to get off Staten Island. The summer before he went away to college, while his high school buddies were getting shitfaced in the Midland Beach parking lots, he took the ferry into the city most weekend nights with his girlfriend Tracy DeSantis. He'd have an inexpensive night planned: a walk around the Village, then a cheap dinner at a place in Chinatown or Little Italy, walk back down Broadway to the ferry. He didn't know where to go, didn't have any money anyway. He didn't care. He just wanted to be there. They took the train up to Times Square, the Upper East Side, Central Park. He wanted to see it all, see every inch of it. He peered in through the windows of expensive restaurants — the bustling downtown hot spots, the posh uptown restaurants catering to tight asses, the steak and martini joints of midtown full of red-faced bankers and nattily attired lawyers — not with envy, but with impatience.

One day, he thought, *one day soon.*

Tracy didn't like the ferry, didn't really like Manhattan. But she liked Peter, probably even loved him in that simple, teenage way, so she went along with his requests. On the way in, he wouldn't linger on the

153

rear deck with her, wouldn't enjoy the illicit pleasure of making out with her, touching her in the dark recesses of the ferry's nooks and crannies. Instead, he'd pull her up to the front of the boat ten minutes before it docked, so they could needlessly line up with the tourists and the boisterous black kids from the North Shore projects, while the ferry crawled to its dock. Sometimes he even dragged her down to the seedy lower level with its surreptitious pot smokers and deranged, piss-soaked vagrants because the ramps down there lowered first, affording that level's denizens a head start into the city, into the night. Peter didn't want to miss anything, wanted everything the city had to offer, wanted the city itself.

On the way home, Peter, glum and a little surly, wanted to linger on the rear deck and stare up at the impossible angles of the Twin Towers, their peaks not visible until the ferry pulled a good distance away. That view, changing incrementally as the ferry drifted away from Manhattan, was simply awe-inspiring. No other description fit. After seeing it, Peter was awed; by the reach of man, by his godlike ambition.

Only when they were halfway across the harbor would Peter's attention turn back to the expectant lips and tongue of the young

Ms. DeSantis. By the time the ferry docked on Staten Island, he was back in her good graces, a short car ride away from getting laid in her basement while her parents slept two stories above. When they lay together afterward, Tracy talked about the benefits and potential pitfalls of staying together when they both left for college, and Peter nodded sleepy assents, all the while trying to re-create the sensation of standing at the back of the ferry and staring up into man-made infinity.

One night he told Tracy that whenever he left Manhattan, he felt like Columbus leaving the New World. He thought he was being poetic, but Tracy said that didn't make any sense. That, if anything, he should feel that way when he left Staten Island because that was the less developed, New World place and Manhattan was the older, developed civilization, like Europe in the time of Columbus. As soon as she said this, Peter decided that they wouldn't be staying together when they went to college. He conveyed guarded optimism for the proposition through the summer, though, to ensure the continuation of the good times in her basement. He broke up with her the night before he left for Cornell. He even managed to make it seem like it was the best thing for both of them.

He watches the ferry until it disappears behind Governors Island. He wants to feel like he used to when he was on that rear deck, ignoring Tracy and staring up at the towers. He wants to be awed again by something. Anything.

But the towers are gone.

And Tracy DeSantis is Tracy Gordon now. He Googled her a few weeks ago, found a Facebook page. Married to a dentist and living in Hazlet. Couple of kids. Still looks good, in the toned and complacent manner of the suburbs. Like Lindsay actually. Seems happy enough. He knows it's a facade, but that's not the point. A path not taken. Maybe he should have listened to her. They could have stayed together, coasted through college, a few casual dalliances here and there — on both sides, no questions asked, no hurt feelings — but stayed together.

He knows he shouldn't do this, torment himself with visions of where his life could have gone. He knows the Internet presents ridiculous, one-dimensional cutouts of people and that his own mind is putting the best possible gloss on what their lives would be like together because of his present misery. He knows the last thing he needs is *another* woman in his thoughts. He'd broken up with Tracy because even though she was smart and pretty and nice, she was too limited . . . too Staten Island. Perfectly happy to go away for four years and then come home. Live the same life her parents had, maybe some incremental improvement. Move to Jersey, sure, but what was that?

A preordained movement. A half step.

Back then, he'd wanted something more. How could you live in the shadow of the greatest city on the planet and be content with that? If Tracy couldn't understand how he felt when they were slouching back to Staten Island, she'd never understand him. He didn't want Staten Island. And he didn't want someone who did.

And now? He wasn't so sure. What was the difference between Hazlet and Harrison anyway? What did being a partner at a law firm and taking home almost a million a year get you in this city?

A better class of shadow. Nothing more.

A Manhattan-bound ferry slides into view. Peter grabs a glass from the cupboard and fills it with water from the tap. He returns to the window to watch the ferry dock, his mind mercifully preoccupied by the early morning happenings of the harbor. The sheer amount of activity is dizzying; dozens of ships dot the dark waters around lower

Manhattan.

Another horn sounds. The inbound ferry has unloaded its passengers, reloaded, and is now departing for Staten Island. The sound perplexed Peter during his first few weeks at the apartment. He'd hear the horn intermittently during the day — in the apartment, walking around Brooklyn Heights — and later the incongruity would gnaw at him. What the hell was making that sound? This was New York City, not Newport.

He figured it out on a frigid weekend afternoon in late January. He was trudging along the Promenade, bare hands shoved into his coat pockets, head down. A light snow falling, the wind snapping as it rose from the harbor's dark water. He paused at the railing, enjoying the punitive blast of wind. He stood there for a few minutes, distracted from the specific woes of his life by the most basic, universal needs: to be warm, to be inside, to eat. He was looking forward to heating up some soup, taking a scalding shower, feeling the warmth return to his fingers. It didn't matter that these were trivialities. He was looking forward to something, something that had a reasonable opportunity of actually happening, and he hadn't felt that way in weeks. He was reassured that he could still feel anticipation, if only for a cup of warm soup in the belly.

Below him, the cars on the BQE flew by, oblivious. A hardy, lunatic soul jogged past him, bundled so completely that he couldn't tell whether it was a man or a woman. He watched the figure until it receded into white haze at the other end of the Promenade. His gaze turned back to Manhattan and its incomplete skyline. He watched an orange ferry slide away from the terminal, announcing its presence in the harbor with a familiar bellow. When he recognized the sound, the small measure of pleasance he'd achieved sank from his chest; he felt a familiar wretchedness rise to take its place. Exposing a finger to the biting air, he traced a clear, unfettered line from the ferry across the open harbor up to the windows of Alberto's eighth-floor apartment. In addition to having unimpeded views of lower Manhattan, the apartment was perfectly situated to receive the sound of the ferry's horn.

Peter laughed, a grim, caustic chuckle that the wind snatched.

Of course he should be reminded of Staten Island every morning. Of course he should. Let the punishment fit the crime or something like that.

■ ■ ■ ■

Dominic burst into Peter's cramped office five minutes before four, ranting that he had another fire drill that he needed Peter's help on. One of his big clients had a whistle-blower and they needed to fly out to Wichita, of all fucking places, and start an internal investigation. Worst of all, the client contact was here, *now,* downstairs in one of the large conference rooms, having a complete meltdown; he needed a little hand-holding, a little stroking, a little everything-will-be-okay, and Dominic needed Peter to be his wingman for this meeting. And then, probably fly out to Wichita tomorrow, Monday the latest, and hit the ground running.

Peter dropped what he was doing, straightened his tie, ran a comb through his hair, and grabbed his suit jacket off the back of his chair. He didn't complain. He didn't groan. He was an eighth-year associate, on the precipice of making partner: complaining or groaning weren't acceptable options. His weekend was already half fucked anyway. So now it would be fully fucked. Lindsay would be pissed, but Lindsay was usually pissed these days. If he had to go to

Wichita, she'd be stuck home alone for the weekend, six months pregnant, trying to corral their daughter, Amanda, who was two years old and driving her mother insane.

He followed Dominic out of his office, shouting back at his secretary, Maureen, to call Mike Williston and tell him that something had come up and he'd have to give him his edits on the brief later that night. Dominic strode through the hall with alacrity and Peter had to hustle to catch him at the elevators.

"Which client, Dom? What's this guy's name?" Peter asked in the elevator down to the conference room floors.

"Oh, umm, Fred Baxter," Dominic said, a thin smile on his tanned, avuncular face. He reached over and folded down the collar of Peter's jacket. Sweat streamed down Peter's face. He perspired constantly, a combination of stress, little sleep, and no exercise. Dominic put a hand inside his own charcoal gray suit jacket and withdrew an immaculate white handkerchief, the initials DD monogrammed in blue satin in the corner. He handed it to Peter.

"Take a minute, Pete; make yourself presentable. You'll want to look good for this."

Peter wiped the sweat off his forehead and

the back of his neck. He looked over at his mentor, who was looking down at the floor. Dominic, usually prone to rambling harangues, had said next to nothing on the ride down.

There was no client waiting. This was it. This was *it.* Finally.

The elevator opened and they walked down the hall toward the large conference room, usually reserved for department-wide lunches. Dominic stopped before the door. He gave Pete the once-over. The realization of what was about to happen had flung open Peter's sweat glands, even more so than usual; he was dripping. He tried in vain to staunch the flow with Dominic's handkerchief

"Useless. Utterly useless," Dominic said with a wink, and then opened the door.

The assembled litigation partners rose to cheer Peter and welcome him to the partnership. A flute of champagne was placed in his hand. Dominic hugged him, kissed his cheek, and whispered in his ear.

"Congrats, Petey. It took me twenty-five years, but I finally got another paesano in here. You got the world by the balls now, kid."

Peter felt like he was in *GoodFellas,* like he was becoming a made man, being welcomed into a Mafia family. Dominic released him. The partners had formed a makeshift receiving line; ninety-odd men (and ten women) in five-thousand-dollar suits, their stern, workplace demeanors temporarily discarded, all waiting to shake his hand. Peter worked his way through the line, shaking hands and swigging champagne. After a half hour of backslapping and congratulatory handshakes, Peter looked around the room at his new partners. Bow ties and braces, cufflinks and horn-rimmed glasses. An entire room of consiglieres, if you thought about it. Not to Mafia dons. To captains of industry, to CEOs of Fortune 500 companies, to the people who called the shots in corporate America, who controlled the peaks and valleys of the stock market. The most powerful people in the country came to the partners at this law firm when they needed advice, when they had a crisis.

From a few seats down, Dominic caught his eye, raised his glass. He was a little drunk, the old hardscrabble litigator from the Bronx. On champagne and on his protégé's success. Peter raised his glass in return, smiled.

No, this wasn't *GoodFellas*. This was much, much better.

■ ■ ■ ■

He staggered back to his office an hour later, euphoric and exhausted and more than a little tipsy. He shook hands with well-wishers as he went. Word had spread. Maureen was waiting for him and she hugged him, real tears in her eyes.

"Congrats, Peter. I'm so happy for you. You deserve this, you deserve this."

Maureen had been his secretary for the past three years; she was competent, had a good sense of humor. She was also in her midfifties and reminded Peter of his mother. Dominic had once told him to never have a secretary who was better looking than his wife. Peter heeded the advice, as he did most of Dominic's counsel. Maureen lived deep in Brooklyn — Marine Park or Mill Basin, he could never remember which — and had lost a nephew, also a firefighter, on 9/11. She felt a kinship with Peter, relished his successes in a way that his own mother couldn't. By dint of working at this firm for so many years, Maureen understood what his making partner meant; his mother wouldn't, couldn't. Not entirely.

The hug drifted toward an uncomfortable length. He tried to ease out of it, but Maureen kissed his cheek and whispered in his ear.

"I'm sure your brother is looking down right now, very proud of you. Very proud."

Peter smiled and stepped away.

"Thank you, Mo."

He paused to allow the emotion to dissipate. Phones rang in other offices. Pages belched out of printers. Maureen wiped her eyes, sat down at her station.

"There will be another reception at five thirty, for the whole litigation department."

"More champagne?" he asked, added a dramatic groan for Maureen's benefit.

"Even I may stay late, on a Friday no less. I know it's tough, Petey, all the champagne, everyone wishing you well, but try to make the best of it."

"That's the Mo I know and love." He walked to the door of his office. "I'm gonna make a few calls, tell Lindsay and my family, so try to make sure the peasants don't come knocking on my door."

"Yes, sir, Your Highness."

"Thanks, Mo."

He closed the door behind him, surveyed his wreck of an office. Piles of paper everywhere. Boxes of documents on the floor. A handful of black stress balls with the Lonigan Brown logo on the floor under his desk.

He exhaled, let the weight of this shift, from a burden on his shoulders to a glow in his gut. He had calls to make, but they could wait. He wanted a few minutes to himself, to let his head steady and clear. He was alone and his mind was unoccupied, and when that happened, he usually thought about Bobby. He walked to the credenza and picked up the picture.

In it, Bobby was holding Amanda and his head was tilted down in a cooing gesture. Amanda was born on August 21, 2001. The picture was taken that day or the next. It was the only picture that Peter had of the two of them: his brother, his daughter. The only picture he would ever have. Three weeks later, Bobby was dead. Peter looked at him now, imagined the words on his lips.

Fuck 'em, bro, they don't know.

That's what he said.

Fuck 'em, bro, they don't know.

Years ago, when Peter was a summer associate at the firm, he'd gone to dinner with a group of summers and young associates. Everyone was talking about where they were from, some girl with a weird *J* name — Jordan? Jade? Jenna? — who'd grown up on Central Park West, laughed at him when he said he was from New York.

"Staten Island, uhh, that's not really part

of New York. You know that, right? I wouldn't walk around the firm admitting that, Pete. They'll think you're support staff. That's bridge-and-tunnel country."

Try the ferry, you stuck-up bitch, he thought but didn't say. No, instead, he turned quiet. His face went hot with embarrassment. He told Bobby the story a few weeks later at the Leaf. Bobby listened intently, his fingers peeling the label of a beer bottle, then rendered his judgment.

Fuck 'em, bro, they don't know.

Peter's hands started to shake. How could Bobby be gone?

Three years on and he still experienced a moment of murderous rage whenever he considered the incomprehensible horror of how his brother had lost his life. He imagined his fingers curling around guilty throats or squeezing triggers to propel bullets into the heads of responsible parties. He had thoughts that scared him, that convinced him he was capable of monstrous reciprocities.

And then the absurdity always hit him. He was a lawyer, not a soldier or vigilante. He went to work in a suit and tie, sat behind a desk, spent countless hours trying to lessen the already insignificant travails of his corporate clients, was paid handsomely to do so. Litigators routinely used the jargon of warfare; they spoke boldly of "going to war" and "skirmishes" and "battles," of "bodies" and "strategic maneuvers," of breaking out the "big guns" or needing "ammunition." They spoke without irony, without self-awareness. Some of them even believed that their personal fate hinged on whether this or that motion was granted or summary judgment was awarded or the SEC decided to close its investigation. The truth was that these things did matter, but not nearly as much as everyone believed they did. Real thoughts of physical violence, like the ones Peter experienced every day, had no place in this arena. They belonged to a different world, one that reached the courtroom only as a shadow of its true self.

And even then, it reached different courtrooms, filled by different lawyers.

After the anger leaked into absurdity and the absurdity drifted into numbness, there was a hole. He looked at the phone. He wanted to pick it up and call Bobby, wanted to tell him that he'd done it, that *they'd* done it, that they were going to Luger's for steak and bacon and enough beer to drown a small village. He wanted to tell him to bring Franky too, because, fuck it, things were too good to be petty. All three of them should enjoy this together. He could almost hear Bobby joking that he was gonna get left behind again, like that time down at Gateway, only this time it would be with a seven-hundred-dollar check in a place that only took cash.

Fuck 'em, bro, they don't know.

He came back to work the Monday after Bobby was killed. Dominic walked into his office, closed the door behind him. He told Peter to go home, to take as much time as he needed, take the rest of the year if he needed, to be with his family.

"He's gone, Dom," Peter replied, his voice hoarse. "He's gone and he's not coming back. And I can't sit at home and think about it because I'll go fucking crazy if I do. I want to work. I need to work. Put me on as many cases as you can."

Dominic didn't try to change his mind. He knew the narcotic power of intense industry. He did as Peter asked. Peter had always worked hard, but after Bobby was killed, he became a machine. He billed 2,700 hours in 2001 despite everything. In 2002, he came up just shy of 3,000 billable hours, the holy grail of large-firm insanity. He was on pace to break that barrier this year. Work had always been an ocean — vast, bracing, capable of overwhelming —

but instead of trying to reach an ever retreating shore, Peter stopped struggling; he simply ducked his head below the surface and surrendered to its numbing infinitude.

His weight fluctuated: ten pounds down, twenty up, fifteen down. He barely slept. His eyes sagged and his hair started to thin. He checked his BlackBerry incessantly, spent the few dinners he took Lindsay to with it tucked below the table, fingers tapping, scrolling through his inbox to make sure nothing demanded his immediate attention.

He woke up one day and Amanda was walking. He came home from a business trip to Houston — six weeks reviewing documents in a windowless conference room — and she was talking.

He gave Bobby's eulogy. He sent Tina money. He held his dead brother's son when he was a screeching purple newborn. He took calls from his mother late at night, listened as she cried softly into the phone while his father snored in the background. His eyes ached expectantly, but he would not let the grief win. The work was always there, waiting to be done, welcoming him back without judgment.

Lindsay pleaded with him to cut back his hours, to take some vacation, to spend more time with her, with their daughter, and he told her he would. As soon as he made partner. When that happened, he promised he would slow down and take a breath. Not a moment before.

Fuck 'em, bro, they don't know.

He thought of that snotty bitch Jordan/Jade/Jenna and her long-ago dismissal of his borough. Where was she now? Not here. Not a partner at Lonigan Brown. But he was. The donkey dago from Staten Island had made it, not the privileged debutante from the Upper West Side.

He'd done it, climbed to the top of the mountain, had the world by the balls. He'd made partner at one of the most prestigious firms in the country.

And Bobby was still dead.

He picked up the phone, dialed his house. Lindsay answered on the second ring.

"Hey, sweetie."

"Linds," he managed to get out, his throat clotted with emotion.

"Pete, is everything okay? Are you okay?"

"We did it," he said and then started sobbing.

The New York offices of Lonigan Brown occupy the uppermost twenty-five floors of a nondescript fifty-seven-story commercial building on the corner of Fifty-fourth and Park. When Peter enters the building at quarter to eight, the lobby is a swarm of unhappy office workers, heads down as they swipe through security monitors and head for the elevator banks. Peter isn't even sure what other companies share the building with his law firm. Hard to imagine he could spend so much time in relative proximity to a mass of people and know nothing about them, but he does. Everyone in New York does.

Peter walks to the last elevator bank, lets a group of women take the first available car, slides into the second unoccupied one, and presses fifty-five. A small screen scrolls through the day's news: market turmoil because of Greece's debt, three cops killed in a shoot-out in Cleveland, the impending March Madness tournament.

Jesus, was it already the middle of March? He doesn't even know who's good this year, hasn't watched a basketball game since last year. Bobby would be disappointed.

The elevator doors open and Peter steps into another lobby. This one is spacious and airy, not cramped and claustrophobic like the one downstairs. The firm's name is emblazoned on the wooden reception desk in deep crimson. These are the Lonigan

Brown colors: deep crimson over chestnut wood. Crimson details that not so subtly evoke Harvard, at which most of the founding partners undoubtedly matriculated. The design serves a purpose: clients can see the stolidity of their counsel, can sense the venerability and stalwartness of this firm.

We have seen your problems before. We will handle it.

Even now, Peter feels the smallest ease in his uncertainty as he drinks in the familiar surroundings. In terms of pure hours, he's spent the lion's share of his waking adult life in these offices. This place is going nowhere. If there is a nuclear holocaust, Lonigan Brown will survive, if only to handle the ensuing litigation.

Peter's wingtips clack on the marble floor as he leaves the lobby. For all the hours they work, big-firm lawyers aren't keen on early mornings. Most associates arrive after nine thirty, the partners after ten. The tardiness is heightened on Mondays because everyone's grumpy, either because the weekend is over or because they never had one in the first place. Other than the two security staff who sleepily man the Lonigan Brown entrance, the place is quiet, unoccupied. He hurries down the hallway to his office. He removes his suit jacket and closes the door.

This has been his practice for the past few months: arrive early, see as few souls as possible, keep the door closed, the head down. Lose yourself in the work. Wait for the day to end. Slither out after the sun falls and everyone's gone home. But that's impossible, because no matter how late he stays — 11, midnight, 2 a.m. — there are always bedraggled associates sitting in their cubicle offices when he leaves, soul-sucked eyes drifting up to him as he slumps past their doors. He can feel their hatred rising as he passes because he is the reason they are stuck there at that ungodly hour. Maybe not him in this particular instance, maybe not even in most instances. But he is a partner, making money from their misery, and they hate him for it. He knows they feel this way. He sat in those seats once himself.

The hate doesn't bother him. It is temporary and, as Dominic once expressed to him, even necessary. *The hate will drive them, Peter; most to leave, but a few to stay. You hated me once. Don't bother denying it.* No, the hate doesn't bother him. But lately the hate is mingled with contempt or even snide bemusement. He's become a joke among the associates, a laughingstock. He can even deal with that. These associates will be gone in a few years, replaced by younger, equally qualified versions. From the same schools, with the same grades, on the same law reviews. The new ones will know about his recent disgrace, but in only a vague, urban-legend fashion, like the way he "knows" that Debby Forsythe, a corporate partner, used to orally pleasure a senior partner back when she was an associate. Or the way he "knows" that Lou McBride, the bankruptcy partner who's making the firm a small mint these days, brings a companion with him on business trips. A companion who is not only not his wife but not a woman.

Gossip has a voracious and varied appetite; it cannot survive on the same meal for long. The smug glances from disgruntled associates will fade.

But the disappointment that sits behind Maureen's eyes?

Crushes him every time he sees her. She tries to hide it, but she can't. It is precisely the look his mother would give him if she knew: a mix of incredulity and disapproval. Makes him feel hollow, like a grave that's already been dug. He avoids Maureen because he can't stand that look. He'd hoped that maybe the story wouldn't make its way to her, would maybe die on the associate vine, but that was a hope beyond foolish.

Everyone knows.

Peter jostles his mouse, bringing his computer back to life. He checks his schedule, looks over some notes he jotted to himself on a call on Friday. He tries to engross himself in work, to submerge himself the way he used to, but he can't even do that these days. Work drugs you only if it's keeping you away from something: like grief or your life. Once it's not keeping you from something, it's just work. Drudgery. Peter has nothing to look forward to but Alberto's couch. Work will not anesthetize such a meager expectation.

His phone rings, startling him. Only someone who knows he's here at this hour would be calling. Or maybe someone who wants to leave a message. Maybe Lindsay. He checks the caller ID. Looks like an international number.

"This is Peter Amendola," he says uncertainly.

"Peter, how are you, my friend?"

A moment passes before Peter recognizes the voice: Alberto Veras, the man whose apartment he's crashing at. Alberto's a corporate partner, spends most of his time in South America. He opened the firm's office in Buenos Aires two years ago. They were barely on a first-name basis before all this.

"Menzamenz, Alberto. Some days are better than others."

"Yes, well, that's understandable. Better days ahead, I'm sure of it."

Peter laughs.

"Well, that makes one of us. How's Argentina?"

"Busy. Unbelievably busy. We should have opened an office here ten years ago. We need another ten lawyers at least."

Each word is spoken with the practiced enunciation of someone who has mastered a language that is not his native tongue. Alberto's voice could soothe a lunatic.

"Wow, that's great."

"Tell my wife. She's used to not seeing me when I'm in New York, but she was hoping it would be different when we opened the office down here. Now, she's telling me to go back to New York so at least she won't have to do my laundry. I didn't think it would be prudent to point out that she doesn't do the laundry."

Peter winces at the discussion of day-to-day domestic jostling. If only he and Lindsay could go back to minor squabbles.

"Probably not."

"Well, in any event, Peter. She's getting

her wish. I'm coming back to New York for a month."

"Oh. When?"

"Next week. Coming in Monday night. Now, if things still haven't worked out, you could certainly stay on the couch for a few days, if you like."

"No, Alberto. You've been more than generous, really. I don't even know how to thank you, actually. No one else has been remotely as kind."

Kind didn't begin to describe it. When everyone else at the firm was treating him like a leper, Alberto offered up his pied-à-terre for Peter to use while he was in South America. Alberto was in his fifties, a silver fox, thin and placid. Had a reputation as a skirt-chaser. Peter guessed that he had some experience with domestic agitation and felt bad for Peter after what happened at the Christmas party.

"Ah, well. This too shall pass. Isn't that what we always tell our clients?"

"Yes, well, thank you. I owe you a very nice dinner at the least when you're in town."

"No problem, my friend. How did you like it, by the way, the apartment?"

"It's fantastic. The views are unbelievable. Got a chance to reacquaint myself with the comings and goings of the Staten Island ferry."

"Isn't that where you're from, Staten Island?"

"Yes, it is."

A long pause, like Alberto's reading an e-mail or someone's come into his office, but Peter can tell it's another question that won't ask itself.

"And isn't that also . . . well . . ."

Another pause.

"Well, this is delicate, but wasn't the girl from there as well?"

Peter's cheeks redden reflexively.

"Yes," he says softly.

"Ahhhh," Alberto says, like he's finally removed a splinter that had been stuck in his foot for months. "Well."

"Yes."

"Well, I suppose that explains a lot," Alberto says.

Peter can do nothing but agree.

"I suppose it does."

She walked into his office at quarter to five, in a manner that only a first-year associate in her infancy at the firm could think was appropriate, and started talking about her *future* at the firm as though he didn't have five phone calls to return and a train to catch. Peter nodded absently as she dithered, trying not to let his eyes wander too frequently to the clock on his computer. He'd promised Lindsay he would make it home at a reasonable hour so the whole family could sit down for a meal together for the first time in weeks and here he was, stuck listening to this girl whose name he'd already forgotten blather on about God knows what. Another first-year who talked too much. A Friday afternoon impediment, one of the many things that were conspiring to prevent him from catching the 5:47 train home and incurring Lindsay's wrath as a result.

He'd met half a dozen first-year associates already that week. They were all the same: earnest, fresh faced, eager to please, completely incapable of doing competent work. They were a necessary evil, one that not only had to be tolerated but humored as well. A year from now, the plucky high spirits would be kicked out of this girl, a casualty of two thousand plus billable hours, most of them spent in mind-numbing document reviews on cases whose greater purpose she would never learn.

But on a crisp September Friday at the end of her first week at the firm?

A bundle of naive optimism, certain that

this conversation was the most important thing in either of their lives. She'd been rambling for minutes, Peter half paying attention, when he heard it. She said it like a native, not saying the first syllable so much as expelling it from her mouth. Eschewing the second syllable entirely and sliding the *n* over to the second word, which slithered out like an afterthought.

STAT Nisland.

Not Sta-ten Island, like the Dutch must have said it four hundred years ago, like you probably should say it. STAT Nisland. Like a challenge. STAT Nisland. Like a threat.

Peter smiled, the mention of his home borough shaking him from his stupor.

"You're from the rock?" he asked, suddenly half interested.

Her obsequious smile pinched for a moment and then relaxed, leaving a genuine grin in its place. She shook her head with humored disbelief.

"You don't remember me," she said.

Peter looked at her with perplexed intent. She was pretty — jet black hair, a soft, round face; large, expressive eyes — and looked somewhat familiar, but only in a vague, ethnic sense. A polished version of every good-looking Italian girl he'd grown up with.

"I'm sorry," he managed.

"Regina Giordano. I won the first annual Robert Amendola Memorial Scholarship. You spoke at the ceremony."

Peter shook his head. His mother had come up with the idea the spring after Bobby was killed, had recruited Peter to help her. A fifteen-hundred-dollar scholarship — a stipend really, just some spare cash to pay for books — in Bobby's name given to a Staten Island kid, the son or daughter of a firefighter, who showed academic promise. She organized a small luncheon to hand out the check. The *Advance* ran a small piece about the honoree, about Bobby as well. It made his mother happy, and for that alone, Peter was willing to pay for the whole thing. Every year thereafter, she asked him to come to the ceremony, but work always got in the way. He'd only been able to attend the first luncheon.

He remembered it now. A buffet at the Staaten catering hall: chicken francaise and pitchers of Coke. He made some remarks, talked about Bobby. They gave the scholarship to a girl, a senior in high school, a nerdy, endearing teenager with frizzy hair in a Catholic school skirt. He looked across at Regina, who was nodding, one eyebrow raised. It wasn't possible.

He looked down at his fingers, did some quick math. Spring of 2002. Four years of college, three years of law school. It *was* possible. More than possible. There was even an extra year somewhere.

Time flies whether you're having fun or not.

"Jesus, Regina. I'm so sorry. I can't believe it's possible. And I didn't recognize you. Look at you. We gave that scholarship to a little girl, not a first-year lawyer."

She laughed and leaned forward. Her silk blouse was unfastened a button lower than what the firm would deem professionally appropriate. Peter got a glimpse of cleavage, noticed a lacy red bra. He forced his eyes north.

"It's okay, Mr. Amendola. I'm sure you're extremely busy. Our mothers actually kept in touch. My mom would give yours updates on how I was doing, what grades I was getting, where I was applying to law school. I actually visited your parents a few times when I was home for spring break in college."

"I'm sure my mother loved that. Absolutely loved it. And please, call me Peter."

"Okay, Peter. Well, your family is lovely. And I still remember what you said at the luncheon."

"Dear God, what did I say?"

"Well, you talked about Bobby, what a great guy he was. Great father. And then you gave me some advice. You said, 'Keep your feet on the ground, but reach for the stars.' "

Had he really uttered such an inane platitude? Possibly. At his mother's behest, he'd spoken at a number of different schools on the Island over the years. In his limited experience speaking to Staten Island students and their parents, he'd decided that straightforward praise of *hard work* as the best avenue to a vague but definitely monetarily associated *success* worked best. As in: if you work your ass off, you'll make a boatload of money. Which was funny, if you thought about it, because the cops and firefighters and teachers you were talking to were living proof of different propositions. Like: take a good city job, retire after twenty, and live on your pension. Or maybe: work hard and you'll make a living, not enough to live anywhere but Staten Island, but a living. That's why the descriptions of success had to be vague. Most Staten Island parents had no idea what to tell their kids to aspire to.

"God, I can't believe I said that," he said, running his hand through his hair.

She let her chin and lower lip droop, leaving her mouth agape in an expression of mock hurt. A salacious thought popped into Peter's mind, unbidden. He exiled it immediately.

"I wrote it down when I got home, it became my little mantra. I even taped it above my desk in college."

Peter groaned.

"You're joking. Really?"

"Yes, yes. I can't believe you're disavowing it. This is like Scalia saying that the drafters' original intent doesn't matter after all."

Clever girl. A little law-school nerdy, but still.

"It's just that of all the things to say to an impressionable young student with her whole life in front of her."

"Why? What should you have said?"

"Don't go to law school."

She laughed again, heartier this time, almost a snort. Her earlier skittishness had dissipated. She leaned back in her chair, comfortable. Her skin was a smooth mocha, her eyes a surprising blue: a touch of light against a dusky background.

"Well, I'm glad you didn't. Because if you did, we wouldn't be sitting here now."

She raised her left hand to remove a

strand of hair that had stuck in the corner of her mouth. He noticed a large engagement ring, felt an inexplicable pang of jealousy.

"So, who's the lucky guy?"

She looked confused. He pointed at her ring.

"Oh, this. I keep forgetting. It happened last week. Right before I started. His name's David. We went to law school together. He's at Hofstadt Klein."

Keep forgetting? She didn't seem overly enthused. Hofstadt Klein was a third-rate firm at best. Of course he'd proposed last week. Couldn't let this girl walk in here without a visible sign of attachment. The older male associates would have been all over her. Probably still would be.

"Set a date yet?"

"No, I don't want anything big."

"The Italian girl from Staten Island doesn't want a big wedding?"

"I'm not your typical guidette."

"No, I guess not. Is David a Staten Island boy as well?"

"No, no, no. He's from Connecticut."

Peter groaned again, this time for dramatic effect.

"C'mon, Regina. The guys from Connecticut already get all the breaks; you can't let them take the nice girls from Staten Island too."

"I'm not that nice," she said and winked at him.

He laughed. This was the first conversation he'd enjoyed with a first-year in years. She was charming. He felt a small measure of pride in the fact that another kid from SI had made it here, to this firm, and that he'd played a role in helping her, albeit a tiny one.

"I'm sure that's not true."

He smiled at her earnestly for a few awkward seconds. Her gaze drifted around his office until his phone rang.

"Well, I'm sure you're busy, Mr. Amendola . . ."

"Please call me Peter."

"Okay. Well, Peter, I know you're busy, but I just wanted to drop in and introduce myself and thank you for the scholarship. And I know it's silly because we don't really know each other, but I've always looked at you as a role model for me, someone whose career I could study and learn from, being that we're from the same place. And I would really love it if we could work together on a case someday. So, thank you again and I'm sorry to have taken up so much of your time."

"Not a problem, Regina. And if anyone owes an apology, it's me. My mind is mush these days."

Maureen's voice buzzed in.

"Peter, it's Lindsay."

"One minute, Mo." He turned to Regina. "I have to take this, I'm afraid. The wife."

She stood and they shook hands. He watched her walk to the door, his eyes drifting down to her ass, its firmness snugly showcased by her pinstriped pants. She had curves, a pleasant change from the spindly, near anorexic look presently in vogue with almost all the young female associates. He called after her.

"Regina, one last question."

She turned at the door.

"Shoot."

"Denino's or Joe and Pat's?"

She shook her head.

"Lee's? Nunzio's?"

"Nucci's."

"Nucci's? Never heard of it."

"You've lost touch with your roots."

He waved her away, smiling. He was about to press the button to accept the waiting call when she called back to him.

"I have a question for you, Pete."

"Shoot."

"Where's your wife from?"

Peter chuckled.

"I plead the Fifth."

She pursed her lips in a mock pout.

"Wisconsin."

"C'mon, Pete. The girls from Wisconsin already get all the breaks. You can't let them take the nice guys from Staten Island too."

"Too late."

She laughed and waved good-bye. He pressed the button and lifted the receiver to his ear.

"Hey, babe, you'll never guess who started working here. Do you remember that luncheon that we went to for Bobby's . . ."

"So," Lindsay interrupted, clearly irritated, "I guess you're not making the five forty-seven?"

Peter glanced at the clock. It was 5:44.

"No, Linds. I guess not. Sorry. Time got away from me."

"It always does."

She hung up.

Peter put the receiver down. He felt a warm tingle in his stomach, realized his cheeks were still pressed in a smile. He felt a charge he hadn't felt in years, the electricity of new attraction.

Flirting, he realized, *we were flirting.*

And then he heard a voice from a different part of him, the practical, married part of him. *Careful,* it said, *careful.*

After Peter hangs up with Alberto, the day grows wheels. Clients return from their weekends and want updates: the latest draft of a brief, the status on a document review, the next steps in an internal investigation. When Maureen cracks the door open to say good night, Peter realizes he hasn't eaten anything all day and that the sky outside his window is almost dark. He prefers days like this, when there's so much going on that he has no time to get lost in his own thoughts. His stomach turns over, reminding him it is empty. He needs some fuel, half a sandwich and some chips.

He walks out of his office, intent on the cafeteria, and nearly knocks over Phil Langley, the reigning fair-haired child of the litigation department. Phil is trim and tidy, has chiseled features that belie his untrustworthiness. He's got upward charm. Treats associates and staff like shit. Kisses the ass of everyone he thinks is important. Peter's never made that cut, even though he made partner two years before Phil. He has a reputation for bad-mouthing his peers, Peter included, to the higher-ups in the department. Peter has little doubt that Phil has exploited Peter's present predicament in every way possible.

"Peter, just the man I was coming to see."

He extends his hand and Peter reluctantly shakes it.

"How are you? How you holding up?"

The falsity of his concern is so apparent that Peter has to suppress an urge to slap him.

"I'm great, Phil. Thanks. On my way down to the cafeteria, so excuse me."

Phil puts a hand on Peter's arm.

"One second, Pete. Kevin's waiting for you in his office. Truman's there too."

"You mind taking your hand off of me, Phil?" he says, louder than he wanted.

A pair of associates — one male, one female — who were chatting by the communal printer fall quiet and retreat to their offices.

Phil releases his grip, leans in.

"Relax, Peter. I'm your friend here. Don't lose your temper."

"Phil, it's probably best that I eat something before this meeting. I haven't eaten all day and I get grouchy when I haven't eaten."

He also needs a few minutes to figure out how to handle this. Kevin is Kevin McCoury, the head of litigation. Truman is Truman Peabody, the head of the firm. This can't be good. His executioners await.

"Okay, Peter. We'll be waiting for you in Kevin's office."

"Thanks."

Peter watches Phil walk off and turn the corner toward Kevin's office. His heart is pounding. He wishes he could walk into Dominic's office, close the door, and bend his ear. Like he used to. Dominic would know what to do, would know what cards to play.

But Dominic is gone, almost a year into a retirement that he appears to be enjoying, contrary to the expectations of nearly all who know him. Golfing three days a week. Spent a month in Rome. Another two weeks in Montana, fly-fishing, of all the fucking things, with his son and son-in-law. Enjoying his grandkids. Peter hasn't seen him since last summer. They haven't spoken in months.

He walks into Dom's old office anyway. The air is still, a little fusty. An abandoned cardboard box sits forlornly on the floor, a crooked Redweld jutting above its lip. Otherwise, the office is barren. All of Dom's personal effects have been removed. Spend fifty years at a place and a year after you leave, there's no trace of you. Peter was supposed to slide over here months ago — into the coveted corner spot, into Dom's spot —

but that's been put on hold, like everything else.

How many times did he step in here for Dom's advice over the years? A hundred? A thousand? On how to handle an impossible client? Whether to make a certain motion? Which arguments to highlight, which to abandon? How to deal with an aggressive SEC lawyer? Dom had seen it all, knew the chessboard and all its pieces. He knew which situations called for honey and which for vinegar. He had shepherded Peter through the tensest moments of his professional career.

And how often did he end up imparting personal advice? About marriage. About raising kids with money without spoiling them. About the firm and the often poisonous personal politics that plagued it. Peter can hear Dom's voice, the gravelly, reassuring susurrations of a man who'd spent his life counseling others.

Pick your battles, Petey. In court. In your marriage. Even here, in this fucking place. You can't win them all. Choose the ones that are important, that mean something, that can improve your position, improve your life. Fight those like you're in the street, like it's knuckles and knives. Win those. But pick 'em well. Only a few mean something. The trick is learning which ones those are.

Which one was this? What would Dom have said about this looming confrontation? Peter rubs the back of his sweaty neck. He knows what Dom would have said. This is a fight that could have been avoided.

Don't shit where you eat.

That's what he would have said.

"Sorry, Dom," Peter says, to the empty room, "but that ship has sailed."

His stomach still empty, Peter sits down across from Kevin McCoury, who is finishing up a call. Phil Langley closes the door and stands sentry in front of it. Behind Peter, Truman Peabody sits impassively on Kevin's black leather couch, legs crossed, suit jacket on. Kevin hangs up, picks up a legal pad, and looks over a sea of piled papers at Peter.

"Well, I ain't gonna pussyfoot around, Pete. You fucked up big time. Put the firm in a bad position. Endangered your partners."

Kevin is a giant, roaring asshole of a man, the type of bellicose litigator who bullies his way to results. His face is fleshy and red and it sits atop a handful of chins. His sleeves are rolled up above his elbows, dark sweat stains sneak out from under the arms of his blue shirt. He spends his days screaming into phones and waddling down the hall while terrified associates scurry into their offices to avoid him. He is the type of lawyer who enjoys living up to the worst stereotypes of the profession. He is also extremely effective.

"Before we get into it, is there a reason that Phil is here?" Peter asks, nodding at Phil, who squeaks out an expression of surprise and hurt.

"What fucking difference does it make? Everyone knows what happened here, Pete. We're not gonna get down into the nitty-gritty of it, if that's what you're worried about."

"That's not what I'm worried about. I just don't understand why he's here. He's junior in the partnership to me, he doesn't have an official position in the department . . ."

Truman interrupts, his voice sliding in over Peter's shoulder.

"Phil has been acting as a firm counsel in this matter, Peter."

"Firm counsel?"

"Ms. Giordano retained counsel some time ago. Given the sensitivity of the matter, we wanted to keep this in-house as long as possible."

"She retained counsel? For what?"

"Jesus Christ, Pete," Kevin says. "I knew you couldn't keep your dick in your pants. I didn't know you were dumb."

Peter swallows, tries to bite down his anger.

"That's not helpful, Kevin," Phil says.

Peter looks over, uncertain. Maybe Phil wasn't lying, maybe he is Peter's only friend here. *Then I'm truly fucked,* he thinks.

Kevin clasps his hands behind his neck, exposing the ponds of sweat spreading from his armpits. He exhales, like he's about to do Peter a favor.

"Okay, Pete, so here's the deal. Devion Labs is looking for a deputy general counsel. Their GC, Marty Newman, is a few years away from retiring and they're looking to groom someone to replace him. They don't think they have anyone in-house. They asked us if we had anyone here who would be interested, maybe get a shot at a GC job. A tryout, so to speak."

He pauses, shifts the position of his hands from behind his head to under his chin. He leans forward, like a man who's about to confess something.

"This is a big opportunity. And if it doesn't work out, you could always come back here."

Kevin pauses again and Phil takes the baton.

"We want you to be the guy, Pete. You know them. They know you. They like you. It could end up being a great move for your career."

He puts his hand on Peter's shoulder, leaves it there. Peter feels blood pounding in his temples. He has to suppress another urge to do physical harm. *She retained counsel?*

"Let me get this straight. You want me to go in-house at Devion?" he says, more to buy time than to clarify.

"Yes," says McCoury.

"In Chicago?"

"Yes," Phil says. "Lot of time in New York, but yes, our understanding is that you'd be working out of their home office in Chicago."

Silence. Everyone in the room seems to be sweating bullets except Truman. Peter is certain that Truman hasn't squeezed out a bead in his life.

"For how long?"

"I wouldn't look at it that way, Peter. You may love it, get the GC job, never come back."

Peter turns to Kevin.

"You said I could come back if it doesn't

work out. How long do I have to stay?"

"A few years."

"A few?"

"Minimum five."

Another silence descends on the room, heavy with the weight of what's been proposed. Peter is trying to process what's happening, but he keeps returning to one thought: *She retained counsel?* Kevin coughs to remind Peter that he hasn't responded.

"I don't know what to say. I'm shocked."

"Don't say anything," Truman pipes in from the couch. "Think about it."

"But what about my family? My kids are in school, all their friends are here. I mean, my family . . ."

Across from him, Kevin raises an eyebrow.

"Maybe you should have thought about your family before . . ."

He doesn't finish the thought. He doesn't have to.

Peter wants to reach across the desk and slam the hypocrite's head onto the table. Taking moral crow from Kevin McCoury? The fat bastard has fucked his way through half the hookers in Manhattan, but the McCoury family photos still sit on the credenza behind him, smiling emblems of a pleasant, tranquil household.

And Truman, the old-line WASP already on wife number three, with mistress number four in the minors waiting to get the call up to the big leagues.

And Phil, well, he didn't know whether Phil fucked around, but he probably did. The little fucker was certainly pleased with himself about something.

Peter's head is swimming. This will complicate a million things, but he's not sure he can refuse. Exile is preferable to execution. His mind turns to the one thing he knows it shouldn't.

"What's gonna happen to Gina?"

A flurry of glances triangulates around Peter's head. A decision is reached and Kevin nods to Phil, who looks down at his tie, suddenly sheepish.

"Ms. Giordano will continue to be paid during this extended, uhh, let's call it a sabbatical. And next October, after her honeymoon, she will come back to work. With a new class. A fresh start, so to speak."

After her honeymoon?

"Wait, she's still getting married?"

"That's what we've been told."

"Really?"

"Let it go, Pete," says Phil, with more sympathy than Peter expects.

Kevin chimes in, glad to play the bulldog.

"Let me remind you, Peter, not to reach out to her. Leave this alone. Leave her alone."

Truman stands, puts a hand on Peter's shoulder.

"You're a good partner, Peter. I know you'll make the best decision for the partnership. Best thing for you is to move on, put this behind you."

He walks around to Peter's side, buttoning his jacket as he does.

"When do I need to let you know?"

Truman frowns, displeased that the conversation isn't over.

"We ain't exactly asking, Pete," Kevin says in a low bellow.

"Kevin, easy," says Phil. "There's no rush, Pete. This doesn't have to be done next week. Or even by next month."

"Just before October," Peter says.

Phil shrugs his shoulders in agreement.

"Bingo," says the bulldog.

When Peter slinks back to his office, his voice mail light is blinking and two dozen new e-mails have arrived, but he's too shaken to work. His shoulders and neck ache; he is suddenly exhausted. His stomach is still empty, but he's lost his appetite. All he wants is to suck back a few stiff drinks, sleep for a month, and wake up in his old life.

The one with two wonderful children and a mostly happy wife. The one with a soft mattress in a big house. The one with suburban boredoms and quotidian worries. The one that had its ups and down, its crises and joys, its mild irritations and simple pleasures.

The one in which he felt moored to things bigger than himself. His family. This firm. Even this city.

His office phone rings and he answers it reflexively. "Peter Amendola."

"Hey, Pete, it's Wade. Are you okay?"

"Hey, Wade. I'm fine. Just tired. What's up?"

"Nothing. Listen, I know things are not good for you right now."

"That would be a mild understatement."

"I know. I'm sorry about that."

"Not your fault."

"Anyway, I wondered whether we could get a drink sometime this week. I wanted to tell you something."

A vision appears in Peter's head: three olives impaled on a toothpick, leaning against the side of a glass full of clear, purifying liquid. He should go home and think this through. Correction: go to Alberto's and think this through. He should get a good night's rest. This is going to be a long, painful week and he should have his wits about him. The last thing he needs is a drink.

But the call of temporary numbness is too strong.

"What about right now?" he says.

"Now? Yeah, I could do that. I'm in midtown anyway. Just a few blocks from your office. Where should we meet?"

"Somewhere I won't run into anyone I know."

"Grand Central Oyster Bar?"

"Good enough. See you in twenty."

Peter retrieves his suit jacket from behind his door, braces himself for the walk to the elevators. He says the words because they always make him feel better, even if it's only a fraction.

"Fuck 'em, bro. They don't know."

He opens the door and strides to the elevator, not bothering to look into the offices he passes.

It was a small matter for a forgotten client. A regional bank, the type of client that had fallen out of favor with the firm's management because really, how many billable hours could you squeeze from a backwater bank in Dover, Delaware? The bank had been acquiring other smaller banks around Delaware, trying to grow so they could compete with the big boys. Or, at least, survive. An employee had been tipping his friend about which banks were going to be acquired and the friend had bought the stock of those banks before acquisition and then sold them immediately after, netting himself a tidy profit, which he'd then split with his friend at the bank. Classic insider trading performed in outlandishly stupid fashion. As soon as the SEC got involved, the bank cut loose local counsel and called Dominic. Only Dominic had retired and the bank had been given Peter's name instead.

So here they were.

The bank's general counsel, a man named Wilson Temple, explained all of this to Peter in excruciating detail during a two-hour phone call. He stated several times that the bank had been founded in 1887 and each time, Peter wondered whether Mr. Temple had served as general counsel for the entirety of the bank's existence. He pictured an ancient, withered shell of a man, hand shaking as he moved a magnifying glass over yellowed parchment.

"Of course, Peter, we aren't entirely unconcerned about cost. In these trying times, a scattergood cannot prosper."

Scattergood? Who was this guy? How the hell did he and Dominic ever meet? If the bank wanted to cut costs, it should keep Wilson Temple off the phone when the clock was running.

"So it would be appreciated if you staffed this matter very leanly, perhaps only yourself and a very junior associate."

An image of Gina appeared in his head, soft and dreamlike.

"I'm sure we can accommodate you on that front, Mr. Temple."

"Excellent."

Another twenty minutes passed before Peter could extricate himself from the call. When he hung up, he exhaled and checked his e-mail in-box. Nothing pressing had streamed in. He looked at his schedule. Nothing pressing until a four o'clock conference call. He had a relatively open afternoon. He could get a little organized, clear his head, and maybe reconcile the internal conflict that had been fomenting in the three weeks since Gina Giordano had walked into his office.

Maureen was sipping tea from a large Styrofoam cup when he walked out of his office. She was always sipping tea, even in the dead of summer.

"Shit, Mo. What are you putting in that tea?"

"Language, Peter."

"Your virgin ears."

She put the cup down, gave him her serious look.

"What's up?"

"I'm going to lunch. My usual."

"Fancy."

He looked down the hall to the closed door of Dom's old office. He'd been gone since June. Didn't feel completely right going to the diner without him.

"Miss your playmate?" Maureen asked.

"Yes," Peter replied, honestly.

"What if your new playmate drops by?" she asked.

"New playmate?"

"Yeah, the one with the long black hair. The one who laughs at everything you say?"

Peter rolled his eyes.

"Good-bye, Mo."

"Umbrella, Peter. It's drizzling."

"I don't mind. I like the rain."

"Bully for you," she said and then turned back to her crossword puzzle.

The Splendid Diner was a greasy spoon joint on Fiftieth Street between First and Second avenues. Years earlier, Dominic had taken Peter here for his "welcome" lunch a few weeks after Peter landed at the firm. Peter was more than a little surprised — other people had been taken to Le Bernardin or Nobu or Sparks — until Dominic explained that since his heart attack, his wife had him on a strict low-cholesterol diet and the one thing he missed, really missed, was bacon and eggs. So he came here once a month to get his fix and he was sorry, really sorry, but he'd been on trial last month and missed his fix and he'd been dying for bacon and eggs and Peter was gonna have to fucking deal with it.

Dominic was the first person at the firm who made him feel comfortable. He wasn't plastic. He was real. You could ask him about the Giants game. You could drop an f-bomb. He ate bacon and eggs in a shithole diner to avoid his wife's wrath.

A waiter came to Peter's booth. It had been a while, but he recognized Peter.

"You waiting for you friend?" he said in an accent Peter couldn't place.

"No, just me today."

"Same as usual? French toast with a side of sausage?"

"No. Two eggs, fried over easy, bacon, rye toast."

The waiter scurried off with the order,

Dominic's old standby. Peter took a sip of his coffee.

Maureen had noticed. Not only noticed but said something to him. That was probably significant. Since their initial meeting, Gina had made a habit of dropping by his office every afternoon, ostensibly to talk about what she was working on, but the work talk inevitably gave way to a flirty repartee that left him breathless and addled. She possessed a sort of beguiling sensuality; when he was in her presence, it was difficult for him *not* to think about touching her. Kissing her. Making love to her.

Even when he wasn't with her, he was thinking about her a lot. Too much. Not in a sexual way. Well, not only in a sexual way. It was like he'd rediscovered an old friend. One he'd grown up with but who also understood his life now. Strange as it was to admit it, it wasn't so different from how he'd felt all those years ago when he first met Dominic. A kindred spirit in a foreign land. Only this time he was the experienced, elder statesman and Gina was the wide-eyed protégée.

Yes, it's exactly like your relationship with Dominic. Except for the fact that you want to drape Gina over your desk and fuck her senseless.

The voice — the pragmatic, caution-urging voice — hadn't grown softer with the passing weeks. If anything, it had gotten louder, developed a sarcastic and crass tone. He'd been arguing with it for the better part of a month.

He wasn't a cheater, he told it; he didn't have the stomach for it. He'd had op-portunities to cheat, the surreptitious invita-tions that every married man detects. From bored neighbors with their suburban malaise and come-hither eyes. From his wife's friends who chased their broods around his pool in revealing bathing suits, flaunting their reclaimed bodies right in front of him. Nothing explicit. Subtle little gestures that indicated a willingness, a restlessness. He'd never pursued any of them.

And he'd spent countless hours on vari-ous cases with a fair share of young, fetch-ing female associates — working late hours, traveling together, lots of tension begging for release — and he'd never given them more than a passing thought. Not in that way.

You're making my case for me.

He loved his wife. Sure, they didn't have as much sex as they used to, as much as he would like, but he didn't blame Linds. It was more his fault than hers. Long hours and unreasonable clients left him tired and irritable. The little energy he had left over was sucked clean by the kids. Six nights out of seven, he wanted sleep or the mind-dulling torpor that a few glasses of really good red wine provided. They'd settled into a routine, one that didn't prioritize sex, and you couldn't blame them. It was clichéd, but it was clichéd for a reason. He and Lindsay had been dating since their second year of law school. They'd gone through the humping frenzy of early love, the safe experimentations of settled monogamy, the clinical coitus of attempted procreation, the semi-abstinence of two pregnancies, the sleep-deprived sparsity of two infancies, the temporary revitalization afforded by procedural infertility. Sex was an important part of marriage, but it was elusive, inconsistent. They'd had peaks and valleys. Were presently in a valley and had been for some time.

So what? What they had together was more important than sex. A true companionship strengthened by their run together through the daunting fire of parenthood. Whenever anything happened to him, the first person he wanted to tell was Lindsay. She helped him noodle through problems of every sort: with work, with his family, with the kids. He'd even been tempted to tell her about Gina, as bizarre as that sounded, because there was very little he didn't share with Lindsay. It felt odd to be thinking about something so much and not telling her.

Agreed. Very odd indeed. Like maybe a warning sign.

He loved his children, Amanda, nine, and Henry, six. He didn't see them as much as he wanted, but when he did, they brought him joy. Amanda was a whirlwind, a precocious, intelligent girl who never ran out of energy or questions. A daughter was a marvelous wonder for a father; she opened a different place in his heart. Henry was quiet and thoughtful; he seemed to be attuned to a different world entirely. He hadn't yet shown much interest in sports, but that might come with age. Even if it didn't, who cared? He was a good kid. He reminded Peter of Bobby. A quieter, brighter version of Bobby.

He liked his life. He wasn't going to throw it away in some predictable midlife crisis, wasn't going to be one of those guys.

Then don't. Find another associate for this case, an obeisant, fastidious drone, preferably one who wears ties.

How was that fair? Gina lost out on a good case — one that would have client

210

contact, would involve witness prep and testimony, actual lawyering — because she was attractive? Because he had a temporary case of puppy love?

You suspect that the feelings are mutual. You hope they are.

He was fooling himself. She was twenty-six, beautiful, and engaged. He was forty, gone lumpy, and going gray. Married with two kids. Maybe she wasn't flirting with him. Maybe she was a flirt, full stop. His ego was probably causing him to misinterpret her gestures.

The waiter dropped a plate in front of Peter and refilled his coffee.

"You need anything else?"

"No, I'm fine."

Peter lifted his fork, creased opened the egg's yolk, and watched the yellow run over the plate. He lifted a pepper shaker with his free hand and gently tapped the metallic top with his index finger, ushering tiny black flakes onto the eggs. He lowered the shaker and grabbed a piece of toast. He dabbed the butter-drenched toast into the flecked yellow and bit it. He'd watched Dominic do this a hundred times, savoring the small ritual of preparing his forbidden pleasure the way he liked it. He wondered what Dominic would advise him to do in this situation.

Call him. Call him right now and lay it out for him. All of it. You know what he'll say.

"You're wrong," he said aloud. Two construction workers sitting at a table nearby turned their heads. Peter put a hand up in apology.

"Sorry. Arguing with myself."

"Who's winning?" said one of the guys, an enormous black man whose gut was trapped below the table. He laughed at his own joke and his stomach heaved, threatening to overturn the table. The other guy rolled his eyes for Peter's benefit. They went back to their food. Peter picked up a piece of crisp bacon, snapped it in half, and put the two ends in his mouth.

The voice was wrong. If he'd learned anything from Dominic, if his entire relationship with Dominic carried a lesson, it was this: look out for your own. Dominic had said as much, had said precisely that, in fact, in this very diner.

"Look out for your own. No one else will. They're too busy looking out for their own."

He didn't mean it in an ethnic or racial sense. Dom had recruited another young associate, Michael Morton — a black kid from the Bronx, had gone to Dom's old Catholic high school — to the firm. He'd ended up on the corporate side so Dom could help only so much, but the guy eventually landed an in-house position at one of Dom's biggest clients. Dom had written a sterling recommendation for Dave Hwang — an Asian kid from Queens, the son of immigrants — and helped him secure a position as a U.S. A in the Eastern District.

"Your own" meant something different to Dom: people who came from similar circumstances. Kindred spirits. A kid from the outer boroughs or a working-class neighborhood in Pittsburgh or Chicago or St. Louis. Or Sydney, Australia, for that matter. Someone who'd worked to get to the firm. Someone who hadn't been handed things.

If Gina didn't fit that definition, no one did. An Italian girl, the daughter of a firefighter, from Staten Island no less. A little rough around the edges, needed some mentoring, a little guidance. Who was gonna look out for Gina at Lonigan Brown? Him or no one. This was bigger than Peter and his petty lustfulness.

He waited a tick for an objection from the killjoy voice. His temples pulsed with blood, but he heard nothing. He took a sip of his coffee, decided to lay out some guidelines.

He would not cross any lines. He would

213

keep everything professional. He would leave this all where it belonged: in his head.

He finished his meal in haste, paid the bill, and walked back to the firm, satisfied by the thoroughness of his internal debate. Maureen was on her lunch break when he got back to his office, but he closed his door anyway before buzzing Gina and asking her to come see him. He did a quick inventory: teeth were clean, the hair combed, the tie straightened. The gut, well, he couldn't do anything about that. Maybe show her a picture of him in college, in pads and cleats, two hundred and ten pounds of muscle. He slipped two Altoids into his mouth and waited.

She knocked and he called her in, his open hand indicating where she should sit. He swiveled to the side and looked at the wall as he spoke. He gave her the details quickly and watched as she struggled to take proper notes. Her smile faded as she wrote, her mind struggling to do two things at once: accurately record what he was saying and comprehend what it meant. A skill every lawyer needed to learn.

Good. She needed to know that if they were working together, it would be all business.

He talked for fifteen minutes, culling Wilson Temple's dissertation down to a brisk recitation of the salient facts. A few times, his peripheral vision caught the flip of yellow paper after Gina's furious jotting had filled it with writing. When he finished, he swiveled back to face her and grabbed one of the black stress balls that littered his office. He flipped it idly between his hands as he waited for her to finish writing.

She looked up at him when she was done.

"Any questions?" he asked.

She looked uncertain, like she had too many to admit or maybe none at all.

"I think I need to digest this a little. I'm sure I'll have questions down the line."

"Good, good. Questions are good. Never be afraid to ask questions."

She nodded, uncertain whether to respond. He squeezed the ball with his left hand, exhaled.

"And look, Gina, I know we've had a few laughs the past few weeks and I've really enjoyed getting to know you. I think you have a very bright future at the firm and I'd like it very much if we became friends and I was able to help your career here."

"Me too, Peter. Nothing . . ."

"Let me finish."

He paused, let the room realign with the new vibe between them.

"The thing is, I take my work very seriously, as you should. And while I don't mind a little joke here or there, the work has to come first. If the work isn't good, isn't top rate in fact, it doesn't matter that we're friends or that we're both from Staten Island. We won't continue working together if the work isn't professional."

She swallowed, nodding sheepishly.

"Of course, Peter, I mean Mr. Amendola."

"You can still call me Peter."

"Okay, Peter. Of course, I will do the best I can. I'll work as hard as I can on this case."

Her eyes welled up. Peter wondered whether he'd been a little too harsh.

"It's okay, Gina. We can still have a laugh, but the work . . ."

"Comes first. Got it," she said and wiped away an incipient tear.

"I'll let you know when we get the documents," he said.

"Okay."

"Great. Thank you."

She stood and he noticed that she was wearing a shortish skirt and patterned black stockings. Someone needed to tell this girl what was and wasn't appropriate to wear to work. Not him. Maybe he could enlist a female partner. He tried not to watch her rear as she walked to the door, but his eyes wouldn't listen. She turned at the door, nearly caught him in a lecherous stare. She drummed the tip of her pen against pressed lips.

"I'm sorry again, Peter."

"No worries, Gina. Looking forward to working with you."

Her face broke into a faint smile and she walked out of his office, her fingers waggling behind her in a coquettish good-bye.

It had gone exactly as he'd planned. He'd reestablished a professional atmosphere, put the kibosh on the flirting. Now he could get back to work. He scrolled through his e-mail, opened one from a needy client, and started to read it. He read the e-mail twice, but he wasn't absorbing anything; he suddenly couldn't concentrate. He tried to banish her from his thoughts, but there she was, marching back into his office in those damn stockings, draping herself over his desk, hiking her skirt up, and begging him to take her from behind. He closed his eyes and tried to shake her out of his head, but that did nothing. She was right in front of him, slick and eager and not taking no for an answer.

His face felt warm. His heart was pounding and he felt blood course through his body and congregate in his groin. His penis stiffened against his leg, an erection that recalled his teenage years when the sight of Amy Landini in a bathing suit could produce a rigidity so complete that it seemed to shrink the rest of him, to literally reduce him behind his cock. But this hard-on was even more intense, fueled by a fantasy that he felt powerless to resist. This was something that needed to be addressed, here and now, never mind that he was at work and it was two o'clock in the afternoon. He needed to get to the bathroom.

He stood too quickly and his erection hit the underside of his desk. He doubled over, gasping for breath, the pit of his groin in agony. The pain spread up to his stomach, sent tingling missives down his legs. He lowered himself onto the floor to let the pain pass. He breathed gingerly for a minute as the pain lessened. He was still hard, still needed release, but his agony had exiled the fantasy and instilled a wincing silence in his head.

A familiar voice filled the void.

Don't say I didn't warn you.

Peter arrives at the bar before Wade, orders a Grey Goose martini. He takes a few hearty sips and feels his troubles start to recede. The bar — an oasis of calm below the madness of Grand Central — isn't crowded. A few tourists, a few midtown traders who had a rough Monday. Peter traps an olive between his teeth and pulls the spear away, separating the orb from its two companions.

He hasn't seen Wade in months. They've been friends since college, though they weren't particularly close at school. They belonged to the same large group of friends, one of those guys who was always around but you never really talked to. But when Peter and Lindsay moved back to New York after law school, they rented a place on the same block as Wade on the Upper East Side. They ran into him randomly on the day they moved in. Wade even helped them with the move. Lindsay liked him; he was quieter and more thoughtful than Peter's other college friends, who were mostly football players still living like college kids, only with a bit of money to fuel their weekends. Male friendship is a product of the simplest things. Does he live nearby? Does my girlfriend or wife like him? It was easy to become friends with Wade, so it happened.

He'd done well for himself in the past ten years. Worked at a small hedge fund, was one of the top guys now. The fund bet against the market in 2007 and '08, made a small fortune. Wade told Peter that he'd done the same in his personal accounts. When Peter asked him what kind of money he was talking about, he was surprised to hear that the amount in question was seven figures, not six. Such catastrophic leaps in net worth were unavailable to lawyers, even big-firm partners. Still, he was happy for Wade. Ninety-five percent happy. Wade had laughed at Peter's slack-jawed expression, said it was a little bit of smarts and a lot of luck. Peter raised a doubtful eyebrow. Wade had buried his wife in 2008, so it was tough to think of him as lucky.

Peter takes another generous sip of booze, plucks another olive from the spear. He misses Morgan, Wade's wife. She was a spitfire, gregarious and bighearted. Peals of laughter exploded from her. The type of girl who reached across tables to give high fives. Her joviality pulled Wade out of his shell, ever so slightly, exposed his quick-wittedness. They'd gotten engaged shortly after Peter made partner. The four of them had gone out for a raucous, celebratory dinner, a pregnant Lindsay playing nursemaid to three lushes. Lindsay didn't like Morgan, they never grew close as Peter and Wade had hoped. She made up her mind after that drunken dinner.

"She's a bit much," Lindsay said to Peter

on the car ride home.

"Oh, I don't think so."

"That's because she's beautiful. If she were ugly, you'd think she was obnoxious."

Peter let it go. Once Linds made up her mind, there was no talking her out of it.

Wade hustles into the stool next to Peter, all apologies. Ran into someone on the street, couldn't get away. Peter doesn't mind. He's halfway through a second martini and starting to feel serene.

"So, how are you?" Wade asks once he's settled, a pint of dark ale in front of him.

"I'm fine."

"Really?"

"No, of course not, but do you really want to hear about it?"

"Of course I do. We're friends."

Wade takes a sip of his beer. Peter looks him over. He's gotten so used to false sincerity that the real item is tough to recognize.

"I fucked up. I fucked up big time. I won't go into the details, but you can probably guess. So, I'm living out of the house, I'm not sure whether my marriage is salvageable, I've seen my kids five times since Christmas, I'm a pariah at my firm, I may have to move to Chicago, and on top of it all, I get woken up every morning by the goddamn Staten Island ferry."

Wade laughs at the last bit. Peter takes another sip of his drink. It felt good to lay out all his problems. At least they were finite, could be listed. Fixing them would be considerably more difficult.

"I know, fucking hilarious right? God-damn ferry."

"I'm sorry, Pete. I really am."

"Not your fault."

He finishes his drink, orders another. When did he start drinking like this? His head feels light and airy, like a balloon that could float away if he loosens his grip.

"So what are you gonna do?"

"I haven't a clue, honestly. Things are so fucked, I can't see a way to make it right."

He takes a sip of his fresh drink. He should probably switch to beer or get something to eat. He's having trouble giving Wade his full attention. His thoughts are drifting to Gina; he's trying to remember the sensation of being with her. It seems like ages ago. This is what happens when he drinks. He gets to think of Gina without guilt, gets to pretend it all didn't turn to shit. He pushes the martini away, grabs a handful of bar nuts.

"Anyway, we didn't come here to talk

about me. What's up?"

"I wanted to tell you something."

"What is it?"

"Well, I'm dating Tina. Still dating Tina."

Peter's brain stalls for a minute. He knows a Tina, but Wade can't mean that Tina. But somehow he does.

"Tina? Bobby's wife?"

Wade looks crestfallen for a beat but recovers.

"Yes, Tina Amendola. I called her after you gave me her number."

Peter puts a hand up.

"Wait, what?"

"You gave me her number last spring. You told her I was going to call her. You set us up."

Peter vaguely remembers doing something like what Wade is describing. He didn't think it was a setup. He thought of it as introducing two grief-stricken souls, sort of a support group or something. But it didn't happen. Wade never called, he remembers Tina saying that.

"But you didn't call her. I remember Tina giving me shit about it."

"I didn't call her initially. Work was crazy. I was in Asia for half the summer. Besides, I thought it was too soon. Two years sounds like a long time, but it's not. I went on one date about a year ago and it felt disrespectful. I couldn't get Morgan's face out of my head."

He takes a long pull from his pint, wipes his lips.

"Anyway, I'm sitting home by myself on Halloween — you know how Morgan loved Halloween, all the elaborate costumes she dreamed up — anyway, I'm sucking back Amstels and wallowing, looking at old pictures: the year she went as Kenny from *South Park,* the year she dressed like Velma from *Scooby-Doo.* So I go to the fridge to get another beer and I see Tina's number, which I must have pinned there months ago. And I know this sounds silly, but it's like I could hear Morgan in my head saying, 'Go for it!' I called Tina the next day."

Wade takes another sip of beer.

"Anyway, we went out and we really hit it off. I mean, she's a fantastic woman. I can't even imagine the courage it took to raise those kids alone. And the kids are great. I mean, Alyssa's at a tough age, you know, those awkward years, but Bobby Jr.'s wonderful. What spirit."

Wade keeps talking, but Peter's gone numb. Not the soft, boozy numbness he was slipping into a few minutes earlier, but a tingling, humming numbness, like his body is steeling itself for action. Realities are realigning in his muddled head to accommodate this conversation. Wade and Tina went on a date. Wade and Tina are still dating. Wade has met Tina's children. Bobby's children. Wade wants to talk to Peter.

A dark urge lurches inside of Peter and he springs out of his seat, grabs Wade by the throat, and brings his face inches from Wade's.

"That's my brother's fucking wife," he hisses, his teeth dangerously close to the flesh of Wade's face.

"Peter, calm down," Wade gets out, but there's real fear in his eyes. Peter wants to pound him, wants to inflict pain. The bartender, an older guy, races down the bar toward them.

"Hey, fellas, fellas," he says, as he waves a bar towel. "You can't do that here."

"My brother's fucking wife," Peter says again, but the bile's already gone out of his voice. The rage has faded. His grip on Wade's neck relaxes, leaving a bright red scratch in its wake. Wade steps a pace back. Peter slumps back into his stool.

"I think maybe you should leave, fella," the bartender says to Peter. He sounds like a character in that Christmas movie *It's a Wonderful Life* that his mother used to make them watch every year. Peter starts to laugh, a heave with more motion than noise.

"It's all right, he's okay," Wade assures the bartender, who looks unconvinced. "You're okay, right, Pete."

Peter nods. The bartender walks away, his gaze still fixed on Peter.

"Well, I may as well get it all out now. I'm in love with her, Pete. I think we have a future together," he says. He takes another half step away. Peter nods, he lifts his hands to his eyes, rubs the tears into his cheeks. The laugh starts again.

"I'm guessing, by your reaction, that you are not too happy with the idea."

Peter can't control his laughter. He breaks out into a cackle. A few of the other patrons cast concerned looks at him. The *Wonderful Life* bartender starts to move back in his direction. Wade leans toward him.

"Peter, what the fuck is wrong with you?"

Peter contains his laugh for a moment, looks up at Wade through red-rimmed eyes. He brings his hands, gently, to Wade's cheeks.

"I'm the last person in the world who should pass judgment, Wade. Particularly when it comes to Staten Island girls. Go with God."

The laugh won't be contained any longer.

It leaks out and starts to rise. It turns back to a cackle and then a howl until the bartender returns and tells them, both this time, that, really, it's time for them to go.

Peter wanted to kill Garrett Holworth, the decrepit, fucking fossil. Eighty-five years old and "retired" for ten years but still hobbling into the office three days a week, ostensibly to work on pro bono cases, but really to cause problems. Like when he lured a paralegal into his office to retrieve something from under his desk and then put his hands under her ass, like a quarterback waiting for the snap. Or when he spoke at a summer lunch and decried the lack of skirts among female associates, emphasizing how one of the first female lawyers at the firm, Amy Donahue, always wore skirts. He even managed to throw in a few references to Ms. Donahue's lovely "bottom."

Or like when he told Gina Giordano that she had the language and bearing of a stevedore, on the Tuesday before Thanksgiving, which had led to Gina's coming into Peter's office at seven o'clock that night for his advice, closing the door behind her, sitting in the chair across from him, and promptly dissolving into tears.

Exactly what he needed.

Peter had survived the SEC's investigation into the Dover Trust and Savings Bank. He'd spent fifteen to twenty hours in close contact with Gina, reviewing documents, prepping witnesses, and explaining his strategy. They'd gone to Philadelphia twice — both day trips, nothing overnight — and brought three witnesses in to be interviewed. Everything had gone well, better than expected. The insider trading issue turned out to be isolated to the one employee. The bank needed better internal controls and more training, but the SEC was being, for once, reasonable. Peter had persuaded them that this was an aberration, an unscrupulous employee taking advantage of a situation that the bank would address. The SEC wanted Peter to keep them informed of the bank's progress with respect to the new policies, but, basically, they were closing the investigation. Wilson Temple was pleased "as punch" and Peter even got a complimentary e-mail from Kevin McCoury for doing a good job and resuscitating business with an old client, one that had the potential for growth.

Gina had proved to be more competent than the average first-year. Her writing needed some work, but she was good with witnesses. That was a difficult skill to learn and she was already better than some senior associates. Besides, his crush — if you could call it that — had settled into something manageable and, with the one exception, there had been no physical manifestations in Gina's presence or at the office generally.

And things with Lindsay had picked up in that department. He didn't like to think too much about the reason for the renaissance, but who really cared? Maybe there was a twenty-eight-year-old trainer from the gym kicking around the back of Lindsay's mind, stirring things up. Would that be such a crime? Of course not.

He looked across his desk at Gina. He hadn't seen her since the SEC called to inform him that they were closing the case, a week ago. Her face looked a bit thin, her cheeks had lost a bit of their meat. He hoped she wasn't moving toward the skeletal look. She wore a gray cashmere cardigan over a black blouse and pinstriped pants. Maybe someone had spoken to her. Didn't matter; she still looked beautiful.

She was quite upset. She'd tried to compose herself twice but couldn't. Garrett may have been the spark, but he'd ignited some hidden reservoir. Peter handed her a box of tissues. She plucked two tissues from the box and wiped her eyes.

"I'm sorry, this is so unprofessional."

"No worries. It happens more than you'd think. This job is not easy. And assholes like Garrett Holworth don't make it any easier."

She sniffled a laugh and a bubble of snot appeared out of one nostril. Christ, even when she was a mess, she was beautiful.

"So what exactly did you say?"

"I'm helping him on one of his pro bono cases for the Metropolitan Museum of Art. One of their employees — his job was to solicit donations, pieces of art, not money, from patrons. This particular guy was working the very wealthy widows of the Upper West Side. And he convinced a few of them to donate some pieces to the museum. He also convinced a few of them to donate some smaller pieces to him personally. Now, the museum's embroiled in this mess and Garrett's helping them sort through it. Allegations are starting to surface that this guy, uhh, may have played on the affections of these lonely older ladies."

She took a breath, looked up at Peter. She'd regained her composure.

"So I said, 'Sounds like a real scumbag.' "

Peter laughed and Gina giggled nervously. He ran a hand through his hair, scratched his earlobe. He adopted a completely casual air.

"This is nothing, Gina. Don't worry about it. Not for another second."

"I'm not so sure."

"I am. Trust me. Garrett's senile, Gina. Has been for years. When I was your age, I spent two hours in his office listening to a rant about FDR. Don't worry about this. Go home, have a nice bottle of wine, and forget about it, okay?"

"Okay. Thank you, Peter."

She stayed in her seat. The tears had stopped, but the troubled look remained on her face.

"Something else on your mind?"

A disobedient tear scurried down her left cheek. She opened her mouth and the tear slipped into the corner. She was working herself up to say something. She took a few exaggerated breaths.

"I feel like I don't belong. Like I'm not good enough for this place. Like I'm fooling myself that I can cut it here. My father keeps telling me that he has a friend in the Staten Island D.A.'s office, that I should go to work there, forget the crazy hours and the stuck-up assholes."

Her eyes widened as she remembered who she was talking to.

"Not you, Peter. I didn't mean you. Jesus, I can't even talk anymore."

Peter put a hand up.

"Gina, relax. I understand. I took no offense. Go on."

She waited a few beats. He recognized her bewildered expression. He'd seen it on a few witnesses over the years, been the cause once or twice during his better cross-examinations. The look of someone who no longer trusts her own tongue. He could see her gears grinding.

"Gina, whatever you say stays in this office. So, relax and tell me what's going on."

Her eyes shone with gratitude and maybe something else.

"It's just that everyone here seems so certain they should be here. It's like they've been given a script that I wasn't given. About what to do and say and not to say. Like, *Don't use the word scumbag.* So, I go home every night and cry and David is sick of it and it's only been two months and I don't know if I can make it another month, let alone another few years. The only thing I've enjoyed here is working with you."

His heart soared a little, despite himself. He understood exactly how she felt.

"And here I am, crying in your office, keeping you from getting home."

She threw up her hands in exasperation and stood to go.

"Gina, sit down, please."

She did as he asked.

Peter brought his hands to his forehead, palms facing in, and dragged them down across his face until they came to rest under his chin. A lawyer's trick, something to buy a few seconds while his thoughts coalesced. He hadn't told this story in years, because Lindsay had tired of it and rolled her eyes every time he started telling it.

"Do you know the word *umbrage*?"

Gina nodded, a little confused.

"Okay, notice how I pronounced it. *Ummm-bridge.* That's the proper way to pronounce the word."

He stood and took a few meaningless steps, like he might have in court.

"Now, growing up, my father used that word all the time. But he pronounced it OHM-braj, like *braciole;* OHM-braj, like a bastardized Italian word. 'Hey, he took OHM-braj.' "

A smile crept onto Gina's face.

"So, my whole life, that's how I say it. OHM-braj. Through college. OHM-braj. Law school. OHM-braj. No one corrects me, maybe because I'm mispronouncing it so badly they probably think I'm saying a different word entirely. I don't use it often, but I like it. Saying it my way, my father's way, it's one of those words that sounds like it should. It conveys exactly what it should."

He sat back down, reclined into the cushy black leather.

"So, I land here, at the venerable Lonigan Brown firm, and it's my second week and I've been assigned to a case with Ned Stone, an old-timer, genteel and soft-spoken. Real gentleman lawyer, belonged to a different era but, unlike your friend Garrett, a genuinely nice guy."

He swiveled back toward her, leaned over the desk. He brought his voice down, sprinkled a bit of the confessional into his demeanor.

"I don't remember what the case was about, but we were in his office, talking about it. And I say it. OHM-braj. Ned gives me this quizzical look — he had these horn-rimmed glasses and his eyes kinda winced behind them — but he lets it go. But then I say it again. OHM-braj. And he puts his hand up and asks, 'Peter, what is that word you keep saying, OHM-braj? I'm not familiar with that word,'

"And I say, with confidence, 'OHM-braj, it means to take offense.' This wry little smile breaks across his face and he says, as kind as can be, 'I think the word you're looking for is *umbrage.*' "

Gina laughed. Her eyes had regained their twinkle. Dried tears glistened on her cheeks.

"Bad, right? It gets worse. I say to Ned Stone, who I later learn went to Exeter, Harvard, and Harvard Law, who majored in English at fucking Harvard, I say, 'I'm pretty sure it's pronounced OHM-braj.' And Ned Stone, may he rest in peace, God bless him, says, 'Perhaps you're right, Peter.' And then I know, I know that I'm wrong, and Gina, I swear to God, it was like a stitch of me had been ripped away. Like the word was everything that I thought was solid and reliable in the world and it had been pulled away from me. I went back to my office and I sat there and I felt like you feel right now — out of place, over my head, unqualified."

Her lips quivered in appreciation. He heard a final whisper from the banished voice, muffled and impotent.

The desk, it pleaded, *keep the desk between you.*

He stood and walked around his desk. He sat in the empty chair next to her. She shifted to face him. He waved to his closed door to indicate the rest of the firm.

"Everyone here isn't sure they belong here. I'm not sure I belong here and I'm a partner. And the other first-years, your colleagues, believe me, they're as scared and uncertain and insecure as you are. They might not be showing it, but they are. Trust me."

He leaned in, lowered his voice. Their faces were closer than they'd ever been. He could see the raw, jagged capillaries in the whites of her eyes, the tiny, inevitable imperfections of her skin. He could smell her.

"The thing is, Gina, some of these kids do have an advantage over you. They grew up with this, their parents did this, they know this world. You don't, not yet. Your father was a firefighter, same as mine. And your mom, what did your mom do?"

"She worked part-time as a secretary at a dentist's office. But mostly she raised us."

Peter nods.

"Exactly. My mom stayed home until Bobby was in high school and then she started teaching. These kids" — he waves his hand toward the door — "their parents were lawyers and bankers and God knows what else. They seem like they belong because they've been in this world their whole lives. You haven't. But you're just as smart as they are, if not smarter. You just haven't been prepared for this like some of them have."

She'd started crying while he spoke. He

reached across and took one of her hands between his two. It was warm and soft, he could feel the heat leeching into his own cold, stiff palms.

"But you belong here. You deserve this."

"Thank you," she said. She looked down at their conjoined hands. He heard a muffled voice out in the hallway. He realized he'd crossed a line. A handful of lines. But he couldn't move his hands. He could sense the possible moving toward the preordained, could feel her anticipation matching his, surpassing it even. Her face inched toward his. Over Gina's right shoulder, he glimpsed the picture of Bobby, head tilted down, almost a nod, and he had the strangest thought, one that settled his mind and cleared his conscience.

We owe the dead our sins.

"Your hands are freezing," she whispered and she was close now, close enough that he could feel the breath behind her words.

"Cold hands, warm heart," he said and then he kissed her.

Peter sits in the back of a yellow cab on the FDR, stuck in the traffic that leads to the Brooklyn Bridge exit. He's asked the cabbie to get out of the right lane — the sucker's lane — twice, but the guy won't budge. He got a ticket last week, he tells Peter, and he won't risk it. Half the reason you get into cabs is so that they can drive like assholes while you sit guiltless in the back and Peter's found the one cabbie in the city with a conscience. The cherry on top of a perfect Monday.

All he wants is to revive his fading buzz with a bottle of red wine and then sleep for twelve hours. He's not going into the office tomorrow. Fuck them.

His cell phone vibrates in his pants pocket. Home.

"Hello," he manages.

"Hello, Peter."

She sounds sad, not angry. He can't decide which is worse.

"Everything okay? Are the kids okay?"

"Fine. Listen, your mom called. She wanted to know if you were still on for lunch on Wednesday, something about collecting your sheets for some pool."

"Oh, shit. I forgot. I'll take care of it."

"She also wanted to remind me that Bobby Jr.'s birthday party is this Sunday."

"Oh, right, right."

A long pause, one that Peter is reluctant to fill. Even his gentlest attempts at reconciliation raise her ire lately.

"She doesn't know, does she?"

"No, she doesn't."

"Well, you should probably tell her."

"Why?"

"Because I still don't know how things will end up, Peter, and she should be prepared. Besides, she might be happy. She always wanted you to end up with a Staten Island girl."

Peter exhales.

"Okay, Linds, I deserved that. I will tell her. Just not right now."

"Why not?"

"Well, because Tina . . . Jesus, I don't even know where to begin. Do you remember last spring when Wade came to the house?"

"Yes, vaguely."

"He was really depressed, felt like he would never get over Morgan. Couldn't bring himself to move out of their place. Couldn't date. Couldn't take vacations because he had no one to vacation with. I think it was right around the second anniversary of her death."

"I remember."

"Well, I gave him Tina's number. I said she might be able to help with the mourning, the grief. I thought it might be helpful."

"That was kind of you."

She sounds sincere but who knows.

"Yeah, well, he called her and they went out."

"Wade and Tina went out on a date. Really?"

"More than that, Linds. They're dating."

"What? That's crazy. Tina and Wade?"

"Yes."

"Tina and Wade?"

"Yes."

"You're joking."

"He just told me. Twenty minutes ago."

"Oh, God. What did you say?"

"Before or after I grabbed him by the throat?"

Her laughter is genuine, knowing.

"Oh, Peter. I'm sorry."

"Who knows? Maybe it'll work."

"I hope it will. They both deserve happiness."

For a few seconds, it feels like it used to, before he ruined it. Then he remembers Chicago.

"Linds, we need to talk. Alberto is coming back to New York next week."

"I'm not ready, Peter. I may never be."

"Linds, the kids. What are you telling the kids?"

"It's a funny thing, Peter. I thought this would be tougher on them, but they barely notice. They're used to not having you

240

around. They're preconditioned. It's not that they don't miss you. They're just used to missing you. I tell them you're away on business and they don't bat an eyelash."

He feels resentful, wants to make a speech about putting food on the table and a roof, a very nice roof, above their heads, but it won't help matters. He swallows hard.

"I miss them, Linds. I miss you."

"That's the worst part, Peter." Her voice cracks. "I miss you too."

"Then maybe I should come home."

"No. I'm like the kids. I'm used to missing you. I've been doing it for years."

She won't be moved any further tonight. The emotion is gone. No anger, no sadness. All business.

"Okay, Linds. What are we gonna do about Sunday? Bobby's party."

"We'll figure it out. Call me later in the week. You can talk to the kids."

"Okay, I will."

"Bye."

"Bye."

He deems the call a mild success. No yelling, no name calling, no unanswerable questions like "Why?" or "How many times?" or "What was it like?" Gina wasn't called a slut; he wasn't called a bastard. The gulf between them had been narrowed, if only by a few inches. Maybe this would be the way. An ocean of distance slowly lessening as time passes and the pain fades. Like the worst settlement negotiations, each side moving glacially toward a position it could live with. Can't come right out with the number, everyone has to inch there.

Peter looks out the window. His cab is barely on the bridge. His buzz has become a headache. The bottle of red wine feels hours away. He suddenly understands the appeal of a flask.

Every night was the same. Gina would come to his office and close the door. She would explain that she couldn't do this anymore, that it was tearing her apart, that David suspected something, that she felt so guilty she could barely function. When she started to cry, Peter would come around his desk to comfort her and soon enough, they were making love on the floor of his office as if it were the most natural thing in the world.

They would lie together afterward and whisper stories to each other about growing up on the Island. He told her about his crazy Irish grandmother in Bay Ridge and how he used to be able to flip over chain-link fences in one motion when he was a kid and how, on the night he got his driver's license, he took Janice Flynn to Wolfe's Pond Park and they made out for two hours, but Janice wouldn't let him get past second base, so on the way home, he got a pain in his groin so intense he had to pull over and get out of the car. Blue balls, he laughed.

That's a myth, she giggled.

That's what Janice Flynn said.

She told him about her great-aunt Tessa, who still played her number — 193 — every day with the last of the Italian boys in Bensonhurst and how her mother sat her down the summer before fifth grade and told her the facts of life and she cried for three days because, even then, without really knowing anything, it seemed like girls got the shit end of the stick. She told him about the Christmas when their street iced over and her whole family — aunts, uncles, grandparents, cousins — had to stay over and everyone got drunk and started crying about her mother's brother Vito, who was the kindest soul who ever lived and was killed in Vietnam two days before he was scheduled to come home. She told him that when she was lying there with Peter, she felt like she used to when her father came into her bedroom when she was a child, whenever there was thunder and lightning, he would race into her room and climb into her bed and hold her and she'd never felt safer in her whole life. Until now.

That makes me feel more than a little icky, he said.

You know what I mean.

And he did. As exhilarating as the sex was, Peter enjoyed the afterglow — lying there blissfully, the only two souls in the world — even more. He hadn't felt peace like that in a long time. Sometimes, he would catch a glimpse of Bobby's picture and that bizarre phrase *"We owe the dead our sins"* would ring in his head. He didn't think Bobby was condoning his behavior. Not exactly. It didn't seem like the sort of thing that Bobby would ever do. (Then again, it didn't seem like the sort of thing that Peter would ever do.) But it seemed like the sort of thing Bobby should have done, if given the opportunity, because really, what difference did it make? Right? Peter tried not to think about it too much.

We owe the dead our sins.

Well, okay then. Worked well enough for Peter.

He kept waiting for something to kick in and make him end the affair: guilt, common sense, a modicum of judgment, basic decency, professional concerns. But for the first time in his life, he felt unfettered by such considerations. Outside of the nightly encounters with Gina, his life went on in the same fashion. He took the train home, he kissed Lindsay, he hugged his kids, he did his work. If anything, he was happier; even Lindsay noticed, commented on it a few times. He spent his days at the office in giddy anticipation of Gina's arrival. He spent his weekends in a weird, lovesick haze, eager to get back to the office but also somehow appreciative of the comforts of his married, suburban existence.

His euphoria was shattered only when he remembered that Gina was spending those weekends with David, was fucking David, was going to marry fucking David, and when that happened, he felt a burning jealousy in his chest that nothing could soothe. He couldn't fucking stand it. Some asshole was going to marry Gina. Spend a life with Gina. His Gina. It wasn't fair. She couldn't marry this guy.

One night, while he watched her slip on her underwear in his darkened office, he told her.

"Gina, you can't marry David."

"Don't talk about him. You don't even know him."

"I don't need to know him. You can't do it."

"Stop saying that," she yelled.

"Keep your voice down," he said. He was still lying on the floor naked.

She slipped her bra on, clasped it closed below her breasts. Watching her dress was the only time he recognized the sordidness of the whole thing, but sometimes it made him excited all over again, led to another roll on the floor, another twenty minutes of peace. He stood and walked to her. She turned away from him. He hugged her from behind, pressed his wobbly erection into the yielding firmness of her rear.

"I can't," she said.

He kissed her neck, slipped a hand down to her breast.

"You can."

"Peter, I can't. I'm meeting David and his parents for dinner. I'm already late."

His fingers found her nipple, hard beneath her bra. She moaned and turned to kiss him.

"Peter . . ."

He laid her down on the couch, removed her bra. He kissed her breasts slowly, his tongue grazing her nipples. His mouth moved south, to the taut flesh of her stomach. Her moans grew more urgent. He reached the small swell of flesh above her pubis. Her hands were on the back of his head, guiding him to the moist patch on her thong when her cell phone rang.

She slid from the couch, her knee catching his jaw and knocking him back. She found her phone and answered it.

"I'm on my way," she said, her voice still hoarse with desire.

Peter sat upright, rubbing his jaw and listening to half a conversation.

"No, I'm not in my office. I'm downstairs, trying to catch a cab."

"You're downstairs? I thought we were meeting at the restaurant."

"I meant I was on my way downstairs. I had to stop and drop something off in someone's office."

"No, not his office. Someone else's office. *No*, David, do not come up. David."

"Okay, I'll be right down."

She'd dressed frantically while talking. She was on the verge of tears.

"Gina, calm down," Peter urged.

"Calm down, calm down? He's downstairs, waiting for me. He wants to come up. He knows something's going on between us."

"How could he know that?"

"I don't know, but he does."

"It's okay. It'll be okay."

"I have to go."

Her face and chest were still flush with excitement. She stopped and took a deep breath. She looked like she was trying to decide something. She turned to the door.

"Peter, I love you," she said, for the first time.

"I love you too," he responded, without hesitation.

She opened the door and a crease of light from the hallway fell into the room, illuminating his naked body.

When the car stops in front of Alberto's building on Columbia Heights, the driver has to shout to alert Peter, who is lost in his own thoughts. He steps out of the car, briefcase in hand, and closes the door behind him. The street is quiet; the only sounds are the wind pushing branches and the low hum of the BQE. He notices a pay phone up the street, fifty feet away, right before an entrance to the Promenade. He's never noticed it before, hasn't seen a public phone in ages. They are like the city's homeless; they seem to have vanished overnight.

Before he knows why, Peter is at the phone, checking for a dial tone. The phone still works. He fishes in his pockets for change, finds three quarters and a dime. He doesn't even know what a call costs these days. He dials information.

"City and state," a sterilized female voice asks.

"Staten Island, New York."

"What listing?" the voice asks.

"Vincent Giordano."

The voice recites a sum and Peter slides two quarters into the slot. He tucks the receiver between his chin and his shoulder. Someone answers on the second ring.

"Hello?"

A female voice. Not Gina.

"Hello, may I please speak to Gina?"

He changes his voice, makes it a little higher. The absurdity does not escape him. The stuff of teenagers, only he's a quarter century past that.

"May I ask who's calling?"

"Brendan."

"One moment, Brendan."

The moments drip by. Peter's heart pounds in his chest. Why didn't he try this sooner? Why is he trying it now? This is pure insanity. He hears the other phone being lifted, hears Gina's voice on the other end saying hello. He hangs up.

What the hell is he thinking? His life isn't fucked enough?

He stands there for a long time, staring at

the phone, clinging to the fantasy that it might ring.

The snow began to fall as Peter walked over to the firm's Christmas party. The forecasters had been predicting a monster storm all week and the city was eerily vacant in anticipation. The firm had even considered canceling the party, but the old-timers who still lived in palatial penthouses off the park would have none of it. They didn't live in the sleepy suburbs north of the city. They didn't have to worry about stalled trains and icy roads. All they had to do was stay sober enough to catch a cab. The Christmas party was a tradition, goddammit, and the flimsy prognostications of a few snake charmers who called themselves meteorologists weren't going to interfere with a hundred and five years of dressed-up debauchery.

Peter chuckled. You had to admire the old-timers. They wouldn't be denied their fucking Christmas party. So the turnout would be light, who cared? More booze for the stalwarts.

The rapidly falling snow cast the semi-abandoned streets in an ethereal veil, inducing whimsical notions in Peter, lightening his melancholy. He'd been gloomy since his last meeting with Gina, gradually resigning himself to the conclusion of their affair.

He knew it was bad when she didn't close the door after walking into his office. She told him, in a hushed whisper, that David had figured it out. She wasn't sure how, but he knew and he'd threatened to call Peter's wife unless it stopped immediately. No more late-night office visits. No more working together. Nothing.

A shiver of fear scrambled up Peter's spine at the possibility of David's calling Lindsay. Somehow, he'd managed to keep his family on the periphery of this whole thing, had managed to ignore the possible consequences if the affair was revealed. The thing had been going on for three weeks. How had David figured it out so quickly?

It didn't matter. He knew Gina was right. It had to end. He'd noticed a few raised eyebrows around the firm. Gina came to his office every night at the same time and emerged two hours later; they hadn't exactly been discreet. No matter that the door was locked and they kept the noise to a minimum. People weren't stupid and there were more than enough of them around at seven every night. It had to stop before people got hurt, before a mess was made. It had to end.

When Gina told him, her eyes were shot through with red and her pallor was the sickly white of the sleep deprived. She'd been up all night, he guessed, brokering this deal with David. Protecting him. It was a fair deal. All he had to do was take it. All he had to do was never touch her again, never taste her again, never fuck her again.

Not possible.

It had to stop, yes, but it couldn't stop. Not yet. Not like this. Not because of David.

So he brokered his own deal with Gina. One last night together. A proper night in a hotel room. He'd laid out his plan: the firm Christmas party, a careful fabrication on her part, they would each attend alone, he would arrange for them to be at the same table, they would leave early, escape together. They were owed that much. They deserved that much. One special night and then good-bye forever. She shook her head yes, a dozen little lurches. She didn't need much convincing. He could tell that she didn't want things to stop either.

Peter crossed Forty-second Street tentatively, his wingtips sliding on a thin sheen of fallen snow. A yellow cab passed in front of him, its speed the stately march of a hearse. He reached the other side and started walking diagonally up the stairs of the New York Public Library's main branch, the site of this year's party. A half dozen black cars were lined up at the curb, waiting their turn to dispense older partners and their spouses into the waiting hands of an attendant. Peter could picture the scene in reverse in a few hours: more snow, wobblier legs. He did not envy the attendants.

When he reached the cover of the building's overhang, Peter ran a hand through his hair to remove some caked frost. His lungs felt renewed by the cold. The snow was a gift, something to ensure a memorable evening with Gina. They wouldn't bother sleeping tonight. He'd booked a room at The Plaza. He would crack a window, let the cold air seep into the room. He'd make love to Gina under the sheets, let the warmth of their bodies serve as a protest to the elements, to the fates, to everything that was conspiring to keep them apart. He would explore her, find all the places he hadn't yet. He'd make it so that they couldn't stop, so that she couldn't end it. This wasn't over yet. He stepped into the lobby with satyric vigor.

He deposited his coat at the check and snagged a flute of champagne from a passing server. They'd turned the vestibule into a temporary cocktail lounge and strung white lights down the marble walls. He nodded hello to a few colleagues and went to look for Gina. He spotted her on the other end of the hall, waiting near one of the makeshift bars, holding a shimmering black purse at her side. She wore a long black dress. Her hair was pulled up in an elegant bun. He could see the astonishing blue of her eyes even at this distance. She looked ravishing. He suddenly understood the expression; he wanted to ravish her, felt a tremor from his groin at the thought. He crossed the distance between them, sidestepping the lion's share of the bankruptcy group and plowing through the small circle of trusts and estates lawyers the firm still employed. These events were pointless; everyone got drunk with the same five people they talked to every day.

When he arrived in front of Gina, he clasped his hands together like an old-world maître d' heralding the return of his favorite customer. She hadn't noticed him weaving through the crowd or his arrival. Her gaze was fixed down at the floor. He took another step closer.

"Gina," he said, almost breathless. "You look . . ."

She looked up at him, startled, and he could see the moist panic in her eyes.

"Peter, nice to see you," she said, in the

most anodyne way possible. Her right hand lifted like a crane and she tapped a man on the shoulder, someone who had been procuring drinks.

"Peter, this is David, my fiancé."

An open hand swung aggressively toward Peter's stomach. He shook it weakly.

"David Geithorn. I've heard a lot about you."

"Peter Amendola, nice to meet you, David."

His voice sounded like water dripping from a faucet.

"C'mon, Peter. Don't sound *sooo* disappointed."

"David," Gina whispered.

He was shorter than Gina. His hair was already receding and a cluster of baby acne had decamped in the middle of his forehead. His glasses magnified his eyes, made it impossible to ignore the rage in them. He wasn't at all what Peter expected. He'd pictured a tall, blond lacrosse player with washboard abs and rocks in his head. David was a nebbish.

"Well, I think we're sitting at your table, Peter. Won't that be fun?"

He stormed away, pulling Gina with him. Peter drained his flute, ordered a vodka tonic. Later, it would occur to him that he should have left right then.

Dinner was held in the grand room of the library, thirty odd tables scattered in haphazard fashion. Without the prospect of spending the night with Gina, the party reverted to what it always had been for Peter: a boring, self-congratulatory banquet, with frequent, long-winded paeans to the singular excellence of the firm of Lonigan Brown. On top of that, he had to contend with David's incessant glaring from across the table and the drunken nattering of Jennifer Jansen, a thirteenth-year litigation associate who, despite repeated and pointed explanations to the contrary, still held out hope that one day she too would be made partner. He refilled his wineglass frequently and by the time Truman Peabody staggered to the lectern to give his annual report on the firm, replete with personalized commendations for partners who had done outstanding work in the past year, Peter was drunk and miserable and half hoping that David would stop glaring at him and just throw a punch already so he could kick the shit out of him.

Truman cleared his throat dramatically and launched into it.

"In the winter of 1894, two young men —

James Lonigan and Lionel Brown . . ."

A low groan passed through the cavernous room. A flurry of hands reached for wine bottles around the tables. At least his table was tucked in the back, out of sight. Peter considered the uneaten piece of pink beef that sat on his plate. His mind turned to the countless affairs he attended growing up on Staten Island: CYO awards dinners, Little League banquets, Christmas lunches. Their combined cost was probably a fraction of the tab for this event. He dug his fork into the cold slab of beef and lifted it off the plate. He waved it at Gina across the table.

"Hey, Gina, at least at the Staaten, they gave you chicken francaise. Am I right?"

Gina stifled a giggle and David's glare narrowed and his temples clicked. The rest of the table looked around in confusion. Peter dropped the beef back to his plate, took another long pull of wine. He excused himself and wandered off in search of the bathroom. When he got back to the table, David was absent and Truman had moved on to the individual citation portion of his speech. He tried to catch Gina's attention, but she wouldn't look at him.

A wave of applause went up as someone from a nearby table rose to acknowledge

Truman's laudation.

"Gina," Peter whispered low across the table. Her eyes pivoted to him briefly, her chin trembling as she shook her head. Another partner rose to accept his round of weak clapping.

"Gina."

Peter scanned the nearby area. No sign of David. Jennifer was snoring lightly beside him, waking only to join the intermittent applause. The other people at the table — two retired partners and their spouses — were either sleeping or riveted to Truman's speech. Peter scurried around the table and slid into David's empty seat.

"Gina, what happened? What's going on?"

"I don't know, Peter. I don't know."

"Did David leave?"

A final burst of applause drowned out her answer. People stood to clap this time, a standing ovation signifying that the speech was over. A high-pitched drone echoed through the room as Truman brushed against the microphone while exiting the lectern.

"Did David leave, Gina?"

The rest of their table was rousing. The party wasn't over, but a large chunk of people started heading for the coat check. The associates in attendance would flee for hipper quarters to finish their night; the tippling partners would continue their debauchery in a dark-paneled bar at a private club. Peter put his hand on Gina's knee.

"Gina."

"Oh, shit," she said and stood. "What the fuck is he doing?"

Peter rose, confused. He heard a noise all around him, a finger tapping on a microphone. He followed Gina's gaze to the front of the room. David's milky face lingered above the lectern, the picture of calm determination.

"Ladies and gentlemen, ladies and gentlemen." The microphone squealed in protest and two hundred heads turned in confusion. Peter looked around. A few people had leaked into the vestibule, but the mass of the party was still standing there, dumbfounded. Terror flooded through him. He wanted to run, but his legs were stone.

"Sorry, a little feedback." David paused, looked down at the floor, seemed uncertain for a second, and Peter felt the tiniest flicker of hope. Then David looked up, his nerve gathered.

"I wanted to make one special addition to the list of noteworthy accomplishments this year. I wanted to single out Peter Amendola, litigation partner, for repeatedly

259

fucking my fiancée, Regina Giordano. Well done, Peter."

He pointed to their table, laid the microphone on the lectern, and started clapping. Two hundred heads swiveled in Peter's direction. He could already sense David's revelation being condensed into tiny arrows — texts, e-mails, even the quaint old-fashioned phone call — and fired in Lindsay's direction. No chance one wouldn't find its mark.

He lurched backward, put a hand on his chair, and vomited the better part of two bottles of red wine onto the marble floor.

After Peter abandons the pay phone, he wanders out to the Promenade and leans against the railing. At least the whole thing didn't hit YouTube, didn't go viral. No, at least that didn't happen. Small mercies.

He looks over at Manhattan, imagines the quiet lapping of the harbor's black water against its bulk. It's still there, unconquered, unbowed. A sliver of rock between two rivers.

We owe the dead our sins.

He was downtown when it happened, at one of the Wall Street firms that never made the leap to midtown. A joint defense meeting. He can't even remember which case.

Some associate wandered into the conference room, vague on details, a small plane had crashed into one of the towers.

He was outside in the street when the second plane hit. When he knew. When everyone knew. His first thought was Franky. He was worried about Franky, not Bobby. Franky with the new job that he'd pulled strings to get. The mailroom job at a trading firm in one of the towers.

What floor, Peter? What floor?

He wandered to the ferry, the most natural thing in the world. What he'd always done. He watched the first tower crumble from the ferry's rear deck, people crying and praying and screaming around him. He took the train, walked to his childhood home, his hand cramped from gripping his briefcase. The front door was open.

A small crowd in the living room: Mom, Dad, Tina. Only when he saw everyone else's eyes did he realize he was also crying. His mother hugged him and over her shoulder he saw Franky sidle in from the kitchen. Thank God.

His mother said something about Bobby. Missing, not accounted for. But Bobby's firehouse was in Brooklyn, well out of harm's way. No. They've heard nothing. He looked around the room and there was still hope in everyone's eyes, behind the tears. Then he found his father's eyes. They were dull and certain. He moved his head from side to side, swiftly, slightly, a gesture for Peter alone. His mother started sobbing into his shoulder.

We owe the dead our sins.

He'd spoken to Bobby on the phone the night before. He was holding his own daughter, a few weeks old. He called Bobby, who was out with Franky, watching the Giants game. They were always closer, even though he and Franky were closer in age. Bobby, the youngest, but the first to be a father. He stepped outside the bar to talk to Peter.

"It's amazing, bro, isn't it? It's amazing. It's not like anything else in the world."

"Yes, it is. It's unbelievable."

Peter brought a hand down to his daughter's thimble of a chin.

"Fucking Giants."

"What?"

"Fucking Giants defense sucks."

"Go enjoy the game, Bobby."

"Thanks, bro. I love you."

The line went dead before Peter could respond.

Peter wipes his eyes. Maybe he needs a change, a fresh start. Maybe it'll do him good to be in a city without ghosts, to be someplace where his past isn't a ferry ride away, where he doesn't feel anchored to someone else's ethos. Maybe Chicago is exactly what he needs.

Out in the darkness of the harbor, an unseen ferry sounds its horn, whether in agreement or objection, Peter can't tell.

CHAPTER 5
THE SERVANTS' QUARTERS

On Wednesday morning, Michael drives Gail to the ferry. Gail offers to take the train, but he's playing golf at Silver Lake with an old firefighter buddy and the ferry is more or less on the way.

"Two birds, one stone," he says and this makes her smile, because Michael loves his little sayings, loves how the wisdom of the ages can be distilled into a sentence. And she loves how he still makes excuses to be around her, even if it's only twenty minutes in the car, neither of them really talking. She looks out the car window on the way; the sky is a medley of grays, has been this way all week.

He wants to play golf in this drizzling misery?

No, he wants to sit in a cart and drink beer. Laugh with a like-minded soul. No matter. *Don't try to understand everything your husband does.* Sometimes she has to remind herself of her own advice.

She wants to tell Michael in the car about Tina meeting someone. About Wade. She won't get a better chance. She should tell him. He would dismiss her wilder anxieties. He would tell her that Tina and the kids aren't moving across the country. He would remind her what Tina always says: that she wouldn't have survived the last decade without Gail. He would kiss her forehead, tell her that all will be well. She should tell him.

But she doesn't. He's happy this morning and she doesn't want to ruin that. This time of the year is rough. Hard not to think about Bobby with everything you do: the basketball tournament, St. Patrick's Day, Bobby Jr.'s birthday. So she sits there and says nothing.

The car winds its way down Victory Boulevard toward the ferry, passing a mishmash of storefronts: Mexican food joints, dollar stores, a joyless beauty parlor half-filled with black women getting their hair done. A few newly refurbished shops dot the otherwise grimy tableau: a wine bar, an antique shop, a coffee place called The Good Bean. The latest doomed attempts at gentrifying St. George. In six months, the graffiti-filled shutters on these new places will be lowered for good and their bewildered owners will hurry back across the harbor to the safety of Manhattan.

Michael stops the car in the drop-off zone. He kisses Gail good-bye and leans across the vacant passenger seat after she leaves the car.

"Tell big shot I said hello."

"I will. Take it easy with the beers. You're driving. Plus, you got the Leaf's Saint Paddy's Day party later."

His face brightens at the reminder. She married a nice Italian boy and turned him into a donkey. With a little help from the FDNY.

"Love you."

"Love you too."

The car pulls away from the curb. Gail blows on her hands, tries to coax some warmth into them. She walks into the ferry terminal, a sudden loneliness her only companion.

Despite the cold, she sits outside on the ferry, on the side that faces the Verrazano. She prefers this side: less crowded, no tourists. The sight of the bridge always stirs something in Gail. She's spent her entire life within ten miles of this bridge, on one side or the other. Some days this makes her proud, some days sad. Today it's a little of both, and there's nothing inconsistent about that, nothing at all. Most of the things people take pride in are a little sad, if you thought about it. Pride is sad. To take pride in something is to proclaim its importance, and really, how many important things are there? How many could there possibly be?

A light rain starts to fall and a few errant drops find Gail, pushed under the overhang by a haphazard wind. She should go inside, but she doesn't. The rain and the cold suit her melancholy. The slow, steady progress of the ferry echoes a commensurate rise in the foulness of her mood. This annual pilgrimage to see Peter is a fool's errand. The ostensible purpose is to collect Peter's entries for the Cody's pool. Bobby used to do it every year, as a way of keeping his older brother in the family's orbit. Maybe have a corned beef sandwich and a pint of Guinness to celebrate St. Paddy's.

But with each passing year, the lunch has become more and more of an obligation to Peter. Gail knows that's how he feels, sitting across from her, not bothering to hide his BlackBerry, ticking off the minutes until he can pay the bill, hurry back to his office, and cross another item off his to-do list. She isn't even sure whether he feels obligated to her or the ghost of his brother. She doesn't care. She's sick of her oldest son humoring her attempts at maintaining some semblance of tradition.

She probably would have cancelled if she didn't have to tell Peter about Tina. She's wasted the last few days, not told a soul, convinced herself that telling Peter first made the most sense. He's the reasonable and clearheaded one. He'll understand, maybe even help her figure out a way to tell Franky.

No one else can help her tell Bobby. She has to do that alone.

After the ferry docks, Gail shuffles off with the rest of the crowd and makes her way up to the Bowling Green station. The wind at the southern tip of Manhattan is ferocious. People sway as they walk. An African man selling umbrellas on the sidewalk struggles to return his sample to a usable state. A flock of middle-school kids scream in joy at their own helplessness. The detached pages of a newspaper rise from the street and hover for a moment before being whisked into Battery Park.

She doesn't mind the wind. It keeps her head down, her gaze lowered, preventing her from trying to see what is no longer there.

■ ■ ■ ■

She doesn't recognize the look on Peter's face. He's sitting across from her, glumly shaking pepper onto a plate of bacon and eggs like he's sprinkling dirt on a grave. He tucks his tie between the buttons of his white shirt and stares down at his plate, like it's a riddle he can't figure out.

Defeated, she realizes, he looks defeated. He doesn't have the answers. His confidence is shot. Something has happened to him, something he didn't expect and hadn't planned on and he doesn't know what to do. A dose of gratification ripples through her, leaving guilt in its wake. She wishes she could say something or simply ask him what's wrong, but she can't. It's never been like that between them. He's always insisted on his independence, on not relying on his parents, not relying on *her.* Too much track has been laid; neither of them has the capacity for the conversation that should happen. She'll have to poke around and see what he gives her.

"Why are we eating here? Why aren't we in the firm's cafeteria or the Pig 'n' Whistle?"

"I like it here," he says, looking around, as though he's mildly insulted on behalf of the establishment. "I thought you'd be glad I still ate in diners."

"I like the cafeteria. I like meeting the people you work with."

Peter lowers his fork, wipes his mouth with a napkin.

"Mom, you like shooting the shit with Maureen. You hate the people I work with. You've never given a fuck about my work, about what I do."

"That's not true," she protests.

"It is unquestionably true. When was the last time you asked me about a case I was working on? When was the last time you asked me anything about work, other than how Maureen was doing?"

"I don't always understand what you do."

He doesn't look up between bites.

"You know exactly what I do. I represent corporations, sometimes individuals, who the government is investigating or who are involved in lawsuits with other corporations. Or, as you would put it: I represent rich people. *Other* rich people."

His response is swift, premeditated. She's forgotten what it's like to talk to him. You have to parse every word. Every question sets the stage for answers he's already decided on.

"Jesus, Peter, what's up your ass?"

He doesn't answer. In the dark rolling wave of his stubble, she notices a few whitecaps. A waiter meanders over and refills their coffees. When he leaves, she tries to change the tenor of the conversation.

"I just always thought you'd end up being a prosecutor. Maybe an assistant U.S. attorney like your friend Matt from law school, and then maybe the district attorney for Staten Island."

His eyes lift from the plate. His fork, coated with egg yolk, hovers below his chin.

"The DA for Staten Island?" He laughs.

"Yes, what's so funny about that? You could still do it, you know."

"Jesus, Mom."

He rubs his left eye, smiles at some private joke.

"Well, it would be an interesting campaign."

"What does that mean?"

"Nothing, Gail, it means nothing."

He does this to irritate her. Calls her Gail.

"It wouldn't be such a terrible life, you know. You could live on Todt Hill, the kids could go to Staten Island Academy. You could join the country club."

Peter stares at her blankly.

"What?" she asks.

"You're not serious."

271

"Well, what if I am? Would that be so terrible?"

"What about Lindsay? How do you think Lindsay would like living on Staten Island?"

"I'm sure she'd like it fine."

Not true and Gail knows it. But Gail can't say what she wants to say, which is *maybe the problem is with Lindsay, not with Staten Island.* No, she can't say that. She tries to think of something that would appeal to Lindsay.

"There's a new Indian restaurant on New Dorp Lane."

"A new Indian restaurant? Well, that changes everything."

"There's a good sushi place on Hylan Boulevard, I hear."

"Ahh, sushi and Indian. I had it wrong. Staten Island's a bastion of diversity and open-mindedness."

His sarcasm flicks a raw nerve. Years ago, Peter said that Staten Island was the servants' quarters of the city. He didn't mean anything by it, was trying to make a point. But the phrase stuck with Gail. She thinks of it every time she sees him. Worse still is the truth of it, as reflected in her own mind. Whenever she comes to the city, she feels out of place, an outsider, the shanty Irish servant traipsing clumsily through the dining room, with its fine china and exquisite crystal. He smiles across at her, satisfied by his peremptory dismissal of her idea. She feels the blood rush to her face.

"Don't give me that shit, Peter. I've seen where you live. Not a lot of plumbers or cops. Not a lot of black people either. Don't give me a lecture on diversity."

His eyes narrow. He's been spoiling for a fight, trying to goad her into one since they sat down, and now he has what he wants.

"True enough, Gail, true enough. But at least it's not a bunch of wannabe gangster gindaloons who wear their ignorance like a badge."

Real anger in his voice. Something is definitely wrong. Now, she's worried about him and angry at him all at once.

"I don't know why you would say that, Peter. I truly don't. You're talking about your own people."

"They're not my people."

He takes a sip of coffee and his face contorts with the presence of a novel thought.

"And what do you care anyway? They're definitely not your people. You should hate them even more."

"You're Italian by blood. I'm Italian by borough."

She watches the anger slide from his face. He dips a piece of toast into egg yolk.

"Italian by borough? That's pretty good. How long you been holding that one back?"

"A few years. Been waiting for the right moment."

"Well done."

He laughs and she smiles. She takes a sip of coffee. She should leave this where it is, let this good mood linger, end on this note. But Peter's intransigence galls her. His whole life is a rejection of her, of his own family, of how he was raised. She doesn't understand.

"I don't know what's so wrong with wanting my family to be close by. I barely see your kids. You never bring them to visit. You act like there's something wrong with us."

"Jesus, Mom. We're coming over on Sunday. The whole family."

She starts crying. How many of these lunches have brought tears to her eyes? Too many.

"That's not what I mean. I don't understand where things went wrong. We should be closer. Bobby would have wanted it that way."

"Jesus, Mom, I'm sorry, okay? I didn't mean to upset you."

"And now Tina's met someone . . . I don't know."

She didn't want to bring it up this way. She's laying it on Peter, trying to conjure some sympathy from him. A pained expression crosses his face. He takes his Black-Berry from his pocket and scans it. His fingers dance frenetically for a few moments and then he puts it away. He looks back at her, his lips rearranged in a sheepish frown.

"I heard about Tina."

"Heard what?"

"That's she dating someone, dating Wade."

How does he know his name?

"I think it's serious, Peter."

"It is."

"How do you know?"

"Wade is a friend of mine. You've met him."

"A friend of yours?" she asks, shocked.

"Yes," he says, eyes averted.

Things are dawning on her. A tiny con-spiracy is forming in her head.

"Did you introduce them?"

He tilts his head down and scratches the back of his neck, a tick he's had since he was a teenager, when he was being evasive.

"Sort of. I gave him Tina's number last year. He lost his wife a few years ago and I thought maybe she could help him, you know, with the grief."

"Jesus, I didn't know that. I didn't know he lost his wife."

Gail feels a softening in her dislike for this man she doesn't know. A widower, someone who's experienced loss.

"Does he have any children?" she asks.

"No, Morgan was . . . Morgan was his wife. She was pregnant when she was killed in a car crash. Four months along."

"My God."

"I'm not even sure Tina knows that, Mom."

"I won't say anything."

She can't even hate this man. Can't even hate the man who is trying to replace her son, trying to take Tina and Alyssa and Bobby away from her. It's not fair. She starts to cry again, tries to hide it from Peter, but she can't. He reaches over and takes her hand.

"Your hands are freezing, Mom."

"Cold hands, warm heart."

His face settles in a rueful stare. He looks at her as though he can't quite remember who she is and then he looks down at their entwined hands.

"Strange," he says, more to himself than to her, "strange the things that you don't realize you remember. That stick in your brain somewhere, waiting for something to stir them. 'Cold hands, warm heart.' Jesus, the things you forget."

He's lost in some tormented contemplation. Gail can't remember him ever being this distracted, this scatterbrained. Not even when he was a kid. The Peter she knows — the Peter who frustrates her — has floated away; it unnerves her.

"What if Tina moves away, Peter? What if the kids move?"

He shakes his head, as though his thoughts could be exiled by physical action.

"He lives in New York, Mom. His job is in New York."

"But he's not gonna move to Staten Island."

"He might," Peter says unconvincingly.

Gail pulls her hands back.

"Right, just like you might."

Peter straightens his seat, pushes his half-eaten plate of food to the side to indicate he's done. He pulls his tie out from his shirt and runs it between two fingers, one behind and one in front. The gesture makes her realize how much of his world she doesn't know. He has his own ticks and habits, his own troubles and annoyances, just as she does. The small things in their lives are not the same. And almost everything is a small thing.

"Well, maybe you and Dad should think about moving somewhere else. Retiring somewhere."

"Sure, Peter."

"I'm serious."

"Where would we go?"

"Go wherever you want. Florida, North Carolina, Arizona. Your cost of living would drop in half."

"What about Franky?"

He sucks his cheeks in and exhales in a low whistle.

"Don't get me started."

"You're too hard on your brother."

"You're not hard enough." His voice is dull, tired; this is ground well trod. "And I'm not too hard on him. I'm the only one who's ever really helped him."

"What do you mean?"

"How soon we forget."

"Forget what?"

His eyes widen and she remembers.

"Oh, that," she says and it comes out the wrong way. She can hear it, can hear herself brushing it aside. *Oh, that.* Like he got drunk and pissed in the sink. *Oh, that.* Like he grabbed someone's ass at a Christmas party.

"Yeah, *that*," Peter says, and his *"that"* gets it right. His *"that"* lands with a heavy thud on the table between them.

"He was upset, Peter."

"No, Mom. He was drunk. Or high. Probably both."

"It was my fault. I shouldn't have said what I said. It was a horrible thing to say. A horrible thing for a mother to say."

She sees herself saying it, the veins in her neck bulging, the words flying out like a taut rope suddenly cut. Franky had been daring her to say it for two years, goading her. But the look on his face when she finally did?

"First of all, he's a grown man who's responsible for his own actions. And second, his little hate crime happened well over a month later, Mom. I know you like to take responsibility for Franky's sins, but this shit is insane."

"It wasn't a hate crime, Peter."

"It was a hate crime. It wasn't charged as a hate crime because I made sure that Franky got competent counsel. And called in a favor. But let's not kid ourselves about what happened. He beat the living hell . . ."

"It wasn't a hate crime, Peter. The guy wasn't even an Arab, wasn't even a Muslim. Franky only thought he was."

Peter stares at her.

"I don't know what's worse. That you think it would have been okay if he was a Muslim or that Franky couldn't even fuck up the right way. Jesus," Peter says, his eyes drifting away from her.

"Enough, Peter. It was my fault."

"Bullshit."

"Tell me there was no connection. Tell me it was a coincidence."

He chuckles behind a hand raised to indicate *stop*.

"You don't know, Peter. I've not been a good mother to him. Even when you were kids, I was always harder on him."

"Not true. In fact, the opposite is true. You were always easier on him."

"What about when you guys left Bobby at the beach? And I played that trick on you. That awful, stupid trick."

"Ah, yes, here we go. The moment-you-ruined-Franky story."

"You don't understand, Peter."

"No, Mom. I do. I was there, remember? I left Bobby behind as well. I waited for you to bring him home, shitting my pants, just like Franky. I was there, literally in the room, when you came in without him."

"But it wasn't your idea. It was his and he knew it."

"The next morning, Bobby had forgotten

all about it. I had pretty much forgotten it. And Franky, sure as shit, had forgotten it. The only one who even remembers it is you."

"I hope you never do anything cruel to your kids, Peter. I truly don't."

Peter winces, takes a sip of coffee.

"Believe what you want to. But stop making excuses for someone who's almost forty."

"He's my son, Peter. I can't abandon him."

He shakes his head again, dismissive. She slaps her open hand down on the table, rattling the saucers that hold their coffee cups, turning a few heads in their direction.

"This is what I mean, this is what I'm talking about. People used to stick together, families used to stay together, live near one another, help one another. They didn't scatter to the four winds. They didn't abandon people because they were difficult."

His eyebrows arch and his mouth settles in a grin. He starts tapping the tips of his fingers together in rhythm.

"Let me tell you something, Gail. What you just said is absolute, complete bullshit. People stick together, families help one another, rah, rah, rah. Bullshit. What about your parents? Did you stand by them? Did you stay in the old neighborhood?"

Her hands start to tremble. She cinches her face into a steady gaze. Peter pauses for a moment, casually stirring some sugar into his coffee, and then proceeds.

"Or did you abandon them?"

A few harsh white spots dot her vision. The tremble trickles down to her legs. Her head feels too full, too heavy; a nosebleed is imminent. She needs to calm down, let the blood in her body rebalance. She reaches for some napkins and shoves them into her coat pocket.

"Do you have your sheets for the Cody's pool?" she asks, in a voice as brittle and cold as cracked ice.

"No."

"Do you want to discuss candidates for the scholarship?"

He laughs, a cackle filled with loathing.

"No."

She lifts her head, fixes her gaze on him.

"I guess we're done then."

His expression softens; he knows he's pushed too hard. She stands and her legs wobble. She puts a hand on the Formica to steady herself.

"Mom, sit down. Finish your meal."

She puts her coat on and heads for the door, ignoring Peter's hushed attempts to get her to sit back down. She walks out to the cross street and raises her hand, trying to hail one of the angry yellow cabs marching down Second Avenue. One detaches itself from the herd, floats over to the curb in front of her.

She gets into the cab and closes the door. At the edge of her blurry vision, she sees Peter hurrying up Forty-eighth Street toward her. The driver asks her where's she going.

"South Ferry," she says, and the driver nods, eases the cab back into traffic. He catches her eyes in the rearview mirror and repeats the destination twice to make sure he heard her right.

She nods in response.

Peter calls while she's waiting for the ferry, conciliatory and ashamed. She listens to his apology and forgives him. She says she was in the wrong as well, though she doesn't feel that way. She can never sustain anger. It flashes — white hot, overwhelming — and twenty minutes later, it's gone. Sometimes she wishes it wasn't so, wishes she could nurse a grudge, linger on a grievance. But she can't. It's not in her makeup. So she tells Peter she loves him and he says he loves her as well and she wonders why it's so easy on the phone between them and so difficult in person. By the end of the call, all is forgiven and forgotten, the conflict between them tucked away and fixed with a label that reads "Things that will never be discussed again."

The automated doors slide open and the throngs of waiting passengers start their shuffle onto the rusted twin ramps that lower onto the ferry. Gail has been lingering in the rear of the terminal, against the side wall, talking to Peter with her head turned to the glass facade. She follows the crowd, hoping she won't lose cell reception. Her anger is gone and all that remains is concern; something is definitely wrong.

"Peter, is everything all right with you? Are the kids okay? Is Lindsay okay? Did something happen?"

His response comes in a thick sob.

"I fucked up, Mom. I fucked up. I don't know what to do. I don't know what to do."

"What happened, Peter?"

A phone rings in the background. He clears his throat, blows his nose. When he speaks again, his voice is almost back to normal.

"I have to take this call, Mom. I'm sorry again. I love you."

"I love you too, Peter."

The line goes dead as she's standing on one of the lowered ramps, the last of the passengers. An impulse to go back to Peter strikes her, but she stands in the center of the ramp, undecided. An overweight, mustached man in yellow rain gear waits behind her, at the crank that raises the ramps, his hands gesturing in irritation.

"Make up your mind, lady. Ain't got all day."

She glares back at him.

"Ho-ho, feisty one."

She walks onto the ferry slowly. When the ramp is pulled up behind her, she turns back to the jiggly-jowled worker and gives him the finger.

The ferry glides across the harbor, uninhabited Governors Island giving way to the low-slung Brooklyn neighborhoods that lead to the Verrazano. The final one is Bay Ridge. The place she abandoned, as Peter put it.

The rain has stopped. A weak March sun is trying to fight through the gray. She closes her eyes, tries to enjoy the solitude. Concern for Peter floats into her consciousness, unbidden. She hasn't worried about Peter in years, but today the weepy apology, his acidic demeanor at the diner, were upsetting.

He'll be fine, she tells herself. He's always been fine. He's a clever boy, a fella whose toast always lands butter side up, as her father used to say. He'll be fine.

At least he knows now, about Wade. One down, three to go. She accomplished something, the trip wasn't a total waste. Then again, he knew already. He introduced them. She can't be angry about that, though. It was a kind thing to do. When he isn't aggravating the hell out of her, Peter is a decent, thoughtful, successful man. That's what the rest of world sees; why can't she always see it? To be a mother is to fail your kids. Just ask Franky.

Anyway, doesn't matter how. Peter knows. The trip was not a waste.

The twenty dollars she spent on a cab down to the ferry? Now that was a waste. Twenty dollars. Dear Christ, how do people live in Manhattan? At least the ferry's still free. This view is still free. Twenty minutes of tranquility. She looks around, but the deck is still empty. Nothing but the gray harbor and the ghost of rain.

She closes her eyes. It's already been a long week. And you have miles to go before you sleep, she tells herself.

"Ma'am?"

Gail wakes, hears the voice, looks up to meet its owner: a young man, stocky, wearing a policeman's uniform. His silver name badge reads ALVAREZ. His smile hides a certain impatience.

"You have to exit the ferry, ma'am."

Behind him, Gail sees the wooden pylons of the terminal's barge. The boat is docked, cleared of all passengers. Except her.

"Why?" she asks. "I want to ride back to Manhattan."

"I know, ma'am, but you still have to exit. Everyone has to leave the ferry now. You can get back on, but you have to exit first."

He says this with a practiced ennui. She can see in his eyes that she's not the first old lady he's had to usher off the ferry. She's not sure when strangers started thinking of her as old.

"But why? What difference does it make? Why do I have to go back through the terminal?"

"Because of terrorism. Everyone has to leave," he says, the impatience no longer hidden.

She stands. Her knees ache with the effort.

"Right. I'm clearly a threat. A suicide bomber."

"Rules is rules," he says, a little more of

287

the Bronx sneaking into his voice. "People are waiting."

"Next time I'll wear a burka. Then maybe you'll leave me alone."

He sighs with boredom. She knows he's only doing his job, but still. A little common sense would go a long way. She walks off the ferry as slowly as humanly possible.

She remembers Michael telling her that he fell asleep on the ferry once, after a big night in the city. When he woke up, he was back on the Manhattan side, had slept through the unloading on the Staten Island side. Each of the boys had stories like that too. Fell asleep on the ferry, woke up back in Manhattan. Must be a rite of passage for the tippling male souls of Staten Island. They all laughed about it, but it made Gail anxious. What if something happened? What if someone did something to them? They laughed at her anxiety. Men don't worry about the same things. Maybe they should, but they don't.

The bustle of the terminal heightens her discombobulation. She's forgotten the labyrinth on the Staten Island side, the assortment of tunnels and walkways leading to various bus lines, to the train, to the curb where cars could pick you up. She wanders toward the tunnel that leads to the train.

She finds a quiet seat, one where she can look out the window, watch the Island slide past.

When she gets home, Michael is holding the phone in one hand and a slip of paper in the other.

"Hold on, T. Here she is now," he says, and then covers the receiver on his chest. "What's this?"

His index finger taps against her to-do list from earlier in the week. The item "tell Bobby" is clearly the object of his question.

"I can explain," she says, though she can't, not really, because she's been dotting her to-do lists with references to Bobby for ten years and Michael's never stopped asking her about it. She takes the phone from him.

"Hey, Tina."

"Hey, you sound tired. You okay?"

"Yes. Went into the city today to see Peter."

"How is he?"

Not good. Pretty bad actually. Scared me a bit. This is what she wants to say, what she would say normally. But already there's a gulf.

"He's fine. I went in to tell him about your new friend, but he already knew."

It sounds snottier than Gail intended, but

she doesn't care. They could have told her. One of them could have told her and saved her a trip.

"Yeah, I'm sorry, Gail. I thought Peter would have told you, but I think there was a mix-up. I don't think he even knew until this week. Wade told him on Monday."

"I see."

She's not making this easy for Tina. She wants to, wants to handle this with a little grace, but she's tired of taking the high road. When does she get to be petulant?

"Anyway," says Tina, "I was actually calling to see how Franky took the news. I was a little worried he might not react well."

Gail pushes a breath out through her mouth.

"I haven't told him yet."

A long pause.

"Okay, are you going to tell him before the party? Because I think it would be better if he didn't find out at the party."

"Jesus, Tina. I will tell him, okay? He will behave himself. I promise he'll behave."

A promise about someone else's behavior. May as well promise happiness or a sunny day or a winning lotto ticket.

"No, Gail. I didn't mean to offend. It's just that Franky can be . . ." She doesn't finish the thought. "And he and Bobby were so close."

Gail hopes Tina learns what it is to love a child who is broken. Irreparably. She wants Tina to feel responsible for that, being the mother of a broken thing. And, just as swiftly, she prays to God that Tina never has to feel that, any of that. She has known enough heartbreak. And Gail hates herself for hoping to add to it.

She speaks softly.

"Tina, I understand what you're saying. I know, believe me, I know. I will tell him. He will be here. And he will not embarrass you or me or any of us. Especially not Bobby Jr."

Gail pauses.

"Because if he does, I will drag him out into the street and murder him myself."

Tina laughs; the tension eases a little.

"I'm sorry for bringing it up at all. I just want everything to go well."

"It will."

"Okay, I feel better."

"See you Sunday?"

"Sunday. Thank you, Gail."

"You're welcome."

Michael has been waiting in the living room, jacket on, ready for the Leaf and the St. Patrick's Day party. When Gail hangs up, he steps into the kitchen, scratching his head.

"Tell Bobby what? Murder who? What the hell is going on?" he asks, with a fair share of impatience. Gail smiles. Michael never wants to know what's going on until the moment he does, and then he wants to know everything. So she tells him.

"Tina met someone. His name is Wade. A friend of Peter's. He's coming here on Sunday for Bobby Jr.'s birthday party. And Tina's concerned about how Franky will react. I haven't told him yet."

Michael doesn't say anything. The irritation on his face dissipates. He walks back to hug her. Don't go to the Leaf, she wants to say. Or what she wants is for him not to go to the Leaf, without her having to ask.

Instead, he says, "Come to the Leaf with me?"

"Nah, I'm tired. I think there are some *Law and Order* reruns with my name on them."

"Pick you up on the couch in a few hours?"

"It's a date."

He kisses her forehead and makes for the door. The door is almost closed, but he ducks his head back in.

"What the hell kind of name is Wade?"

Sometimes Michael knows exactly what to say.

She sits down on the couch and turns on the television. She hopes it isn't one of the episodes where she's not sure at the end whether the guy was guilty. She wants an episode where there's no ambiguity about guilt or punishment. One that ends with a long sentence imposed. With justice served.

Chapter 6
Brothers and Sisters
I Have None, But This
Man's Father's . . .

Michael Amendola still enjoys his sleep. It does not elude him as it does his friends. He listens to the complaints of his friends with a wry smile and stays silent. He can't imagine a worse way to respond to a complaint than by confessing to its absence. Better to nod agreeably and fake commiseration.

The old men go on and on about how they're up three, four times a night to take a leak, how they can't fall back to sleep, about how they lie in bed and close their eyes and try to think about something pleasant, a blonde on a beach or a warm fire or a brunette on a beach, ha ha, because old men are always reminding someone that they're still virile, but none of these things work and they end up waiting for the first hostile red digit of the alarm clock to add a line and transform from an outrageous five to a more agreeable six so they can stagger out of bed and begin their days.

Michael does not suffer in this way. He falls asleep with little trouble, especially if he's had a few drinks. His bladder pulls him out of bed to the bathroom in the wee hours more than he'd like, but he drifts back to sleep without much effort. If he thinks about blondes or brunettes or beaches, it's because he wants to, not because he has to. He wakes when he's meant to and if neither the world nor his wife is calling him, he is not shy about rolling over and spending an extra half hour in the warm spot Gail has left on the other side of their bed.

It used to trouble him, his lethargy in this manner. He wasn't lazy in other ways; the opposite in fact. It seemed like a defect of youth, one that he should shed. He imagined that he'd eventually become like his father, an industrious man who woke with a start in the predawn blue and ran headlong into each day. But it never happened. The years went by and there were wailing babies, the demands of the firehouse, his stint in the service, the occasional call in the middle of the night. Each of these demanded his attention — sleepy-eyed, dutiful — but none of them changed the preference.

It used to trouble him but it doesn't anymore. He's an old man, that's what he tells himself, and old men have earned their foibles.

This morning he woke to the sound of Gail in the shower but has been unable to slide back to sleep. He listened while Gail prepared for the day, hoping he would drift off. When she kissed his forehead, he opened his eyes.

"Can't sleep?" she asked.

"Can't sleep."

"I have absolutely no sympathy. How was the party?"

"Same shenanigans as usual. Happy Saint Paddy's, by the way."

"Don't remind me. Just another Thursday."

"You gonna go to the city, Goodness, watch the parade?"

"Bunch of drunk donkeys painting the streets green with their vomit? No, thanks. Glad I went to see Peter yesterday."

"We didn't even talk about that. How was big shot?"

She paused before answering.

"Same as usual. All wine and roses."

He sensed something in her hesitation, but let it drift. Gail did many things for him and one of them was act as a filter for bad news. She only told him things if necessary.

Like the new boyfriend thing last night with Tina.

"Good for him."

"You and the boys dropping off your sheets today?"

"Yes."

"Will you be home for dinner?"

"Not sure. What are you making?"

"Traditional Irish fare: baked ziti."

"Can we play it by ear? I'll call you, let you know."

"Sure, sure. Some slut of a waitress is gonna sweet-talk you into corned beef and cabbage. You and the Irish girls."

She smiled and her eyes expanded merrily, taking Michael back a few decades. He reached a warm hand up to her hip, an old man reminding his wife that he can still be stirred in that way and that she can still do the stirring.

"Come back to bed with me, my Irish girl."

But she didn't. She rose out of his grasp, said she was running late, and winked at him before leaving the room. From the stairs, she shouted back up at him.

"Maybe later."

"Tease."

There will be nothing later. He knows that. He can still be stirred on occasion.

She can still be stirred on occasion. But aligning those occasions so they coincide? A tricky business made trickier by his unwillingness to employ pharmacological aid and her unwillingness to be cajoled into something in which she's mostly lost interest. This used to bother him — the diminishment, near extinction, of their sex life — but it doesn't anymore.

The fact that it doesn't bother him is what bothers him now.

He has a mild hangover and his usual remedy, more shut-eye, is unavailable, so he gets out of bed and goes to the bathroom to fetch a handful of Advil. His right shoulder is achy and both his ankles click as he walks. He curses his teenage self, cavalier and invincible, for pinballing around football fields without regard for either of their bodies: that young, pristine one or this old, dilapidated one. He takes a long, satisfying piss and washes his hands. He splashes some water on his face.

He is startled when he looks in the mirror. Most days, he barely notices his reflection. He shaves in the shower, uses the mirror only to make sure he doesn't look like a buffoon: no shaving cream hanging from an earlobe, no gush of blood from a nick, no patches of hair the razor didn't find. But some days, he looks up and his father stares back at him. Today, he sees Enzo. A question sits on his lips, unspoken.

"Not today, Dad."

His father's face remains impassive, patient.

"Not today, Dad. Please, I just want to enjoy today. Take the sheets in, have a few beers."

His father waits.

"I wanted a different life. Okay. Simple."

His father shrugs.

Michael raises his right hand, extends his index finger, watches its doppelgänger extend to meet its maker. He pushes on the mirror once, raises the finger to his reflection again, presenting his evidence.

"This. I was tired of this."

His father smiles.

Michael is woken by a finger jabbing his shoulder. He knows this jab well. It is not a rough gesture, not particularly insistent. It is simple, purposeful. It carries a message.

I have let you sleep as long as possible.

He opens his eyes, pivots to a sitting position. He senses the shadow of his father hustling out of the still-dark room, embarrassed that he must rouse his son in this fashion. Michael looks at the window, sees the hint of daylight creeping around the shade. It is not yet six o'clock. He yawns and stands.

His parents are waiting for him in the kitchen, already dressed, breakfast behind them. His father sips coffee while his mother cooks him peppers and eggs. He finds them like this every morning, as though they were living according to some clock he cannot see, cannot fathom. His mother slides a plate in front of him, kisses the top of his head.

"Grazie," he says, then, "thank you."

His parents look at him, unsure why he keeps saying everything twice, first in Italian, then in English. Michael's not a big talker, in either language. Neither are his parents. Their English is still choppy, experimental, despite their twenty years in this country. And they know that long conversations in Italian make their son uncomfortable. Silence reigns, and in that silence lives a heavy, expectant love.

It has always been this way. From an early age, Michael could sense the oppressive neediness of his parents' love. He was their universe, the polestar of their existences, the only outlet for their hopes and dreams. Just the three of them. No cousins, no aunts or uncles. No neighbors dropping over for coffee. Once a year, a distant relative of his father's, Umberto, would drive down from Buffalo to drop off a dozen jugs of homemade wine, receive a few bundles of Enzo's dried salami and sausage. He would spend a few nights and even though Umberto wasn't particularly warm, Michael relished those visits. If nothing else, Umberto distracted his parents for a while, let Michael escape the glare of their incessant affection.

He finishes his breakfast, takes some coffee to go. He kisses his mother good-bye, has to hurry to catch up to his father. Enzo is shockingly impatient in the mornings, as though they were running late, even though they almost always finish their prep work an hour before the first customer of the day arrives. They drive to the store in silence. When they enter, the smell — the slick, acrid scent of blood and bone — always shocks Michael. He thought he would eventually stop noticing it, but he hasn't. Others love it. They tell his father, make a great show of sniffing the air when they walk in. Michael doesn't understand why he hates it so; he wonders whether florists ever get sick of the scent of fresh flowers.

They go about their business. Periodically, Enzo peeks over Michael's shoulder and notices an error. *You are moving too fast, not watching your knife. You are slicing the bacon too thin. You need to find the joints on the chicken thigh before you start hacking into it. Now the bacon is too thick.* Michael nods, mutters curses in English under his breath.

As usual, they finish well before the store opens, but Enzo cannot sit still. He fiddles in the display case, straightens boxes of pasta, sweeps up the floor for the third time. Michael sits and reads the paper, ignoring Enzo's beseeching looks. If there were something else to do, he would do it. He is not lazy. But fussing about and making work is craziness. So Enzo sweeps while Michael reads and the silence grows tense.

The tension dissipates as soon as the first customer shows up. The day speeds up, the store fills with other voices. A few speak Italian, but it's mostly English. The conversation is light, expedient. The Verrazano Bridge, only a few months away from being completed, is a frequently discussed topic. Some people say it will be a good thing: it will bring more people to the Island! Others think it will be bad, very bad: it will bring more people to the Island! Most people agree that it's beautiful. Also, of course, wonderful that it was named after an Italian.

"Michael," one woman asks, "you just

graduated from high school. What do you think?"

He thinks, *If I hear one more person talking about the fucking Verrazano Bridge, I am going to walk to the middle of it and jump off.*

"Could be a good thing. I don't know. Maybe not."

The woman nods as though he's said something profound.

"Smart boy," she says to Enzo, who looks at Michael with intense pride. Michael looks at the clock. It's not even noon.

He makes some deliveries: Seaside Boulevard, Old Town Road, Garretson Avenue. Enzo won't let him drive — he knows how but doesn't have his license yet — so he has to use the store's busted old bike, even though it's ninety-two degrees and the air is thick. By the time he gets to the houses, he's dripping with sweat and he can smell himself through his clothes. He knows the women he delivers to: Mrs. Scotto, Mrs. Villa, old lady Meehan. Mrs. Villa is young, maybe five years older than he, and pretty. She invites him in for a glass of water, tells him to call her Lisa. He stares at her cleavage while she complains about her mother-in-law. He takes his time finishing the water.

On the way back to the store, he stops at Nunzio's for two slices and a Coke. He eats the slices in a rush and then sits at the counter, sipping the Coke, wishing the minutes away. When he gets back, Enzo looks irritated even though the store is empty. He hands Michael a paper plate with his lunch: sliced salami on a roll. He inhales that, slaps his hands together to remove the crumbs. If this was the job — Lisa Villa's tits, pizza, salami — he would be happy. If he could somehow get *his* salami between Lisa Villa's tits, he'd be really happy. He needs a few bawdy thoughts to get him through the day.

The afternoon is quiet, only a handful of customers. At five o'clock, Enzo looks outside to make sure no one else is coming and then turns the sign from OPEN to CLOSED. Michael sweeps up while Enzo counts at the register. He licks his fingers between bills, counts out the change, checks the scraps of paper where he tracks his customers' accounts on credit. He does some math on another scrap, concentrates while he's adding. When he's finished, he looks up at Michael and smiles.

"Una buona giornata," he says. "A good day."

His parents are more chatty at dinner, their tongues loosened by a few glasses of Umberto's wine. His mother asks about their day and Enzo re-creates, in meticulous detail, the not very exciting day they just experienced. Michael lived the day in English and now he has to relive in it in Italian. He inhales long strands of linguine coated with garlic and oil. He downs the glass of wine, asks to be excused. His parents look at him, then at each other, uncertain what to make of their son's recent restlessness. He retreats to his bedroom even though the sun is still up. He was supposed to hang out with Tiny tonight, but Tiny is spending almost every night with his girlfriend Laura Gentile. Tiny is off to college in the fall and he has sworn to Michael that he is getting into Laura's pants before he leaves. Michael wishes he had a girlfriend, had some goal to pursue, even something as basic as trying to get laid. He turns on the radio, lies on his bed. The Mets are playing the traitor Giants, Marichal is pitching. There's no score yet.

He misses baseball, misses football too. Being part of a team, the simple joy of camaraderie. The brothers he never had. That is all done now. There is no school to return to in the fall. No college lies in the distance. He was never a good student, but school was, at least, somewhere to go, something to do. And nothing made him feel the way sports did.

He is eighteen years old and as far as he can tell, all his days going forward will be the same: the waking jab, the silent house, long days at his father's shop, cutting up meat, coming home smelling of blood. Unless.

Unless what? He doesn't know. He doesn't have a plan, but he has blind hope. Maybe something will happen. Maybe a man will wander into the store, like the look of him, offer him a job. Maybe he can take another look at college, take some classes at night. Maybe he can help out coaching football at New Dorp in the fall. Maybe Lisa Villa will ask him to stop staring at her tits and just screw her already. He lets these hopes, vague and unformed and ridiculous, brighten his day's final thoughts.

But the next morning, his slumber is disrupted by a gentle jab of his shoulder. He slides to a sitting position. His hopes have vanished in the night, leaving a resigned emptiness in their wake.

This is your life. This will be your life unless . . .

Something happens. He draws a very low draft number. He'd considered enlisting — anything to get away from an endless line of *buona giornatas* — but the conflict in Vietnam, slowly escalating, made him hesitant. He's doesn't want to go, but he's no dummy. He knows when something's inevitable. He's a working-class kid, 1A, no deferments to use, no evasive magic to conjure. His parents have no connections, no strings to pull. He figures it's a matter of time anyway. He volunteers for the draft. In October 1964, a month before the Verrazano Bridge opens, he ships out to Fort Sill in Oklahoma for basic training.

His first night there is the first night he's ever slept off of Staten Island.

Down in the kitchen, Michael finds a freshly brewed pot of coffee. He pours himself a cup, sits down at the table. His entry sheet lies below an envelope filled with crumpled twenties. Gail has filled in a few. He picks it up, takes a sip of coffee, peruses her entries. She always has too many underdogs, too many high seeds making the Final Four. This year's no different.

Who's he kidding? He's never won the pool, never even come close. Doesn't matter; it's a tradition. Today's little expedition — collecting all the entries from the Leaf, driving them over to Cody's — is one of his favorite days of the year. Bobby used to come with him, the young pup hanging out with the old-timers. Franky would meet them at Cody's. Peter could never get away from work, but Bobby would still collect his entries, call him when there was a sense of the total number. Two hundred thousand, half a million, seven hundred thousand. Up, up, up. Never mind the economy. The Cody's pool was recession proof.

Michael has a different plan this year. He's going back to the way they used to do it, when the boys were kids, when the pool was just starting to spread across the Island. He and the boys would each pick one Final Four team. Then Gail would choose the winner and the final score. Only one entry for the whole family. They would watch the games together, the boys living and dying with every missed free throw, every sloppy turnover. As soon as one of their teams lost, the boys would be despondent, but Michael didn't mind. He didn't expect to win. The tradition — the ceremony — was what mattered. Relying on one another, everyone contributing. A team effort. They fell away from that over the years. They wanted to put in their own entries, put in a bunch of entries, increase their chances of winning.

He likes the way they used to do it. And he's thought of an added bonus: doing it this way will help keep Tina in the loop, part of the family. Tina can make Bobby's pick. Or maybe she can have Bobby Jr. make it. Doesn't matter. Gail told Michael last night about Tina's new man. He's happy for Tina, but he knows Gail's worried about what it means. This is a way to ensure that Tina stays included in the family. It's only a little thing, he knows that. But the ceremony means something. It'll mean something to Tina and to Gail. They'll understand.

He looks down, inspecting the sheet. He'll pick the first team, from the East bracket. He checks the high seeds: Ohio State, North Carolina, Syracuse, Kentucky. He's never liked the coach at Syracuse. Too much of a whiner. He looks further down to see if there are any other Big East teams: Villanova's a 9 seed, Marquette, an 11. Long shots. Hmm. Kentucky's coach is an Italian. He'll stick with the paesan. Kentucky it is. He enters his choice on the last line of the sheet, so he'll know which one is the family entry.

Peter always chose second. There's no time to go see him, so he'll call. He puts on his glasses. He picks up the house phone, realizes he has no idea what Peter's number is. He looks around on the cork board that hangs near the fridge, finds a weathered slip of paper — "Peter's office #" scribbled in Gail's handwriting — tacked under a grocery list. He dials the number. A receptionist answers.

"Peter Amendola's office."

"Yeah, uhh, can I talk to Pete? It's his father."

"Hold one moment."

The line goes quiet for a few seconds. When Peter picks up, his voice is sharp.

"What's wrong? Is Mom okay?"

"What? No, Peter . . ."

"Are you okay?"

"I'm fine. Listen . . ."

"Oh, Christ, what did he do now?"

"Who?"

"Franky."

"Franky didn't do anything. Jesus Christ, Peter, calm down."

"I am calm. So everyone's okay?"

"Yes, why would you assume something was wrong?"

He hears Peter exhale.

"Dad, in all the time I've worked here, I think you've called me three times. One was when Grandpa died. The other was when Franky got arrested. This is the third."

"I don't think that's right."

"You're right. You called me once from the Leaf to settle an argument about whether someone could sue the Interweb, as you put it."

"I think you're forgetting other times."

"It doesn't matter. What's up?"

"Listen, do you remember how we used to do the pool? I'd pick a team, then you'd pick a team, then Franky, then Bobby. Just the one entry. So I was thinking that this year, we'd go back to that."

"To be clear, you're calling me about the Cody's pool?"

"Yeah."

"Dad, I don't have time for this right now."

"Peter, I just need you to pick one team. It'll take five seconds."

He looks down at the sheet.

"You have the West regional."

"Just give me the one seed. I haven't watched a game all year."

"But that's Duke."

"So?"

"We hate Duke."

"I don't hate Duke."

"Well, Bobby did. You can't pick Duke."

"Okay, Dad. Who's the two seed?"

"San Diego State."

"Jesus Christ, San Diego State? No way a team from San Diego makes the Final Four. Who's the three seed?"

"UConn."

"Fine, give me UConn. Big East team, been there before. Good coach."

Michael fills in the second entry.

"Good. Thank you, Peter."

"Okay, Dad. Gotta run."

He starts to say good-bye, but Peter has already hung up. He puts the receiver back in its cradle. He inspects the sheet again: a 3 seed and a 4 seed. He will get Tina's pick next, stop by their house on his way to the Leaf. And Franky's pick on his way to Cody's later.

Was it possible that he'd only called Peter three times in fifteen years? Maybe. Gail usually did the calling, handled the chitchat. Still, he talked to Bobby all the time when he was alive. He talks to Franky frequently, even though there have been rough patches over the years. But he's never been able to talk to Peter, they've never been able to connect as adults. He never needed anything from Michael, nothing of substance anyway. Bobby and Franky were both like him in some respect, wanted the same things. Peter was different. He never wanted his parents' life.

A son who didn't want to be like his father. Michael understands that.

■ ■ ■ ■

From his bedroom, Michael can smell his mother cooking his favorite dish: braised lamb shanks with garlic, onions, and tomatoes. If he missed one thing during his time in the army, it was his mother's cooking. But since he came home six weeks ago, twenty pounds lighter than when he left, his mother has been trying to fatten him up. Lamb shanks used to be a rarity, once a month maybe, if Enzo had a few left over on the days when he was lucky enough to get lamb. By Michael's count, this will be the tenth time they've had lamb since he came home; he's getting a little sick of it.

He's tried to explain to them, several times, that he was never in harm's way. Not really. He was only in Vietnam for six months, only discharged his weapon twice; neither situation escalated into a full-blown engagement. He'd thought the army was going to be an efficient, egalitarian organization, but it was like anything else run by men: subject to their own predilections and peccadilloes. One time, his transfer to Vietnam got postponed because the base had a baseball game coming up and he was their star third baseman. One time, he mentioned to his CO that he was an only child and his name got moved from one list to another. Mostly, things hadn't really heated up until he was gone. They were heating up now. Boys were starting to get killed. He'd been lucky in a way, to serve so early, even though it hadn't felt like it at the time.

His parents will not listen, do not care. They know only that their beloved boy is safely home. His father has even abandoned his usual waking jab in favor of a gentle shake. Some mornings, Michael even waves his father off, tells him he'll meet him at the shop, falls back to sleep. Enzo is puzzled, but lets it go. His boy is home, has served his country, is entitled to a few indulgences. Besides, Michael's presence at the shop is superfluous. In his absence, Enzo hired a young boy, Enzo Annunziata, to do the deliveries and he doesn't have the heart to let him go now that Michael is home. So old Enzo handles the cutting and the counter and young Enzo makes the deliveries and Michael sits there, watching them scurry around and wondering how it's possible that he went halfway around the world, spent two years in three different countries, and came home to find that nothing had changed.

Not true. The world has changed. Michael

has changed. But his parents have not changed. Their love for him, which was always stifling, is now suffocating. He doesn't miss the army — the food was terrible, there was too much bullshit — but he misses aspects of it: the camaraderie, the sense of purpose. He missed being home too. Missed his parents, missed his friends, missed the kindhearted but streetwise sensibilities of Staten Islanders. He did not miss the shop.

He hears his mother call up to him, tell him in Italian that dinner is ready.

"Il tuo preferito," she adds. His Italian is rusty, but he knows this one.

Your favorite.

Tiny picks him up after dinner. It's the night before Thanksgiving, the biggest night of the year. Michael has been itching for a night out since he got home.

"Where we headed, Tiny?"

"There's a big party over at the Feeney house. Jerry is shipping out next week."

The Feeneys are a well-known clan on the Island. Seven boys, all good athletes, all tough as nails. A little crazy. They live in a sprawling wreck of a Victorian at the top of Forest Avenue. The father is a living legend, got the Silver Star in WWII, is some kind of a big shot in the fire department.

"Is that the one we played against?"

"No, that was Ryan. I think he's in the army now."

"Who was the lunatic who got thrown out of Curtis for stealing the principal's car and taking it on a joyride?"

"I think that was John. Maybe Tommy."

Michael opens the window, smells the ocean.

"Laura Gentile's gonna be there," Tiny says.

"Jesus Christ, Tiny. Give up the ghost."

Tiny never got in Laura's pants before he went away to college, but he hasn't stopped trying. Every holiday, every summer break, he renews his efforts, never mind that he has a steady girl back at school.

"Ye of little faith."

"No man is getting in there until a priest says he can."

"We'll see. I'm close."

Michael looks over at his friend, wonders how so much drive and determination could be packed into so slight a package. Tiny's nickname actually fits him; he is short and thin. He is handsome, in an almost impish fashion, and does not lack for confidence. The teasing and ridicule that often plague short men is not a problem for Tiny. As soon as he steps onto the field or the court or the diamond, all the jokes stop. He is fast and fearless and he delights in making larger men look ridiculous.

Michael knows; he was one of them.

Before the first day of freshmen football practice, Michael and a few other guys were mocking Tiny, calling him a midget and asking him when he was due back at the North Pole. Then practice started and no one could touch him, never mind tackle him. They played football together for four years and somewhere along the way, they became fast friends. Tiny was quicksilver in the open field and Michael blocked as hard as he could to get him there. As a senior, Tiny was first team all-city at halfback. His success garnered perks: a football scholarship, write-ups in the *Advance,* the attention of attractive young ladies, and a measure of fame on the small-town Island.

Michael isn't envious of Tiny, not exactly, but he wishes he had some of his confidence, especially with girls. The army made him a man, in more ways than one, but he could really use a bona fide girlfriend. He needs something to distinguish the long, silent days that languish between shakes on his shoulder.

"There are gonna be a lot of girls at this

party, Mikey," Tiny says, as though he could read his friend's mind. "Lot of girls looking to welcome home an army man."

The party is in full swing when they arrive. Despite the cold, people are out in the front yard talking, drinking, making out. Music — the Stones — blares out of an open window. Michael looks up as they sidle past the revelers out front; the house is enormous, but it looks like it could collapse at any moment. As soon as they're inside, Tiny abandons him in search of his ever-elusive prey. Michael wanders from room to room for a bit, bumping into old friends, yelling to be heard over the music. He runs into Danny Olsen and they reminisce about the Thanksgiving Day game they played in a torrential downpour. He throws a friendly shoulder into John Feeney, still clearly a lunatic, who launches a mock punch at him. He talks to Amanda Panek for a bit until her boyfriend shows up. He chats a while with Paul DiZinno, a high school buddy who's also recently returned from a two-year stint in the army.

The house is packed, the party a little wilder than the ones he attended before he left. People are drinking with abandon, the girls are a little more flirtatious. There is an edge in the air. The prospect of Vietnam casts a long shadow. People are nervous. Michael feels unsettled, like he's somehow both older and younger than everyone at the party. The house is thick with hormones, overheated. Too many bodies in the same place at the same time.

Michael walks into the less populated kitchen, steps out onto the back porch to get some air. He is a little drunk. From the back porch, he can see the lights of Manhattan. He watches a ferry slink toward the city, takes a sip of beer. His gaze wanders over the low bulk of Brooklyn. He leans over the railing to get a better view of the Verrazano.

"Checking out the ginny gangplank?"

He turns, startled, and sees a bright red ember floating in the darkness on the other side of the porch.

"Incoming," says an older man's voice. A second later, a can of beer flies out of the shadows. Michael raises his right hand just in time to snag the can.

"Good hands."

"Thanks."

The ember disappears, then blazes full. He watches the red circle rise and move toward him until a burly man with a bald head and a thick, reddish brown mustache emerges from the shadows, a cigar trapped between his teeth. He walks up, stands against the railing next to him. He's holding a large, yellow container — a Polly-O cheese tin, with the parrot in the chef's hat — in his right hand. He takes the cigar out, raises the container to his lips, and drinks deeply. He points the stub of the cigar out toward the bridge.

"That fucking bridge is gonna ruin this Island."

He turns back to Michael, looks him over.

"You played ball against one of my boys."

"Yes, sir. I played football against Ryan. Baseball too. Michael Amendola."

The man snaps a finger in recognition.

"That's right. Amendola. Fullback."

"And third base, sir."

"Stop calling me 'sir.'" He puts the cigar back in his mouth, moves the Polly-O container to his left hand, extends his right. "Gus Feeney. Pleasure to meet ya, kid."

They shake. He smiles at Michael, his whole face creasing into an exuberant Celtic grin.

"You blocked for that little fucking rabbit Terrio."

"That's right, Mr. Feeney."

"Shit, kid. If you don't start calling me Gus, I'm gonna put this fucking cigar out in your eye."

He raises the cigar in mock menace, laughing as he does.

"What are you doing now, kid?"

"I just got out of the army."

"Well, hell, crack that beer, Private Amendola. Congrats."

Michael opens the beer, takes a long pull.

"Were you in Vietnam?"

"For six months."

"See any action?"

He wants to say yes, wants to impress the legend. But he doesn't want to lie.

"Not much, sir. Gus. I got lucky."

"Don't be ashamed of that, kid. Better to be lucky than good."

He drapes his elbows over the railing, leans over. The wood creaks; Michael worries for a moment that the whole railing might snap, sending them both sprawling into the yard.

"So what are you doing now?"

Michael takes another sip of beer.

"My father has a store, a butcher's shop, on Hylan Boulevard. I'm working there."

Gus spits a large loogie out into the darkness.

"You like it, working there?"

"I hate it. I absolutely hate it."

He has never said this out loud to anyone, not even Tiny. He's a little drunk, yes, but it's more than that. Gus Feeney is a legend for a reason; the man has charisma. Michael has known him all of five minutes and already wishes he were part of the family, wishes he had seven brothers, wishes he had a father like Gus Feeney. He met men like Gus in the army — men who could lead other men — but they were all pricks. Gus is a rough-and-tumble uncle, a jovial soul who can give you a kick in the ass when you need it. Michael can just sense it.

"You'll be all right, kid. We'll get you straightened out."

The back door opens and another reveler staggers out onto the porch. A scrawny, blond-haired kid, completely tanked. He walks over to the space between them, a crooked smile on his face. When he reaches the railing, he leans over and pukes. Michael watches Gus put his hand on the kid's neck.

"Get it out. Get it all out, son."

The kid vomits, sporadically, for another minute. After a few dry heaves, he rises up, wipes his mouth with the back of his hand.

"You okay?"

The kid nods.

"Good. Take a sip of this."

He gives the kid a sip from his container. He looks over at Michael, winks.

"No man should go into the army sober."

Gus pulls the container away, whirls the kid around so he faces Michael.

"Jerry, this is Michael Amendola. He played ball against Ryan. Michael, this is my youngest, Jerry."

Jerry smiles, extends the same hand he used to wipe the vomit from his face. Michael shakes it. Gus points his cigar at Michael's chest.

"We're gonna make a firefighter out of him."

The following Saturday, after Enzo closes the shop, Michael goes to the Feeney house to start training for the firemen's test. Gus and his sons run him ragged, but he loves every minute. The following spring, he takes the test. In September 1967, after Gus pulls a few strings and gets his name bumped up the list, Michael enters the academy.

He graduates the same week that Jerry Feeney comes home from Vietnam in a box.

Tina looks happy, a little glow in her face. Michael gives her a peck on the cheek, a quick hug.

"To what do I owe the pleasure?" she asks, as she shuffles some papers off the kitchen table. He sits. "Coffee?"

"Don't bother yourself."

"It's already made. I'll zap a cup for you."

"No work today?"

"They have me down to three days a week. Barely enough work for that."

"You could run that bank."

She takes a mug out of the microwave, hands it to him.

"I'll tell 'em you said that."

He sits down across from her. She looks like she did back in those early years with Bobby: never far from a smile. Some people aren't meant to be unhappy, doesn't suit them. He's always thought of her as family, the daughter he never had. He's happy she met someone.

"So what's up?"

He takes the sheet out of his pocket, unfolds it, slides it across to her.

"So when the boys were young, we'd only put in one entry for the family. Each of us would pick one team and Gail would choose the winner. I don't know why we stopped doing it that way, but we did. Anyways, this year, I'm going old school. I already picked my team, so did Peter. I figure you could make Bobby's pick. Sound okay?"

Her face widens in a broad smile.

"Sure. Sounds great."

She looks down at the paper.

"You know I don't have any earthly clue who's good. There's not as much basketball watched in this house as there once was."

"Doesn't matter."

"Which region?"

"You have the Southwest."

Her finger moves down the list, pausing occasionally.

"What's this?" she asks, pointing to a line that has two teams instead of one.

"That was a play-in game. VCU won, so you can ignore the other team."

"Good. I'll take VCU."

"But they're an eleven seed, Tina."

"Hey, you asked for my pick. That's my pick."

He pulls the sheet back across the table, scribbles in her pick.

"Can I ask why?"

"Those are my mother's initials. Valentina Cara Ummarino. VCU."

"Can't argue with that."

He has what he came for, but he wants to sit with Tina, have a chat, let her know he's happy for her. Glad to see a smile on her face.

"You hungry, T.?"

"Always."

"I'll make you some peppers and eggs."

"No, Michael, I can cook you some eggs."

She stands, moves to the fridge.

"Tina, sit down. I want to cook. Please."

She returns to her seat, assumes a pose of complete relaxation.

"Can't argue with that."

He slices bell peppers while Tina sits at the table. He doesn't cook that much anymore. He misses it, the satisfaction of providing for others in the most basic way possible. He used to cook all the time at the firehouse, making communal meals for hungry brothers. He pours some olive oil into a pan, takes the eggs from the fridge.

"Hey," he offers, eyes still on the pan. "Gail told me about your new friend. I think that's great."

"Yeah?"

She sounds surprised. He looks over at her, winks.

"Yeah, I do."

"Thank you, Michael."

"Well, you're welcome."

He pushes the sliced peppers and onions into the pan. They crackle in the oil, start to fry.

"What about Gail? How do you think she's taking it?"

"She's happy for you too, but you know, you get older, you don't like change as much. You want things to stay the same. But, in her heart of hearts, I know she's happy. I think she's worried about how Franky's gonna take it."

"That makes two of us."

"The two of you worry too much. He'll be fine."

It occurs to him that this is something he can do, something he can take off Gail's plate. He's gonna see Franky later. He can tell him, face-to-face. Let him know that no nonsense will be tolerated.

He adds the eggs to the pan, watches them scramble into shape. He sprinkles on some salt and pepper. He uses a spatula to slide the peppers and eggs onto rolls, walks over to the table with two plates, hands Tina one. They eat in silence for a bit.

"Delicious," she says, between bites. He's almost finished with his sandwich.

"I miss cooking. I used to do it all the time at the firehouse."

"Can I ask you something, Michael?"

"Of course."

"Why did you become a firefighter?"

The question catches him off guard. He hasn't been asked it in a long time.

"Well, it's hard to say exactly."

"I don't mean to pry. I just mean, how did it happen?"

"No, I understand. It's a fair question."
He pauses, takes a sip of coffee. "Gus
Feeney."

Tina laughs. "Is that a person?"

"Yes."

"Who was he?"

"He was a real character, a Staten Island
legend. A big, boisterous guy. He had seven
sons, all of them became firefighters. All
except Jerry. He was killed in Vietnam.
Anyway, Gus had all these sayings. *The
Feeneys have fought fires on every block in
the five boroughs* or *There will be a Feeney
fighting fires until this city burns, and because
of us, it never will.* He had three brothers
himself, all FDNY. The department is lousy
with Feeneys. I'm sure Bobby worked with
a Feeney at some point."

He tosses the last scrap of his sandwich
into his mouth.

"Tell me more," Tina says.

"They had this great old house at the top
of Forest Avenue, overlooking Silver Lake.
The house was on the verge of falling down,
but no one seemed to care. The house was
always full, someone was always laughing.
You could see Manhattan from the back
porch. Gus would sit out there in the summer, like a king surveying his kingdom. Beer
in one hand, his feet perched on the half-

rotted railing. He used to drink his beer out of a Polly-O cheese container, you know, the yellow ones?"

"That's hilarious."

"For whatever reason, Gus took a shine to me and he made being a firefighter seem like the most noble thing imaginable. Underneath the jokes, there was a sense of purpose. He took the job seriously, even if he didn't take himself too seriously. He didn't even consider it a job. It was a calling, something sacred. Hell, you know how firefighters are. The good ones, anyway. I was twenty years old, fresh out of the army, and had no idea what the hell to do with the rest of my life. Gus seemed to have things pretty sussed out."

Tina nods, satisfied.

"Thanks, Michael."

He glances at his watch. He needs to get to the Leaf.

"Sure. Any other questions?"

"Actually, yeah. One more."

"Marone."

"Something I always wanted to know."

He exhales in mock frustration. "Go ahead."

"How did you meet Gail?"

"Gail never told you?"

"No. And Bobby didn't know."

He stands.

"Sorry, can't tell you."

"C'mon."

He walks to the door. She follows behind, whining. "Why can't you tell me?"

He turns back, gives her a good-bye peck on the cheek.

"I made a promise."

This was typical Tiny. He meets a girl — God knows where he met all these girls, but he did — and asks her out. She's from Bay Ridge, suggests a bar in the neighborhood. The girl, Sheila, wants to bring along a friend. Tiny says fine. Enter Michael. They drive over the Verrazano together, Tiny scheming, Michael hoping the friend isn't a complete horror show. Simple enough.

Except when they show up at the bar, it turns out that the friend is an absolute fox, makes poor Sheila look like a consolation prize. Most guys would shrug their shoulders, play the cards they'd been dealt. Not Tiny. He gets one look at the friend and decides to make a play for her. Screw gallantry, screw Sheila, screw Michael, screw the best-laid plans of mice and men. He starts flirting with the friend, who responds in kind, leaving Michael to deal with a rightfully pissed-off Sheila. He's tried a few different times to engage her, but she keeps ignoring him, glaring at her friend and Tiny. He waves a hand in front of her face.

"Hey, I'm going to get a beer. You want something?"

"A Tom Collins," she says, eyes still fixated on the treasonous couple.

Michael wanders down the bar, looking for an open space. He needs this like he needs a hole in the head. It's been a rough week. His father was finally getting over the firefighter thing — it had only taken a year! — and then Michael tells his parents he's thinking of moving out. Now, his mother isn't talking to him. They would never fully understand. He can see the questions piling up on their faces, not getting asked. *Why would anyone risk their life for strangers? Doesn't this life make you happy? Why do you need to move out? When are you going to meet a nice Italian girl?*

Michael waves at the bartender. He's about to shout his order when the guy sitting on the bar stool next to him tries to stand up and starts to fall backward. Michael reaches over, steadies him. The guy is in his early fifties, weighs next to nothing. He mutters something incomprehensible, slumps onto Michael's shoulder. He is completely ossified.

"Sean," the bartender yells. "Sean. Wake the fuck up. Sean."

Sean does not respond.

"Sorry, buddy. Can you hold him there for a sec? I'll call someone to fetch him. He lives two blocks away."

The guy reaches under the bar for a telephone. Michael glances over his shoulder. Sheila is laying into Tiny. The friend is looking down, sheepishly. Tiny catches Michael's eye, gives him a beseeching look.

"I'll walk him home."

The bartender looks at him like's he's half cocked.

"You sure, pal?"

Screw Tiny.

"Positive."

"Two blocks down and make a right. Halfway up the block. Three-sixteen Eighty-ninth Street. Press the button for Maguire."

Michael gets him outside. Fresh air partially revives the stumblebum. His eyes open, taking in his new companion.

"You're not Goodness," he slurs.

"Let's go home, buddy."

They make their way along bustling Third Avenue, bypassing small crowds of revelers. When they reach Eighty-ninth Street, Sean starts laughing, pushes Michael away, sits down on a stoop. After a few seconds, Sean stops laughing, looks around bewildered, like he's just landed on the moon. Michael considers leaving him there — the guy's nearly home and Michael's pretty confident it's not his first rodeo — but decides against it. He cajoles Sean back onto his shoulder and they continue down the block. When they get to number 316, Michael looks at the names on the panel, sees Maguire 1C. At least he won't have to get Sean up any stairs. He presses the button, ready to explain, but the buzzer sounds. He carries Sean, now nearly comatose, into the dimly lit lobby. They cross a black-and-white-tiled floor to the apartment door. Michael knocks three times. He slaps Sean's cheek a few times, trying to rouse him.

The girl who answers the door has the bluest eyes he's ever seen. So intensely blue that it's hard for Michael to answer her stare.

"Jesus Christ," she says, more tired than surprised.

"Goodness," Sean roars, awakening. "Goodness, I'm home."

He stumbles up the single step into the apartment and hugs the girl.

"Okay, Dad, here we go," she says, helping her father into the apartment. The door is nearly closed when she sticks her head back, eyes blazing.

"Wait right there," she says. The door slams shut.

Michael stares at the closed door, unsure what to do. He's more than done his duty, no reason in the world to wait around. But he waits anyway. A minute passes. Two. Five. He's pretty sure he's been forgotten. As he turns to walk away, the door opens. The girl steps into the hallway, closes the door behind her.

"What's the big idea?" she says, angry.

"What do you mean?"

"Aren't you a little young to be one of my father's asshole drinking buddies?"

"Hey, take it easy. Your father — Sean, is that his name? Your father fell off a bar stool into me. I walked him home."

"Are you some kind of pervert?"

"Jesus Christ. Are you out of your head? The man was legless, in no condition to get home by himself. I walked him home. Tried to do a good deed. That's it. That's all. Good night, Goodness."

He turns. She reaches out, grabs his arm.

"Hold on. I'm sorry. It's just, you know, this isn't the first time he's come home like this."

"You don't say."

"Hey, he's not a bad guy, my father. He

just shouldn't drink."

He steps back, exhales, rolls his neck around. She's a few years younger than Michael. A little plain-looking. But those eyes.

"Hey, I'm sorry too. What do I know? I've been there before, had a few too many. We all have, right?"

"Well, thank you. For walking him home. He's fallen a few times, hurt himself."

"You're welcome."

They stand, uncertainly, nothing left to say.

"I'm Michael, by the way."

"Gail."

"I was really hoping your name was Goodness."

She fights down a smile. He feels a flutter in his chest. He'd do anything to make this girl smile, make this girl happy.

"Buy you a beer?"

"Sure."

She picks a quiet bar, middle-of-the-street joint on Fifth Avenue. A handful of solitary customers nurse drinks, pick absently at nuts and pretzels. The jukebox plays older music: The Moonglows, The Platters, Frank Sinatra, Perry Como. Michael and Gail sit in the front, around the curve of the bar. Gail is halfway through her first beer when she talks.

"I love this bar."

"Yeah. Why's that?"

"Only bar in Bay Ridge my father hasn't ruined for me."

"Oh."

Michael finishes his beer, orders another. The bartender refills his mug, walks down to the other end of the bar. Gail looks over at him, assessing.

"You know this is never gonna work out."

"Why's that?"

"Because if we get married and have kids and live happily ever after, we'll never be able to tell our kids how we met. *Daddy walked Mommy's drunk of a dad home because he could barely see.* C'mon."

"Why do they even have to know, our kids? I don't know how my parents met."

"Really? I know how my parents met."

"How?"

"My mother walked my father home because he was drunk."

Michael smiles, takes a sip of beer.

"What if I promise not to tell anyone?"

"Cross your heart, hope to die, stick a needle in your eye?"

"Yes."

"Say it."

"If things work out between us and we get

married and have kids and live happily ever after, I promise not to tell anyone, including our seventeen children — I want a big family, by the way — how we met. Sound good?"

She shrugs, finishes her mug of beer.

"Still might not work out."

"Why's that?"

"I haven't decided whether I like you yet."

The Leaf has the hushed stillness of an establishment slowly recovering from an epic night. The bar is darker than usual for a weekday, with just the artificial light from the televisions flickering off the bottles behind the bar. A few bands of dust-specked sunlight stream into the smallish dining area adjacent to the bar; the tables are empty but ready, the plates and cutlery arranged and waiting for lunch customers who are unlikely to come. The whole place is festooned with green and white St. Patrick's Day decorations that are looking a little sheepish, a little sad, now that their purpose has been served. Today is officially St. Patrick's Day, but the Leaf's party was the night before and the Island parade was a week ago Sunday and well, the day itself seems like a bit of an afterthought. Besides, it's the first day of the NCAA tournament and the Cody's pool takes precedence.

Michael pauses after he walks in, captures a dry, barking cough between his wind-chilled hands. His eyes drift to the massive 9/11 memorial poster behind the bar, with the icon of the towers in the foreground and the list of names blurred in the background. Somewhere on that poster is Bobby's name. He looks away.

Two customers sit halfway down the bar turned toward each other, an empty stool between them. He knows them both: Jack Walsh, a retired NYPD detective, who has been drifting from functional heavy drinker to full-blown alcoholic in the year since his wife died, and Tiny Dave Terrio, still his best friend after all these years. A cup of steaming coffee rests on the bar in front of Tiny; Jack is holding a rocks glass filled with whiskey and ice.

"Michael," says Tiny.

"Tiny, Jack."

A handshake for Jack, a hug and a kiss for Tiny.

"Tell me something, fellas, why is it that ginnies have no problem kissing other men but won't go down on their wives?"

Typical Walsh, sex and tribes from the go. Michael considers a joke about wives, remembers that Jack's is dead, and stays silent. Tiny doesn't.

"It's not that we won't go down on our wives, Walsh, it's that we don't need to. We have the equipment to get the job done without resorting to tricks of the tongue."

Laughs all around.

What's left of Tommy Flanagan slides out from the back room and slithers behind the bar. When Michael left last night, Flanagan was wearing an oversize green leprechaun hat and doing shots of Jameson with a couple guys half his age. The morning has not been kind to Mr. Flanagan. Michael takes a twenty out of his wallet, puts it under a coaster. Tommy places a bottle of Budweiser in front of him.

"Thanks, Tommy. Shot of Jameson on this fine Saint Patrick's Day morn?"

"Fuck yourself, Amendola."

Chuckles all around, except for Tommy.

"So I guess Tommy got the gold. Silver?"

"Phil Linetti," says Tiny.

"Basis?" asks Michael between sips from his bottle.

"He made out with crazy Gabby at the bar for a good hour. They left together."

More chuckles, Tommy included this time.

"Dear God. Bronze?"

"Probably a tie between everyone else in

the place," says Tiny. He takes a sip of coffee.

"Did you hear about the kid from Tottenville?" Walsh asks Michael out of the blue. His face is a bruised mélange of red and purple and small flakes of dried skin are peeling away in batches. His tone is aggressive and challenging lately, even to his friends.

"No."

"Killed in Afghanistan. Twenty years old."

"Jesus."

"Old enough to die for his country, but can't walk into a bar and order a beer. This country is fucking insane."

"What was his name?" Michael asks.

"Liam Curcio," Tiny says reverently.

"Of course it was. Of course it was. Micks and ginnies are the only white men still dumb enough to die for this country."

Walsh sounds drunk. It's tough to tell these days. Tiny and Michael exchange knowing glances. Walsh is never too far from a rant about one group or another. Most of his rants used to be about the "fucking niggers" but, now, all his rants are about the "fucking sand-niggers."

Progress, Staten Island style, Michael thinks.

"What about the kid from South Beach

last year?" asks Tiny. "Olchenski, wasn't it? Isn't that Polish?"

"Russian," says Flanagan.

"Either way. Same difference."

"What do you mean?" asks Walsh, angry that the conversation has drifted away from him.

"Well, Walsh, micks and ginnies aren't the *only* ones getting killed."

"Fine, fucking polocks too. Micks and ginnies and polocks."

"Hey," says Flanagan, "what about the kid from the Bronx a few weeks back? Raheem something or another."

"Jesus H. Christ, Tommy, I said white men. The only white men still dumb enough to die for this country."

"So if the niggers and the spics and the micks and the ginnies and the polocks are all dying for this country, Jack, who isn't?" asks Tiny.

Walsh turns back to Tiny, an ugly look on his flushed face.

"The fucking Jews."

Tiny and Flanagan snicker. Tiny nudges Michael as if to say "Walsh is a piece of work," but Michael is half paying attention; the name Curcio has been flipping around in his head, looking for traction.

"Shit, I was in a firehouse with a Steven

Curcio from Tottenville."

Tiny shakes his head.

"That's his uncle. His father works for Con Ed. Mother's a nurse."

"Farrell kid?"

"Tottenville. *Advance* all-star in baseball."

"Liam Curcio. Rest in peace," Tiny says, his mug raised.

"Liam Curcio," they all mumble in reply. They clink glasses.

An impromptu moment of silence passes.

"His father lost his mind when he found out, apparently. Inconsolable."

"Any other kids?" Michael asks.

"A daughter. Senior in high school."

"Small mercies," Michael says.

"A-fucking-men," chimes in Walsh.

Another silence, drinks at lips.

"Jesus, lose your kid, can you imagine?" Flanagan says, leaning over the bar and trying to sound profound. Michael stares at him.

"I don't have to imagine," he says. He feels Tiny's hand on his shoulder.

Flanagan backs away, embarrassed. Michael wanted to get here, but he's already had enough of the Leaf, enough of Walsh's drunken vitriol and Flanagan's hangover. He finishes his bottle of beer and zips up his jacket.

"Ready to go, Tiny? We have all the sheets?"

Flanagan reaches below the bar and pulls up a manila folder and an envelope filled with cash.

"Twenty sheets total. Four thousand dollars."

He pushes both across the bar to Michael. Tiny puts up his hand.

"We can't leave yet. Knucklehead's dropping off a few sheets from his office."

Michael groans. Knucklehead is Tiny's son-in-law, Tony Ragolia. Married to his daughter Maggie. An asshole of the highest order: full of himself, doesn't shut the fuck up. He's the last thing Michael needs this morning. Tiny shrugs his shoulders.

"Hey, Mikey, what can I do?"

Michael unzips his jacket. He looks up at the television. The first game is about to tip off. Cody's accepts entries until five o'clock on the first day of games. If one of the favorites goes down early, everyone will be scrambling to change their sheets.

"I'll take another beer, Tommy."

Flanagan flicks off the bottle's cap in an opener that hangs down from the other side of the bar. He pushes the beer over to Michael.

"On the house, Mikey. I'm sorry," he says,

softly, so Walsh can't hear.

Michael smiles. Flanagan's not a bad guy. A lifer behind the stick. Never had kids. Doesn't know. Couldn't. The things you do, the sacrifices you make, the decisions made for their benefit.

"No worries, Tom. No worries at all."

He is a newly married man, grateful and growing more so each day. Grateful that he came back from Vietnam in one piece, grateful that he has a good city job and a good wife, grateful that his parents are healthy, but mostly grateful for a bit of news that pushes a smile across his face whenever he thinks about it.

He's going to be a father.

His gratitude is an oddity in these times, in this place. Anger is the prevailing mood of the day. The future is unclear, the fabric of things seems to be coming apart. Things that once seemed solid fall to dust overnight. New York City is in decline, sliding toward a precipice. The drugs have gotten worse, more insidious, and they've started turning up in places no one expected. White people are leaving in droves, to Long Island, to New Jersey, to Westchester and Connecticut, to other cities entirely.

Let it burn, they say, and let the niggers

and the spics and the faggots burn with it.

He doesn't want the city to burn. His job is to ensure it doesn't burn. He loves this job. This job gives him moments he cannot describe to his new wife, moments when he feels as though he were dancing at the razor's edge of humanity, moments when he feels as though he were an ancient Greek hero, descending into a blazing hell to save souls. A knight in modern armor, fighting not the dragon but the dragon's breath and all the horror it spreads.

It's not all roses. Sometimes the people he is trying to save throw bottles. Sometimes they spit at him. He has seen things on this job. A crib and its occupant charred beyond recognition. A woman just out of the flames, convulsing so violently that it takes two men to hold her down. He has seen abject fear in the eyes of a comrade who sees his life — his wife and his kids, his house and home, his Sunday football, his six-packs and White Owl cigars, his summers at the beach, his friends and his laughs — slipping away from him. This comrade has seen his own funeral. He has attended it time and again. He has heard the bagpipes keening. He has seen the uniformed body in the casket, he has seen the casket closed as well, he has comforted the widow. He can see Michael attending his funeral, can see Michael contemplating it even as Michael looks into his eyes and says, "You're gonna be fine. I'm gonna get you out of here."

He tells Michael this weeks later in the hospital. His lungs on the mend, his life rescued.

"I saw you attending my funeral, comforting Terry."

"I would have enjoyed comforting Terry."

They laugh because that's all you can do. When death taps you on the shoulder and you manage to slip away, you laugh. To do anything else would be madness.

How do you feel when you walk out of the hospital room and his family is there? When his wife hugs you and you feel her wet tears on your chest? When his daughter hands you a picture she drew for you of you carrying her father out of a burning building? When his son thanks you and runs in to see his daddy and you know that you made this moment possible, that you created it?

You feel like a god. Anyone who says different is lying.

So Michael has to remind himself what Gus used to tell him: that feeling like a god is as dangerous as the fire itself. He is only a man, one with a new wife and a kid on the way. A man who doesn't want to see the city burn, but who doesn't want it to burn him or those he cares about either. A man who can't afford Westchester or Connecticut, who can't fathom Long Island, who doesn't want New Jersey.

Michael knows what to do, where to go. He knows a place that is still safe, an idyllic patch in the ravaged city. Right over a bridge. Staten Island. He's always intended to return. After they got married, he and Gail moved into an apartment in Bay Ridge, a temporary concession to Gail's desire to be close to her parents and to the demands of his job. They had no car. They had no money. It was easier to live in Brooklyn, easier to get to work and to save money. But it's been almost two years in that tiny, cramped apartment and he is sick of it. He wants some space, some fresh air. It's time to put their plan in motion, time to look for a house on Staten Island.

Actually, this is his plan. He has never articulated it to Gail; he has assumed her acquiescence. An apartment is fine for the two of them, but he wants his children raised in a proper house.

An opportunity has knocked, as they say, and though it's sooner than he would have liked, you have to strike when the iron is hot, as they also say. He is fond of his sayings. He grew up in a house where the adages were in Italian, so the English ones hold more allure for him. A house for sale in Great Kills. Cheap.

Why the discount?

"Older couple, no kids. Died within a month of each other. They were renting from the bank. No one can remember why we own it in the first place. Couple lived there for forty years. We want to sell it," whispers Tiny Terrio into the other end of the phone. Tiny works at a bank on Staten Island. The bank that wants to sell the house. A bank that could give them the mortgage, Tiny mentions, if they can move quickly and if they have ten thousand dollars to put down.

Michael hangs up the phone and frowns. He is nine thousand dollars short. The door to their apartment opens and Gail walks in. Her blue eyes are blood-shot and her face is blotchy. She has been crying.

"I'm pregnant," she says.

There are no coincidences in life. Michael isn't sure if this is a saying or not, but it's what he believes. You do not get a phone call from your best friend about a house in one minute and your wife telling you she's pregnant in the next for no reason at all.

The next day Michael has off, Enzo picks him up and they drive across the Verrazano together.

The bridge is beautiful, a majestic baby blue span in the sky, soaring above a strip of water called the Narrows, giving all who cross it a panoramic view of New Jersey, then Staten Island, Jersey again, New York Harbor, the Manhattan skyline, the low-lying infinitude of Brooklyn, and finally, a glimpse of eternity in the Atlantic Ocean. It is a bridge that explains New York, reveals why it soared to greatness in the first place. It's a bridge that should be loved, but somewhere deep inside him, Michael is starting to hate it. He is starting to think that Gus Feeney was right: it's going to ruin Staten Island.

The car descends on the Staten Island side of the bridge and Michael feels peaceful, happy to be in a place more green than gray. They meet Tiny on a dead-end street in Great Kills. Wirra Lane. It's a little farther out than Michael would like. His parents' house, in Dongan Hills, is ten minutes closer to the bridge. The house is run down, will need some work. The backyard has been neglected for years. Weeds and bushes grow unimpeded. But the structure is sound. There are three bedrooms, a basement, a nice-size kitchen with a quaint bay window. It's two quick turns from Hylan Boulevard, the thoroughfare that runs the entire length of the South Shore. They'd need a car, obviously, but if they had one, they could be at his parents' house in four turns. The street is a good one; there's space between the houses. When they drove up, a flock of young kids was playing Wiffle ball at the end of the street. Not a lot of car traffic. Bicycles lie unguarded in front of houses.

They stand outside, the three of them, and consider the house.

"Tiny, excuse," Enzo says. He puts his heavy butcher's hand on Michael's shoulder and guides him to the side of the house. Michael looks over his shoulder at Tiny, who is leaning against his car, gently pulling at the knot of his tie. It is humid; they are all sweating.

"Take it," Enzo says. He smells of sausage, of chicken and pork, of bone and blood. His English regresses when he's being urgent. "You take it."

"Dad, I can't afford it."

"You borrow from us."

"We can't pay you back soon."

"Doesn't matter. You pay back when you can."

Enzo looks at the house. He still has an immigrant's eye for deals. Michael almost tells him about Gail right then, but superstition holds him back; it's very early. He looks at his father and wonders: How did you land here, Enzo, of all places? Not Brooklyn or the Bronx. Not Little Italy or Bensonhurst or Pleasant Avenue. Here. It is one of many questions he will never ask his father.

Enzo smiles. They hug.

"Is good. Is good. *Bellissimo.*"

They walk over to Tiny, who's smiling as well. They all shake hands. On the way back to Brooklyn, Michael thanks his father, reminds him that repayment will be a long time coming.

"Is okay. You work at shop."

Michael nods, the slightest stain spreading across his happiness. Enzo has never understood Michael's fascination with being a firefighter. But he has never said what he thinks: Why risk your life for strangers? He will wait for Michael, will hold on to the shop. He still thinks he can cajole his son back into the fold. Michael knows better. He will work at the shop, he will do what needs to be done. And then he will walk away because that is not the life he wants. He sees the smile on Enzo's face and smiles in return. He knows what his father is thinking, knows his father is wrong.

Enzo drops Michael outside the Tankard, a restaurant where Gail waits tables a few nights a week. He walks in, says hello to the regulars he recognizes. He is brimming with the confidence of a man whose future is certain. He orders a beer, places a ten on the bar. Gail walks over, still shaken by the unexpected news, still not herself.

"You're a happy camper."

"I am."

He takes a sip of beer. He may be only a man, but he is a good one, a good husband. He is a solver of problems, a finder of solutions.

"We're buying a house."

She turns her chin up and to the right. Her eyes narrow. She makes this little face whenever she's not sure whether he's serious. He clinks his bottle against the brass rail she's leaning on. The happiness is flowing out of him. She can tell he's serious.

"On Staten Island," he adds.

"What?" she says, which is what she says when she doesn't know what to say.

"I found us a house." His confidence is starting to slip.

"What? What?" Louder this time, a few patrons turn their heads.

"A house," he says, embarrassed now and

growing a bit angry. "On Staten Island."

"Jesus, Mary, and Joseph."

"Peggy and I are thinking about packing it in," Tiny tells him, as they pull onto the West Shore Expressway. "Selling the house, moving to Florida."

"You shitting me?" Michael asks.

"Thinking about it."

Until the last few years, life has been a little kinder to Tiny. Football got him to college, which got him a job in a bank, first on Staten Island and then in Manhattan. He married Peggy Dunn and they had two kids, both girls. Tiny wasn't rich, not exactly, but money wasn't ever a real concern. The family vacations were a bit nicer. His daughters, Maggie and Maria, went to the best colleges they got in to, regardless of price. All the while and in spite of the differing financial circumstances, he and Michael had remained friends. No easy thing, Michael has come to realize, having seen too many friendships ruined by money, or the lack of it, by one party or the other.

But a few years back, Tiny put the bulk of his savings under his son-in-law Albert's control. When the market crashed, Albert panicked, did something stupid, did something else stupid to try to cover up his first stupidity, developed a substance abuse problem, and maybe banged one of his employees. Long story short: there was an indictment and a divorce and Maria is presently living with Tiny and Peggy, sleeping eighteen hours a day. Albert is wearing an ankle bracelet and awaiting sentencing and Tiny is worth a lot less than he used to be. His house is probably his largest asset; real estate prices on the Island are up a thousand percent, easy, over the past thirty-five years. Michael figures he could get half a mil for their shack. Maybe more.

But Gail will never leave.

He had to drag her to this Island and now, he'd have to drag her off. He would leave if she would let him. This is not the place he grew up, not even the place his kids grew up. He and Gail live in the shadow of tragedy, in the overcrowded, overdeveloped ruins of a once spacious paradise, surrounded by morons who act like they're constantly auditioning for a reality television program that prizes stupidity, classlessness, and thuggish bravado. He would have left years ago if not for Gail.

He raised the idea a few years back, brought it up casually, on a quiet Sunday afternoon, just the two of them sitting at the kitchen table. Like the idea had just occurred to him. He'd heard about a retirement community in North Carolina. Not one of the old-fogy Florida types they parodied on *Seinfeld,* but an active, vibrant community. A place that catered to Northeast retirees. With what they'd get for their house, they could afford a huge house right off a golf course and still pocket a hundred grand, easy. He knew two guys — ex-FDNY, from Queens — who'd moved down there and were loving it. The weather was great, the people were nice. Even the pizza was tolerable. Gail stopped licking envelopes and stared at him, trying to see if he was serious.

"What about the bagels?"

"We can have them FedExed."

"What about the Leaf?"

"I'm sure there are other Leafs."

She laughed and he grinned. He was thinking it was going well, maybe she was even considering it, and then the questions turned serious.

"What about Franky?"

What about Franky? he wanted to say. Franky was a grown man, beyond their control. If he was going to get his act together, *he* was going to get his act together. Not them. But he'd lost this argument enough times. He tried a different approach.

"He can come with us. They need nitwits in North Carolina."

"Michael, be serious."

"I am being serious. He can come with us. There are jobs down there. Would probably do him good to be out of the city."

The truth was that Franky would find trouble no matter where he was. But if he was going to be Michael's headache one way or the other, better he be his headache in a place where Michael could roll out of bed onto a golf course.

Gail stretched her arms and looked out the window, like she was contemplating the idea of leaving. Michael put the brochure on the table and was about to slide it across the table when he felt Gail's eyes on him. He looked across at her.

"What about Bobby?"

She hadn't been considering anything. She'd merely been waiting to drop the hammer. He stammered out a few half words, more noise than language. Finally, he cleared his throat and looked across at her, and said, as calmly and softly as possible:

"He's dead."

She looked at him, incredulous, for a few seconds and then her hand smacked down on the table.

"Jesus, Mary, and Joseph. Thanks for reminding me, Michael. I'd nearly fucking forgotten."

She stood and walked away. A few days later, he threw the brochure in a garbage cylinder outside a deli he never frequented, like a teenager trying to dispose of a pregnancy test.

The car slows in a thicket of traffic after they merge onto the Staten Island Expressway.

"You okay, Mikey?" Tiny asks.

"Yeah, fine. I'm a little distracted. Tina met someone."

"Nice guy?"

"Don't know. Haven't met him yet."

"Oh."

"His name is Wade. He's coming to the house on Sunday."

"Wade?"

"Wade."

Tiny's face furrows in uncertainty, like he can't figure what that means, but he's pretty sure it's not good.

"I saw her a few weeks ago. She came over to try to get Maria out of the house. She looked great," he says, a hint of salaciousness creeping into his voice.

"You're a dirty old man."

"I can't notice? I can't look?"

"That's my daughter in-law, you sick son of a bitch."

Tiny laughs.

"She's not my daughter in-law. Hey, Mikey, you stop noticing, you die. Nothing wrong with looking."

Only Tiny does more than look, or, at least, he used to. Michael saw him with another woman once, years ago, back when he and Tiny were both young men. He was in the city, at some retirement booze-up, bouncing around from place to place. He and a few FDNY guys were walking along Second Avenue, between places, and Michael spotted Tiny inside a restaurant, sitting and smiling. By himself, Michael thought. He was wearing a jacket and tie, looked like hot shit. He told the other guys he'd catch up. He never saw Tiny in the city; it gave him a little thrill to see his friend in a different element. Michael walked into the restaurant with vague ideas about playing a joke or making a scene, but the hushed closeness of the place made him realize he was halfway drunk. He mumbled something to the maître d' and took a few steps toward Tiny's table.

Then he saw her: young, pretty, definitely

not Peggy. It could have been a business meeting, but Michael knew it wasn't. Tiny was pouring wine with his left hand and his right hand was on the woman's bare back. His face was flush and he was in full Casanova mode. Michael stopped and turned around. He walked out of the restaurant and hustled after the other guys. He thought that maybe Tiny had spotted him but wasn't sure. Tiny never brought it up, in any event, and Michael never told anyone, not even Gail. Thinking about it later, Michael concluded that this was not an isolated event; Tiny looked too comfortable, the whole scene almost seemed rehearsed.

Michael looks over at Tiny as he guides the car onto the ramp for Clove Road. He's never felt envy toward Tiny, never begrudged him his successes. They've known each other for more than fifty years. With a few exceptions — Michael in the army, Tiny away at school — they've probably seen each other almost every week during that time. He's as close to a brother as Michael has ever had.

And there was only one person whose judgment Michael trusted more.

He finds Gus on the back porch, smoking a cigar he isn't supposed to be smoking. Gus is staring across the bay at the base of Manhattan, where the tips of the Twin Towers are shrouded in fog. A few weeks ago, some Arabs detonated a bomb in the North Tower, killing six people. But it could have been a lot worse.

"I guess they thought they were gonna bring them down."

Gus jumps, startled by Michael's voice.

"You scared me. Thought you were Nancy."

He looks back across at the towers.

"Guess so. I don't know, Mikey, this world, I don't understand it anymore."

"That why you're so intent on leaving it?"

Michael points to the cigar. Gus is much thinner than he used to be, thinner even than the last time Michael saw him.

"I'm eighty years old, you dumb ginny bastard. Let me enjoy myself. Make yourself useful, anyway, and fetch me a blanket."

Michael goes inside, grabs an afghan, lays it on his mentor's lap. He sits down next to him, takes in the view, always breathtaking. Two ferries pass in the harbor.

"I was on my way to drop off some entries at Cody's, figured I'd drop by and see if you croaked yet."

Gus laughs. After a few seconds, his laughter stumbles into a coughing fit.

"Don't make me laugh, you bastard." He stubs the cigar out in an ashtray on the table between them. "How's it looking?"

"They're saying two hundred grand, maybe more."

He reaches under his blanket, pulls out an envelope, hands it to Michael.

"Just one sheet. With my luck, I'll finally win this year but be too dead to collect."

Michael laughs. Gus reaches over and grabs his arm.

"Mikey, if anything ever happened and I did win, you'd make sure that Nancy, you know —"

"*Marone,* Gussy. Of course. You're not gonna die," he says, patting his mentor's hand. "And you're definitely not gonna win."

"You little prick."

"Learned from the best."

Gus leans over.

"Listen, Mikey, there's a bottle of scotch in the kitchen, in the pantry, behind the cereal boxes. Go get it, bring back two glasses. I hear we have something to celebrate."

Michael retrieves the bottle, trying to ignore the decrepit state of the house. Dirty dishes are piled on the counters. Cabinet doors dangle off their hinges. There's a hole near the sink and not a small one. The house was always a wreck, but now it's dangerous. Feels like it might fall down at any moment. When he gets outside, he pours them each a finger of whiskey. Gus shakes his glass in irritation.

"Don't be such a miser."

Michael pours him another finger. They clink glasses.

"Congrats, Mikey."

"Twenty-five years."

"You did the most important thing, kid. Came home at the end of every shift. That's the trick."

"Went fast."

"Tell me about it."

They take sips, look out over the city. The whiskey tingles Michael's tongue, sends warm emissaries to his extremities.

"City's changed, mostly for the better," Michael says. He looks over, sees Gus pulling the blanket up over his chest. He can still remember the night he met the legendary Gus Feeney. Now, the legend needs a blanket to stay warm, has to sneak cigars when his old lady is out.

"Everywhere but here. That goddamn bridge."

The population on the Island has risen steadily since the bridge was finished.

There's construction everywhere; it's like some of the builders have personal vendettas against trees. The Island is starting to lose its small-town feel.

"You were right, Gussy."

Gus takes a long pull on his glass, closes his eyes.

"So, Mikey, what are you gonna do now?"

"Play some golf, relax, enjoy myself."

"Seriously, what are you gonna do?"

"I am serious."

"You're a young man, Mikey. You need to find something else to do. Otherwise, this" — Gus raises his glass — "is what you'll do."

"I'll figure it out."

"You want me to make some calls, set you up someplace in the city, a cushy consulting gig, advising companies how to respond to fires, something like that?"

"I'm done commuting to the city."

Gus takes a long pull, motions for Michael to refill his glass.

"Your father still have that shop?"

Michael can see his father holding an apron, triumphant at last. A quarter century, an entire career; these mean nothing. The shop is still waiting for him.

"I'm sure I could get a few shifts at the Leaf if I wanted."

"You're gonna bartend?"

"Maybe, I don't know, Gus. I'll figure it out."

"The shop, would he give it to you? Or sell it on the cheap?"

"Of course. He's been waiting thirty years to give me that fucking shop. I'm not gonna be a butcher, Gus. That ship has sailed."

Gus reaches over and pokes him in the shoulder. Hard. Michael turns. There's something close to anger in Gus's eyes.

"Hey, jackass, don't look a gift horse in the mouth."

Tiny waits in the car while Michael goes to fetch Franky. He lives on the second floor of an old Victorian in Westerleigh, above an elderly widower whose lack of hearing and genial nature are the only things that have prevented his eviction. Michael goes up the back staircase, knocks on the door. Franky answers, holding a beer in one hand and a few entry sheets in the other.

"Daddy-o," he says, giving Michael a hug. He smells sour, over-ripe. Not from the beer this morning, but from too much generally. He's half pickled; he doesn't look well.

"A little early, no?" Michael asks.

"It's almost three. And, what, you didn't have a few pops at the Leaf already?"

"Fair enough. You ready?"

"Give me two minutes. C'mon in. The games are in full swing. You want one?"

"No, I'm all set."

They walk into the living room, which is less of a wreck than the last time Michael was here, nine months ago, looking for drugs. Franky has his sheets lined up in rows on a coffee table; envelopes of money lay scattered about. The television is on, the volume is low. Butler, an 8 seed, is playing Old Dominion, a 9 seed. Ten minutes left in the second half. A nail-biter. Michael reaches into his jacket, pulls out his sheet.

"So, Franky, I'm only putting in one entry sheet this year."

"Really?"

"I'm doing it the way we used to do it. I pick a team, Peter picks a team, you pick a team. I asked Tina to pick for Bobby. I'll call your Mom later and ask her to pick the winner."

"Nice. Old school."

"So it's down to you."

"What region?"

"Southeast."

"Okay, let's see. Who did everyone else pick?"

"Not gonna tell you."

"I like it. Nice."

He picks up a sheet, starts perusing the teams, talking to himself out loud.

"You and Petey definitely went chalk. Always have. I have no clue what Tina did, but Maria Terrio went to Notre Dame, so she probably picked them, in which case we're all screwed anyway. But you gotta have faith, right? Okay. Pitt? No. Florida? Maybe. BYU? No fucking chance. Wisco? Maybe."

Michael smiles at Franky's logic. This is what he wanted. This is what he remembers: the boys treating the pool like it was a sacred thing, an institution. Franky looks up at the television. The game is tied, looks like it's gonna go down to the wire.

"I'll tell you what, Daddy-o. These two teams are really, really good. Whoever wins this game could give Pitt a real fight and then, who knows? Give me Butler. If Old Dominion wins, we can change when we're in line."

"You want Butler?"

"Good young coach. Scrappy team."

"Butler it is."

Michael looks down at his completed entry: Kentucky, UConn, VCU, and Butler. A snowball's chance in hell. But, hey, they call it gambling for a reason. He feels good. With a little luck, they won't be out of it by the time Sunday rolls around; if any of these teams are playing during little Bobby's party, they can root for them together.

Franky sits on the couch, organizing his entries, counting money. Michael should tell him now about Tina and her new friend. He won't get a better chance. They're alone and Franky's more or less sober. But he can't bring himself to do it. He doesn't want to ruin the good mood.

"I'm gonna go wait in the car with Tiny. Hustle, Franky."

"Two minutes, Pop."

Tiny is dozing lightly when Michael gets back to the car. Michael smacks the driver side window, startling his friend.

"You prick," he says when Michael gets into the car. He looks around for Franky. "Everything all right?"

"Fine. He'll be right down."

Michael's cell starts ringing. He looks at the caller ID — the Leaf — and answers.

"Hello?"

"Hey, it's Tommy."

"What's up?"

"Listen, did you guys put the entries in yet?"

"No, we're five minutes away. We stopped to pick up Franky."

"Because a couple of guys just came in

and said that Cody's was closed, that the pool got shut down."

"What?"

"That's what they said."

"That's bullshit. It has to be."

"I don't know, Mikey. They sound pretty sure."

Michael sees Franky emerge from the back of the house, a panicked look on his face.

"I'll call you back, Tommy."

Tiny rolls down the window. Franky leans in, his breathing is ragged.

"Yo, Tony Brennan just called me. He says the pool is fucking done. Ovah."

The far end of Forest Avenue is pandemonium. Traffic is backed up for six blocks before Cody's and the sidewalks are filled with men holding sheets of paper and screaming into cell phones. Michael watches as one guy tosses a handful of sheets into the air in exasperation. A few other guys do the same and then a few more follow suit. Soon, every guy on the street is tossing sheets into the air. The sheets start blowing all over the street, getting caught in bushes, obscuring windshields, collecting in the gutters. Some of the cars in front of them start making U-turns despite the cramped conditions.

"Jesus Christ, this is fucking mayhem."

An entry sheet flies onto the front windshield and sticks there. Michael inspects it.

"Shit, Tiny, this guy had Bucknell in the Final Four."

They laugh. Franky runs down the sidewalk toward them, returning from his recon. He opens the rear door, slides into the backseat.

"So?"

"Sign on the window says 'Closed. No Pool This Year.' "

"That's it?"

"That's it."

"What about the Laundromat next door, where they used to take the entries?"

"That's open, but the Chinese lady in there is as confused as everyone else. She's screaming at people to get out. I think someone's gonna throw a garbage can through the front window of Cody's."

"What about all the entries they already collected?" asks Tiny.

Franky shrugs his shoulders.

"Don't know."

A guy gets out of the car in front of them and starts yelling at someone on the other side of the street. A fight, or possibly several, seems imminent.

"What are you gonna do, Franky?" Michael asks.

"Tony told me that a bar up on Victory may run a replacement pool. They're accepting sheets. You want me to take yours up there?"

"No, not sure what the other guys from the Leaf want to do."

"Okay, I'll call you later. Later, Tiny. See you Sunday, Dad."

Franky closes the car door, walks back up toward the crowd. Michael never got a chance to tell him about Tina.

"What should we do, Mikey?" asks Tiny.

Another set of sheets gets tossed into the air and the wind catches them, sending them flying past the car.

"Not sure, Tiny, but I think better on a bar stool."

If Michael hears "A Holly, Jolly Christmas" one more time, he's gonna put a fist through the jukebox. Old man Dunn, the drunk at the end of the bar — his only customer for the past forty-five minutes — has played it at least six times. He has half a mind to declare last call, kick Dunn out, and close up shop, even though it's only midnight. It's a Tuesday night, a week before Christmas; a late crowd is unlikely.

Then again, what's waiting for him at home? A pissed-off wife and a cold bed. He and Gail haven't spoken in months, haven't slept together in who knows how long. He pours himself another draft, refills Dunn's rocks glass. He takes a dollar from his tip cup, slides out from behind the bar, walks over to the jukebox. He'll play his own goddamn songs.

The front door opens. Michael looks over, sees his father enter the bar. A light dusting of snow lies on the shoulders of Enzo's coat. He takes his hat off, shakes it free of snow. He walks down to Michael, hugs him hello, kisses his cheek. Michael's in shock; he's never seen his father in a bar before. Enzo takes a stool at the far end of the room, away from the door. Michael retreats behind the bar, money still in his hand, confused and a little nervous. Eight months ago, he retired from the FDNY. Seven months ago, Enzo offered to sell him the shop at a very discounted price. They haven't spoken since.

"Do you have any wine?" Enzo asks. His English has improved over the years, since Maria died.

"None that you'd like."

Enzo looks at the shelves behind Michael,

searching for something he might enjoy.

"Zambuca. Just a small glass."

Michael pours him a drink, slides it across the bar. Enzo reaches for his wallet.

"On the house, Dad."

Enzo raises his glass. Michael retrieves his mug, does the same.

"Alla salute."

They drink. Enzo rubs his hands together, bites his lip. He takes another sip of his drink. He's nervous as well, searching for the right words.

"It took a long time, but I understood the other thing. Fighting the fires. Good thing. Noble. But this" — he points down the bar at Dunn, who is slumped over, sleeping on crossed elbows — "this. I do not understand this."

He reaches for his drink, downs the remainder. He looks at Michael, beseechingly, hoping for some explanation. When it's clear that Michael isn't going to say anything, Enzo continues.

"Tomorrow, I go to Italy. For a month. When I come back, I need an answer."

He stands, picks his hat off the bar. He looks at Michael, holds his gaze.

"Whatever you chose, Michael, I love you. Your family, your wife, your boys. *La mia famiglia. La mia vita.*"

He reaches over, pats Michael's hand. He walks out into the night, doesn't look back. The sound of the front door closing momentarily wakes Dunn. Michael refills his mug, goes back around to the jukebox. He surveys his choices as an adolescent anger builds within him. He's a grown man, being given a curfew like a teenager.

When I'm good and ready, he thinks. Not a moment before.

Tiny and Michael retreat back across the Island to the Leaf. The bar is packed, but Michael secures a table in the back for the two of them. The word has spread. The whole bar is buzzing with the news. Tommy Flanagan, just off his shift, comes over with a round of beers and the latest gossip.

"So what's the word, Tommy?" Tiny asks.

"Heard the Feds shut it down. The guy who won last year was some Serbian lawyer. But he was in the middle of a divorce. So his wife told her lawyer that Devin Cody brought eight hundred thousand dollars to their house one night last year and the Serb lawyer hasn't listed it anywhere in his assets. So her lawyer called the Feds. One thing leads to another."

A guy from a neighboring table, wearing a blue hoodie, interjects. "The lawyer wasn't

Serbian. He was a Croat."

"A Croat?" asks Tiny.

"You mean Croatian?" asks Michael.

"No, not Croatian. Fuck, Vinny, what was the lawyer again?" he asks the guy sitting across from him.

"Albanian," says Vinny, before returning to his own conversation.

"That's it, lawyer was Albanian, not Serbian."

The guy turns back to his table.

"That's bullshit," whispers Tommy. "How the fuck would an Albanian even know about college basketball?"

"But what, a Serbian would?" asks Tiny.

"Yeah, sure, Wagner had those four Serbian guys a few years back. The big kid, what was his name?"

"They weren't Serbs, Tommy. They were Croats," Michael says. They all laugh.

The afternoon limps into the evening. The Leaf takes on the contradictory character of an Irish wake: somber but festive. A stream of refugees from Cody's trickles in, mixing with some Paddy's Day revelers. The place fills up with a menagerie of blue collar guys: firefighters, cops, construction workers, Local One electricians. After a while, the whole bar is glowing with the camaraderie of half-soused strangers killing time together. The tourney is in full swing, but most of the crowd isn't even watching the games. Fresh rumors about the pool arrive with every soul who walks in the door.

A couple of mob guys tried to shake Devin down. Four ex-cops threatened to start a war with the mob guys. Someone called him in the middle of the night and threatened to kidnap his daughter. Some asshole actually reported the winnings on his tax return. Devin's wife ran off with a nineteen-year-old and he's heartbroken. Devin ran off with a nineteen-year-old and the early entry money. He left some of the money with a nun and she gambled it away.

Tiny and Michael order burgers. They eat them in silence, unwilling to yell to be heard over the dull roar of the bar. They watch the games, have another round of beers. At eight-thirty, Tiny asks for the check.

"That's it for me, Mikey," Tiny announces. "Want a ride?"

He should go home. But it's been a long day, a sad day, and he wants to put a shine on it. He's never known when to call it a night, has always chased a good time, a few more laughs with the fellas.

"I'm gonna stay for a little bit."

He walks Tiny out the back door to his

car. They embrace.

"Florida, huh?"

"Someone told me Laura Gentile moved down there after her second husband died."

"Never gonna happen."

Tiny winks at him.

"Ye of little faith."

When Tiny drives away, Michael walks around to the front of the bar. A crew of guys stands outside smoking. He bums a cigarette from a regular he knows. He hasn't had a smoke in years, but the day is calling for it. He stands off a little to the side. A few entry sheets drift past; some guys must have brought their sheets back here before abandoning them.

The pool is done. Another thing that made the Island cozy is no more. Michael's been putting in entries since the mid-eighties, back when the pool was a couple thousand if you won. The boys grew up with the pool. They all loved it, especially Bobby. All over the tristate area, the news will spread: on Wall Street, out to Jersey and Long Island, up to Connecticut. No more pool. It got too big, drew too much attention.

And now it's gone.

He takes a few drags on the cigarette, drops it on the sidewalk, and steps on it. His head swims from the smoke.

It starts to drizzle, driving the smokers inside. Michael walks back into the bar. The crowd has thinned a bit and separated into pockets: the still raucous, the silently stewed, and the unsteady in between. Michael finds an open spot at the bar, next to Tommy Flanagan and a few other guys he knows. He puts a twenty on the bar and heads for the bathroom.

The bathroom is empty. Michael relieves himself of a day's worth of beer. He goes to the sink, washes his hands. When he looks up, he sees his father staring back at him from behind the smudged mirror.

If you'd taken the shop, maybe Bobby would still be alive.

Not his father's voice. His own.

His chest tightens. It feels as though his ribs are closing to protect his insides. His eyes water. He goes to one knee, a half kneel, his hands holding opposite ends of the sink. He's having trouble breathing. Little whirling dots blur his vision. He feels faint.

The door to the bathroom opens. Michael scurries to his feet. The tap is still running. He leans down, spoons cold water onto his face, the back of his neck and his arms.

"You okay, pal?" the guy asks.

"I'm fine," he answers. "Dropped a quarter."

He usually wakes with the thought. Most days, it's there, on the back of his eyelids, waiting for him somewhere between asleep and awake. It's better to wake with it, to have the sadness already there, the thought already accepted and just go about his day. But today, the slippery bastard hid all day, attacked when he least expected it.

He washes his hands, walks back out to the bar. He takes a long pull on his beer, waves the bartender over.

"Jameson," he says. "A double."

Enzo pours out two glasses of wine, slides one over to Michael. Gray hair sneaks up out of his shirt and down out of his nose and ears. He smiles.

"Alla salute."

Michael takes a sip.

"Listen, Dad. Tomorrow night is Bobby's last high school basketball game. It would mean a lot to him if you came. Would mean a lot to me."

"Of course. I'll be there."

They sit in silence for a bit.

"Something else, Michael?"

Three months have passed since Enzo walked into the Leaf, gave him a deadline.

He has not been a good man these past months. Not a good husband, not a good father, not a good son. He has been living in a fugue, angry for reasons he still doesn't understand. But he is a humbled soul now. His hands start shaking. The words pour out.

"I was wrong, Dad. I was wrong, I was a jerk and I'm sorry. I had some kinda stupid midlife crisis, but I'm ready now. I have the money. I'm not a firefighter anymore, I have to accept that. I want something to pass along to my boys. I want the shop."

Enzo rubs a finger over a drop of spilled wine. He considers his son.

"It's okay, Michael. Is better this way. I sell the shop and then, when I go, you use the money, use it how you want it."

"No, Pop," he says, an unexpected urgency taking hold of him. "You don't understand. I want the shop. I really do. I'll buy it. We can talk price. I know I made you wait, so I can pay whatever you want, well, maybe not whatever you want, but we can make it work. I'm sure —"

Enzo raises a hand. Michael stops talking. He feels panicky, an only child's overdue realization of his own selfishness. Enzo gulps down his wine, puts the empty glass on the table. His eyes are sinking moons.

"Is too late, Michael. Too late. Enzo An-nunziata bought the shop. We closed last week."

It is late when Michael leaves the Leaf. He is drunker than he's been in a good long while. The rain has given the street a sheen. Wads of wet paper — more entry sheets — line the gutter. He starts to walk home. The streets are empty, most of the houses are dark. The only sound is rain hitting pavement. By the time he gets home, he's soaked.

Gail is in a deep sleep on the couch. A library book is draped open across her chest. He lifts the book from her chest and saves the page with a mass card, the way she does. He kisses her forehead gently, try-ing not to wake her. He's too unsteady to risk guiding her up the stairs.

He walks upstairs, stands outside Bobby's room. He closes his eyes, listens at the door, hears nothing.

He walks into the bathroom, takes off his wet clothes. He tosses them over the shower rod, spreads them so they'll dry. He walks to the sink. He runs the tap, splashes some cold water onto his face. He looks at his reflection.

He sees an old man who's had too much

to drink. An old man who didn't follow his father. An old man whose sons followed him: one into a different life, one into the bars, one into the flames. He exhales, wipes his face with a towel, takes a last look in the mirror.

He sees an old man, cold and tired and ready for his bed.

CHAPTER 7
ALL WOULD BE FORGIVEN

Friday is clear, blustery. Gail spends the morning cleaning the house in advance of Sunday's party and the early afternoon halfheartedly watching the second day of games of the NCAA tournament. The news has spread like wildfire, putting the whole Island in a funereal state. Gail has gotten four calls herself, Michael another half dozen. No more pool. At noon, Michael says he's feeling squirrelly, gonna go for a walk, which means the Leaf. She wants to ask about Franky, how he behaved yesterday, but she doesn't. There's enough bad news for one morning.

No more pool. Bobby would have been devastated. He would have been sitting here miserable, probably commiserating with Franky. Still watching the games of course, but miserable. She gets an idea: she'll call Franky, invite him over. *They* can commiserate. And she can tell him about Tina in person. Easier to pass along news like that with a firm hand on the shoulder, a steely gaze in the eyes. Easier to say what needs to be said. To tell him that he can be angry about this, upset about this, but that he can't be either of those things on Sunday. He has to behave, and if he can't, he shouldn't bother coming at all, which, God help her, is what she's hoping happens.

She picks up the phone, dials his house. Straight to voice mail. She leaves a message, casual and nonchalant, asking him to call back. She's still holding the phone when she gets another idea. It's been two days and she can't quite shake the defeated look on Peter's face. Defeated by what? She thinks she knows, but she isn't sure. She glances at the clock. Not even three. Peter is definitely still at work. She calls his house. Lindsay answers on the second ring. Her voice is neutral.

"Hello?"

"Lindsay, it's Gail. How are you?"

"I'm fine, Gail. How are you?"

"Hanging in there. Is Peter around? I wanted to tell him about the Cody's pool. It's a silly thing, but I thought he'd want to know."

"He isn't here. He's probably at work."

Probably? A little sarcasm.

"Of course, of course. Getting senile. Sorry. I don't want to bother him at work. Just have him call me when he gets home."

Gail waits for a response. When it comes, Lindsay's voice is sharp but unsteady.

"He isn't here, Gail. Do you understand what I mean?"

Gail knows what Peter did.

"I think I do."

"Good. Well then, I'll talk to you soon."

Gail's eyes start to water. Two women separated by a phone line. Each on the verge of a nervous breakdown. And still, they can't connect.

"Lindsay," she says.

"What?"

She almost breaks down, blurts it all out. About Tina, Wade, needing to tell Franky and Bobby and not having told them, even about Maria and Enzo and how she named Bobby and her mother and father and even about the stupid fucking pool. She almost says all the things she would normally say to Tina.

But she can't. This isn't Tina. Too much water has passed between her and Lindsay. They've never had that kind of relationship and it's too late to start now. A desperate feeling seizes her. Sunday can't be just Tina and Wade and her and Michael and Franky.

They need buffers.

"Will I see you and the kids on Sunday?"

Lindsay sighs.

"I'm not sure, Gail."

"Please, Lindsay. It would mean the world to little Bobby."

This isn't fair, what she's doing to Lindsay, but she can't help it.

"We'll try . . . okay, Gail? No promises."

"Okay, thank you, Lindsay."

"Good-bye, Gail."

They hang up. Gail holds the phone, contemplates calling her oldest son. She dials the number, is about to call when she changes her mind. She puts the phone back in its cradle, wanders to the kitchen table, and sits down.

"Oh, Peter."

She can see the guilt now, sprinkled throughout their interaction. She would not have guessed it. Peter doesn't seem the type. Probably isn't the type, not really. She knows her son. This wasn't some casual fling, some meaningless rut. There was some heartbreak on his face as well.

"Peter, Peter."

Certain things suddenly made sense, like Peter's absence whenever Gail called the past few months. He wasn't living at home. She couldn't blame Lindsay for that. She would have done the same thing as a young wife.

And now?

She doesn't know, she's not so certain. These things happen, even in the soundest marriages between the best-intentioned people. Even when there's love. A long-dormant guilt stirs in her stomach.

She was so angry. Seething. She has to remember that. She wanted to kill Michael, something every wife says. *I could kill him.* And she really could have. She couldn't stand the sight of him. But memory does a disservice to anger. She can't re-create the feeling. It wasn't an explosion of temper, the face going hot and the heart rate jumping. That's easy enough to summon. Christ, an unruly kid in class or an obnoxious driver leaning on the horn can conjure that feeling.

This was different. Two people sharing a bed and a life, growing distant. The rift feeding on the silence between them. These things happen, people fall into a rut, struggle to get out. Every marriage has its lulls. But then it went to another level. He made a decision, without her input, without consulting her. A decision about *their* lives, not just his. And he wouldn't even do her the courtesy of explaining it. It was his fault.

Even now she believes that.

Don't try to understand everything your husband does. Sound advice.

But this was beyond anyone's comprehension, not just hers.

She was thrilled when Michael retired. Twenty-five years served, a good pension and benefits secured. She wouldn't have to worry anymore, wouldn't wake up in the middle of the night with the flames from a nightmare still dancing in her head. And the timing could not have been better. Enzo was ready to hang up his butcher's smock, ready to hand a profitable business over to his only son. The place practically ran itself. The same four people had worked at the store forever. Enzo even had a younger butcher who did most of the blood and guts work these days.

The young butcher's name? Enzo.

Only on Staten Island.

A few weeks after Michael retired, his father came over for Sunday dinner and laid out the proposed transition. He wanted to run the place through December, one last Christmas with his customers. In the new year, Michael would take over. Enzo wouldn't interfere, wouldn't stop in every day and look over his shoulder. It would be a clean break; he wouldn't get involved unless Michael requested. He asked only that Michael keep on his employees.

As for a price, Enzo said, he was an old man who needed little. He'd saved more than he would ever need. But he didn't believe in handing things over for nothing, so he wanted something, a token amount, enough for him to take a long trip back to Italy, spend a month in the village where he was born, another month in the village where Maria was born. Michael sat and listened, and when Enzo was done talking, he poured three glasses of wine and they toasted the future.

She was giddy. A livelihood was being passed on, something that could be passed on again. Maybe Franky could learn the business. Bobby too. They would have something of their own. They wouldn't need to rely on others, wouldn't need to run into burning buildings or chase down criminals to earn a paycheck.

The extra money wouldn't hurt. They could get a new car, help Peter pay off some student loans, maybe even think about a place upstate, a little cabin to get away from it all. Life would be a bit easier.

Besides, Michael would need something to fill his days. She knew enough retired cops and firemen to worry about how he would spend his time. A forty-seven-year-old retiree who liked his beers was a dangerous thing.

He wouldn't have to rush in. He could enjoy a few months off, golf with his friends. They could take a trip together. Gail had gone back to teaching when Bobby reached high school, but she had her summers off. She'd always wanted to see Ireland and for years Michael had promised to take her. Now they could do it.

They made love that night. She lay awake afterward, spinning out the possibilities in her head. Maybe she could stop teaching, work at the store. Maybe Franky could start right away, never mind college, which was a waste of his time and their money, if she was being honest. Maybe Peter would get into Columbia or NYU for law school; he could live at home, commute, make a few extra bucks working for his father. She fell asleep thinking they would remember this night forever, the end of one chapter in their life, the beginning of a new one. She would remember it later for a different reason, as the last time she and Michael had sex for nearly a year.

She woke the next morning with a nervous enthusiasm, a feeling that slowly ebbed over the course of a strange and lonely summer. Peter stayed in Ithaca, got a job as a research assistant for some professor plus a few shifts waiting tables at the local hamburger joint. Franky was supposed to take summer classes at CSI, but one of Michael's old FDNY friends had a landscaping business down the shore in Spring Lake and offered Franky twenty dollars an hour and a bed in a basement.

Bobby was home, but he was a vagabond, barely in the house, in constant search of hardwood floors or asphalt blacktop. In the spring, he'd had a late growth spurt, three inches in as many months, and become a basketball junkie; he talked about little else, spent all his free time practicing or playing. Last year, he'd been a bit player on the team, inserted into the games sporadically: a minute here, two minutes there. He barely stayed in long enough to break a sweat.

But most of the key players had graduated and Coach Whelan had dangled the promise of increased playing time under the noses of all the rising seniors as an incentive to make them practice over the summer. Bobby had taken the bait.

The other boys had played football and baseball, games Gail knew and understood. She enjoyed them, except for the more brutal aspects of football. Basketball was foreign to her, a fast-paced mess whose best players — no point denying it — were inevitably black. She didn't understand Bobby's fascination, but there was little doubt that he loved it. And unlike baseball and football, it was his; he didn't have to toil in the shadows cast by his older brothers.

He got a job at a local basketball camp, an underpaid counselor to a bunch of fourth and fifth graders. After work every day, he hitched a ride to play pick-up games at P.S. 8 or I.S. 59 or hopped on the train down to Cromwell Center, arriving home every night with a ball in one hand, a half-empty jug of yellow Gatorade in the other and the smell of dried sweat coming off of him. Sometimes, when she stumbled across him in the house, Gail experienced vertigo — he seemed to be bobbing up and down — until she realized he was intentionally rising to the tips of his toes and lowering himself over and over, his calf muscles twitching with the effort and his lips moving in silent count. When she asked him what he was doing, he said, "Calf raises, duh," like this was a perfectly normal activity that everyone should be engaging in whenever they had a free moment.

The only consistent time they spent together was in the mornings. She drove him to work and some days she lingered in the parking lot, watching her goofy man-child of a son interacting with his charges, a referee's whistle hung around his neck, a smile etched on his face. Watching him with the kids was a joy, put her in a good mood that lasted until she arrived back to an empty home, another short note from Michael on the fridge.

Went golfing. Back later.
Went to meet Flanagan.
Went to AC with Tiny. Back tomorrow.

Back tomorrow?

She'd expected an adjustment period. The man had fought fires for twenty-five years. He wasn't used to explaining his whereabouts all the time. He was entitled to blow off some steam. She understood that but she'd hoped that he would spend some of his free time with her. She'd declined the opportunity to teach summer school because she thought they'd spend some time together, maybe take that trip to Ireland. But Michael showed no interest in spending any time with her. When they did interact, he was surly or aloof, always hustling off to

392

do this or that. He suddenly seemed to have an endless list of errands to run and for a while, Gail worried that maybe he was having an affair.

But when he came home at night, she smelled beer, not perfume, and that was cold comfort. She tried not to think of her father, tried not to think *this is how it starts,* and for the most part, she succeeded.

Michael was not her father. Michael was a good man. A good man going through a rough patch, had lost a bit of his identity, was finding his way. Taking over for his father would be a good thing, would give him something to do, a new identity. All would be well in January. She had to bite her lip and let him stumble a bit. He'd earned that much.

She filled the summer reading books and listening to baseball games on the radio and dropping in on the neighbors, mostly Diana Landini, she of the legendary low-cut blouses. They sat on Diana's screened-in back porch and played hearts, a pitcher of powdered iced tea sitting on the table to slake their thirst. Gail listened to Diana complain about her husband, Joe, who the entire neighborhood suspected of carrying on a long-term affair. For several years, he had been spotted at various pay phones —

in Keene's Pharmacy, on the corner of Hylan and Richmond — slipping quarters into the slot and looking, for all the world, like a man who was trying not to be seen. If Diana suspected something, her complaints revealed nothing. They focused on Joe's personal hygiene.

"The man's breath always smells like ham, Gail. It's not natural. He doesn't even eat ham. And his snoring, dear God, he sounds like a wild animal caught in a trap. It's no wonder I'm down in the kitchen eating Entenmann's at three a.m. every night."

To accentuate the point, she slapped the mass of exposed thigh that slipped out from her khaki shorts. The rest of Diana's body had expanded in the years since poor Mr. Greeley had keeled over leering at her cleavage. Everything else on her body was like her breasts now, plump and oversized, but Diana still dressed to draw stares. Men still looked, but their looks were now accompanied by the rueful shake of a head, lamenting what had been. It gave Gail a secret, guilty thrill.

Gail threw in a few desultory, household complaints about Michael: socks on the floor, dirty dishes in the sink, drops of cold piss on the toilet seat. She took a sip of iced tea. Diana leaned back, her eyes made small by the girth of her cheeks.

"Jesus, you look great."

"Stop."

"Really, you look fantastic." She paused, refilled her glass. "You lucky bitch."

Gail rolled her eyes in disagreement, but it was true; she looked better than she had ten years earlier. Before the kids, she'd been skinny, devoid of the curves that turned male heads. And three pregnancies had taken their toll: varicose veins, a stubborn pouch of fat in her lower stomach, a softening and slackening of the major muscles. Any attempts to coax her body back to leanness had always been thwarted by the demands of motherhood. She barely had time to brush her teeth, never mind spend forty-five minutes trying to imitate Jane Fonda doing aerobics in a garish body suit.

So she spent fifteen years as a frumpy, disheveled mess. Who cared? Not she and not Michael and that was all that really mattered.

Midway through her forties, her body had coalesced into a curvaceous version of its former self. Her thighs, her hips, her rear were all thicker but contoured; four years of walking at night had transformed fat into muscle. Her small bust had navigated the ravages of time and gravity far better than the showstoppers of Diana Landini and her big-busted cohorts; it was still only a handful of tit, but at least it was in the right place. She was no rare beauty, she knew that, but age, in its fickle generosity, had treated her well. There were a few wrinkles, a few gray hairs, but they conveyed a contrarian idea: well-worn beauty. Beauty that had survived.

It happened to men all the time — bit of gray or white bestowed an air of wisdom, compensated for any physical decline — but women were stuck with the absurd monotony of male desire: young and thin, except where it counted, thank you very much. Anyway, she'd lucked out. Time had touched her, but gently. And her eyes hadn't changed at all. If anything, the gleam within had grown more brilliant. In jeans and a sweater — her standard attire — she was pleasant to look at. Maybe even desirable, she allowed herself, on her better days.

She noticed the looks men gave her. In the supermarket. In the street. Even at school. Mr. Torrenson, the high school baseball legend turned gym teacher, walking past her classroom a few times a day for no reason at all. Mr. Williams, the principal, dropping in on her classes "to observe her teaching method."

Right. Observe her ass while she wrote on the chalkboard was more likely.

Men were so transparent, especially teachers. Last year at the faculty Christmas party, Torrenson, a mess of black chest hair sprouting out of his half-unbuttoned shirt, had put his hand on her ass in a dimly lit corner of the school cafeteria. He leaned down, his thick tongue sliding between ruby-stained teeth, and whispered in her ear.

"Good God, Gail. I'd love to take you to the Victory Motor Inn and toss you around a room for a few hours."

Then his tongue landed in her ear, encasing it in warm, brackish drool.

She reached back, grabbed his meaty wrist, and removed it from her backside. She took a half step away. Her voice was low but firm.

"Danny, I think you've had too much to drink. You're forgetting about your wife and kids."

He grinned, the dopey wide smile of an inebriate, and moved off in the direction of Edna Adelstein, the frizzy-haired music teacher who'd grown accustomed to being his backup plan at such events. When Gail left shortly afterward, Torrenson's left arm was draped over one of Edna's ham-hock shoulders, a clear plastic cup holding a pint of thin red wine at his lips.

Torrenson's advance hadn't shocked Gail. Torrenson was a well-known lech. What surprised her was the lowness of it: The Victory Motor Inn? With its room-by-the-hour pricing and pink bedsheets? Quite an offer.

She never told Michael, couldn't see any point. Torrenson was a pig, but not worth making a scene. And it was nice, in a way, to be desired. Gail had never encouraged that kind of attention, but it was flattering, she had to admit.

Maybe she should have told Michael, sparked a little jealousy in him. Let him know that other men had taken notice, even if he hadn't.

He grew more and more distant as the summer progressed. Something had come between them. It wasn't a woman, she was sure of that. But what could it be? She didn't know and not knowing scared her as much as the gulf between them. She wanted the summer to end. She wanted to go back to work, establish some semblance of routine in the house.

One night, a little before Labor Day, she came home from Diana's and Michael was outside on the back patio, grilling a sausage wheel and some peppers for dinner. He turned and smiled when she stepped outside.

"Hey, here you are," she said.

"Hey, here I am." He rotated a green bell pepper with tongs. "Long legs is home too. We can all have dinner together."

"Great, I'll open some wine," she said, before stepping back inside, her mood a bit lighter. "Been a while."

It was nothing. A late summer barbecue, sitting at the kitchen table while the light outside refused to die. Sausage and pepper sandwiches on fresh bread. Bobby had taken a shower, smelled like soap for once instead of sweat. Michael was his old self again, laughing and smiling, touching her bare leg under the table whenever Bobby said something goofy. The closed intimacy of family sharing a simple meal.

She'd worried for no reason. Michael had been in a funk, that was all. Gail sat there, floating from the wine and the return to normalcy. This is what she'd imagined the whole summer would be like. She took a sip of wine, looked absently out the window as a car braked in the street to let a neighborhood kid retrieve a Wiffle ball. By the time she turned back to the table, it had already started to fall apart.

"Coach Whelan," Bobby was saying, "says that I'm gonna be the starting center this year. Probably team captain."

The words came out in a panicky rush. His eyes searched for Gail's, looking for support. She watched Michael, whose face betrayed nothing. But she knew it was bad.

"But if I play football, I have to sit out the first five games, including the Thanksgiving eve game, and I can't be captain."

Bobby looked at his father, awaiting a reaction. Gail swallowed.

"So, no football," said Michael. "That's what you're saying."

Bobby's eyes shifted to meet hers.

"Well, I guess, umm, I can't be captain if . . ."

"Even though you made a commitment, even though your teammates are relying on you. That doesn't matter to you."

Bobby reached for a glass of water, took a long sip.

"I don't look at it that way, Dad. I'm the backup tight end. I barely play. I'm gonna start on the basketball team this year."

Michael wasn't listening, was staring at the window.

"You'd rather run around in your underwear playing a nigger's game."

"Michael!"

He pushed his chair away from the table and stood up.

"Michael, sit down, please," she said. She glanced over at Bobby, who was fighting back tears and choking down anger at the same time.

"Why? He's already made up his mind," he said, waving a dismissive hand in Bobby's direction. He walked out of the kitchen, out of the house. She turned back to Bobby, who was crying openly, on the verge of sobbing.

"Bobby, he didn't mean that. He's upset that you're not playing football, that's all. You should have told him earlier."

"When?" Bobby asked, his head tilted sarcastically, a tick picked up from his father. He stood, embarrassed that he couldn't stop crying.

"Bobby, sit down. Let's finish eating."

She reached a hand across the table, but he stormed off and a minute later, she heard the familiar boom of the Wu-Tang Clan coming from his room.

"Fucking dandy," she said, to the empty table. She finished her glass of Chianti in one swallow.

Weeks passed. The older boys came home for Labor Day, sensed the tension in the house, and quickly departed: Peter back to college, Franky back to the job, college on hold for another six months. Gail went back to work. Bobby went back to school. Michael went back to his routine of sleeping in, disappearing for hours at a time, and spending every night at the Leaf, in the company of hiccuping half friends. He went away for Columbus Day weekend, a golf trip down to Myrtle Beach with a few of the boys from the Leaf.

She spent the weekend pacing the house, rehearsing her remarks, preparing her arguments. She jotted down a few points on a piece of yellow paper, kept it in her pocket for easy reference. A summer of silence followed by a month and a half of bitterness? She'd had enough. He'd had his fun; it was time for things to get back to normal. As the weekend limped along, she replayed the events of the past few months and a sense of dread seeped into her. Their fight had distracted her, masked an absence that was conspicuous in retrospect: Enzo. She hadn't seen him all summer, wasn't sure Michael had either. Was there a dispute about the price? Had Enzo decided he wanted to hold on a little longer? She didn't know what was wrong, but now she was certain it had to do with his father.

She came home from school the Tuesday after Columbus Day and Michael was waiting for her in the kitchen, his golf clubs propped up in front of the refrigerator. His face was red from sun and booze. He sat with his back straight, like he was expecting a confrontation. She sat across from him.

"How was the trip?" she tested.

"Fine. Few laughs."

"Good. Glad."

She felt like she was sitting in her kitchen with a total stranger.

"We need to talk," she said.

"Agreed."

She reached into her purse and pulled out the folded piece of yellow paper. Her list of points had spilled onto the other side of the paper.

"Before you start, Gail, I need to tell you something."

She'd convinced herself there wasn't another woman but was suddenly unsure. He spoke with the tentative air of a husband who'd lapsed.

"What is it?"

He eased the brim of his baseball cap back on his head, scratched the place where his hairline began.

"Danny offered me a couple of nights behind the stick at the Leaf. Tuesdays and

Fridays. Every other Sunday afternoon."

"Okay," she said, relieved but confused.

"I'm gonna take them."

She stared at him and he averted his eyes. Whatever it was, he hadn't told her yet. Or maybe she hadn't heard it. Tuesdays and Fridays?

"Bobby's basketball games are gonna be on Tuesdays and Fridays," she said.

"Really?" he asked, as though he hadn't attended every one of them last year. "I forgot." He took his hat off and scratched the top of his head. "Well, I can ask Tommy to switch me from Tuesdays, but I'd hate to give up Fridays. Busiest night of the week."

"If anyone would know, it'd be you," she said, unable to resist the shot. She was irritated — Bobby would be upset, though he wouldn't admit it — but it was better than another woman. She looked down at her list. From the miasma of scribbled, angry words, Enzo's name flashed up at her. She looked back at Michael.

"Wait, are you gonna keep these shifts when you take over the shop?"

She didn't understand until the words were out of her mouth. He looked down at the table, ran his right hand in circles over its surface. He wouldn't return her gaze.

"Michael, what are you telling me?"

"I think you know exactly what I'm telling you."

He looked at her, mind made up, no discussion necessary.

"I don't understand this. I don't understand this. Why?"

He shrugged his shoulders, as though she were asking why he preferred vanilla ice cream to chocolate.

"I don't want to be a butcher. Don't want to smell like blood all the time."

"You want to be a bartender, instead? Spend your time with drunks and winos? Smell like the inside of an ashtray all the time?"

Her tone was manic. He shrugged again.

"I don't know what to tell you, Gail."

"Michael, this is insane. This makes no sense."

He stood, yawned.

"Your father will be heartbroken."

"Well, sons don't always do what their fathers want them to. Such is life."

The line sounded prepared, like he'd been waiting weeks to drop it. She wanted to slap him. Slap his face until his cheeks bled.

"You're not talking about Bobby? Tell me this is not about Bobby not playing football?"

He looked at her. His face was the picture

of calm.

"No, Gail, no. It's about me not wanting to be a butcher. That's it."

He yawned again, stretched his arms.

"I'm bushed. I'm gonna take a nap."

She looked down at the floor, filled with a sudden, seething hate for him.

"You are such a fucking asshole. Such a fucking asshole."

He walked away without responding. She heard his feet on the stairs. She noticed his golf bag. She stood and kicked it as hard as she could, sent it skittering across the linoleum. Not satisfied, she lifted it up and turned it over and the clubs dropped out, one after another, producing loud clangs as they fell to the floor. When the noise died, the word *divorce* was in her head, in a way it never had been before.

Gail laughs at the memory. Her eyes drift to the spot on the floor where she spilled all his golf clubs.

We knew nothing, she thinks. We were young and dumb and we knew nothing.

She's hungry. She had a buttered roll for breakfast and nothing for lunch. And day-dreaming about food hasn't helped. She puts on a jacket and walks out to the car. She knows exactly what she wants: chicken cutlet hero with the fresh muzzarell and red peppers, oil and vinegar. She usually shops at the Enzo's in Eltingville — it's closer, has a better selection because it's bigger — but when she needs a sandwich, she goes to the original.

The chimes above the door startle to life when Gail walks in. The display counter — antipasti, trays of prepared dishes, a selection of cuts of meats — is on the right. Opposite the display counter are shelves that hold boxes of pasta, jars of tomatoes, loaves of fresh bread. The smell is heavenly. She looks at the wall above the counter and spots the black-and-white picture of Enzo — Maria's Enzo — standing outside the shop when it first opened. If you look closely at the picture, you can see a glimpse of Maria in the shop window, staring out at the photographer. Gail knows. On a handful of occasions, she has asked Enzo — the new Enzo — to take the picture down so she can inspect it more closely. The only other customer is an old lady who is pointing out the precise stuffed peppers she wants to an impatient teenager behind the counter. He picks up a pepper with tongs and turns it so the woman can inspect it through the glass. The lady peers at it for a few seconds before nodding her head yes.

He lets the oil drip off the pepper and places it in a plastic container, joining a single companion.

The new Enzo strides out from the butcher's station in the back, an easy grin on his granite face. His head is a failed experiment in human geometry: the crooked nose, the forehead with three sides, the lantern jaw that juts out farther on one side of his face. He wears his hair in a tidy flattop that only accentuates the misshapenness of his other features. His eyes are little black stones pasted on a quarry wall.

"Gail," he booms, before coming around the counter, his arms open. He's startled the old lady, who turns to him in shock. The teenager slips two peppers into the container while the old lady is distracted. Enzo stops and puts his hand gently on her shoulder.

"You've scared me, Enzo."

"I'm sorry, Mrs. Avello. I'm sorry. I was excited to see my friend. Paul, the peppers are on the house and give Mrs. Avello a package of fresh mozzarella for her husband."

"Thank you, Enzo."

He glides past her toward Gail, a silent giggle on his face. He hugs Gail. He smells like the old Enzo. God, the things she misses.

"What's going on, Gail?"

"Nothing at all. How's by you?"

"Menzamenz. What can I get you? Usual?"

"I'm a predictable woman, Enzo."

He laughs, slides back behind the counter. The old woman shuffles away.

"Take a break, Paul. I'll take care of Mrs. Amendola."

Over the years, Gail has noticed that she is Gail when he is on one side of the counter, Mrs. Amendola when he is on the other. She's always liked Enzo, long before he bought the store that Michael didn't want. She still likes him, even though he turned one store into four, made a small fortune on the other Enzo's reputation. He's shrewd and ambitious. Can't fault him for that.

And respectful. Keeps the picture of Enzo on the wall, has never renovated or updated the original store. Gives her money every year for Bobby's scholarship.

"How's Michael?" he asks, his back turned.

"Good. Bummed about the pool."

"I know. It's crazy. Customers have been complaining all day. What a shame."

"How's Michelle doing? Hear back from

colleges yet?"

He turns, eyes wide, proud father.

"Son of a gun, I forgot to tell you. Got into Cornell. Ain't that a thing. My daughter in the Ivy League. Like Peter."

"That's great. Congratulations."

"Hey, if she turns out halfway like Peter, you know? Hey, we're happy. She's happy, right? All that matters."

"I'll give you Peter's number. She should call him. He'll give her the lay of the land. He loved Cornell."

"Would you? That would be great."

He wraps the hero in white paper, puts it in a brown bag, stuffs some napkins inside, hands it over the counter. She reaches for her purse. He waves her away. She hasn't paid for a sandwich in years.

"Your money's no good here."

"How you gonna pay for Cornell if you keep giving away sandwiches?"

He points a finger to the picture above him.

"Hey, you know. I owe. Your father-in-law. May he rest. I owe."

The chime on the door rings again. Enzo's eyes drift to the door, to new customers.

"Thanks, Enzo."

"Take care, Mrs. A. Give my best to Michael."

She sits in the car, in the parking lot, and opens the wrapper. She takes half the hero out and takes a bite. She does this sometimes, eats a sandwich in the car. She's not sure why. Tina teases her, says she has a crush on Enzo, that she's waiting for Enzo in the parking lot like a teenager.

She's not one for crushes, not one of these women who pretend to pine for the good-looking cop or fireman (or butcher) in the house down the street. No, she's not one for crushes. Not anymore.

She pulls a pepper out of the sandwich, eats it.

She hasn't thought about him in years.

Danny McGinty. He was easy on the eyes, no doubt about that; a tall, dark Irish charmer with salt-and-pepper hair and the sturdy build of an ex-athlete whose vanity wouldn't let him go entirely to seed. Always a nice smell — cream and wood — hanging from him. Some of the other mothers feigned weakness in the knees when he passed. He made a lot of money and his wife was a high-holy bitch; that was the gossip.

Gail had never paid him much mind, just the odd *hello* or *good-bye* or *nice game* or *how were your holidays?* If anything, she found him a little off-putting; he seemed pretty pleased with himself. If she wasn't so angry at Michael, nothing would have happened, no matter how good-looking or charming Danny was. She was furious, though. Her anger was palpable and Danny must have sensed it. Some men have that sense. They can sense discord or wanderlust or boredom or anger. Danny had that sense. She thought it was something special, a real connection between them.

An empty space beside her, filled in by fate. She thought that Danny had been sent to her, that his appearance at that specific moment in time — when things between her and Michael were so bad — was a sign of some sort.

She couldn't conceive that it was calculated.

The same six parents sat together at every game: Paul and Dana Baddio, John and Mary Keegan, Gail, and Danny. Bobby was the starting center (and, as Coach Whelan had promised, the team captain). Vinny Baddio was the starting point guard, Pat Keegan the starting shooting guard. Danny's son, Kevin, never played. Their sons were the only seniors on the team, except for Terry Kovak, whose father was doing a two-year bit in the federal pen for commercial bribery and whose mother was trying to hold down the fort in his absence.

Gail could have sat alone or with Nancy Duggan, who she knew from church and whose son Matt was the only sophomore on the squad, but she didn't. Nancy Duggan was tough to take, always going on and on about Matt getting a basketball scholarship, like the kid was gonna end up in the NBA. Matt was a very good player — sophomores rarely made the varsity — but this was Staten Island, not Brooklyn or the Bronx, and Nancy Duggan needed to get a fucking grip. And as for sitting alone, well, she didn't feel like sitting alone. So she sat with the Baddios and the Keegans and Danny. And she and Danny sat next to each other because neither of their spouses attended the games. Simple as that.

Danny knew the game, knew it well. Had played college ball at Fordham, according to John Keegan. Was some helluva player, back in the day. When Gail watched him striding across the gym or taking the bleachers two at a time with his long legs, she could see it, see the young Danny, lithe and lean, leaping in his short shorts. He came to the games straight from his job, something

413

on Wall Street, the only man in the gym in a suit. His breath was always fresh, smelled like peppermint. He chewed gum incessantly, offered a stick to Gail at the start of each game, but she was too nervous to do anything but bite her fingernails and watch the action, uncertain exactly what she should be watching.

The team wasn't supposed to be any good. A rebuilding year, if such a thing existed in high school. Last year's team had been one of the best on the Island, laden with seniors and blessed with some size. This year's team was green: mostly juniors new to varsity ball, a handful of inexperienced seniors, and the precocious sophomore, Matt Duggan. Worse still, they had almost no size at all. At six four, Bobby was the team's only legitimate big man, the only player capable of mixing it up with the big boys from the North Shore. He played the whole game, never seemed to leave the court. She knew that he'd improved, but his role on the team was a bit mystifying. He rarely touched the ball on offense, spent most of the game under the baskets, jockeying for position so he could corral the ball and then swiftly give it to a teammate.

Danny assured her that Bobby's role was important, even vital.

"He's doing all the little things, setting screens, getting rebounds, diving for loose balls. Plus, he has to guard the other team's best post player, who usually has a few inches on him. And he's scoring ten, twelve points a game, without demanding the ball. Putbacks and layups. It's easy to notice Matt because he's scoring and Vinny's got the ball in his hands most of the game, but the reason they're winning is Bobby."

And they were winning. Not every game, but more than anyone had expected. They played hard, they didn't back down. Danny's instruction helped Gail enjoy the games more.

"Watch his footwork, Gail. See how he helped, came over to pick up Matt's man, altered that shot?"

"See how he spun off that guy to get that rebound?"

She started to appreciate the finer points of her son's play. He was unselfish, dedicated to the team, and indefatigable. His relentlessness frustrated his opponents, drove them to commit silly fouls. He was tough too. Not afraid to mix it up. He was such an easygoing kid off the court, it surprised Gail that he had a mean streak. He stood up for his teammates, without hesitation. One night, a burly black kid on

Port Richmond knocked Vinny to the ground with an elbow to the head. A dirty play, the whole gym gasped. And there was Bobby, right in the kid's face, not backing down, even though he was a good forty pounds lighter. Some shoving back and forth before the refs broke it up. She reached over, instinctively, to grab Michael's knee, say something like "That's your son," but it was Danny's knee that she found. He looked at her.

"You okay?"

She pulled her hand away.

"Yes, I'm sorry. His father would've been proud."

Danny nodded.

"Gotta stand up for your teammates."

He looked down between his knees.

"Where is Michael anyway?"

She exhaled. She lifted her pinky to her mouth and gnawed gently on the tip.

"Good question."

She knew the answer. He was at the Leaf. Every Tuesday and every Friday. Behind the stick, not watching his son play basketball. Not watching the final high school season that any of their boys would ever play. Not sitting next to her. Whenever she thought about it, she got so angry that her stomach clenched. He'd ruined so much already.

Bobby's games were the one bright spot in an otherwise dismal time. She wouldn't let him ruin this.

She'd been wrong about Danny. He was nice. Lovely, actually. A little cocky, maybe, but hey, a guy with his looks and his money could have been far worse. Besides, he had his sadnesses, she could tell. A sullen son. A wife who didn't come to any games. What kind of mother didn't come to her own son's games?

She knew that answer too. A selfish jerk. Someone so caught up in his own bullshit that he didn't notice that his son loved this game. Loved it fiercely. Never mind that he was pretty darn good at it too.

You could say what you wanted about Danny, but he was at every game and his son never played, not unless it was an absolute blowout. It had to be hard for him that his son wasn't very good at a game he'd excelled at. A game that he loved as much as Bobby did, she could tell, by the gleam in his eye when he explained a 1-3-1 zone or a pick and roll.

He told her as much, told her that basketball had been good to him. Got him a scholarship to Fordham, kept him out of Vietnam. Through basketball, he met a guy who worked on the floor of the New York

Stock Exchange. The guy took a shine to him, offered him a job. He had his own company now, had made more money than he ever could have imagined. He didn't say it in a bragging way, said it like he'd been the right combination of lucky and good.

He told her other things too. That he was raised in Far Rockaway, the youngest of six children, the boy his father kept trying for, God knows why, because Danny spent his childhood trying to avoid his father's drunken rages. That he gave up drinking himself when he was in his early thirties. That he liked it a little too much, didn't want to become his father. He didn't elucidate, didn't need to, not with Gail.

"A good-looking Irishman who doesn't drink and has lots of money? Where do I sign up?"

Out on the floor, a whistle blew, louder than usual. Gail half expected the ref to point up in the stands at her.

Flirting, Amendola #40, flirting with a married man.

Her cheeks turned red. She'd crossed a line. She resolved not to do it again, no matter what.

The holidays. A pause in the season. The older boys came home. She and Michael temporarily broke their silence, acted civil in front of the boys, fooled no one. The whole family decorated the tree joylessly, quickly, eager to be away from one another. Gail couldn't even listen to Christmas songs; they seemed to be written for people living different lives entirely.

Michael gave no explanation for Enzo's absence at Christmas; the boys barely noticed. Gail tried to go see him, but the shop was closed, the house empty. He didn't answer the phone. She asked Michael, a little concerned.

"He's in Italy," he said, his voice cold and sharp.

She usually loved the holidays: a week off from school, the whole family back together. But that year was dreadful. The boys, Bobby included, spent as little time in the house as possible, and who could blame them? She was miserable and Michael was gruff. The whole house reeked of unhappiness. After the first few days, they dropped the illusion of normalcy and went back to silent glares.

She missed Bobby's games, missed basketball, missed Danny too. She knew that was a bad sign, a dangerous one, but she was too angry to care. She spent New Year's Eve alone, on the couch, making her way through two bottles of Chianti and watching the ball drop in Times Square. She woke up the next morning, still on the couch, a single resolution in her fuzzy head:

Flirt with Danny as much as humanly possible.

The first game back and Danny was late. Worse still, Nancy Duggan slid into Danny's normal spot at Gail's side, spent the first quarter chewing Gail's ear off about how Coach Whelan was misusing her son, playing him at small forward when it was clear that he should be the point guard. Never mind that the Baddios — whose son *was* the point guard — were sitting right in front of her, well within earshot. Never mind that the team's record was 8 and 3, a fair bit better than anyone had expected. Never mind that Matt Duggan had struggled through the first half of the season, looking overwhelmed and skittish most of the time.

Gail listened halfheartedly, her eyes drifting to the gym's entrance. Where was he? She'd waited two weeks for this night and he wasn't going to show up? The enormity of her disappointment was unnerving.

Out on the court, the ref blew the whistle and pointed at Bobby. He gaped at the ref incredulously, the picture of innocence. In the past year, his gangly limbs had thickened with muscle, but his face was still comically boyish. His second foul. He'd have to sit out the rest of the first half. She watched him trot to the bench, a frustrated look on his face. He sat down, his back to her; a sickle of bright red acne ran out from under his maroon jersey and curved onto his neck. She brought her right hand to her mouth, started to run her front teeth over her fingernails.

Without Bobby, they were having trouble keeping Wagner off the boards. A Wagner player grabbed an offensive rebound, took a low, steadying dribble, and rose for a putback off the glass. Another whistle. And one. Bobby flapped a towel in exasperation on the bench. She looked up at the scoreboard. Tie game, 22–22. Four minutes left in the first half.

This was supposed to be an easy win, but the whole team was out of sorts. Pat Keegan couldn't hit the broad side of a barn and Vinny was turning the ball over at an alarming rate. The Wagner player made his foul shot: 23–22. Gail bit down on the knuckle of her thumb.

A few seconds later, Vinny threw another ill-advised pass; this one sailed out of bounds. Nancy Duggan exhaled in frustration, a little too forcefully. Gail noticed Dana Baddio's ears turn scarlet in front of her.

"Jesus, they need to take Vinny out of the game, let Matty run the point for the rest of the half," Nancy said, ostensibly to Gail, but loud enough for the crowd. Gail glanced at the Baddios nervously.

Paul turned his head.

"Nancy, I'd appreciate it if you kept your opinions about Vinny to yourself. He's doing his best."

Nancy rolled her eyes.

"Jeez, Paul, you can't be so thin skinned. It was a bad pass."

"Yes, it was. I'm sure Vinny knows that. We do too. Enough."

"It's not his fault, Paul. Coach Whelan should have Matty playing point guard."

Dana exploded off the bleacher, swung around, and put her finger in Nancy's face.

"Shut the fuck up, Nancy. Shut the fuck up. I'm sick of hearing about your fucking Matty."

Paul reached a hand over to corral his wife.

"Dana, take it easy. Calm down."

Nancy swung her hand, knocking Dana's finger away. Dana lunged, her hands reaching up for Nancy's neck. Gail stepped in, tried to move Nancy away.

"Nancy, move. Jesus."

Paul was holding Dana at bay, but it was taking some effort. Dana tried to wriggle out of her jacket so she could get at Nancy. Other parents noticed the commotion; some of the players on the Farrell bench did too.

"Fuck you, bitch."

Dana's face was red, maniacal. Gail tried to hustle Nancy down out of the bleachers. *Jesus Christ,* she thought, *there may actually be a fight.*

Nancy finally stopped resisting, stepped down, and walked off the bleachers to the other side of the gym. With a little help from the Keegans, Paul calmed Dana down. The whole gym had been watching, even a few of the players on the court. Dana turned to Gail, apologetic, the fury gone as quickly as it came.

"I'm sorry, Gail. I just couldn't take another fucking word."

Gail laughed nervously.

"It's okay, Dana, most excitement I've had in weeks."

Her heart was still racing. She looked up and there was Danny, looking sharp in a blue pinstriped suit and beige overcoat. In all the commotion, Gail hadn't even noticed him come in. He waved hello to the whole group. He sat down next to Gail.

"So," he said, a wry little grin on his face, "I miss anything?"

Two weeks of intermittent practices and holiday indolence had put the whole team in a torpor, but they somehow pulled the game out in the last few minutes. Gail watched, distracted, not sure how to act around Danny. He was quiet too, his charm shelved for the night. She felt like she was on a first date, as ridiculous as that seemed. After the game, they all moved down to the court, the usual crew huddled together, discussing the game. Nancy Duggan waited on the other side of the gym, giving Dana a wide berth.

Gail stood, not listening to John Keegan's complaints about the referees. She was despondent. She'd thought for sure there was some connection between Danny and her, but she'd been wrong. They didn't even have anything to say to each other. The whole thing had been foolishness. A bit of fantasy. Stupid.

"Gail?"

He touched her arm.

"Yes."

"You okay?"

"Grand."

He pulled her gently out of the larger circle, lowered his voice. He put his hand in his coat pocket, took something out, and placed it in her hand.

"Late Christmas present."

She looked down: a tiny box wrapped in solid red.

"What is it?"

"You'll see."

He leaned down and kissed her cheek. A surge of desire welled up inside her. The smell on him. Jesus.

"Merry Christmas."

She wanted to say something clever, something flirty and witty, but there was no opportunity because the team had begun emerging from the locker room in small groups; the huddles of parents were break-ing down or expanding to accommodate their presence. Danny's son, Kevin, was one of the first to emerge — bench players always were — and his sulky, disgruntled air did not square with the larger group's geniality. He walked straight up to Danny, ready to go.

"Say hello to Mrs. Amendola."

"Hello, Mrs. Amendola."

Kevin pulled on his father's arm, urging a hasty departure. Danny snuck a wink to Gail. She watched him walk across the gym, his hand draped over his son's shoulder, his mouth near his ear, giving counsel she wished she could hear. Gail put the gift in her coat pocket, rejoined the other parents.

"What's the matter with that kid?" Paul asked her, nodding in the direction of Kevin and Danny.

"His mother's nuts. Certifiable," Dana said.

"So sayeth the woman who nearly got into a donnybrook this evening."

"I never said I wasn't nuts. Besides, you knew who you were marrying. You can take da girl outta Bensonhurst, but you can't take Bensonhurst outta da girl."

She kissed her husband, her anger a distant memory. Gail winced. How long since she had kissed Michael? A long while.

Bobby and Pat Keegan emerged from the locker room, walked into the semicircle. The usual congratulations and idle commentary ensued. After a few minutes, Gail and Bobby broke away and walked toward the exit. Gail tucked her hands in her coat pocket and felt the gift. She was curious, but she couldn't open it in front of Bobby.

Only Bobby was no longer beside her. She turned and he was five paces back, leaning down to talk to a short girl who was staring up at him with lovesick eyes. Gail watched their interaction with a smile. When Bobby noticed her watching, he shuffled over.

"Can we give Tina a ride home?" he asked. Gail tried to remember whether he'd ever mentioned someone named Tina. No, he'd never mentioned the name. Or any girl's name, for that matter.

She'd been a little worried, in fact, at the lack of girls' names. Peter and Franky had shown interest — could barely hide their interest — at much younger ages and each had had a girlfriend, of sorts, by their sophomore years in high school. But Bobby had said nothing on the subject, had shown no progress in that arena, and he was a senior. Gail wasn't worried about his proclivities — she'd found a magazine shoved between his bed and the wall; was disturbingly relieved when she opened it and found the right kind of naked pictures — but he didn't seem to possess any ability or desire to interact with actual, living girls. He barely seemed to notice them and he never talked about them, no matter how delicately Gail tried to raise the subject.

Yet, suddenly, here was Tina.

"She lives in Eltingville, on Winchester," he added, the words flying out of his mouth.

"I hope it's not too much trouble, Mrs. Amendola," said Tina.

"No trouble at all."

She was a sweet girl, cute as a button, and unfailingly polite. Everything was Mrs. Amendola this and Mrs. Amendola that. When they reached Tina's house, Bobby got out of the car and walked her to the door. They didn't kiss or hold hands. When he got back in the car, he offered no explanation. They drove home in silence and as soon as they walked in the door, he went straight up to his room, stopping briefly at the fridge for a plate of chicken cutlets and a jug of the ubiquitous yellow Gatorade. Gail waited in the kitchen for a few minutes, wondering whether she should say anything at all. She slipped the tip of her index finger into her mouth, gnawed at the worn nail.

She had to know.

She opened the door slowly in case he wasn't decent. He was lying on his bed, still clothed, flicking a basketball up at the ceiling. His feet dangled off the edge of the bed. Thick headphones covered his ears, but he removed them when he saw her.

"Jesus, Mom, you scared the hell out of me."

"Who's Tina?"

His cheeks reddened, but the smile was irrepressible. She took another step into the room.

"Bobby, is Tina your girlfriend?"

He kicked his legs up at the ceiling like he was pedaling a bicycle. He started laughing; threw the ball against the ceiling and it ricocheted downward, hitting his stomach and then bouncing across the room. He sat up in bed.

"Not just my girlfriend, Mom. The love of my life. The girl I'm gonna marry. The mother of my children."

He was dead serious. *Right,* she thought, *sure. Heard this story before.*

"Easy, Romeo," she said. "She seems very nice."

"Thanks, Mom."

She walked across the hall to her bedroom, euphoric from Bobby's long-awaited progress with the ladies. Another worry crossed off the list. It had turned out to be a good night, the first one in a long while. She looked at Michael's empty half of the bed and felt a kind of gloom creeping over her, threatening her good mood.

Not today. He wouldn't ruin today. She wouldn't let him.

The gift! She'd forgotten all about it. She sat down on the bed, reached into her pocket, and took out the tiny, rectangular package. She removed the red wrapping with a quick rip to find a small black box.

With two fingers, she eased the lid off the box. A shiny, metal object lay inside. She tilted the box and the item fell into her palm. It took her a few seconds to identify it: a nail clipper.

A nail clipper?

She found a tiny note tucked inside the box. A schoolboy's shaky printing on it.

Gail, Take it easy on those nails. It's a long season!!! Danny.

She brought her hands up for inspection. The tips of her fingers were all red and raw. Her nails were the jagged edges of broken plates. She giggled and fell back onto the bed. She fell asleep in her clothes, jovialities flecking her dreams for the first time in months.

She brought the nail clipper to the next game. Danny was waiting for her, his knees jutting up to meet his elbows, a knowing smile on his face. She took out his gift and waved it at him.

"You dirty dog."

He laughed and tapped the wood on the bleacher beside him in invitation. She sat down next to him and he laid a hand on her shoulder and gave it a hearty shake, like they were old friends. His hand remained there throughout the lazy pregame layup lines until the Baddios walked in before the opening buzzer and sat in front of them. They watched the game together in restless silence, their thighs pressed together, nervous energy pulsing between them.

The game was a blowout; Farrell cruised. Without any real drama, Gail's fingers remained out of her mouth until Bobby went to the foul line in the third quarter. Despite hours of practice, he was mediocre from the foul line and whenever he was sent there, Gail's stomach tightened with nerves, no matter what the score. This game was usually so fast, so team oriented, that it jarred her whenever the action halted and an individual was singled out to perform a seemingly simple task. Bobby's first shot clanged off the side of the rim. He shook his head in frustration. Gail lifted her left hand and moved it toward her mouth, but Danny intercepted it.

"Uh, uh, uh," he said. "You've been a good girl all game."

She laughed and squeezed his hand. Dana Baddio looked back over her shoulder at them with a raised eyebrow. Bobby sank his second shot, and Gail wriggled her hand away from Danny and clapped softly.

Alone in bed that night, she felt a longing come over her, a need borne of deprivation and anger and new attraction. Months had passed since she'd slept with Michael; she would not sleep with a man she was not speaking to. The anger had stifled any carnal yearnings, but, that night, she put her hand between her legs and found an impatient wetness waiting. She closed her eyes and thought of Danny's crisp breath and all the places she wanted it to find.

Afterward, she scurried down to the basement, tiptoeing past Bobby's room, to deposit her soaked underwear in the washer. In the damp, cool air of the basement, she was overcome by an acute sense of adolescent shame. She bawled while the washing machine chugged, her bare feet growing frigid against the hard cement of the basement floor. When she finally calmed, she walked back up the stairs, a queasy feeling in her stomach. She slipped into bed and a lifetime of admonitory sermons sprang to her memory. She remembered her childhood parish priest, Father Kenny, a tiny sprig of a man who railed and spit his way through mass. She remembered his voice, could nearly hear him saying, "Thou shall not, Gail."

Her shame came from the thoughts of Danny, not the masturbation. She'd long ago reconciled her faith with certain aspects of the human condition. Touching herself was okay, her thinking went, as long as she thought of Michael. Sometimes your husband was away, sometimes he was stuck at the firehouse. What could you do?

God help her, it had never been an issue. Michael, or the thought of him, had always been enough. The other women laughed at her. They talked about Tom Selleck or Tom Cruise or whomever was that moment's heartthrob. They talked about closing their eyes and thinking of someone else, anyone else. And Gail had never understood. Until now.

Thou shalt not, Gail.

She fell asleep by focusing on the prickly sensation of warmth returning to her feet. When Michael came into the bedroom hours later, unsteady and smelling of beer, she was lost in a deep, troubled sleep.

The games ticked by, each one like the last, in the stands if not on the court. The six parents talking in the quiet pauses of each game, the conversation revolving around the action on the court.

"This number 22 is a punk."

"Terry's off tonight."

"Why aren't we pressing this team?"

"That was a charge, ref!"

Every so often, Bobby made a play whose importance wasn't readily apparent to Gail: he set a solid screen or threw an outlet pass or grabbed a rebound he had no earthly right to get. When that happened, Danny leaned over, put his hand on her back, and whispered in her ear.

"Bobby's playing like a man possessed tonight."

"Jesus, that screen rattled teeth."

Sometimes he put his hand on her back for no reason at all.

After each game was the same as well: the lonely bed, the soiled underwear, the cold, unforgiving basement, the shame, Father Kenny.

Thou shalt not, Gail.

The vision of Father Kenny grew more intense, but also more comical.

Thou shalt not, Gail.

She started talking back to him.

Perhaps I shalt, Father. Perhaps I shalt.

She was always asleep by the time Michael came in and if he woke her, by accident or design, she feigned grogginess and turned away from him.

It was a good season. Saint Peter's beat them twice, each time by a dozen points, but the games felt closer, like a play here or a bounce there and the outcome may have been different. They lost a heartbreaker to St. Joseph by the Sea, on a prayer at the buzzer, and got destroyed by Curtis on a night when the whole team was off. After the losses, Bobby was sullen and he sought comfort not with her, but with Tina. And that was depressing and thrilling.

He was the team's heart and soul: its leading rebounder and second leading scorer. First, by a wide margin, in charges taken, balls dived after, floor burns suffered, and elbows swung. One night, Danny mentioned casually that he knew a few scouts, that he could probably get Bobby a scholarship to a Division II school: University of New Haven or Sacred Heart or Molloy College. Gail nodded, excited but uncertain.

Bobby had never been a student. CSI, then a city job, was the assumed route. But that night she watched him snatch a rebound and thought maybe, just maybe, basketball could be his road to a different life. Maybe, with Danny's help, he'd have options. Maybe even work on Wall Street, like Danny, make a boatload of cash. Danny had said as much himself.

"Would love to have a kid like Bobby working for me someday. Kid who works that hard will always find a way to be useful."

She was glad someone was showing an interest in Bobby. His own father didn't seem to care a whit. Silently, she beseeched Michael to show her some sign of love, give her some reason for not doing something that was taking on an air of inevitability. He was oblivious, hopeless, clueless. He'd turned into her father in the space of six months, but she would not be her mother. She would not rage silently and do nothing.

One night, Danny cupped his hands around her ear, but instead of praise for Bobby's play, he said, "Jesus, you look beautiful tonight."

She pretended not to hear him, but it was hard to ignore his hand casually resting on the curved muscle of her inner thigh.

She couldn't concentrate at work; her mind kept drifting out the window into idle daydreams like those of half the students she taught. She thought of Danny's blue-gray eyes and the feel of his fingers thrumming on her thigh. The whole thing was madness, some bizarre echo of high school; two middle-aged adults playing at teenager. She barely knew him and yet, twice a week, it took all her self-restraint not to turn and start kissing him in a gym full of people.

Bobby and Tina became a couple. They started holding hands and kissing in public, sometimes a touch more aggressively than Gail thought appropriate. She was certain that what she saw was the tip of the teenage iceberg; more expansive explorations were undoubtedly taking place behind closed doors, when no one else was around. She thought Michael should probably say something to Bobby, something about protection at the very least, but she wasn't speaking to Michael and neither was Bobby, so she let it lie. She wasn't going to give Bobby a lecture about safe sex and waiting for marriage, not when she spent her nights fantasizing about another man.

Besides, the euphoria vibrating between Bobby and Tina was infectious. Witnessing young love, in all its absurdity, was a powerful aphrodisiac. Gail started thinking that maybe she and Danny were meant to be together. Maybe there was an easy, clear path for them to be together. The boys were basically out of the house. Michael had no interest in her.

She knew these thoughts were ludicrous. She didn't believe in adultery, had only recently come around to the idea of divorce. But sitting next to Danny, watching her son play basketball, felt right in a way that she couldn't explain. Even the ghost of Father Kenny had stopped haunting her.

Still, beyond some heated leg pressing and intense flirtation, nothing had happened. She had no reason to see Danny other than at Bobby's basketball games and the season had dwindled down to a precious few games: the Catholic school play-offs and something new this year, a March Madness-style tournament for the Island championship.

If something was going to happen, it would happen soon or not at all.

The play-off game took place on a Friday afternoon, at Bishop Ford in Brooklyn. The gym was half empty due to the early start. Some of the usual parents couldn't make it because of work, Paul Baddio and John Keegan included. Danny came straight from his office in downtown Manhattan, wearing a charcoal gray suit, a blue shirt with a white collar, and a blue silk tie. He strode up the bleachers with a confident smile and sat down beside Gail. Dana Baddio and Mary Keegan walked in together before the opening tip and took seats on the opposite side of the gym.

Gail and Danny were alone, nervous. The first quarter of the game passed in silence, as though they didn't know what to do with this sudden, unexpected boon.

The game itself provided little to comment upon. Bishop Ford was bigger, faster, better coached. They played with energy and discipline; their players' movements were somehow both fluid and precise. On offense, the ball zipped from player to player, scarcely touching the floor. On defense, they contested every movement, harassed each dribble or pass. They were relentless. One of their players, whose jersey bore the appropriate last name Long, was nearly seven feet tall and rail-thin, with spindly arms that reached out and effortlessly rebuffed half of the shots that Farrell attempted.

Bound for Kentucky on a full basketball scholarship, Danny said. Gail watched as Bobby tried to box him out, but there was nothing for him to stick his ass into. Long slithered around him, gathered the errant Bishop Ford shots, and deposited the ball in the basket as easily as other people would drop a coin in a parking meter.

Midway through the second quarter, the game's outcome was no longer in doubt. It took on the air of an exhibition as Ford's backups battled with Farrell's starters and the lead stagnated at twenty. Whenever

Farrell made the slightest run, Long was inserted back into the game and, soon enough, the lead was twenty again.

With two minutes left in the first half, Coach Whelan called another useless time-out. Danny reached over, gripped her hand. His gaze was still focused on the court.

"I don't know how to say this, Gail, so I'm just gonna say it. I've been lucky, by and large, in my life. I've caught some breaks, made a few of my own. Mostly, I've listened to my gut. If my gut told me to do something, I did it. I've learned not to doubt my instincts. The one mistake I made in my life, I didn't listen to what my gut was telling me."

He exhaled, a doleful sigh. Gail's stomach was in ribbons.

"I married the wrong woman. I knew I shouldn't have, but I did. Such is life. I didn't care for the longest time, didn't care until I met you. There's something between us, Gail, I can feel it. I know it in my bones. I wish we'd met thirty years ago. But we didn't. And I'm not gonna ignore what I feel. I can't."

He told her all this in an unbroken rush of words, his eyes drifting from the court up to her. The halftime horn sounded, punctuating his last statement, like he was trying to squeeze it all in, beat the clock.

Gail watched Bobby jog off the court toward the locker room, the inevitability of his team's defeat already gnawing at him. She noticed, for the first time, Tina in the stands behind Farrell's bench, looking glum.

Danny gazed at her.

"Jesus, your eyes. I could live in those eyes."

She wanted the game to be over, wanted to leave right then.

"Danny . . . I don't know how, I mean, I'm, Michael and I . . ."

She nearly started crying.

"It's okay, Gail."

"I'm sorry."

"Excuse me, one second, Gail."

He stood and walked down the bleachers to shake hands with a young man wearing glasses and holding a spiral notebook. Gail looked down, her hands were trembling. The doubts she thought conquered were rallying for a late charge.

She looked out across the gym. Through the small, slitted windows at the top of the opposite wall, she could see the day dying outside, the last strands of light falling away. Michael could have come to this game, she realized, and with that, all her remaining doubts surrendered. Her mind became a mantra of simplicity, like a child's first instructive reading tome:

I will sleep with Danny. Gail will sleep with Danny. Gail will be with Danny. Danny and Gail will be together.

Danny returned. He told her that the young man he was talking to was an assistant coach for the Sacred Heart basketball team. They had an open spot and the guy liked Bobby. The coach wanted to see tape. Gail nodded.

"Will you have dinner with me tonight, Gail?" Danny asked.

"Yes," she said.

"Ever been to Peter Luger's?"

She shook her head no.

"Best steak you'll ever have."

The second half passed in a blur. The final buzzer came abruptly, waking the entire gym, it seemed, from a stupor. Gail and Danny both stood, clapping for no reason, and watched the teams exchange handshakes. She glanced at the scoreboard. 79–41. A blowout. She'd barely paid attention.

They walked down the bleachers and Danny introduced her to the young coach. He gave her a card, told her he'd be in touch. She and Danny joined the other parents in a large, joyless circle, the season's usual alliances abandoned in favor of solidarity in this cruel, merciless land.

"Jesus, that was an absolute ass-kicking."

"What about that kid Long? It wasn't even fair."

"No way number 24 is seventeen."

Their sons didn't linger in the locker room, didn't keep them waiting. They wanted to get away as quickly as possible, back across the bridge and safely ensconced in the warm, convivial comforts of the Island. The city boys had whipped them, as they usually did, at least in this game, and they wanted to go home.

Bobby was surprisingly chipper, had already shaken off the sting of defeat. He told Gail that he'd catch a ride back with Pat Keegan and he asked for a few bucks because the whole team was going to dinner at Denino's. She gave him a twenty and watched as he walked over to Tina.

Now she was truly unfettered. Michael would be working. Bobby would be out. She looked at Danny and he was smiling at her, like a little boy who'd lined up all his dominoes and whose finger was poised over the first, crucial one. The parents slowly shuffled out of the gym, more disappointed, it seemed, than their sons. She felt a hand on her shoulder. She turned.

"Mom, Tina took the ferry, then the train,

and the dinner is kinda team only and there's no room in Pat's car anyway and I was wondering if you could give her a lift home so she doesn't have to take the ferry alone."

Tina was irritated at the fuss.

"It's okay, Mrs. Amendola. It's no problem. I like the ferry."

What could she say?

"Don't be silly, Tina. Of course I'll give you a ride home."

She fished in her purse for the car keys, handed them to her son.

"Bobby, walk Tina to the car. I need to use the restroom."

They walked out of the gym, arguing in lowered voices. The gym was nearly empty, but Danny lingered back, sensing a disruption. They stepped into a small, dimly lit alcove between the bleachers and the exit doors.

"I have to drive Tina home," she said, with teenage petulance.

"Okay, meet me after."

"Drive back to Brooklyn?" she asked. Something about that rankled her. Something silly, like having to pay the toll twice. He laughed.

"It's okay," he said. "We can do it another night, Gail."

"No, no. I'll come back."

He put his hand on her arm, gave it a squeeze.

"It's gonna be okay, Gail. Everything will be okay."

She kissed him. A long, exploratory kiss, the kind she and Michael hadn't shared in years. She pulled away.

"Wait for me," she said.

She walked out of the dim, dusty space. Outside, in the parking lot, it was cold and dark. Only a few cars remained. She saw Tina standing outside the car, shivering. She walked to Tina, hands thrust in her jacket pocket, her tongue tingling from the taste of spearmint.

The car was quiet until they were halfway over the Verrazano.

"That kid Long was unbelievable."

The sound of Tina's voice startled her; she'd been daydreaming about Danny.

"Yes," Gail said. The traffic on the bridge was heavy. The car inched over the span in short spurts.

"So, you're pretty friendly with Mr. McGinty?"

Gail stiffened. Was it that obvious? She tried to sound casual.

"Not really. He's helping Bobby get a

scholarship. That man at the game was an assistant coach, he thinks Bobby could play at Sacred Heart in Connecticut."

Tina laughed.

"Bobby's not going to Sacred Heart," she said, with a sarcastic certainty out of step with her usual politeness. She looked out the passenger window, her face turned away from Gail.

"Well, there are other schools interested as well. Mr. McGinty" — she nearly called him Danny — "says he could get a scholarship to a number of Division Two schools, maybe even a low-end Division One school."

Tina laughed again.

"Bobby won't go away to school. No way."

"How do you know?" Gail asked, a little annoyed at Tina's presumptuousness.

"He'll never leave Staten Island. He loves it here. All he cares about is the Staten Island tournament. That's why he wasn't that upset today."

The car behind them honked. Gail pulled up in line. She didn't need this. She didn't need traffic. Or a chat about Bobby. She needed a straight line. No distractions. She needed not to lose momentum. Of all the fucking nights.

"What do you mean?"

"All Bobby wants is to become a fireman, like his dad. Be a firefighter, live on Staten Island, coach CYO."

She'd managed to banish Michael from her thoughts. She opened her eyes wide, tried to suck all the moisture of out her eyeballs.

I will not cry. Gail will not cry. She will sleep with Danny. Gail will sleep with Danny.

"He'll go to CSI, play on the team there, join the FDNY as soon as he can." She laughed again, nervous to be playing the expert. "That's what he tells me, anyway."

Gail cracked the window to pay the toll. Cold air spilled into the car, stinging her eyes. She rolled the window up and, with her thumbs, pushed the tears into the tight flesh beneath her eyes. She laughed to disguise her agitation.

"You may be right, Tina. What do I know? I'm only his mom."

Tina flushed with embarrassment.

"No, Mrs. Amendola, I didn't mean that."

Gail turned to her. Tears meandered down her cheeks. She saw Tina's embarrassment turn to confusion.

"Are you okay, Mrs. A?"

"I'm fine. Please call me Gail."

Behind them, a few horns honked.

"Jesus, all right, take it easy!" Gail yelled,

447

startling Tina. She pressed down on the gas and the car raced forward. She glanced at Tina.

"Anyway, Mr. McGinty is only trying to help."

A long pause. When Tina spoke, her voice had returned to the peppy, polite tone Gail was accustomed to.

"I'm sure you're right. I think he helped Jack Kelly get onto the SUNY-Potsdam team last year."

The name sounded vaguely familiar.

"Jack Kelly?"

"He was on the team last year. Blond hair. Kinda short," Tina offered.

Gail remembered him now. Scrawny thing, never saw the floor. He barely played in high school. How could Danny have helped him get onto a college team?

Then she remembered the laugh.

The year before, during one of the games, someone had been laughing like a loon in the stands behind her and Michael. An obscenely loud laugh, sounded fake. She'd glanced over her shoulder and saw where the laughs were coming from: Jack Kelly's mother, Terri, a recent divorcée with bottle-blond hair, wearing skintight, leopard-print leggings. She'd forgotten, but someone was sitting beside Teresa, whispering crisp, mint-scented jokes in her ear.

The cause of the high-pitched cackles. A helper of boys, companion to their lonely mothers.

Danny.

When Gail gets home, Michael is in the living room. Not the Michael she didn't speak to for six months. Not the Michael she nearly cheated on. Not the Michael who wanted to bartend.

No.

This Michael served his penance: he attended Bobby's last few high school basketball games after Gail threatened to divorce him if he didn't. This Michael went to his father to claim his inheritance only to find it was too late, that Enzo had already sold the business to the other Enzo. This Michael watched that other Enzo turn one store into four and make a small fortune with his father's business. This Michael is humble and heartbroken and watching basketball with a glum, disinterested look on his face.

"Hey, back from the Leaf?"

"Yeah, I think maybe I'm spending too much time at that place."

"You don't say."

She laughs. He giggles. He's a little tipsy.

"Franky called."

"I assume you didn't tell him."

Michael's smile slackens into a frown.

"No, I didn't. I was thinking, Gail. Maybe we should just ask him not to come. None of us needs a scene."

"He's little Bobby's godfather, Michael."

"I know, but maybe it's better if he's not here."

Gail lifts a finger, starts chewing on a nail. "You gonna call him back?" he asks.

"Tomorrow. I'm too tired tonight."

She holds up the bag to change the subject.

"You hungry?"

"Actually, yeah."

She tosses the bag to him.

"Half a hero left. Chicken cutlet."

He doesn't ask where it's from. He doesn't have to. This is part of his penance too; he has to spend the rest of his life eating sandwiches from a store he could have owned.

She fetches a plate from the kitchen, hands it to him, sits down next to him on the couch. She puts her head on his shoulder, pulls an afghan over her legs. He eats the sandwich with his right hand, puts his left on her back.

"Who's playing?" she asks.

"I don't even know," he says, between bites.

He took her to Ireland the fall after Bobby's senior year. They hit the tourist spots in the west: the Cliffs of Moher, the Lakes of Killarney, the Burren. In Galway, Gail bought each of her boys a cable-knit fisherman's sweater. Outside of Cork, they leaned over and kissed the Blarney Stone, even though someone told them that the locals liked to piss on it. They enjoyed the people, enjoyed the pints. Michael said it was the most beautiful place he'd ever seen.

For years, friends had told her that Ireland felt like home even if your family had left two centuries ago. And she always thought it was nonsense, a bit of nostalgia and a lot of advertising, but when she was actually there, with the misty rain and the stereotypical shades of green and the beyond-friendly people, she did feel something. Not that it was home. She knew where home was. More like some small part of her still belonged there, and that part's joy at its long-overdue homecoming was as pure and clean as anything she'd ever felt.

They stayed a few extra days so they could drive up to Donegal, see the nowhere town where Gail's great-grandparents had emigrated from. They spent a night in a harbor town named Killybegs, got drunk with some locals, staggered back to their B and B in the wee hours of the morning, laughing.

When they got into bed, Gail listened as Michael's giggles eased down into heavy breathing. He lay there, not sleeping, building up his courage. She knew what he would ask. Seven months had passed since she'd bitten Danny McGinty's lip behind a bleacher in Brooklyn. Things had mended but not completely. Every moment between them since had held the absence of an answer to the question he couldn't bear to ask. She wasn't even sure how he knew about Danny, but he did. He coughed.

"Gail," he said. She listened as the sound of her name died down. The room returned to silence. He couldn't bring himself to ask. She answered anyway.

"No," she said. "Almost, but no."

They lay there for a moment, in the moist, cool air, an ocean away from their lives, and then Michael started to sob. He turned to her and cried on her stomach. He begged for her forgiveness and though she had largely forgiven him already, she forgave him again, completely this time. She forgave herself too for what had happened and what almost happened. She forgave the both of them, turned the page on the shop, Danny McGinty, the whole thing.

She didn't know. Apologies were pointless, forgiveness unnecessary. Soon enough, absolution would be plentiful, incomplete, haunting, useless.

All would be forgiven in the shadow of the atrocity that loomed.

CHAPTER 8
THROUGH THE MIRROR

In the wincing half moment between awake and asleep, Franky Amendola's mind is pure, unified by interlaced desires: he wishes that he were dead and his brother alive. This will be the best moment of his day, because in this moment, he knows he would do it. He would sacrifice his life for Bobby's. In a heartbeat. Without hesitation. No questions asked. He has no doubt, no misgivings or second thoughts. He would do it. Were it that simple, he would do it.

And then, with merciless alacrity, he is reminded of the impossibility of the proposed exchange: his own death would not restore his brother. He controls only one half of the equation. Knowing that his own death would be useless removes most of death's allure, and the thought of his mother standing over a grave removes nearly all of the rest. But the tiniest sliver of suicidal impulse lingers, impaling itself into some dark corner of his consciousness, a splinter he cannot remove.

He is awake now, shaking off the dewy futility of a well-crafted and oft-visited fantasy and confronting a multitude of unfortunate realities, each stemming from one central, indisputable fact: he is severely hung over. He pissed himself in the night, soaking the jeans he fell asleep in, as well as the sheets and the bed; the room smells like the bathroom at a brewery. His head is a tender piece of meat that an angry iron-worker spent the night driving a stake into. The skin on his face feels too tight for his skull, as though a tiny, ill-tempered goblin were pulling on his ears in an attempt to have them meet in the back of his head. He suspects that while he was sleeping, some-one lodged razors at various points in his throat. His stomach, perhaps sensing the discontentments of its brethren, is merci-fully quiet.

But complaints are on the way.

He coaxes his torso into an upright posi-tion. He coughs into his hand and wipes it on an unsoiled portion of the sheets. He reaches over and cracks the window. On the windowsill, his personal effects are arranged in a neat little row: his keys, his cell phone, his wallet, an untidy wad of mixed bills, a pack of Marlboros. He must have emptied his pockets before passing out.

He can't remember how he got home last night; a vague but unrelenting anxiety makes him think he would probably regret some of his actions if he could remember them. He tries to isolate his last clear memory. He was at Kelly's with Denny Hogan and Tommy Acevo, watching one of the tournament games, Marquette versus Purdue. He was feeling good, not too hammered, when Hogan started with the shots. The game was at halftime. He got off his stool to walk to the bathroom. Hogan was in the bathroom too. They were laughing about something. In a good mood.

And then, nothing. A little slice of death. A dip in the black river.

"Fuck," he says to an empty room. He remembers that Purdue was getting four and a half. They were winning at halftime. That's what they were laughing about. But he can't remember how the game ended. He picks up his cell phone tentatively, checks his dialed calls. Fuck. Lot of calls to one number and he doesn't remember making all of them. He dials it again.

"Sports," says the Hispanic female voice on the other end.

"TR three, three, three."

"Password?"

"FA."

"How can I help you, FA?"

"Balance?"

"FA, your figure is minus six hundred ninety."

"Six ninety?" he says, incredulous.

"Yes. Anything else, FA?"

"No."

"No action on this call. Thanks, FA."

Fuck. He was up six hundred after Thursday and flat yesterday after the afternoon games. Now he's seven hundred in the fucking hole and he can't even remember how he got there. He closes his eyes, slides down to a lying position. He wishes a gorgeous, big-titted nurse would come into his room, give him a few Vicodin, wrap him in clean, nice-smelling sheets, put him to bed on a sea of pillows, and then suck him off while he drifted back into oblivion.

He waits a few pained beats and when it's apparent that no nurse is on the way, he rouses himself and staggers to the bathroom. He takes a long piss — how could his bladder still be holding this much? — and throws back a handful of Advil with some tap water. He looks at himself in the stained mirror above the sink. His eyelids are puffy, his eyes tiny slits of bruised gray. He looks like something that has been dragged from the sea and left to rot on the beach.

He retreats to his bedroom, slides his piss-soaked jeans and underwear onto the floor, takes an unsoiled pillow from his bed, picks an afghan off the floor of the living room, and lies down on his couch, which isn't terribly comfortable but is dry.

He doesn't want the buxom nurse anymore. He wants to be lying next to Tina, like he did one night, eight years ago, in what Franky assumed was a prelude to something but which never went anywhere. She needed a night out, that was all, and who better for a night out than Franky? They went to Denino's for a pie, had a few pitchers of beer at the bar afterward. They ended up back here, half trashed, giggling. He put her on the couch and she asked him to lie with her and he slid in behind her, a platonic cuddle. She was tiny, the littlest thing, and his body nearly engulfed her.

When they woke, his standard morning erection was full and flush against her rear and his right hand was touching her breast and he kissed her neck softly because why shouldn't that be the way, why shouldn't he step in for his brother? Isn't that what they used to do, back when? But she said, "No, Franky, no."

And then she stood and was gone before another word was spoken and it was never discussed again. She had asked him to lie with her, not the other way around, but it didn't matter because he felt awful, worse even than usual. Tina had always liked him and he'd fucked that up too, like everything else he'd fucked up, and he knew then that they would never end up lying on his couch together again. Which is all he wants now. To lie on the couch with Tina and shroud her with his body.

He can't have the things he wants so he'll take sleep instead. A few hours of it, to escape this brutal stitch of sobriety.

When Franky wakes up a few hours later, he feels better. His head is still throbbing but less insistently, as though the ironworker has wrapped his head in layers of soft cloth to make up for the all-night spiking. The tiny goblin has abandoned his efforts to relocate Franky's ears; only the corners of his eyes feel stretched. And most important, the funereal thoughts of his first waking have downshifted to the usual, post-binge blues.

He sits up on the couch and yawns.

He doesn't understand why he tortures himself by reliving that one stupid night with Tina every time he wakes up lonely and hung over. He woke up with a hard-on. It happens. But nothing *happened.* That's the important thing. He's not a scumbag. He doesn't even think about Tina in that way the vast majority of the time. She's great, she's like a sister, and yeah, if pushed to an answer on the crucial question, that answer would be yes. But that doesn't mean anything. She's got a trim, tight ass and cute face and perky tits. Bobby had good taste, can't fault him for that, but you can't fault Franky for noticing either.

He shouldn't be thinking about this, about Tina's ass or tits. He shouldn't be thinking about Tina in that way at all. He's just so goddamn horny, he can't help it. His thoughts are like this sometimes after a big night and he's had a few big nights in a row. He needs to clear his head.

There's only one way. Rub one out. Clean the pipes, cleanse the system. Then shit, shower, and shave. Then get some food into his stomach. He goes into the bedroom to get the moisturizer and returns to the couch. His stomach rumbles as he lies down. Maybe he should eat first? That's the problem with a hangover: it leaves several body parts in need of immediate attention but renders the head useless in deciding which should be first.

He squeezes some of the white lotion onto his right hand and brings it down to his flaccid penis. He closes his eyes and starts stroking. He fiddles around for a bit, hoping the physical stimulation will spark something in his head, but he can't think of anything; the constant availability of free porn on the Internet has destroyed his once vivid erotic imagination.

Is there literally no one in his present life who he can envision fucking in some semi-plausible manner? He looks down at his unresponsive penis, its drooping head quivering slightly as if to say yes.

Christ, he thinks, this is beyond pathetic.

He reaches into his memory bank for something reliable, a fully conceived scenario already cooked up and ready to go. The Amy Landini bikini fantasy.

He goes to visit Joe, but Joe isn't home and neither are his parents. Amy's like seventeen and he's fourteen. She invites him in and gives him a glass of lemonade. She's just broken up with her boyfriend. They're sitting on her couch, the plaid one in the basement. Her black hair is pulled back in a ponytail. He's wearing swimming trunks and she's wearing a pink and black bikini, the top of which can barely contain her enormous tits.

An erection starts tenting his trunks.

The well-worn fantasy produces the desired effect. His penis thickens and elongates, but the hangover prevents him from reaching a satisfactory stiffness; all he can muster is a droopy facsimile of a proper hard-on. He increases the pace of his strokes but to little effect; he remains stuck at half-mast.

He gets off the couch and walks into the bathroom, bringing the lotion. He splashes some cold water on his face.

C'mon, Franky, relax, he tells his reflection. Relax.

He puts some more lotion on his hand, closes his eyes.

He's on the couch with Amy Landini. She's in the black and pink bikini. An erection starts tenting his trunks. She takes her bikini top off and kneels on the floor in front of him. She slides his huge, throbbing cock between her enormous tits.

"Franky, it's so big. I never knew."

He has a proper hard-on now. Feels like he's stroking solid oak.

"I can barely get my mouth around it. Ohh, Franky." She's overcome with lust.

"I need to fuck you, Franky."

She slides down her soaked bikini bottom and straddles him. Her tits are in his face and she starts to ride him, moaning, a little in pain.

"Franky, Franky."

Franky brings his other hand up to a slender, suddenly smallish breast.

"Franky."

Her voice sounds tender now. They're not rutting anymore, they're making love. She holds his face with her tiny fingers. She leans down and kisses him. He can't see her face, can only feel her soft brown hair on his chest. She's a sprite on top of him, the littlest thing.

"Tina," Franky whispers.

He ejaculates and a muted sensation ripples through him, more release than euphoria. The wave loosens his muscles, easing the tension in his neck and shoulders but leaving a hollow feeling — scooped out and shameful — in its wake. He can't bear to look at himself in the mirror. He runs the faucet and cleans the sperm off the sink basin. He turns on the shower and steps in, even though the water hasn't warmed yet. The shock of the cold water is punitive, pleasing in its way. He dips his head under the stream, lets it bombard the back of his neck.

He didn't even feel like drinking yesterday. A few pops to ease the spike in his head and then a nap, maybe watch the night games at home and catch up on some rest.

But then he ran into Denny and Tommy and one thing led to another and the day slid away from him.

He needs to calm it down. He's been on a toot, which is fine; he planned it anyway. Has always taken the first two days of the tournament off, the way Bobby and he used to. But then he got ahead of himself, started on Wednesday night with a few of the boys from work, guys he doesn't even really like, but fuck it, he'll drink a coupla beers with any thirsty soul. Got a little more banged up than he anticipated and then strolled into St. Paddy's Day still jaunty and tasting whiskey in the back of his throat, rolled right into it and then no fucking pool and who wouldn't need a few stiff ones to get over that and there we go. A good time, he needed it, no doubt about that, but he needs to calm it down a little and he will. He'll be fine.

The problem is he's still drinking like he's on the bump, but he's not on the bump, hasn't been for six months. He's drinking and nothing else, so he's drinking too fast and without the adrenaline boost to boot.

He steps out of the shower, grabs a towel. That's exactly what he needs right now: a little bump, something to put a shine on the day, chase away these stupid fucking blues.

He's got nothing in the apartment. Probably for the best. One good bump begets another.

He needs a day or two off from the sauce to clear his head, which is fine because he needs to go to the mall today anyway to get something for little Bobby's birthday. The thought of taking the bus depresses him and he can't fathom spending thirty bucks on a cab, not when he's seven hundred in the hole. There's only one person he can cajole into driving him to the mall.

He picks up his cell and dials Kieran's number.

"Hello?"

"Fuckwad."

"Who is this?"

"Fuckwad."

"Franky?"

"Who do you think, fuckwad?"

"Stop calling me that."

"Okay, cocksnot."

"You're an asshole, Franky."

"Whatever you say, fuckwad."

"I'm hanging up, Franky."

"Whatever you gotta do, fuckwad."

The line goes dead. Franky chuckles to himself. Tormenting Kieran Kielty is one of the few things he still takes pleasure in. Kieran is an old friend of Bobby's, one of his charity cases. A sad sack, a lost soul. He graduated in the same class as Peter, but was still keeping the book at high school basketball games when Bobby was a senior. One time, he showed up for an Amendola family Super Bowl party with a half-empty box of white powdered doughnuts as his contribution; everyone pretended not to notice the white powder caked in the corners of his mouth and sprinkled down the front of his shirt. He was fat and disheveled and kind of a whiny pain in the ass, but Bobby always included him; he even made him part of his wedding party. After Bobby was killed, Franky took it upon himself to look in on Kieran, treat him the way Bobby would have.

Well, maybe not exactly the way Bobby would have.

Still, he made it a point to hang out with Kieran every few months, go to a movie or take him to dinner, even invite him over when the whole family got together for Sunday dinners.

But in the past few years, the fat fuck had somehow managed to convince a girl to marry him, get promoted at his job, even buy a house. Now when they hung out together, it seemed like Kieran was doing Franky a favor instead of the other way around. So every once in a while, Franky had to put him in his place, restore the natural order of things. He'd wait a few minutes, then call Kieran again, semi-apologize, and bribe the fat bastard by offering to buy him lunch. Worked every time.

The phone rings and Franky answers reflexively.

"Fuckwad! Back so soon?"

"Francis?"

Only his mom calls him Francis.

"Hey, Mom, what's up?" he says, sheepish.

"Who were you expecting?"

"Joking around with Kieran Kielty."

"How is Kieran?"

His mother has a soft spot for Kieran, but she would have asked after whomever he mentioned, no matter who it was. He and Bobby used to joke about it.

And how is Adolf doing? Still have that silly mustache?

"He's fine."

"And Megan?"

How the fuck should he know how Kieran Kielty's wife was?

"Fine, I think," he says, unable to hide his irritation. "What's up with you?"

"Out doing the shopping for tomorrow."

"What's on the menu?"

"Well, your father was gonna grill, but it looks like rain so it may be pasta and gravy. Some antipasto."

"Get those breadsticks that you wrap the salami around."

"I will."

"You heard about the pool?"

"Sad."

"Tell me about it."

A few beats pass. Franky can hear the sound of people ordering from a butcher's counter in the background.

"Everything all right, Franky?"

"Right as rain. Was wondering, what should I get little Bobby?"

"Oh, Franky, whatever you get, I'm sure he'll love."

"I know, but what's he into these days?"

"He's starting baseball in a few weeks. Tina says he's into dinosaurs again, but . . ."

Her voice trails off. A few more silent beats. It's his turn to ask.

"Mom, everything all right?"

"Listen, Franky, there's something I need to tell you."

"What's up?"

"Tina's bringing someone tomorrow."

His face feels hot, all of a sudden.

"Like a boyfriend?"

"Not 'like' a boyfriend. A boyfriend."

He stands up and walks into the kitchen, opens the fridge. One fucking Heineken? It'll have to do.

"You met this guy yet, Ma?"

"No, not yet."

The first swig of beer tastes like broken glass, but the second is manageable. The third is almost pleasant.

"It's a little fucked up that he's coming, no?"

"I'm not sure how I feel about it."

"I think it's fucked up."

"Well, we need to respect her wishes. It's her son's birthday and she thinks it's important that her friend is there."

"What's this asshole's name?"

"Franky, he's not an asshole." She waits a beat. "His name is Wade."

"Wade?" he says, as sarcastically as possible. "Let me guess, he's not a firefighter?"

"No. He's not."

"Not a cop, either."

"No."

"And with a name like Wade, he sure as shit isn't from the rock."

"No," she says, the wind kicked out of her sails.

"Of course not."

The fucking Heineken is empty and he's got nothing else, not even a drip of Jameson.

Or even Powers. He'd do a shot of paint thinner if he had it. He wants to punch the wall, punch it until his knuckles bleed and his bones crack. This is bullshit.

"He's a friend of your brother's."

"Bullshit. I know all of Bobby's friends. He doesn't have any . . ."

He realizes she's talking about Peter.

"He's a lawyer?"

"I'm not sure. I don't think so."

A friend of Peter's. Great. Another stuck-up asshole. Tomorrow was gonna be tough enough with Peter and his judgment and disapproval.

"Franky, I need you to do me a favor."

"What?" He nearly shouts at her.

Her voice lowers to a whisper.

"I need you to show up sober and I need you not to cause a scene."

His temples are pounding. He tries to coax another swig from the empty bottle.

"Was it really necessary to ask me that?" he say, knowing it probably was. Her disappointment is the one thing he cannot tolerate and they both know it.

"I'm sorry, Franky."

"Yeah," he says, searching for something to say. "Yeah, me too. I'm fucking sorry too."

He flings the phone onto the couch.

Fine. He'll be sober tomorrow. He'll be a

fucking saint.

But today is a different story.

By the time Kieran picks him up at Kelly's to drive him to the mall, Franky is four beers in and the day has been draped in a soft gray blanket. He has decided not to give a fuck about Wade or Tina or Peter or his mother; he'll make a day of it and fuck the rest. It's all bullshit anyway. When Kieran's busted blue Camry pulls in front of the bar, things are already looking up; he put four hundred on North Carolina minus three and they're up seven at the half. He does a quick shot for good measure before walking out into the harsh daylight of early after-noon.

"Christ, Kielty," he says as he gets into the passenger seat. "Is it possible that you're even fatter than the last time I saw you?"

Kieran looks out the side window, away from Franky. He takes his Coke-bottle glasses off with one hand and pinches his nose with the other. He *has* gotten fatter; he's wedged between the seat and the steer-ing wheel and the lower folds of his stomach are peeking out from below his powder blue golf shirt. His face is a sheen of greasy acne and his brown hair is pocked with yellowish-white spots.

"I'm not taking you unless you're nice to me," Kieran says, still facing the street. When he hears Kieran's voice, Franky realizes that he's close to tears.

"Kieran, Christ. I'm only busting balls. That's what friends do."

Kieran puts his glasses back on and wipes his nose with the back of his hand. A thin film of snot attaches to the meaty bulge where his thumb and index finger meet.

"Megan says that you're not a real friend to me. That you use me when you need me. Like today."

Franky doesn't need this, doesn't have the patience to reason with this whimpering half-wit. If he only had a fucking car. He swallows hard, puts a hand on Kieran's shoulder. He hopes no one inside Kelly's is watching through the window.

"Kieran. I'm sorry I was rude."

He tries to sound sincere. Kieran's eyes — huge and hopeful behind his glasses — shift toward him.

"It's all right. Megan doesn't think I stand up for myself."

The unabashed meekness of Kieran's voice makes Franky want to smack him. He reminds himself that Bobby loved Kieran, would have wanted him looked after.

"Megan doesn't know what the fuck she's

talking about. We've been friends for years. Remember when we went down to Atlantic City for the weekend? Or the night we ended up at FlashDancers and I paid that Russian chick to give you like, what? Twenty lap dances? Megan doesn't know about that, right?"

Kieran's face goes a shade whiter than usual.

"You're not gonna tell her?" he asks. It takes Franky a beat to recognize that his concern is serious.

"Jesus Christ, Kielty. Of course not. That's my whole fucking point." This was beyond useless; it was like talking to an infant. "Megan doesn't understand everything about how guys hang out. Like how guys bust each other's balls."

"I don't bust your balls, Franky."

"But you could, kemosabe. You could. And that would be fine."

He watches as the logic circulates through Kielty's enormous cranium, eventually turning his gray lips up into kind of a half smile. Franky smiles back.

"Okay?"

"Okay."

Kielty puts the keys in the ignition. He looks over at Franky again, his hand paused in mid-twist.

"You'll take me to Applebee's for lunch?"

Jesus H. Christ, Franky thinks, *that's exactly what you need. Another meal.*

But he nods agreeably.

"Applebee's. Chili's. McDonald's. Burger King. Whatever the fuck you want."

Kielty's smile expands. He turns the key and the car struggles to life. The fog of good cheer has been lifted during this conversation, a combination of Kielty's incessant simpering and the sunlight glaring off the hood. And the mall is a twenty-minute ride. Franky needs a restorative shot. Maybe two.

"Hold on, Kieran. We've been talking so long I need to piss."

He gets out of the car and walks back into Kelly's. He puts a crinkled ten on the bar and orders a Jameson. He checks the score in the Carolina game.

Tied with twelve minutes left. What the fuck happened?

The daytime bartender, some bald grump with no personality, pours the golden liquid into an impossibly small vessel. Franky downs it with a quick shift of the head, the whiskey tingling his lips and tongue.

He walks to the bathroom as the beer and the booze slosh around his otherwise empty stomach. He needs to eat something. He's getting ahead of himself. He's right back

474

where he was last night before the curtain fell: no pain, not a care in the world. He takes a long piss, one hand pressed against the wall.

He walks back to the bar, claps excitedly as a Carolina player nails a three. He needs another shot. One more will do the trick, keep the day rolling in the right direction. He watches the bartender pour the whiskey, watches as a meniscus forms at the lip of the glass.

"One more," he says as he lifts the shot glass. "One more then out the door."

By the time they reach the mall, Franky is furious. He spent the entire car ride listening to Kielty lament the end of the Cody's pool in the most simplistic, repetitive fashion imaginable. His buzz has started to drift and his stomach is in full protest after being ignored all morning. But it's not any of that.

It's his mother and her fucking favor. Show up sober and not cause a scene? Seriously, was that really necessary? Bobby's his nephew, his godson. Did she really think he would ruin the kid's fucking birthday? Wasn't he here now, at the goddamn mall of all fucking places suffering through the company of Kieran fucking Kielty, all so he could get the kid a proper present?

The whole thing could drive a saint to drink. And he was no saint. He knew that much about himself.

He hates the mall, hasn't been in years. Everywhere he looks, he sees the reasons why: chain-wearing guidos with spiked-up hair, over-tanned mothers in bright, skin-tight jumpsuits, a group of cocky black teenagers wearing red Yankee hats, the labels still attached, the brims as straight as diving boards. There are more Russians than the last time he was here, but that was no surprise; they were moving onto the Island in droves, always looking for beachfront property, no matter how shitty the beach. Thank God it was a Saturday. At least there wouldn't be any fucking Hasids.

He spots a Foot Locker a few storefronts down and heads for it. Kielty is a few paces behind him, trying to avoid cataclysmic collisions with other obese mall goers.

Then Franky sees something and, for a second, he thinks he's hallucinating. He shakes his head, but there they are: a cluster of women in hijabs, that tongue-clacking filth ricocheting between them. He stops walking as they approach. They float right through him, one momentarily disengaging from her two companions, stepping outside him and then returning to her friends after she passes him. He watches them glide away, only their feet visible beneath the long draping sheets.

Kielty catches up with him, follows his gaze.

"What's up, Franky?"

"Fucking Arabs?" he says, loudly.

"I guess."

"There are fucking Arabs at the Staten Island Mall now?"

A few passing teenage kids looked at him uncertainly, like maybe he's making a joke or they're being filmed. Kielty shrugs his shoulders, sending his entire upper torso jiggling.

"I guess."

Franky looks around, sees mostly regular people milling around, flitting into stores, carrying shopping bags, sipping from over-size Styrofoam cups. But in the cell phone store across from him, he notices an Arab with a mustache comparing cell phone chargers. He's wearing an old-fashioned New York Giants jacket, the once shiny blue now faded and dusty. A small, dark-skinned boy holds his hand.

Arabs in the Staten Island Mall. Un-fucking-believable.

"It's finally done. They finally destroyed it completely," he announces to Kielty and a handful of confused passersby. "This Island is completely and totally fucked."

He walks into Foot Locker, hands raised in exasperation.

"Look, they have the new 'Melo jerseys," Kielty says, holding up a kid's blue and orange jersey so Franky can see. "These are pretty sweet. Little Bobby'd love this."

Franky eyes it doubtfully. He feels better now that he's in the Foot Locker, surrounded by sneakers and mesh shorts and all the other accoutrements of athletic endeavor. He feels like an athlete even though he hasn't shot a ball, not even men's league, in five years. Somehow, in here, it doesn't matter. His belief that all he needs is a new pair of kicks and five weeks to train and he could be back in game shape seems reasonable in this place. The tools are available; all he has to do is decide to do it.

Plus, Carolina covered, cutting into the hole he's in. The day is maybe halfway salvageable. He shakes his head at the Carmelo jersey.

"Can't do it, Double K. Every gindaloon on the South Shore will be wearing one. Every fat little Ant'nee who fancies himself a baller will be rocking this."

A little frown from Kielty.

"What?"

"You're Italian. So is Bobby Jr. So was Bobby."

"Half Italian, but not a gindaloon. Half Irish, but not a fucking donkey either. It's not complicated, Kielty. Don't hurt yourself thinking."

"I'm hungry," says Kieran, partly to deflect Franky, but mostly because it's true.

"Me too, Double K. Thirsty as well."

He spies another jersey, a throwback number 33 with Ewing stenciled on the back. He takes it from the rack.

"This is the winner. Old school."

"Will he know who Patrick Ewing is?"

"Doesn't matter. His pop's favorite player."

"I don't know, Franky. Is he even a Knicks fan?"

" 'Course he is. He's from New York."

"Yeah, but the Knicks have sucked for basically his whole life."

"Doesn't matter, Kielty. You root for your teams, no matter what. You don't jump on and off the bandwagon when it's convenient."

"I know, but he's a kid."

"So?"

"So maybe he likes a different team."

"Like who?"

"Like the Heat."

Kielty holds up a Miami Heat jersey, the name WADE in black letters on the back. Wade. He'd nearly forgotten about Tina's new friend. What the fuck kind of name was Wade anyway? A douche bag's name. His throat is dry and he can feel his leg twitching.

"I'm not getting him a fucking Heat jersey like some goddamn front-runner," he yells, startling Kielty, who quickly puts the offending jersey back.

"Okay, Jesus, Franky. It was just a suggestion."

"Here's a suggestion: shut the fuck up."

Franky stomps to the register, clutching the Ewing jersey. He drops it on the counter and gives the girl manning the register a smile. She has a bit of a horse face, and her black hair is pulled back in a severe ponytail, making her face seem even longer. Skin is almost orange. Franky can't decide whether she's attractive or hideous. Maybe a little of both. He really needs to get laid.

She lifts the tag with long, pink fingernails and swipes the gun over the bar code.

"Fifty-two, twenty-seven," she says between snaps of her gum.

"For my nephew," Franky says as he reaches for his wallet. She smiles, bored. He pulls out a credit card and hands it to her.

"Excuse me," says an accented voice from behind him, "is this on sale?"

Franky turns and the Arab in the ratty Giants jacket is standing there, holding a baseball glove. The young boy stands obediently at his side.

"You're gonna have to ask a salesperson," says the girl.

Franky stares daggers at the guy, hoping the man will say something to him. He'd love a fight. God, would he love a fight. To grab this filthy fucking Arab's head and slam it into something. Nothing would make him feel better. When he slammed that cabbie's head onto the hood of his own car, he'd felt a rush stronger than anything the bump had ever given him. Every violent impulse he'd ever had succumbed to in one cleansing moment. So he'd done it again and again and once more, for good measure. None of the bullshit afterward mattered: not his mother or Peter, not the handcuffs or the courtroom. It was a worthwhile trade. Standing over that terrorist sack of shit as he bled into his own hands and prayed for mercy from his worthless god. He would do it again. He would do it today.

And how did that start? With words. He was walking away, skipping the fare, but walking away, and then the dumb shit opened his mouth.

You are disgrace to your mother.

Am I now?

Words could lead there. That's what he wants now. He wants this guy to say something. Anything. He needs this, more than a drink or a snort or a fuck.

Please, Lord, he thinks, let this guy say something to me.

He takes a half step closer to the man.

"Please, they told me to ask you," says the man, his eyes darting between the girl and Franky.

"She said to ask a salesperson, you filthy camel fucker," Franky says, leaning into the guy. The man moves his son to the other side of his body, putting himself between Franky and the kid. Franky can hear Kielty behind him, breathing heavy and nervous. He can see fear in the man's eyes, can sense it even coming from the girl behind the counter. Everyone's nervous but him. His body has adjusted to the adrenaline surge. He's humming, keyed up, ready to go. He smiles at the man, a nasty, derisive lip curl.

"Let's get out of here, Franky," says Kielty. "C'mon, they're gonna call security."

"Say something," he says to the man, whose son is hiding behind him now. "Say something."

The man doesn't respond. He keeps one hand on his son and raises the other like he is trying to soothe a wild dog.

"Say something," Franky says. He can feel tears starting to slide from the corners of his eyes. He knows the man won't say anything. The blood in his body starts to throb less insistently.

"Franky, please," says Kielty.

He reaches over and grabs the plastic shopping bag that holds his nephew's birthday gift. He turns and walks out of the store without speaking, the sudden emptiness in his chest in desperate need of liquid attention.

At a table near the bar, surrounded by faux sports memorabilia and bargain-basement kitsch, Franky watches Kielty devour a plate of buffalo wings, unsure whether he should be disturbed or impressed. The fat fuck simply inserts a blue cheese–slathered piece into his maw and then removes a scrap or two of bone, his teeth somehow having shorn the wing of all meat and flesh and sauce. It doesn't even matter whether the piece is a drumette or one of those annoying rectangular pieces with two bones; Kielty is a machine. His face is covered with orange buffalo sauce. Some things, at least, never change.

Franky chuckles, drains his mug.

"You're a piece of work, Kielty."

"What?" he says as he uses a small army of mini wipes to clean his hands.

"Applebee's? Where we going next, Olive Garden?"

"I like Olive Garden."

Franky flags down a waitress, orders another beer.

"You want another?"

"I'm driving. I'll have a Diet Coke."

"Some fucking drinking buddy you are."

The waitress leaves with their orders. She isn't much to look at, but Franky finds himself checking out her ass as she walks away. Christ, he really, really needs to get laid. He turns back to Kielty.

"The one thing you can get on Staten Island, no questions asked, any time, day or night, is fantastic, out-of-this-world Italian food. And yet, you like Olive Garden."

Kielty shovels some blue cheese into his mouth with a piece of celery.

"I like their never-ending pasta bowl with the spaghetti Alfredo."

"That's exactly what you need."

The waitress drops off his beer in a fresh mug, thinly encrusted in ice. He hates this place, but the beer is damn cold. He orders another. If he has to drink alone, he'll set a proper pace. He looks at television over the bar. He bet the second half over in the Florida State game, but it doesn't look like much has happened. A dopey white kid with a floppy haircut sinks a foul shot. If the over comes in, he'll lay one more bet, try to get flat.

"When are you opening up your bar?"

"Me and Denny Hogan were talking about that yesterday. Gotta pick the right spot. Would love to be on Forest, but maybe Victory could work. He looked at a place down by the ferry, but I don't know with the projects and all."

"Staten Island Yankees games could bring in business."

"How many games do they play a year? Twenty, thirty tops?"

"It's something."

"Yeah, guess so. Maybe. I don't know."

He doesn't tell Kielty that he still needs to come up with most of his end. He's managed to save a little since he got off the blow, but he's still almost sixty grand short. He was thinking about asking Peter for a loan, but the thought of the sanctimonious lecture that would accompany the money is too depressing. He can't handle that bullshit.

Plus, Peter might say no. He takes a sip from his mug. No sense ruining the day thinking about this.

The waitress brings another full mug to the table, places it behind Franky's half-drained one.

"Hold on, doll," he says before he empties his mug. "Save you a trip."

"Thirsty boy," she says as she picks up his discard. She isn't bad looking after all. Her eyes are a little too big or maybe just too close together, and she has curly hair, which isn't his cup of tea, but if you were in a poke, she'd do for a poke. Any port in a storm.

"They talk of my drinking, doll, but never my thirst."

It's an old line but reliable. She laughs.

"Next one's on me," she says over her shoulder as she drifts away.

He feels good. A little flirting never hurt the old confidence. And the rest of his day is wide open. Nothing to do but ease into the sunset. Maybe take a certain waitress home for some proper rogering.

He checks the score of the game. He needs seventeen more points. Five minutes left. Tough but doable. A Florida State player banks in a three as the shot clock is running down. He'll take it. Fourteen points. Four minutes, thirty odd seconds.

His cell phone vibrates in his pocket. He checks the caller ID: Mom. Fuck that. She was out of line and she knows it. That why she's calling. Let her stew in her own guilt.

The waitress arrives with their burgers. Franky was starving before, but the beers have dulled his appetite. He picks at a few fries, Kielty dives into his burger. Franky raises his empty mug at the waitress.

The other team, Kent State, is down twelve with three minutes. They need to start fouling and he needs ten more points. All he needs is a few made fouls shots by Florida State and some quick shots by Kent State. A Florida State player bricks the front end of a one and one.

"Goddamn it. Hit your fucking foul shots."

The waitress deposits the mug in front of him.

"Good luck," she says with a smile.

"I need all I can get, doll."

Kent State misses a three, fouls immediately. Double bonus now. He still needs ten. Two and a half minutes. The same player — an enormous power forward with hands like stone — steps to the line. His first shot doesn't even hit the rim. Air ball.

"What the fuck? Can't anyone shoot foul

shots anymore?"

Kielty struggles to rotate his head around the flabby mass of his shoulder so he can look at the game. He turns back to Franky, a sudden sincerity creasing his face.

"Franky."

Stone-hands somehow makes his second free throw and the point guard on Kent State dashes up the court for a quick layup. Two minutes and change. He needs seven.

"Franky."

"What?"

Kent State fouls right away. Television time-out.

"I think you were out of order before."

"What?"

"I said you were out of order at the mall with that guy."

Franky's eyes shift from the television down to Kielty.

"Excuse me?"

"I think you went over the line. The guy was with his kid."

Franky glares at him until Kielty looks down at his shoes.

"Jesus Christ, Kielty. You're worried about the feelings of future terrorists? You are one sorry, misguided soul."

Kielty takes a doleful bite of his burger. He can't stay angry at such a pitiful fuck.

"Besides, you were a little out of order yourself."

Kielty looks up.

"No, I wasn't."

"No, no, no, no, no. You insulted him a little bit. You were a little out of order yourself."

Kielty stares at him, dumbfounded.

"*GoodFellas?* DeNiro? The shine box scene?" Franky says.

"I never saw it," Kielty says quietly before taking another bite of his burger.

Franky shakes his head in mock solemnity.

"Jesus, Mary, and Joseph, Kielty. I mean, really. I don't even know where to begin."

He remembers the game, turns back to it, and does some quick math. He needs two more points. Thirty seconds left and Florida State has the ball, but Kent State isn't fouling. Florida State is going to run the clock out.

"Oh fuck. You have to be fucking kidding me."

"What?" says Kielty.

The game clock whittles down to single digits.

"Don't do this to me. Don't fucking do this."

He's gonna lose, be right back where he started the day, plus the vig. With three seconds left, the ball is passed to some benchwarmer, only in the game because the outcome is no longer in doubt. No one even bothers to guard him. He takes two lazy dribbles and nonchalantly flicks up a jumper from fifteen feet. Nothing but net. The second half over comes in.

"*Yesss!* C'mon now, son."

He stands and throws a halfhearted punch that smacks Kielty's shoulder.

"Ouch. Jesus, Franky."

Kielty rubs his shoulder, pouting. Frank leans in, hisses in his ear.

"Yeaaaaah, muthafucker."

The waitress arrives with a fresh mug of beer. He takes a hearty pull, laughs at his own good fortune.

"Aren't we a happy camper?"

Franky smiles.

"We are indeed. Sweetheart, you don't, by any rare chance, have a cigarette I could bum?"

"Your lucky day," she says, pulling a pack out of her waitress apron.

"It's starting to feel that way."

Outside, it smells like rain. The sun has disappeared behind a drift of smoke-colored clouds and the wind has some bite. Franky wishes he'd thrown on something more than a pair of gray sweatpants and a T-shirt. He takes a drag of the cigarette, looks out over to Fresh Kills, where the dump used to be, where they sifted through the remains from the towers, where the city is planning to put an enormous green space. There was a time when this whole area smelled like garbage, when people walked out of the crisp, air-conditioned mall only to have their nostrils invaded by the scent of rotting cabbage. Or worse.

The dump seemed like a curse at the time, its fetid stench drifting over the whole Island on hot summer days. But that time seems sacred now. Innocent. Before, well, before everything. Having to live with the smell of garbage seems quaint. Beats living in the shadow of things that once were.

Christ, he misses Bobby. More today than in a long while. He misses him every day, but on certain days, the hole is so clearly defined that he can almost feel it being traced on his chest. Bobby would have understood the appeal of letting the after-noon drift away on a sea of beer. He would have laughed and celebrated the absurd backdoor cover at the buzzer. And he sure as shit would have picked up on the *Good-Fellas* reference. He would be standing next to Franky now, looking out over the hundreds of shiny cars parked next to a sea of covered shit, and laughing.

Actually, no, he wouldn't. He'd be inside, fuming, and Tina would be out here, smoking with Franky. A little buzzed herself. Flirting. Nothing serious. A conviviality, an understanding, that didn't need to be spoken. Like brother and sister but not quite. The tiniest hint of something else. How could there not be? She loved Bobby and he was Bobby's brother. There would have to be something there, would almost be unnatural if there wasn't. They would share a vice, share some laughs, and then walk back in together to his brother and her husband, whose cheeks would be tinted red with jealousy.

He could have stepped in, could have helped Tina with the kids at least. But after that night on his couch, she kept him at arm's length. And then everything happened: Thanksgiving at Peter's house, the arrest. That was all years ago now. She could have given him another chance, given him an opportunity to show that he had changed. Instead, she's with some asshole named Wade.

He takes a last drag, drops the cigarette to the ground, and steps on it. He checks the message his mother left on his cell.

"Franky, I'm sorry about before. I'm sure you've been doing much better and I'm proud of you. I'll see you tomorrow."

He holds the phone open, trying to decide whether he should call her back and make things right. Tell her how much he misses Bobby.

He knows his mother; Gail Amendola is a woman very familiar with the effects of alcohol on the men in her life. He's had enough to drink that she'll notice, even over the phone. He can't talk to her now, in his condition, though when he's in this condition is the one time when he can nearly articulate his loneliness, the one time when he feels reckless enough to reveal the scar on his soul, to let her know what a mess he is.

He closes the phone, turns back to walk inside.

What could she say anyway? What could she possibly say that she hasn't already said?

In his absence, Kielty has asked for the check. His wife needs the car and they need to run some errands, he explains to Franky sheepishly, expecting a tongue-lashing. Franky yawns, feels the fatigue of three days closing in on him. This is one of those times, when all the signals are aligned together, indicating that the sensible thing to do would be to simply go home and go to sleep.

He's exhausted. His ride is ready to go. He's had enough but not too much. The melancholy is coming on. It's still early. He could even nap, maybe go out later if the mood struck. Even his thirsty side can't argue with that logic.

"Okay," he says, in a rare surrender to common sense. "Okay, Special K, let's go home."

He checks the damage, throws down a few twenties. When he stands, his legs feel heavy, soaked through with some coagulant. He follows Kielty to the door. He's about to walk out when he feels a tap on his shoulder.

He turns to find their waitress holding the plastic bag from Foot Locker.

"You forgot something," she says with a busted smile.

"Thanks," says Franky, taking the bag back into his hands.

"You guys leaving already?"

"Yeah, Kielty here has to get home to the wife."

"What about you? You need to get home to the wife?"

He looks down at her. She's short, barely comes up to his chest.

"Not me. I'm footloose and fancy-free."

"I get off in a couple hours. I was thinking maybe you'd buy me a drink."

"A couple hours?"

"You could wait at the bar."

Franky glances over, spots the bartender pouring a gold-colored draft into a mug. It looks glorious under the yellow light. He looks back at the waitress. He still can't decide whether she's cute, but he would definitely fuck her.

"I'm Denise," she says, flicking a strand of dirty-blond curls behind her ear.

A coltish breath fills his lungs. He can feel the day pulling him back: the prospect of some pussy, the allure of another half dozen drafts, the nirvana of not giving a fuck. What's waiting for him at home anyway? A piss-soaked bed.

"Franky, I need to go," Kielty pleads.

"*Vaya con Dios,* Special K. I'm gonna stay for a while. Thanks for the ride."

He gives Kielty a hearty slap on the back. Denise spins away, still smiling. Franky walks back to the bar, his whole being reinvigorated by a powerful second wind.

The afternoon takes on a sheen. Beers slide down Franky's throat, each one easing the passage of its followers. Minutes compress, then slip away en masse. A few expand, he counts one silently while inspecting a coaster with a fascination usually reserved for rare archaeological artifacts.

The bartender, Harold, is a surly prick, which would be fine if this were some old-school joint, but it's not. It's a fucking Applebee's so Harold should be happy beyond measure. But then again, hey, it's an Applebee's, so Franky feels for the guy. He's not so bad after all. He buys Franky a round. Long time coming, but still. Harold's all right by Franky.

Denise flits by from time to time, checking in on him. He's starting to slur, just a little, but he's fine. He sticks to beer, his buzz settles into a steady, floating euphoria. He bums a few more cigarettes from Denise, smokes them outside. He calls the bookie service. His balance is under two hundred. He lays seven hundred — doesn't think about the amount, just says it — on UCLA minus three and a half. Isn't even sure who they're playing. He walks back in, realizes the daylight is dying.

He navigates his way back to the bar. The place emptied out in the late afternoon but is filling back up for the dinner rush. He tries to make small talk with some guy at the bar, but the guy is a fucking loser. The ends of his fingers start to go numb. He thinks that maybe the people around him are staring at him, but he isn't sure. He pushes his empty mug across the bar at Harold. The beer is getting him nowhere fast.

"A wee one, Harold," he says when Harold puts his refilled mug down. "Mr. John Jameson."

Harold pours him a stiff one in a rocks glass, a double gulper. The whiskey clutches his chest and lands hard in his stomach. He swallows twice, tastes vomit climbing up the back of his throat. The urge to puke passes, stifled by will alone. He swallows again, feels better. He takes a sip of beer and when he turns, Denise plops on the stool next to him, her shift finally finished.

She doesn't want to drink where she works, so Franky leaves a ten on the bar for Harold and they leave. It's dark outside, a nearly full moon is slung low in the sky. Franky follows Denise to her car, a little unsteady in the dimmed light. When he gets in the passenger seat, Franky realizes he's well beyond buzzed. He's drunk, dancing near the cliff of a blackout. His thoughts are fuzzy and flickering and he cannot hold them. He doesn't want to speak, can't speak. His tongue is thick with drink. Denise looks over at him, incipient disappointment creasing the corners of her mouth.

What did she expect? She saw how he was drinking.

"You okay?"

"I'm fine," he replies with a roll of his neck.

"Little buzzed?"

"A little."

His voice doesn't sound right, it sounds like its coming from the back of his head, not his mouth. He cracks the window.

"Just need some fresh air."

She smiles and he can see, even in his state, hope trying to fight off doubt. She's lonely, he can tell. Who else would invest a Saturday night in his drunken ass? Now he feels bad about what hasn't even happened yet, about ruining this unlucky soul's night. He makes a silent vow to make Denise — lovely, kind Denise — happy in some small way.

"I'm fine," he says again. "Let's hit it. The night is young."

She starts the car.

"Where to?"

"You pick."

He can rally, he's roused himself from a stupor before. He needs to catch his breath. Maybe they're going someplace far. The drive will do him good. The car smells nice.

Denise's bed probably smells nice too. Soft pillows. He winks at Denise and his eyelid fights to stay lowered. He chuckles.

"What is that anyway?"

"What?"

"The bag."

Franky looks down at the plastic bag in his lap, unsure what it holds. He opens it and sees the Knicks jersey.

"A gift for my nephew. My godson. It's his birthday."

She purrs in response and this irritates him.

"How old is he?"

"Nine. He's gonna be nine."

Suddenly, the car feels too small and he knows there will be no rally. He's had too much, the damage is done. He's stumbling closer to the edge, sending pebbles into the darkness. He shouldn't have done that shot. Inkiness seeps into his head, obscuring things, hiding patches of time. The needle skips.

They're at a bar, sitting at a table. He doesn't recognize the place, doesn't remember getting here. Is he crying? He is. And Denise is staring across at him, pitying and horrified. He lurches to his feet, nearly stumbles. The room spins, a kaleidoscope of faces, contorted and twisted.

He is in the bathroom staring at the floor, trying to steady the world. The latticework between the floor tiles is lifting off the ground, tiny ghost lines vibrating in the air. Someone is staring at him. He is on the floor, struggling to rise. The man reaches down to help him.

"I'm fine," he hears himself say.

The sink and mirror. Water on the face. A hand on his back. A demonic smile in the mirror. His own.

In the backseat of a car. Where is Denise? Gone.

"Bitch."

"What?"

Franky follows the sound of the voice to the front seat. Someone is driving this car. A fat man wearing a Yankees hat. Listening to The Doors. Waiting at a red light.

"Take me to Kelly's."

"I think your night is done, buddy."

"Fuck you, fatso."

The car screeches to a halt. The driver moves well for a fat man. Some hand wrestling at the door. A kick or two. Laughing and heavy breathing. A blow to the head. Out. Onto the ground. Flesh of the face meeting gravel. Stinging pain, felt through the haze. The fat man throws a plastic bag at him. The car tears off.

Up. To his feet.

"FUCK YOU, FAT MAN."

A black boy on a bike, arms resting on handlebars.

"Yo, fat man fucked you up."

He lurches but the boy glides off, effortlessly, laughing. He leans down for the bag, starts walking.

Walking, walking. Trees and darkness, a park. Face feels torn below the eye. Crying again. He has been wronged. So terribly wronged. He doesn't remember the details, knows only that he has been wronged. An injustice committed. Someone will pay. Someone has to pay. Who?

More walking. He watches his feet move below him. Left, right. Left, right.

The fog is starting to lift. Everything is being recorded, albeit on grainy film by a negligent observer. He sees a street sign, knows where he is now.

Forest Avenue. Kelly's isn't far.

He sits at a bar. The world has returned to him and he to it. He is beyond drunkenness, has reached a state of numbness so complete it resembles sobriety. He lifts his mug to his bloodied lips and the beer slides in.

"Another one, Franky?" asks Pat. A friendly face in a storm. No judgment here.

He nods, lifts a towel filled with ice to his torn cheek.

He feels a fingernail jab his right triceps.

"I knew your brotha."

"What?" he says, shifting the towel below his eye so he can see who's talking to him. A woman with spiky blond hair in a butch cut, built like a softball player. Something alluring in the face, despite a stud in the nose. Not lacking for confidence. She was pretty once.

"Your brotha, Bobby." She jabs his triceps again, which bears a tattoo. ROBERT E. AMENDOLA. RIP. 9/11/01. NEVER FORGET.

He shifts in his stool to face her. Her eyes float up to meet his. She's almost as drunk as he is. A kindred spirit.

"You knew Bobby?"

"Yup." She takes a sip of her vodka drink. She leans in. "I gave him a blow job in the back room of the Leaf."

Franky snorts.

"Was that back when you liked boys?"

She punches his shoulder.

"Be nice, asshole."

"What's your name?"

"Chrissy Nolan."

"Patty Nolan's little sister?"

"That's right, muthafucker."

She gives him a sloppy high five.

"Well, Patty Nolan's sister, you're a fucking liar. My brother never . . ."

Before he can finish, she leans over and sticks her tongue in his mouth. The movement knocks the ice out of the towel and the pieces fall to the floor. He kisses her back, roughly. He can taste his own blood in his mouth, but she doesn't seem to care. They make out, unabashed, for what seems like hours. The rest of the bar is watching them, but he doesn't care. He needs this, needs someone to take care of him, to tend to his wounds.

She licks the lobe of his ear, whispers into it.

"Let's go to my place."

"Let's go," he says.

Another car ride. Teeth and tongues. Giggling and groping. A stranger's room. Soft light. An urgency, clothes removed. The exhilaration of unfamiliar flesh. Something sad and sordid drifting below the scene. The fleeting revelation of penetration, staggered thrusting. Over and done with.

Sleep, that dogged hit man, finally catches

his quarry, puts his man down.

He's climbing behind Peter. Bobby is behind them, anxious. A narrow tunnel. He can see light from above filtering around Peter's body. Bobby's fingers touch his calf in the darkness. This has already happened. Not like this but almost.

"Where are you guys? This isn't funny. I'm scared."

Bobby's finger taps his calf. Franky laughs, puts a finger to his lips. Crouching and hiding, shorts and scabby knees.

"We can't leave him, Franky. Mom'll be pissed."

"Pussy."

"Where are you guys?"

Tap on the calf. Lifting the leg, leaving him in the dark.

"C'mon, guys."

On the bikes, Peter looking over his shoulder.

"We should go back."

"Pussy."

An impulse, nothing more. Some devilish whim, succumbed to.

"Where's Bobby?"

Eyes down.

"Where's your brother?"

The sun not set, not yet, but going. He shrugs.

"Peter, where's your brother?"

She knows who to ask.

"We left him."

"WHAT? You did WHAT?"

Her face crimson with rage. Clutching the keys, out the door. A slow turn of the head.

"What if she doesn't find him?"

"Don't be such a pussy."

Waiting, waiting. The sun below the horizon, the light dying. Waiting. The phone rings, startling the conspirators. Peter answers.

"Hello?"

"She's not home right now."

"Good-bye."

Tears on his face. Waiting. The street is a dark rug, tiny strands of light weaving through it. Waiting. Nothing. Darker still. Nothing. The light is gone. Still no Bobby. No car lights flashing in the street.

He kneels, an impromptu confessional, might buy him a reprieve.

Bless me, Father, for I have sinned. I left my brother Bobby at the beach.

"Shut up, Franky. You're drunk," Peter says, softly, with a smile. He's older, wearing a sweater, ready to carve the roast.

"I know what you're all thinking." His

voice, older, but the boy waits. "I know what you're all thinking."

The words preordained, rehearsed, already spoken. The déjà vu of all dreams.

"I mean it, Franky, leave. Now."

A car on the street turning into the driveway. Waiting.

"Franky, stop it, please," Tina says from the other room. "Please."

The sound of a car door slamming. One door.

"It's what you've all been thinking for years, since the day it happened."

The doorknob turning. He's scared now, more frightened than he's ever been. The door opens. His mother. Alone.

"Where's Bobby?"

"I couldn't find him."

"It should have been me, that's what you're all thinking. Say it."

Don't say it.

"Out, Franky. Get out of my house."

"You wish it was me. Not Bobby. Say it."

Don't say it. Please don't say it.

"Where's Bobby?"

"I couldn't find him."

"*Say it,* Tina, you can say it. You should say it."

His mother walks in, kneels down, holds his cheeks with her hands.

"Say it, Mom. I know you want to. You wish it was me. You wish it had been me, instead of Bobby. Say it."

Don't say it.

His teeth crack in his mouth, drift into the air. Her voice is steady, an arrow in flight.

"You're right."

Franky opens his eyes. He's on the edge of a small bed, pushed there by Chrissy Nolan's awkward bulk and selfish sleeping habits. His bloody cheek is stuck to the bedsheet; he pulls it away delicately but it still stings. He slides out of bed, in search of the bathroom. He stumbles in pain. He looks down, spots an ugly raspberry on his thigh; he must have landed on that as well.

He inspects his face in the mirror. His left cheek is shredded, oozing yellow and puckered red. With his pinky, he pries a small black pebble out of it. His left eye is swollen nearly shut. How the hell is he gonna explain this? Fuck it, worry about it later.

He takes a piss. His prick is tender. She was enthusiastic, he remembers that much. Maybe he should stay, try to sleep a little more, go another round with Chrissy in a few hours.

Something she said last night is gnawing

at him, about giving Bobby a blow job. No fucking way Bobby would have fooled around with that skank. No fucking way. He was only ever with Tina. If anyone would know whether Bobby got a BJ in the back room of the Leaf, it would be Franky. He has half a mind to stick around to make sure the bitch isn't spreading false rumors.

No, he should go. Get out while the getting's good. He has little Bobby's birthday party later.

The present! Where the fuck is the present?

He sneaks back into the bedroom. Nothing. He goes to the kitchen, naked and cold. On the counter next to the fridge sits the plastic bag holding Bobby's present. Small mercies.

He moves quietly back to the bedroom. Chrissy hasn't moved an inch, is still snoring like a bear. He grabs his clothes from the floor. He dresses hastily, clumsily, in the kitchen; grabs the bag, shoves his feet into his sneakers, and leaves.

He walks out into gray silence. He looks around, unsure where he is. All he knows for sure is that he's still on the Island; they didn't cross water last night. At the end of the street, a stoplight switches needlessly from green to yellow to red. He follows the sidewalk up to the intersection, rain finding its way to him through the barren branches of trees. When he reaches the corner, he can sense the sun slowly rising behind the clouds.

Another day, infected by all that preceded it.

CHAPTER 9
ALL TOMORROW'S PARTIES

A drizzly Sunday, a day to stay in bed. Michael obliges, but Gail cannot. She has one last thing to do. She drives to the beach.

She's been avoiding this all week, sparing herself the anguish. Losing herself in daydreams. She can't put it off any longer. This afternoon, Tina is bringing a man to her house and she cannot let this man — this *stranger* — cross her threshold without telling Bobby. He has to know.

She winds her way through Gateway park down to the little spit of land that juts out into the bay. She parks the car and steps out into a cool spray; the wind pushes rain in from the bay. A bit of fog obscures the water, but she can hear the gentle lapping of the tide. She looks across the inlet to the marina. Boats sway gently in their docks. A few gulls fly idly overhead. Two other cars in the lot, but not a soul in sight. Still places on this Island where you can achieve a bit of solitude, lose yourself.

She found him here once, red-eyed and furious. A scared little boy. His older brothers played a prank, left him behind. The typical boy nonsense — two older brothers picking on the runt of the litter — but with a hint of real cruelty. It was Franky's idea, Peter the reluctant co-conspirator. She found him on the beach, crying in the darkness. So angry.

"Why?" he asked. "Why did they do it?"

One of those questions. He may as well have asked her about the cruelty of life. And then she realized that he had. She held him and he sobbed into her chest. Held him as some tiny, tender part of him turned to stone. Only a sliver, but still.

She cleaned him up, took him for a cone, drove him home in the front seat. She told him to slink down in the seat as they pulled into the driveway. A second prank, crueler on account of the prankster. But she had a lesson to impart. She told Franky she couldn't find Bobby, even though he was safe and secure, giggling in the car in the driveway.

Wisdom *is* cruelty, thinly disguised. She often thinks she lost Franky that night. He didn't stop sobbing for hours, not even when it was clear that Bobby was fine. After that little escapade, Peter kept Franky and his bad ideas at a distance. Drifted away from his brother, as he would later drift away from the whole family. Nothing dramatic, nothing formal. A simple recognition: Franky was an anchor, not someone he wanted to be tied to. Best to leave him alone.

Bobby, bless him, went the other way. Forgave Franky, almost immediately, and they soon became thick as thieves. Stayed that way, more or less, until Bobby was killed.

As for Franky himself, it was like she'd alerted him to his capacity for cruelty, alerted him to his true nature. That's how she thinks of it, never mind that he woke up the next morning like nothing had happened. Went straight back to the same song and dance.

To be a mother is to blame yourself. Take on their failings so they don't have to. Her little lesson caused all of Franky's problems. A fine bit of nonsense. Bullshit of the finest grain. She knows that.

But the look on his face when she walked in alone . . .

Damn it.

She's getting distracted, excoriating herself over Franky. Wasn't Peter there as well? He shook it off: took his punishment, apologized, and moved on. Doesn't matter. This isn't about Franky. Or Peter.

She needs to tell Bobby. He deserves this time with her, alone, without his brothers.

She talks to him all the time. In the house, in the car. Whenever she needs to. Nothing profound. Just a chat, like he was sitting beside her. Sometimes she thinks the words; sometimes she says them out loud, softly. Michael has caught her a few times, in mid-sentence; looked around the room to make sure he wasn't crazy, that there wasn't actually someone there he couldn't see. He never says anything, though. He's a good man that way, Michael. Respects a person's right to be crazy in their own fashion.

Yes, she talks to Bobby all the time. She talks to the infant who slept beneath the sausages hanging in his grandfather's attic. She talks to the lovesick teenager who bobbed up and down, doing calf raises. She talks to the inconsolable boy she once found here. She talks to all of them. And more.

But she can't tell any of them this. She can't tell them that life is crueler than she imagined, that its cruelties are like the stars: infinite, unfathomable.

She has to tell the man who is gone. Only he will understand.

She empties her mind. She flips up the hood of her slicker and cinches it. She starts to walk. The sand is moist, easier to traverse. She exhales.

Ease into it.

The mist feels good on her face. Suits her mood, the task at hand.

Go on now.

The rain is punitive, restorative. A confession of sorts.

Nearly there.

What a day.

"What a fucking day."

Michael is standing in the doorway, eyes closed, drinking in the sun. The phrase strikes her, makes her smile. He isn't big with the curses, not around her anyway. He looks back at her, winks good-bye. She does not know this yet, but his face will never quite look the same. A blemish of sadness will dot it forever more.

He is right, though. A beautiful day. Makes the heart ache, how beautiful it is. How blue the sky. Flawless. Spectacular. A cliché. A prelude.

And the air. Feels like crispness itself, the change of seasons captured in a breath. Invigorating.

She can't even enjoy it. She is furious, driving Franky to the train in silence. Living at home again. Another false start into his life. Second day of a new job, secured by his brother, running late already. She can't even look at him. He sits there, hung over and glum. She can smell the booze on him. She stops at the station.

"Bobby and I had a nice time last night."

Well then.

She doesn't answer. She drives off as soon as the door closes. She glances at the clock. 8:27. She is going to be late for work.

Work, lateness, responsibility, hangovers, anger. These all still matter.

We are still innocent.

And, then, we are not. The world changes in the space of hours. Time untethers itself.

She is home with Michael, watching in horror together, unsure what to do, unsure what this means. For their country. For their city. For their little patch of nothing that sits in its shadow.

She does math. The train to the ferry. The ferry to the city. He couldn't have gotten there. She knows this, nothing else. She will feel better when she sees him, but distance is distance and speed is speed. And late, for once, is a good thing.

"Is Bobby working today?"

Slightest quiver in his voice. She looks over. He is doing his own math. He is calculating distances, average speeds, estimating traffic. His sums are not as tidy, his answers not as comforting.

"I don't know."

"Call Tina."

She feels her soul drain from her chest.

"Michael, dear God, Michael."

Somewhere deep inside of her, a howl is born. She will live with it until the grave.

They watch. They can do nothing else.

The city gasps.

Twice.

Mother of God.

The house fills with people. Tina, Franky. Peter wanders in later, shell-shocked. He was downtown when it happened, he says. Everything he saw is trapped behind his eyes. He is speechless.

All the people she loves collected under one roof.

Except one.

Hours pass. Information trickles in, none of it good. The house thickens with despair.

She thinks this: she would know. She would *know*. She would feel it somehow. And she doesn't. She looks at Michael, but he won't look at her. She would know, there would be some sign. She hammers in a nail of hope, pegs everything on it.

Tina teeters between hysterical and numb.

Gail pulls her into an empty room.

"You cannot lose this child," she says. Their eyes, clouded by tears, meet. They both know what she's asking. What she's demanding. Tina nods, bites her lip.

"He is gonna walk through that door any minute now."

She believes this. She can see it. The door will open and he will be standing there. This will revert to something terrible, unspeakable, tragic. But something that happened to others.

Neighbors and friends bring food in aluminum trays. The Landinis, the Hudecs, the Dales. They tell her they are praying, they have tears in their eyes. The trays are accepted and heated in the oven. They are placed on the table and the lids are removed. The food — chicken parm, penne vodka — lies there, uneaten. The sun is nearly down when Tiny Terrio shows up. He sobs in Michael's arms, as though it were his son who was missing.

The day turns to night, then back to day. No one moves, speaks. They cry, hope, pray. Tina sleeps on the couch in ten-minute intervals. Every time she wakes, she looks at the door. The ghost light of the television plays the same images over and over. They cannot watch. They must watch.

In the morning, Michael makes some calls. He still has some connections in the department. Every few hours, the phone rings and Michael answers. The calls are brief. He returns to the living room with another name. A friend of his or friend of the boys'. Someone from the neighborhood. Someone who went to school with the boys. Men they know. Some have sat in this living room, watched this television. Mostly firefighters, but others too, men who worked in the towers. It is early, but one thing is already clear: Staten Island has been hit hard.

The phone rings. Another name is whispered. The list grows.

She knows her son's name is being whispered in other living rooms across Staten Island, across the city. Other phones are being answered and her son's name is traveling from lips to ears. Men with stern faces are saying his name. She can almost hear it: Bobby Amendola.

More information trickles in. His company was there. He was there. Seen, entering one of the towers.

She doesn't care. The information is meaningless. She would know. She would know. She will not abandon hope. They are still finding people. She decides, then and there, that she believes in miracles.

She goes to church. The pews are filled, people kneeling, hands clasped.

She makes the sign of the cross, walks the aisle, feels it shift and move beneath her feet, like a ship at sea. She stumbles into a pew.

She prays until her kneecaps ache.

Please, Lord, she prays, please. Please.

She drives home. She walks back into the living room. No one has moved. The television is showing something different. A Palestinian woman is clucking her tongue and raising her hands.

She's *celebrating.*

And then Gail is gone. She feels something she's never felt before. A rage so explosive she has this exact thought: I will cut out your heart and eat it. She is screaming, she is being restrained. They take her upstairs, Michael and Peter, and they hold her until she sleeps. She sleeps for twenty minutes, no longer.

When she wakes, her body is throbbing with one thought: Bobby is dead. Murdered.

Enough.

She stops walking, kneels down into the soft sand, keeps her eyes closed. She can sense him now: the man who would have been. The man he never got a chance to be.

She tells him about his kids, how they're doing. She tells him that the Cody's pool is no more. She tells him a joke that Michael told her on St. Patrick's Day. She tells him she'll be back to wish him a happy birthday in a few weeks. Finally, she tells him that his wife has met someone, that it's serious and he's a nice guy and he's good with the kids.

She lets it sink in. He nods, smiles, is gone.

She stands, wipes wet sand off the knees of her pants. She dries her eyes. She looks out over the water, watches the rain pucker the surface of the sea in a thousand places. She turns, starts back in the direction of the car.

She'd never understood the purpose of a grave. She's seen bodies lowered into the ground, been to more funerals than seemed fair. Still, a cemetery seemed impersonal, even cynical. The rows of headstones, the afterlife reduced to an efficient use of space.

What she would give for a grave.

She doesn't feel the way some of the other families did, about Ground Zero, sacred ground and such. She feels no bond with Bobby there, no desire to visit where her son was murdered.

But she understands. We all should get

whatever we need.

Someone once told her that the greatest pain in life was having to bury a child. She nodded in agreement, oblivious.

Try not having a child to bury. Try having to share your child's death with the rest of the world. Try having the world debate the meaning of your child's death. Try having people speak and write about your child's death vaguely, in some shapeless way, as though he were not flesh of your flesh and blood of your blood. Not a man. Not a father or husband. Not a son.

Let it go, Gail. What needed to be done is done.

She opens the car door, sits on the seat, legs still outside. She takes off her sneakers and smacks them together a few times. Wet sand falls off in clumps. She turns the ignition, checks the time. She'll have to hurry if she wants to make the early mass.

Tina watches from the front steps as Wade parks the car. When he gets out, she feels a pang of frustration; he's overdressed, wearing a green and brown houndstooth blazer, a crisp blue shirt, and dress slacks. He's dressed for a Broadway show when they're going to a kid's birthday party on Staten Island. Jeans and a sweater would have been more than enough. She has some clothes in the house, could give him something more casual to wear, but then, she realizes, he'd be wearing Bobby's clothes to his mother's house. Probably not the best idea.

She blows a wayward strand of hair out of her face. Nothing about this is going to be easy. There will still be hurdles, stumbles, failings. Love does not protect you; it exposes you. The last ten years are a testament to that sentiment.

Wade reaches back into the car, takes out two bouquets of flowers and a small gift bag. He waves. She waves back. He walks casually toward the house, an easy smile on his face. Her frustration drifts away, is replaced by a raw longing. She'd like to rip those stupid clothes off his back and screw him senseless. She invited him over early to get the kids reacclimated before the party, but now she wishes there was no party to attend, no kids in the house. She hasn't seen him all week, not since last Sunday, and she's been stuck in a dewy, lovesick haze, daydreaming about sex, the dirtiest thoughts insinuating themselves at the worst possible moments. Embarrassing to be distracted in this way, at this age.

It was a long drought, she tells herself.

Just before Wade reaches her, she glances

left and right, makes sure there are no nosy neighbors out on the street so she can kiss him properly. Not a soul. He stops on the step below where she stands so their heads align. He kisses her, slides a hand to her waist.

"I missed you," she whispers, after a long kiss that ends too soon.

"Missed you too."

He hands her a bouquet of flowers.

"They're beautiful." She eyes the other bouquet. "Who are those for?"

"Mrs. Amendola."

"I don't think so."

"Why?" he says, inspecting the flowers to see if there's something wrong with them.

"She'll think you're trying to kiss her ass."

"I guess I am, after a fashion. Don't people like it when you kiss their ass?"

"Not Gail."

He looks confused for a beat, but then the smile returns. He hands her the other bouquet.

"Your good luck," he says. He pulls an envelope out of the inside pocket of his blazer. "I got Bobby Yankees tickets, but maybe I should give them to him now?"

"Good idea. And that?" she says, pointing out the little gift bag.

"Just a little something. A little treat.

From Henri Bendel."

"For Gail?"

"No, for Alyssa. I figured Bobby would be getting all the gifts today so she might feel left out."

She smiles, relieved. She opens the front door, gestures him in.

"Is that okay?" he asks, as he walks past.

"Yes, of course," she says, before adding. "Her ass you can kiss."

She closes the door behind him.

The rain picks up in the early afternoon, wiping away any lingering chance of a barbecue. Gail will cook, is grateful for the distraction. Baked ziti and meatballs. Some appetizers. No one will go hungry in her home.

She chops some tomatoes and fresh mozzarella, sprinkles some pepper and salt on the plate. She slides slices of eggplant into egg, then bread crumbs. She fries them in a pan with oil. She wraps pieces of salami around breadsticks, like Franky asked. She cuts aged provolone into bite-size squares. She puts stuffed peppers on a plate.

Alone in the kitchen, she feels thoughts pressing up against her skull, demanding attention. All week, she has tried not to think about this. Told herself that she had to tell the boys first, tell Bobby, and then she could deal with her own feelings. Now everyone has been told. Bobby has been told.

So what does she think?

It is too soon. There. It needed to be said.

Not true, but she can't help it. That's how it feels. An insufficient amount of time has passed. This was not just anyone. This was her son. This was Bobby. The kindest soul you ever met. He chose Tina, chose her when he was seventeen and never looked back. And now she's choosing someone else. Not fair.

She can't lose Tina, Alyssa, Bobby Jr. To someone named Wade. Not fair.

Ingiusto, she hears Maria say, from a different life.

She smiles, rolls the veal and pork between her hands into a ball.

Ingiusto indeed.

Around one, she pours herself a glass of Chianti. Earlier than she'd like to start drinking, but the day calls for it. Michael comes into the kitchen and helps himself to a glass. She swears the man has radar, can tell immediately if someone in a twenty-mile radius is about to imbibe.

"Can't say I'm looking forward to this."

"Do you want to talk?"

He raises his glass, smiles, and walks over to her.

"What is there to say?"

They clink glasses, each takes a sip.

"I love you."

"I love you too."

While Peter is waiting in front of Alberto's apartment for Lindsay and the kids to pick him up, his cell phone rings. He checks the caller ID: Dom. A call he's been dreading for weeks. There's no one he wanted to talk to more, but he could never muster the courage to call. He answers anyway.

"Hello, Dom."

"Petey boy, how we holding up?"

"Well, I'm not sure what you know, but —"

"I know enough to know that you've probably had a shitty winter."

He'd been holding onto a ridiculous hope that maybe Dominic hadn't found out. He does nothing but disappoint people these days. This is the man who paved the way for him, who supported him for partner, showed him how to play the game.

"I don't know what to say, Dom. I'm so sorry."

"Stop it. You don't have to apologize to me. We're friends. Can you see the light at the end of the tunnel?"

"I don't know, Dom. I can't see my way out of this one."

"How so?"

In the background, Peter can hear the sounds of grandchildren misbehaving, mothers chastising. A family gathering, not unlike the one he's about to attend.

"Well, things still haven't, well, I won't bother you with family stuff, but —"

"Lindsay still hasn't forgiven you. Shocking. Okay, what else?"

Peter smiles despite himself. He misses Dom's peremptory summations of a problem. He remembers a time in Dom's office — he was still a young lawyer, second-, maybe third-year — when Dom explained why he let clients ramble but not associates. *They're paying me to listen. I'm paying you to talk. When you're on the other side of the desk, you can go on and on for as long as you like. Until then, get to the fucking point.* God, he thought he was miserable then — the long hours, the competition among associates, the stress about every little misstep — but he misses it now.

"Well, the firm asked me to be seconded to Devion. I'm not sure exactly what's going on. Whether they want me to leave or maybe —"

"You know exactly what's going on. The firm is trying to extricate itself from this mess as cheaply and quietly as possible. They could fire you, ask you to leave, whatever; that might be cheap but not quiet. They could pay this girl, make her sign a confidentiality agreement. That would be quiet but not cheap. They're looking for a way out."

His head really was on the chopping block, Peter realizes, and Dom saved him, proposed this idea. Talked his old client, Devion, into the arrangement. He notices the family car a block away on Montague, waiting at a red light.

"You're still looking out for me, Dom. I don't know what to say."

"What I did always tell you, Petey. Look out for your own."

Peter laughs.

"That's kinda what got me into this mess, Dom."

"Well, Petey, as my dearly departed brother would have put it: the fucking you get is never worth the fucking you get."

"Wish you woulda told me that six months ago."

"That lesson you have to learn on your own, Petey. One day, after I've had too many martinis, I'll tell you about my first secretary, Dawn Rezaluk. Nice Polish girl from Greenpoint. My wife still won't eat pierogi."

Peter laughs again. He wishes he were in Dom's office, late on a Friday afternoon. The week on its death knell. A bottle procured, a quick drink before the train home, the weekend, the family. The light turns green, the car moves slowly toward him.

"I just wish I could find a way to fix things with my family."

"Jesus, Petey, I can only give you the cards. I can't play them for you."

"What do you mean?"

"Isn't Lindsay from Wisconsin, over the border from Illinois? Her parents still live there, right?"

"Yeah, so?"

Of course. Devion is in Chicago. Lindsay's parents are an hour's drive north.

"You think Lindsay would maybe like to be closer to her parents?"

"Yes."

"It doesn't solve everything, Petey, but it's the only play you have."

Peter detects the tiniest flicker of hope struggling to keep in his chest. Maybe he can make this right.

"The only problem, Dom, is that I'll have

to live in Chicago too."

"Penance, my boy, penance."

"Ain't that the truth."

"Stay in touch, Petey."

The car eases in front of him as he hangs up the phone. He can see the faces of his children inside. They look uncertain, happy to see him but nervous. He smiles at them, then turns his gaze to Lindsay. Her face is partially obscured by the reflected sheen of his own image. He can see only her chin and her lips, quivering.

Peter's family arrives first. Lindsay is gaunt, stricken, unable to completely hide her anger. Gail wants to take her aside, give her a hug, tell her this will pass, but it's not her place. Probably not a good idea to weigh in at all. Besides, they've always hated each other, the tiniest bit. No sense trying to bond over the trials and tribulations of middle-aged womanhood, especially when Gail's son is the cause of the sudden unsteadiness.

The kids look a little wobbly. The prim serenity they've known all their lives has disappeared in the last few months. They're not used to raised voices and slammed doors. Life has thrown them its first curveball. Peter slouches in behind the kids, carrying presents, sins etched on his face. He looks around the house dazed, like an astronaut returning to a planet he doesn't recognize.

They'll get through this. Lindsay can barely feign civility, but she's here. If she wasn't here, Gail would worry. But she is. Peter has some groveling in his future, some stormy nights and queasy mornings. But they'll get through it. Lindsay's a good mother. No questioning that. She'll do what's best for the kids. And that means Peter.

Gail retreats to the kitchen. Let Michael thaw the room. She can't do all the heavy lifting. She loses herself in the cooking. She turns on a burner below a pot of salted water. She takes the ziti out of the pantry. She wipes a thin film of sweat from her forehead, takes another sip of Chianti. She is at the stove, stirring sauce, when she feels a hug around her midsection.

"Hello, Bob-a-loo."

She kisses his cheek and leads him back to the living room. They are making their way in: Tina and Wade, with Alyssa lumbering behind. One big happy family. She can tell by the way they walk in, by the frisson between Wade and Tina, that it is more than serious. It's a done deal. Tina will marry

Wade, a tall, thin, rich man who's good with her dead son's kids.

Wade looks delicate, a piece of fine china. He's wearing a blazer and an expensive watch. He is polite and respectful, calls her Mrs. Amendola. She is polite in return. She remembers what Peter told her, that he lost his wife. She'll like this man soon enough, she can tell.

But not today.

The adults settle in the living room, the kids escape down to the basement. The television is on but muted; college basketball players race up and down the court. Gail stays on the periphery of the conversation, popping in from the kitchen every few minutes with some more antipasti. She refills wineglasses, picks up used paper plates. She looks at the clock, wonders where Franky is. She has no idea what to expect. He could show up sober. He could show up legless. He could not show up. None of these would surprise her. She gets a panicky throb in her chest and her eyes drift to Michael, who lowers his hand, motioning for her to stay calm.

Michael locks the door in the bathroom and lets the tap run. He takes out his cell phone and dials Franky's number. It rings four times, then goes to voice mail. His voice is calm, firm.

"Franky, this is Dad. If you're drunk, do not show up. Please."

He closes the phone. He never imagined he'd be making calls like that. Telling his grown son not to come to his house if he's intoxicated. He thought fatherhood would be like his job: you put in twenty, twenty-five years and then you retire. Enjoy the benefits. But it doesn't end. Not until you're in the ground.

He doesn't want today to be ruined. He's happy for Tina. This guy, Wade, isn't half bad. Maybe not exactly his kind of guy, but he's nice. Smart too. She deserves to be happy. She's had her share of unhappiness and then some. They all have.

He puts his hands under the tap, splashes some water onto his face and the back of his neck. He looks in the mirror, sees his father staring back at him. He closes his eyes and, for a moment, he can see it: a butcher's smock, his sons behind the counter, locking up the shop, coming home smelling of blood. A smaller life maybe, not as exciting. Less mayhem, less fire, less death.

He opens his eyes, sees an old man, thinking about what might have been.

■ ■ ■ ■

At five, Gail puts the food out on the kitchen table: ziti and meatballs, a salad, a loaf of bread, an extra bowl of sauce. She calls the kids up from the basement, invites everyone into the kitchen to eat. Everyone files in, makes a plate, and disperses back to the living room. They sit and eat with their plates on their laps. Gail watches Wade struggle to eat in this fashion. He can't quite get the hang of it, doesn't look entirely comfortable. He notices her gaze, gives her a shrug and a smile. He plucks a large piece of meatball with his fork and tucks it into his mouth.

The front door opens. Every head in the room turns. Gail sucks in a breath. Franky walks in, holding a plastic bag, the right half of his face covered with gauze. His eyes skip around the room, to the nowhere spaces between faces. He's sweating bullets. He mumbles something about tripping while jogging, scraping his face on the sidewalk. He is introduced to Wade and manages a handshake, head down. Gail exhales.

He's sober. His face is mangled and he's clearly hung over, but he's sober. Small mercies.

She doesn't ask any questions, doesn't want to know. No sense getting into it. They've been cruel enough to each other over the years. He makes himself a plate, settles in the kitchen near her, away from Wade. She takes a tall can of Budweiser from the fridge, offers it to him. He doesn't bother pretending he doesn't need it.

She stands in the doorway, watching and listening. Wade dotes on Tina, keeps a hand on her back, fetches her whatever she needs. He is charming, even funny. Franky stays in the kitchen, drinking cans of Budweiser at an incautious pace. He can't stand Wade, the person or the idea. This makes Gail happy. Someone should feel that way, even if it can't be her.

The demise of the Cody's pool is discussed at some length. Several theories are proffered; Gail hears something about a nun with a gambling problem. Even Lindsay laughs at that. Wade says there are a few guys from his office who'd been putting in picks for twenty years. Michael blames the mayor. Peter says it had to be the IRS. Eventually, Franky can't resist; he sulks back into the living room to add his thoughts, something about a Croatian lawyer who got divorced.

When he does, Tina comes into the

kitchen to see Gail. She is trying to restrain herself, but she's a little giddy. A few glasses of wine have loosened her up.

"So what do you think?"

She is in love, Gail can tell, because how else could she ask such a stupid question. *He's a fraction of the man my son was; you're a fool for thinking he will make you happy.*

"He seems very nice, Tina."

"Right?"

"Lovely."

She can't resist.

"Does well for himself too, I hear."

"I guess, I don't really know."

Tina frowns and Gail feels guilty. She reaches over and grips Tina's hand.

"I'm happy for you, Tina."

"Thank you."

They hug. Gail can tell this is a good-bye of sorts. Tina has come for her tacit approval, nothing more.

"Thanks for everything, Gail."

Not Mom. Just Gail.

"You're welcome, Tina."

They turn off the lights when it's time for cake. Gail lights the candles and carries the cake into the living room. Unprompted, Michael sings "Happy Birthday" at the top of his lungs, the same way his father used to, purposefully off-key. Everyone laughs. Gail looks at him. He's a little tipsy, smiling. He's happy. She places the cake on a tray in front of Bobby Jr.

"Make a wish," someone shouts. Bobby Jr. closes his eyes, pinches his face into a determined scowl. The candles flicker; the only thing visible in the entire room is Bobby's face. He furrows his brow, concentrates harder. Gail can almost hear wishes being made silently, around the room. A moment passes, then he opens his eyes wide and blows out the candles. Everyone cheers.

While they eat cake, Bobby opens his presents: toys, clothes, video games. After everyone has given him their gifts, Franky sheepishly hands him a plastic bag.

"Sorry, Bob-o, didn't get a chance to wrap it."

Bobby pulls the jersey out of the bag, looks at the name on the back.

"Ewing?" he asks, quizzically.

"Patrick Ewing. He was your father's favorite player," Tina offers, a tear sliding down her cheek. Wade puts a hand on her back. Bobby pulls the jersey on over his shirt.

"Awesome. Thanks, Uncle Franky."

"You bet, Bob-o."

Franky leans down and hugs Bobby, making sure the unsullied side of his face is the half that touches Bobby's cheek. Gail's and Tina's eyes meet, briefly, then retreat, two mothers watching their sons.

When Peter's family gets ready to leave, Franky slips upstairs. He walks down the hallway, but the walls seem too close together; he keeps drifting into one side or the other. He can't tell whether he's buzzed or punchy or plain exhausted. He takes a sip from his can and pushes open the door to Bobby's room. He feels at peace here, closer to Bobby than anywhere else but not painful somehow. He doesn't have to imagine Bobby or try to remember him in this room; he's simply present.

Franky leaves the can on the dresser and steps toward the bed. He takes his wallet and his cell phone out. He has a new message. It can wait until tomorrow. He slides under the covers, savors the cool feeling of enclosure. He nods to the poster of Patrick Ewing.

"Good night, Patrick."

He showed them today, showed them all. They doubted him and he made them eat their doubts. He showed that asshole Wade too. What kind of a fancy fuck wears a blazer to a birthday party? Asshole.

His face hurts so he switches positions, lays the other cheek against the pillow. If he did it today, he can get right. He can be a better son, a better uncle. A better person, for Christ's sake. He just needs someone to believe in him. Bobby believed in him and the world took him away. It's not his fault. But he'll get right. He'll make things right.

In the flicker of seconds before slumber, Franky's word is true. In this moment, these things will happen. His eyelids close in peace, his mind intent on redemption. Tomorrow is a long way off; it remains unborn, perfect.

It is late when they leave. Peter's family has already left, right after cake. Franky is staying over, sleeping upstairs, probably already in Bobby's bed. Tina hugs Michael and Gail. She walks out to the car, Alyssa's head resting on her shoulder. Wade says goodbye, says thanks, and carries Bobby Jr. down the steps in his arms. Another man, a stranger, is carrying her dead son's sleeping child down her front steps. The steps Maria hobbled up, the steps her sons ran down as kids, the steps Michael stood on the day that changed everything.

Gail's throat catches and makes a soft

noise. Michael asks her if something is wrong.

"It's nothing," she says. She hears Maria's voice in her head: *nulla.*

He puts his hand on her shoulder.

"C'mon, let's go inside."

"Go on, I'll be right in."

She watches Wade lay little Bobby down on the backseat, then get in on the driver's side. Tina waves a last good-bye through the windshield. Gail raises a hand in response. The car backs out of the driveway and into the street. They drive off slowly.

The rain has stopped. The branches of nearby trees sway, then ease into stillness. The street glows in the gentle hum of front door lights. Somewhere on the block, a car door is closed. Footsteps echo off pavement. The noise drifts down, disappears. The street is empty, the night hushed.

Gail lingers on the top step, hoping something will break the silence.

EPILOGUE:
BOBBY

You've been waiting for this night, this moment, for months. Years. The Staten Island version of March Madness. Top eight teams on the Island. You beat Moore in the quarter finals, upset Peter's in the semis. Tonight is the final. You're playing Curtis, best team on the Island. They kicked your ass earlier in the year and you'd love some payback. But win or lose, this is it: the last high school basketball game of your life.

The opening buzzer sounds and is swallowed by the hum of the crowd. Your head spins and you can barely hear, never mind understand, what Coach Whelan is shouting at you and your teammates. His voice is hoarse and his face is red. Behind his glasses, his eyes are rigid with conviction.

"Your night," he's screaming. "This is your night."

A throng of hands descends on the middle

of the sweaty huddle and you see your own join it.

"TEAM."

You rise from the bench as the huddle disperses. Your head goes dizzy from the crowd. The gym is packed. People are milling along both baselines because there's nowhere left to sit.

A few brazen teenagers dash across the floor as the teams break huddle, sprinting for seats their friends are trying to hold for them on the other side of the gym. You feel a hand grip your arm just before you hit the court. You know it's Coach Whelan. His words are hot and wet, delivered straight into your left ear in an animal whisper.

"Bobby, if you control the boards, we win this game. Control the boards, control the paint. We win. Your night. This is your night."

You nod at him. He releases your arm and slaps your ass onto the court. You experience a moment of uncertainty because the way you feel right now is similar to the way you feel when you're alone with Tina. You can even feel something stirring deep in you, at the very root of you, and it's not sexual exactly but pretty close. You experience a fleeting recurrent anxiety that this makes you abnormal somehow, maybe even gay, even though you know you're not, you're certainly not. Anyway, there's no time for these thoughts because here's your summer friend and winter enemy Ray Henderson, all six feet eight inches of him, coming toward you with a smile and his hand out for a pound.

You give him the pound but not the smile because if you put aside the hops and the height, if you ignore the twenty points a game he scores, if you look into his heart, you know this: Ray Henderson is a bitch. If you hit him hard early, if you don't let him run and dunk and throw your shot into the stands, if you box out and give him a few head fakes, draw a few early fouls, if you make him work, Ray Henderson will disappear. You know this. Your teammates know this. Christ, his teammates know this. You are not worried about Ray Henderson.

But Toughie Johnson is a different story. Toughie isn't even a summer friend because Toughie has no friends. Toughie is mad at the world. He is not nearly as talented as Ray Henderson, not even as skilled as you, but Toughie is, well, a tough fucking nut. He will push and elbow and throw his body around. He will pull your shorts and your shirt and if he could figure out a way, he'd bite you too. He's only six two, but he's a fucking bull and if you don't keep him off the boards, he'll score twenty on putbacks alone. You will start off guarding Ray tonight, but you will need to account for Toughie as well because Terry Kovak, your teammate and frontcourt mate, will need a break. Terry will do what he can, but he's slow and he can't jump a lick, and Toughie is a bad matchup for him, so you'll end up guarding Toughie at some point tonight and then you'll need to be smart. You'll need to goad him into dumb fouls. You'll need to slither and slide around him. You'll need to use the two inches you have on him. You'll need to give him more reasons to be mad at the world.

Toughie doesn't offer a pound to you or anyone else. He ties the white string on his maroon shorts with a menacing sneer and you're angry now. Fuck him. Fuck Curtis. Throw the ball, ref.

But it's not time yet and your anger turns back to butterflies. You give perfunctory bumps to Curtis's other players: their shooting guard Danny Lynch, their small forward Omar Owens, their point guard Delvin Freese. You know them all. You play with Owens and Freese down at Cromwell in the summer; you've played with Lynch at P.S. 8. Strictly a spot-up shooter. He won't venture into the lane. And Vinny will be guarding Freese. Nothing to worry about there.

Owens is the only one you might have to worry about. He's inconsistent but occasionally makes electrifying forays to the basket that result in momentum-changing dunks. You might have to put him on his ass early, but you also have to be careful with your fouls. Coach Whelan has told you all week that he needs a full game out of you, that he'll only be able to give you a thirty-second blow here or there. At best.

You've finished your circle through the opposing team. There are a few awkward seconds of silent nerves, everyone's hearts beating through their chests, muscles twitching in anticipation. The refs are making sure the clock is working. You glance at your own teammates: Kovak, Pat Keegan, Vinny Baddio, Matt Duggan. They have your back. They're ready. They know what they need to do. They're all nervous, stomachs churning, Duggan especially. You look at each of them with a steady gaze, watch them find strength in your certainty. You turn to Vinny, who's standing behind you, standing where Ray will try to tip the ball because even though you'll do your best, there's little doubt that Ray will win the tip.

Vinny is preternaturally calm. He is exactly where he wants to be. He gives you a slow, steady nod.

You steal a glance at Coach Whelan, who shakes a fist in solidarity, exiling the nerves from your body. His faith in you is all you need. You are ready now. Your legs stop tingling. Your stomach stops flipping.

Your hearing returns and you realize the sound in the gym is thunderous. The crowd has risen to its feet, waiting for the tip. You scan back to where you know your family is sitting. You see your mother, right hand already up at her mouth, biting her nails. You see your father next to her. He missed most of your games this year, but he's made the last two; you'll never tell anyone how much this means to you. You see your grandfather behind them, proud and nervous and laughing. You see Franky; he meets your gaze. You see Peter, home from college on break, excited, envious.

You see Tina a few rows below them, straining to see over the people in front of her. Her friend Stephanie is talking into her ear and Tina is trying to ignore her, trying to focus. She is more nervous than you. You want to go to her later, tired and triumphant, and lay your head in her lap.

You hear another sound from the buzzer.

The clock has been fixed. The refs jog to their positions. One of them blows his whistle, testing, and walks slowly toward the narrow space between you and Ray Henderson, the space where he will toss the ball up and you will both leap to touch it. You put your right foot in the assigned portion of the tiny circle on your side of mid court. Ray does the same. All the slack on the court goes taut; every body in the gym tenses.

You go deaf again as your eyes focus on the bright orange sphere that is resting in the ref's hand. It consumes your vision, the orange blinding you, so like a fire, burning intensely; you never noticed before.

The moment sticks: the ball cradled in the ref's palm, all the people in your life who matter collected in one place, to support you. You at the center, the fear drained from your body. The whole game before you, your whole life before you, an uncountable number of precious moments laid out in front of this one, shadows waiting to take shape, like the kids you assume you'll have, like souls not yet in existence.

If you close your eyes, you can almost see them.

ACKNOWLEDGMENTS

My deepest thanks to: early readers Kevin Snover, Don Steinman, Dave and Michelle Donahue, and Ann Shields for their insight and support; Patricia Smith, who gave me a chance and some much needed hope; Keith Gessen and Keith Dixon, who each gave advice and guidance at critical junctures; Clare Ferraro, Paul Slovak, Nancy Sheppard, Carolyn Coleburn and everyone at Viking; Laura Bonner at WME; my agent, Claudia Ballard, who was rightfully insistent that I make the book better and patient while I did so; Allison Lorentzen, wonderful editor and friend, who set me on the right path well before she knew it would lead back to her.

Mom, Dad, Kris, and Kev: thank you all for your love and support.

M, A, and K: early drafts of chapters drifted into my head while I pushed you, sleeping, in strollers.

Martine: words cannot fully express my gratitude. Thank you for this wonderful life. All my love.

Finally, I'd like to thank the people of Staten Island: who's better than you?

ABOUT THE AUTHOR

Eddie Joyce was born and raised on Staten Island and now lives in Brooklyn with his wife and three daughters.

The employees of Thorndike Press hope you have enjoyed this Large Print book. All our Thorndike, Wheeler, and Kennebec Large Print titles are designed for easy reading, and all our books are made to last. Other Thorndike Press Large Print books are available at your library, through selected bookstores, or directly from us.

For information about titles, please call:
(800) 223-1244

or visit our Web site at:
http://gale.cengage.com/thorndike

To share your comments, please write:
Publisher
Thorndike Press
10 Water St., Suite 310
Waterville, ME 04901